Rosalind Stopps has always wanted to tell the stories of the less heard. For many years she worked with children with disabilities and their families.

She has five grown up children, three grandchildren and an MA in creative writing from Lancaster University. Rosalind's short stories have been published in five anthologies and read at live literature events in London, Leeds, Hong Kong and New York. She lives in South East London with large numbers of humans and dogs.

When she is not writing fiction she is, mostly, reading it or working as a host at London's South Bank Arts Centre. *Hello, My Name is May* is her debut novel.

D1050265

Hello, My Name is May

Rosalind Stopps

ONE PLACE. MANY STORIES

HQ
An imprint of HarperCollins*Publishers* Ltd
1 London Bridge Street
London SE1 9GF

This edition 2019

1
First published in Great Britain by
HQ, an imprint of HarperCollins*Publishers* Ltd 2019

Hardback: 978-0-00-830256-6
Trade Paperback: 978-0-00-830257-3

MIX
Paper from
responsible sources

FSC
www.fsc.org   **FSC™ C007454**

This book is produced from independently certified FSC™ paper
to ensure responsible forest management.

For more information visit: www.harpercollins.co.uk/green

This book is set in 11.5/16.5 pt. Sabon

Printed and bound in Great Britain by
CPI Group (UK) Ltd, Croydon, CR0 4YY

For Dom and Tom, with love.

CHAPTER ONE

September 2017
Lewisham

I could hear the words in my head but they wouldn't come out.

I'm fine, I wanted to say, you can leave me here, I'll be OK. It was the blood, that was all, I could smell blood, and I've always hated that. I wanted to explain to them. It makes me feel funny, but not funny ha ha, I would have said but they've got no sense of humour, young people. I didn't like the way the man was looking at me. I'm not just a stupid old woman, I tried to say. I may not have been speaking very clearly but there was no need for him to look at me like that. I tried to tell him, don't look at me like that, young man. I wanted to say it in quite a stern way but my mouth was doing that thing again of not working properly, as though I was drunk or I'd had something nasty done at the dentist. All that came out was a slur of s's and some spit. I noticed he didn't like the spit much, ambulance man or no ambulance man, he didn't like that at all. I'd say he flinched, leaned back a bit, but he couldn't go far because he was kneeling next to me on the floor.

It made me laugh that, him kneeling, it's not a thing you see much. Reminds me of going to church when I was a kid, I tried to say, but the spitty thing was still going on. Try to relax, he said to me, try and calm down, deep breaths, we'll get you sorted. I gave up on talking, tried to roll my eyes instead but of course that made him call his colleague over, the young woman with the thick ankles. She was wearing a skirt and I was surprised at that. I'm sure they're allowed to wear trousers these days and if I was her I would have done. Cover up those ankles. I might have rolled my eyes again. They probably thought I was dying or something, because it was all rushing around after the eye rolling, no more of the calm down stuff, just lobbing me onto a stretcher like I was already gone and couldn't feel anything. At least I was wearing trousers, I thought, and it made me laugh. It felt like a laugh inside. I don't know what it looked like on the outside.

I might have gone to sleep for a moment or two after that. I'm surprised I was tired because I'd been doing nothing but lie around on the floor resting since I fell. I didn't know how long I had been there but it must have been quite a while. Someone told me later I'd been there for two whole days and two nights. I'm not sure if that's right or if it's just another one of the things they say to old people to keep them in order. I'm still thinking about that one. I certainly remember watching the clock on the wall and thinking that it was going slowly, and that I might need to wind it up or put a new battery in it. I couldn't remember which. And I can remember hearing someone push something through the letterbox. It was probably only a flyer for some kind of pizza place or a nail parlour but I tried to shout. I thought it was just a fall, you see, I've got big feet, clown feet I've been told, plus I've always been rather clumsy so I thought I had just fallen over the coffee table. I was wedged in between the coffee table and the sofa and the smell of blood was horrible. Turned out I'd only bashed my head a bit, no stitches needed, but at the time it smelt like an abattoir and that's what I mainly remember.

Two days. I nodded like I agreed with them but two days, honest. I'm not sure about that. I'm going to ask some of the others when I can, I'm going to ask them how long they lay on the floor for if they had a stroke, and if just one of them says, two days, it will be obvious that it's something they say to everyone, the two days thing, a big old lie. I've caught them telling lies a couple of times so I won't be at all surprised.

I don't remember much about the ambulance journey. There's the smell, I remember that, the blood from the cut on my head, and another smell, a dirty smell that showed up in the ambulance. Maybe it was a smell from the person who had used the ambulance before me. They needed to work on that, clean it up a bit better. I'm sure the smell couldn't have been coming from me. Who smelt it, dealt it, that's what they used to say in the shop I worked in when I was a student. It reminded me of the day one of the boys in packing brought a stink bomb in during stocktaking. It brought tears to our eyes, but none of us girls said a word, in case we got teased.

I didn't say anything in the ambulance. I just went to sleep and the next thing I knew, the young man who had been kneeling by me and the well-meaning woman with the thick ankles, they'd gone. It would have been nice if they had said goodbye or cheerio or something so that I'd known they were going. I'd got used to them being there and I felt lonely without them. They should have said something but they didn't, or they didn't do it loudly enough, so when I woke up there was a different woman. She had a badge on that said, 'hello, my name is Agnita'.

Hello yourself, can you not speak then, I wanted to say, have you got badges for other things you want to say? I imagined a person covered in badges, all of them saying useful things like, would you like a cup of tea, or, mine's a pint. Count me out, I thought, I'm not wearing any badges, they can't make me. And they didn't, but get this, what they did was even worse. They wrote it, on the wall above my bed. 'Hello,' it said, 'my name is May. Please talk to me.'

I couldn't believe it. Please talk to me, indeed. As if. I don't need anyone to talk to me, thank you very much and if I could just untwist my mouth enough I'd tell them so in no uncertain terms. I haven't had anyone to talk to for a long time, no one except for my daughter, Jenny, and she's so quiet I can hardly hear her. Speak up, I always say, speak up or I'm going to read my book and ignore you. That makes her nervous, and I'm sorry about that but there's no point mollycoddling a grown child. No point at all.

I fantasised for a while about scrubbing the words off my wall. If I could just stand up for a moment I'd make sure there wasn't a trace of writing left. There wouldn't be any 'please talk to me' then, I can assure you.

They tell me I've got the sequence of events all wrong. They say that I went to the hospital first, had scans and saw doctors and that sort of malarkey, and that I only came to the nursing home later. I don't know why they say that. I've got no idea at all, so I don't argue, I just keep quiet and watch them all. It's not something I'd forget, is it, a whole trip to hospital and everything that goes with it?

Honestly dear, you've been unwell for longer than you think, said the one with the purple streak. (Hello, my name is Abi.)

I hate being called 'dear' and I don't trust any of them. It'll be a cost cutting thing. It's my guess that they just cut out the middle person and bring the old people straight to the nursing home, save money on hospital beds. They tell the poor old dears they've had some treatment but they don't remember and everyone is happy. That's the thing with me, you see, I'm quite clever underneath this old lady exterior. That's what it feels like, an outfit I'm wearing.

As if I woke up wearing a fancy dress costume complete with wrinkles and grey hair, and I can't take it off. Inside it's different. Inside me I'm about thirty, with occasional forays backward and forwards. I don't think the other old people are like that. I've watched them. It's real for them.

I didn't see any of the other old codgers that first day. As far as I remember I was on the floor in my front room, in the ambulance, and then this room. I'm not complaining. It's all very nice and everything, this room, clean and bright, but it smells of gravy at all times. It's like living in a gravy boat I wanted to say, one big gravy boat sailing away into the night, full of old people on their last trip. I'd like to be able to say that to Agnita, she's the one I'm supposed to go to if I have any 'issues'. She's not a nurse. Mentor friend, they call it but she hasn't got a badge that says that.

So that first day, she sat with me for a while, telling me this and that about St Barbara's, that's the name of this gravy boat. St Barbara is the patron saint of miners, firemen and prisoners, she said, so that's appropriate. I didn't listen to everything she said, but I liked the sound of her voice, all soft and lilty like a bedtime story. She told me that she came from a part of the West Indies that used to be Dutch, and that was why her accent was unusual, I remember that. I remember it mainly for the frustration I felt, wanting to let her know that I was a true Londoner, not racist like the other old people. They weren't proper Londoners, I could tell at a glance. They seemed more like the sort of people who'd moved to London from Hull. A sea of bad perms, crimplene and right-wing nonsense. The most important people in my life have been people of colour, I wanted to say but all that came out was spit.

Come on now May, there's no need to be alarmed, she said, I'm a trained carer. Something like that anyway, but it wasn't fair, I wasn't alarmed. Well I was, but not by her, I don't know why people always think it's about them. Trained carer, I wanted to say, trained carer? An untrained toddler would have been able to see that I was actually alarmed by the fact that I couldn't talk. I couldn't join in with the conversation I hadn't asked for in the first place, and I didn't want to be having it anyway. I must have got a little upset after that. She looked offended, and that's bonkers. How could anyone be offended by an old woman who spits instead of talks?

She left me alone for a while, but she left the door open. I could see two rooms across the corridor. One had the door shut, and the other was open. I couldn't see who was in it but I could hear the television blaring so I knew it was occupied. And I could see people moving up and down the corridor with trolleys. Pill trolleys, cup of tea trolleys, book trolleys. This was clearly going to be a place where they didn't leave a person alone for five minutes. I wasn't sure what to think about that. I've been lonely in my life, I'll admit it, but I've learned to like my own company too.

I slept again then, and when I woke up I realised exactly

what was going on. I didn't have a voice, that was the long and the short of it, I was trapped until I could make myself understood. That was a difficult thing to come to terms with. No one could understand me and while there was a kind of freedom in that, it was not a freedom I wanted. I was set apart from the rest of the world, a separate kingdom with my own self as ruler and subject. I was going to have to make my own rules; work hard.

I'd heard a radio programme about someone famous who had had a stroke and then practised and practised and got themselves better and climbed Everest for charity or something. I should be able to get better a lot more quickly, I thought, because I didn't want to climb any mountains at all. I just wanted to go to the toilet unaided. I wanted to manage the whole process without swinging through the air on a hoist, or being helped by two carers while I lurched along with a three legged stick. I wanted my dignity, that's what I wanted the most.

I never thought that going to the loo would be such a big deal in my life, but in between toilet visits not a lot happens in here. There's TV, and meal times, and therapy of various sorts, but the other people are very dull. Mostly of the common or garden vegetable variety; no conversation to speak of. I need to practise my talking, that's what the speech and language therapist says, but it's hard to do that when I'm surrounded by people who are either busy working or busy dying.

There's one, I've never seen her, I guess she keeps to

her own room, but every night at about seven o'clock she starts shouting for her mother. If it was me in charge, I'd get someone to dress up as her mother and give her and the rest of us a bit of peace, but I don't think they've thought of that. I'm thinking about doing it myself, when I can get around a little better. I could just put my head round her door and say, there there, it's all OK dear, Mother's here. She might stop calling out, she might sleep better and then we'd all be happy.

There was a shouter on the ward where I had my Jenny. It wasn't her mum she was calling for, more like she was asking for divine intervention as far as I remember. God, please help me she kept calling. I'd had my baby by then, but I could still hear her, we all could, the new mums. There was one across from me, she kept muttering, God help her, whenever the shouting woman went quiet, and for some reason that made us all laugh. It was good to have a laugh together, made me feel like one of the gang. A conspiracy of women, that's what we were, that's what Helen called it and I didn't mind at all that Alain often missed visiting hours. He wasn't the only one, having babies was women's work back then. I'd read the books of course, I wanted it to be different for us but I knew how hard it was for him.

It will be different, Alain used to say, we won't be like all the others. I've got to make things right for all of us, we're a family now. He had interviews for jobs as far as I remember, it wasn't that he didn't want to come. The visiting hour was short, literally an hour, I think.

I understood. When he did come though, oh, all the other mothers took to him. He'd go along the ward saying hello to them, commenting on how pretty their babies were, that sort of thing. He always brought flowers, every day that he managed to come in, and he usually cried at the sight of little Jenny.

She's so perfect, he said, I'm sorry I just can't help it.

He loved to sit and look at her while she was sleeping. It worried him when she cried. I got into the habit of telling Jenny to be quiet, and if I'm honest, I never really stopped until she was grown up. I've had a lot of time to think about that in here, and as soon as I can get the words out properly I'm going to tell her. I'm sorry, I'm going to say, I don't know whether it's my fault that you're so quiet now, but if it is, I'm sorry, and I think you should spend the rest of your life shouting, just to make up for it.

She's been to see me quite a few times in here. It's nice to see her but the last thing she needs is me getting all sloppy over her, so I've tried to keep myself to myself. It's the spit. Any attempt at talking and it's there, splishing and splashing out of my mouth like one of those water slide things they have in outdoor swimming pools. I thought of that when Jenny was here the other day. She used to love going down the water slide on holiday and I wanted to remind her of that and explain why I was spitting at the same time but of course it all came out in a wet jumble and she had no idea what I was trying to say.

Do you want a drink, she said, or the toilet, it's OK Mum, I'll call the nurse.

They're bloody not nurses I wanted to say but it came out as a growl and then she pressed the buzzer and I was being swung through the air to the toilet like I was a sack of old bones, which I suppose I am. The swimming pool, I wanted to say, remember the water slide and how many times you went down it? You were so tired you'd often fall asleep eating your dinner on that holiday. Mush mush mush spit dribble slobber, that's what comes out. All anyone can guess is drink or toilet, that's the only things that I'm supposed to care about now. Like one of those dolls Jenny used to have, where you poured the water in the mouth and put a nappy on the other end so it could come out. That doll always creeped me out and now I know why, it was my fate, waiting for me.

Don't try to talk Mum, it's OK, Jenny says and I try so hard not to cry that I knock the water out of her hand as she offers me a drink.

Now now, May, one of the carers says, there's no need for that, your daughter has come to visit you, let's be nice. It's not fair, I think, it's not fair and if at that moment I could have blown the place up I would have, daughter or no daughter. I've never liked things that aren't fair.

When I was at school there was a fashion for biros with more than one colour, and you clicked a button to change the colour of your writing. I didn't have one, so when Carol Eliot's got lost, it was me everyone thought had taken it.

I didn't, I didn't, I said, but the teacher still insisted on searching my bag based on 'information received'. It wasn't there of course, but some of the girls believed it anyway, and for months they held their pens to their chests when I walked past.

I stopped trying to remind Jenny of the water slide, I stopped trying to tell her I was sorry, I turned my face to the wall and waited for her to go home. I was very sad when she had gone.

I've got to get out of here. September is usually my favourite month. There's a feeling of new year, new possibilities, but no fireworks. Sunshine. I think I was reading in the garden only last week or the week before, when I was still at home and everything was different. I think I was, only I've got into a muddle over dates. I'm sure I was at home with all my body parts working when the children went back to school, I heard them walk past my window and then there's a blank part and now they tell me it's the twenty-second of September. The thing is, as you get older, you don't look at the date every day like you do when you are at work. You take things a bit more slowly, you wind down a little. It doesn't mean I've been ill for nearly three weeks just because I wasn't noticing the date, and I'd tell them that in no uncertain terms if I could.

Something a little different this evening. Just after the tea trolley and before the pill trolley, they came round shutting all the room doors. I thought it was just mine at first, and that maybe I was in trouble, or Jenny had complained about me or something, and they were teaching me a lesson. But I listened hard, I've always had good hearing, and I heard them shutting all the doors, up and down the corridor. We were banged up. A lockdown. I knew the words because I've always liked the prison shows on TV. I listened, and I could hear them roll a trolley down, I could hear those trolley wheels. I'm quick, and I realised what it was. It was creepy. The death stretcher, that's what it was, the last journey, the only way out of here. Poor old bugger whoever you are, I thought. I wondered for a moment whether I should show respect by bowing my head or something.

They opened the doors a few minutes later. I think it was only a few minutes. I tried to make my eyes as questioning as possible but same old, same old, Kelly just asked me if I'd like a drink or a wee. I jumped (figuratively) at the chance of a bit of a hoist and a nose, so I made a particularly enthusiastic sound in the appropriate place. It sounded a little like, yeeeeuuugggsshshshsh.

They always use the hoist when they're busy. It's quicker. It can take me half the day to get across the room otherwise, even with two carers helping me.

Come along now, May, Kelly says.

She has that voice on that means, I'm busy and you're a nuisance. If I had a way of having a tantrum I'd have one. I'd sweep all the tissues and the polo mints and the orange squash right off that tray, and lob the sticky toffee pudding left over from dinner right at Kelly's hair. She's got this complicated hairstyle, all winding plaits and Princess Leia and it would look just the thing with a handful of custard and sponge on the top. It's the assumption, that's what I don't like, the assumption that whatever I do, I'm doing it as part of a plan to disrupt their lives as much as possible, ruin their busyness. I know it's only a short time since I went to the toilet last, and that when I got there I couldn't make much impact anyway, hardly a trickle. But it's my right to go to the toilet whenever I want to, I know that much.

So Kelly and Lee-An strap me into the hoist and lift me up, swing swing, into the air and across the room. Talking all the way about hair extensions. I've got used to carers talking to each other as if I wasn't there. It's restful sometimes, listening to chatter about wallpaper and children, dinners waiting to be eaten and holidays planned. I don't mind, most of the time, but I'm sad this time what with death rolling past my door so recently. I'm lonely, I'm not sure what hair extensions even are, and I miss Jenny. She might be nearly forty and as quiet as a mouse, but she's my only family and I can't help thinking that it would have been nice if she could have stayed a little longer. I'm on my own, after all. She has a long journey to get home and she doesn't drive, that's true and I should remember that but I'm upset.

I can't have a proper tantrum but I manage a side swipe to the left that knocks the half-drunk mug of tea to the floor as they swing me round. You'd think it was some kind of chemical, the way they carry on, something from a Batman film that could burn through floors, walls and bones. She looks at me, Kelly, not a look that anyone would want to receive, especially from the person who is operating the hoist that gets you to the toilet. I look away, settle down a bit into the sling, so that she can see there isn't going to be any more drama.

Something catches my eye. The room across the corridor, not the one with the open door and the booming television, but the other one. The one that's usually closed and silent. There's someone in there, a man I think. It's difficult to tell once you get old. The person is tall, because I can see the back of his head over the top of the chair he is sitting in. There's something familiar about the tilt of his head as he faces the TV. As if he's breathing it in, listening hard. I can hear a man's voice and the hollow sound of questions being asked. I'm not sure until I hear the music, dum diddy dum, all threatening and serious, but I'm right, it's *Mastermind*.

Alain used to love that show. He was good, too, he often got more right than the contestants. *Mastermind*. I haven't thought about that show in ages.

CHAPTER TWO

September 1977
Hull

'May,' called Alain as he opened the front door, 'May, do you want the good news or the really, really good news? Don't worry about the lovebirds,' he said as May looked towards the top of the house, 'they're out, I saw them in town. And we won't have to worry about them for much longer, I promise. We'll have our own place soon, our very own with no housemates to worry about.'

May smiled. She hadn't minded living with the student couple at first, in fact she had liked having other people around, but as the baby's birth got nearer, May felt a nesting instinct. She wanted to be on her own with Alain and her bump, thinking about baby things and preparing. She didn't want to make conversation or worry about how she looked. In fact, she didn't want to think about the world outside of her bubble at all.

'Go on then,' she said. 'I could use some good news, anything you like, bring it on.'

She washed her hands and moved away from the stove.

'That smells great,' Alain said. 'Let me guess, tomato mince?'

May blushed.

'I'm going to learn some new recipes,' she said. 'I'm working on it.'

Cooking did not come naturally to May, but she had bought some old recipe books at a jumble sale and she was trying. Her mother had gone for the easy stuff, baked beans, fish fingers, frozen peas, and that had always been good enough for May until now. Now she had a husband and a baby on the way, and she wanted to do it well.

Alain put both arms around her and lifted her slightly off her feet.

'No need,' he said, 'men can cook too, you know. I'm going to cook every night when this little one is born.' He dropped to his knees and kissed May's pregnant stomach.

'Hello, little tiny,' he said in a quiet voice. 'Any chance of some kicking for your old dad?'

'He's been quiet today,' said May, 'probably waiting for you to come home.'

'He?' said Alain. 'He? Isn't that a bit sexist? If she's a she, she'll be listening and she'll think we want a boy.' He stood and kissed May on the side of her neck. 'I'm happy with anything,' he said, 'boy, girl, alien, I'm just so happy that he, she, or it, is there.'

May was happier than she had been for ages, possibly forever. It had all been so quick, meeting Alain, marrying him and getting pregnant, only not in that order, and sometimes she still had to pinch herself to make sure it was real.

'So, the good news things in order. First, it's *Mastermind* on TV tonight and we can watch it together, score sheets and everything. I read in the *Radio Times* that one of the contestants is going to answer questions on the poems of T.S. Eliot for their special subject. I bet we know all of the answers between us.'

May smiled. It still seemed amazing that Alain liked the same sort of things that she did, and that he understood her so well, so intimately. May and her mother used to watch *Mastermind* together, especially when she was ill.

'Did I tell you,' May asked, 'about the last time Mum and I watched *Mastermind*?'

'You did,' said Alain, 'but I'd love to hear it again.'

'Really?' said May. She was worried that she was boring him. It still seemed inexplicable to her that someone like Alain would look at her twice, let alone marry her. He was six years her junior for a start, handsome, funny and clever. He knew about politics and poetry and he could play the guitar and sing like Paul Simon. Everyone who met him loved him. Her mum would have loved him too, she was sure of that.

'Really,' said Alain. 'Come on, you sit down and I'll take over the cooking. I'll tell you my other piece of news later – it's worth the wait.'

'No,' said May, 'no, go on, I want to hear it now, right now.'

She put the memory of her mother out of her head. Sorry, Mum, she thought. I'm not ignoring you, but I'm moving on. It's OK, she could imagine her poor old mum saying back, smiling even though she'd been dismissed, go on, you have a good time.

'Are you OK, merry May?' Alain said. 'It must be so difficult for you, I'm sorry if I forget that sometimes. I read an article the other day about grieving, and it said that it's even more difficult to grieve when you're pregnant, because everything is invested in the future, all your hopes and dreams, but that's hard when the loss is still there to make you sad. I think that's what it meant, anyway.'

Fancy that, May thought, reading articles for her sake, how lovely. Alain lit a cigarette. May decided not to mention again how much she hated the smoke now that she was pregnant.

'So, here's my good news. I've got a job! I've got a job, just when we were starting to panic, a real job with real money and everything. And a flat! We won't have to live with Love's Young Dream upstairs any more, it'll be just us: me, you and Jiminy Cricket in there.' Alain patted May gently on her bump, and looked at her. She could tell he was keen to see her reaction.

'Al,' May said, 'Al, I can't believe it. Where? Teaching? How come there's a flat? I don't understand.'

'OK, OK, well, I haven't only been applying for teaching

jobs. There's nothing around now, term has started and there are loads of good teachers without jobs, we both know that. I didn't want to tell you, because I wasn't sure if it would come to anything and I didn't want to get your hopes up. But my dear May, my merry May, I got out my special skill, my superpower, and it's going to save us.'

May wondered for a split second whether Alain had been drinking. She didn't know what he was talking about. They were both teachers, newly qualified, in fact they'd met in college only nine months ago. He'd never mentioned applying for other jobs or having a special skill and May realised again how little they knew about each other, how quickly everything had happened.

'You don't know,' said Alain, clapping his hand to his head in a pantomime gesture. 'Perhaps I never told you about my superpower. You're going to be so surprised.'

Alain rubbed his hands together. May waited.

'I can speak Welsh, that's my hidden talent, my special thing. I can't believe I didn't tell you before, but I guess I didn't?'

'Really?' said May. 'Proper Welsh? But you come from Sevenoaks, we went to see your nan there.'

May was surprised. Surely it would have come up before, a whole language? She wanted to believe him, but it seemed so strange. They had talked about languages, and swapped stories of German and French exchange visits, and he had never mentioned this hidden talent.

'So the lady isn't buying it. Have I ever lied to you? So

disbelieving for one so young. Well, maybe not so young, but...'

May felt unreasonably upset. She hated any mention of her age, absolutely hated it, and now she felt stupid as well. Of course it was true that he spoke Welsh, why would he lie to her?

'Oh May, I didn't mean to upset you, I was just joshing, come here.' Alain sat down at the kitchen table and pulled May on to his knee.

She wished that she wasn't so emotional, so girly, so weak. She hadn't been like this before she got pregnant, she was sure she had been tougher. Why couldn't she just ask him why he had hidden it from her?

'Oh lovely girl,' Alain said, followed by something in a lilting language that May presumed must be Welsh. 'See, I can still do it! I was at university in Wales, you know that, a little college in Lampeter, and Welsh was on offer to all the students there. There weren't many English students, in fact hardly any, I don't know quite how I ended up there but I did and I took the Welsh option and I loved it. And now I've got a job from it and it's such a good start for us. It's with the Welsh Film Board. I bet you never even knew there was such a thing, did you? Go on, admit it. But there is, and I'm going to be one of their translators. They have a small team, you see, who translate the major new releases into Welsh. They either oversee the dubbing process, or they write subtitles. It's a dream of a job and that's not even the best bit.'

Alain turned to May. She could see the excitement shining in his eyes.

'What is the best bit?' May asked. It must be a pregnancy thing, she thought, some altered reality thing that made her feel as though she was playing along, as if none of it was true.

'I'm glad you asked that,' Alain said, 'very glad indeed. It's as though you could read my mind, thank you, missus, lady with the lump, you're a picture of beauty even when you're stirring the mince. I'll tell you, seeing as you asked so very nicely. There's a flat with it, that's the best thing. Look, I've got all the details here.'

Alain reached into the bag by his side and pulled out a sheaf of papers and photographs. May stood up, conscious of how heavy she must feel on his lap. He handed her the papers and May gasped. The pictures were amazing. May could see a large house with a long driveway set amongst trees. She had been so worried about where they would live when the baby was born. The panic she felt had increased with every week of her pregnancy, until it was there all the time like a malevolent parrot attached to her shoulder. May felt the weight of it lessen.

'That's it, merry May, that's the Welsh Film Board house. And our flat is inside, imagine! There's a Land Rover that everyone can use to get to the end of the driveway, and from there it's only a few minutes into Bangor, it will be such a great place for the baby to grow up, May, imagine.'

Wales. May had spent a seaside holiday in Wales once,

in a caravan. She had always wanted to go back. Just the word conjured up pictures of sunny beaches and picturesque hills. Compared to Hull, it sounded like paradise. She looked again at the trees and the big, friendly-looking house.

'Will it matter,' she said, 'that I don't speak Welsh? I mean, if everyone else does.' May trailed off, painfully aware of how boring she must sound. She wasn't good at languages, Alain knew that.

'I'll learn, of course,' she said, trying to sound more together, less pathetic, 'I'll pick it up, I'm sure.'

'Oh darling, you will, you will, and we can bring the baby up to be bilingual, maybe call her Myfanwy or Glendower.'

That's going a bit far, thought May, I'm not sure about that at all. She would have liked to say something about the names they had already chosen, but Alain was so excited and really, he was right, it was a great opportunity. A flat in a big house, with trees and grounds and space for the baby, no housemates. May could hardly eat for excitement. It was going to be OK.

Later that evening, after *Mastermind*, May snuggled up to Alain on the rickety sofa. He was knitting, following a pattern he'd made himself.

'I love you because you knit, do you know that?' she said. It was true. May adored the fact that he knitted, loved the way his mouth pursed as he was tackling a difficult part of a pattern. The little creatures Alain had knitted for the baby marched across the mantelpiece in a line. There was

Pooh, Christopher Robin, Eeyore, Tigger, four hedgehogs and a family of dogs with sticking up ears.

'The baby will love them, and I love them,' she said. 'Tell me a story.'

'Ah, well, Eeyore, there, he loves babies. Not to eat, you understand, he loves to wash them and feed them and generally look after them. It's his thing, his private passion.'

'Like speaking Welsh,' May said.

'Yes,' said Alain, 'exactly like that. Only more difficult to follow through, because at least a person can speak Welsh in their head, or to a wall or a dog. But looking after babies, well, you need a baby for that. Eeyore tried to get his hands on one, but no one would trust him. "You're too damn miserable," they said, "it'll rub off on the baby." One of his friends, I think it was Tigger, bought him a doll, a little woolly baby he could practise on. Do you think that worked?'

'No,' said May, 'I think Eeyore would have wanted the real thing.'

'Spot on,' said Alain. 'You couldn't pull the wool over Eeyore's eyes, if you'll pardon the pun. He was so sad. All the creatures with babies kept away from him; they still saw him on adult occasions, obviously, nights out, that kind of thing, but at home he was alone, and he longed for a baby and a family of his own.'

'Didn't he want a wife as well?' said May.

'I'm not sure about that,' Alain said. 'I think he thought he wasn't good enough, wasn't worthy of a wife. He had terrible depression, you see, and I think he thought that only the love of a baby would cure it. Hang on, I've got to concentrate here, this bit is fiddly. It's the tail.'

'Let me see,' said May. 'Oh look, it's a tiny Eeyore, I didn't realise, it's so sweet, is it his baby?'

'It is,' said Alain. 'I thought I'd give him what he wants.'

I'm happy, May thought, he's a sweet man. It's normal to have little niggles.

'Do you think it will always be good?' May said. 'I mean us, our relationship, will we always be happy like this?'

She stretched out and patted Alain's head.

'No,' Alain said and for a moment May's stomach clenched, 'it'll be better, I promise, even better than this. We're never going to need anyone else.'

May wondered for a moment about friends. Surely we'll need other people sometimes, she thought, friends with babies, that sort of thing.

'Just us, merry May,' Alain said.

CHAPTER THREE

October 2017
Lewisham

The door across the corridor has been closed for days. Whoever he is, he likes his privacy, that's clear, although sometimes I get this prickly feeling. In the back of my neck, as if I'm being watched. I look out when I can but there's nothing much to see from my room except passing ghouls leaning on sticks or walking frames or being pushed like babies. There are trolleys, of course, and if I could talk I'd try some conversation openers about them. Trolley dolly, I could say, or, have you got any gin on there? I used to know a whole song about hostess trolleys but I can't get it out, even when I try really hard, one word at a time. I wouldn't mind how it sounded if I could just say something. I read about someone once, had a stroke and when they started speaking again, they had a Russian accent. I'd even be happy with a Hull one.

It was an odd place, Hull. Always an ill wind blowing.

An east wind off the sea. I'm glad I've ended up here. The Thames, that's my idea of a river, you can keep the Humber. Maybe it's because I'm a Londoner, I try to sing when they bring the lunch. It's a small token of identity but that Kelly, I really do not like her, she holds my good hand down where I'm trying to make it conduct the imaginary band, and stuffs a spoonful of soup in my mouth. I hate soup. Food is food and drink is drink and let's not get the two things mixed up, that's what I say. What I used to say.

Jenny understands me sometimes. She's the only one who does, and she doesn't seem to mind about the spit thing. She leans in close, listens hard and then answers me. I've never been so glad to see her as I am these days. She comes most evenings, after work. She's a teacher, my Jenny, like I was. It must be genetic, I tell her, only that always makes her frown and I think it's because she doesn't like being compared to me. I can't blame her.

We're doing an autumn display for the assembly hall, she said last night, leaves hanging from coloured hoops and some big firework paintings.

She used to love fireworks when she was little, my Jenny. All the kiddies did. The smell of burning and the excitement, choosing all the little fireworks one by one and imagining what they would be like on the night. All fakery, all up in smoke but she liked it.

Bonfire? I tried to say, then just, fire?

I'm sure she understood. I'm sure she knew that I was asking to go to see some fireworks, in my chair. I saw the shadow pass across her face and I read what was behind it. Please don't ask me to do more than I can do, it said. I wished I could say more, maybe beg her to take me. She would probably have given in in the end, she's weak like that, but I wasn't going to get carried away. Not for a stupid firework display, with its oohs and aahs and heads pointed at the sky till the necks hurt. I'm glad when Jenny goes home.

Hull Fair was always on in October. It probably still is. Such a big thing, loads of streets shut off and all the children bundled into their coats for the first time that year and eating candy floss. I went with Alain. We didn't have many dates before I got pregnant but for a little while afterwards we had some lovely ones. He used to say he was carrying the courtship into the marriage, or some such nonsense. I ate burnt cinder toffee, I remember the taste even now. I'd been sick a lot in the pregnancy, and I couldn't keep much down at all, but that toffee, it tasted like something magic. Angel food, as long as angels don't have teeth. He won me a Womble, Alain did, throwing darts at a target. He always had good aim, Alain, and I was as pleased as a child with it. I hadn't ever done anything like that before, been to the fair with a boy. A man. I was as giddy as a girl.

I was older than Alain, but much less experienced. I'd spent most of my teens and twenties being the kind of girl that was asked along by other girls as a last resort. The kind of girl who went home on her own at the end of every evening out, unless one of her friends was extremely unlucky. A fat girl, if I am completely honest. A fat jolly girl with loads of pals and three similar navy blue dresses, worn in rotation. I see the fat girls now and they wear anything they like, bright pink leggings, crop tops, mini-skirts, shorts. I don't know what I think about that, but I do know it wasn't a thing that could have been done in the early seventies. Fat girls bought their clothes from the fuller figure range at Arding and Hobbs, Clapham Junction, or Binns in Hull. There were Peter Pan collars and ruches and tucks that were supposed to hide the fat, only they didn't.

I did have a boyfriend once. Brendan. He was a bit like me, awkward and tubby so everyone thought it was the best match, the cutest thing but he got handsome, almost overnight. That's how I remember it, one moment he was like me, waistband straining and T-shirt too tight, and the next he was slim and tanned and could take his pick. He chose Cherry, picked her right away and I didn't blame him at all. It made sense to me.

I stopped being a fat girl in 1976. Summer 1976 to be exact, when I started my teacher training year and everyone was singing 'Dancing Queen'. It wasn't my sort of music, but I used to put it on the record player every morning anyway, and I'd dance along to get my metabolism going. I was still doing it when I met Alain that Christmas, only I never told him. I was as slim as all the other young women by then, and I could see in the mirror that I was looking OK, but I couldn't believe he chose me. He could have had anyone.

I've put the song into my head now, like a fool. I try drumming it out with my good hand on the tray over my bed, that always used to get rid of it. I'm hoping to send the blasted song packing but instead I've knocked over the cold soup that was sitting on my tray. It's splashed all over the floor, the bed and even up the wall a little.

Kelly comes in. What have we got here, she says, what's this? She pulls the bed covers back more roughly than she needs to and I don't have time to make sure I'm decent underneath. What would happen if we all threw things we didn't like, huh? Who would do the cleaning up then? I didn't, I try to say, it was just that Abba song, that was all, I needed a drum roll but my hand wouldn't do it.

We don't need all that slobbering now do we she says, if you can't speak properly best say nothing.

By the time she's cleaned me up and settled me back into my chair we've used up at least half an hour. Even better, the head honcho, or shift supervisor or whatever they're called, she comes in and has a bit of a go at Kelly.

Why are you doing that on your own, she says, you should have called for help.

I didn't want to take anyone away from their own jobs, Kelly says, but head honcho sees right through that.

It's not your decision, she says, it's policy and that's what we do here. She has a sniff in her tone that you could hear from across the river. But she's good with the patients, or inmates, or whatever it is we are. It's all, are you OK Mrs Beecham and I try to say, Ms, but she takes it as a yes.

Splendid, she says, splendid, shall I get the girls to bring you some more soup? I shake my head at that one, don't even try to speak.

Fair enough, she says, let Kelly here know if you want anything else, won't you.

She isn't keen on that at all, Kelly, but she doesn't dare to be rough any more. She has a killer look when she puts the blanket round my knees, but it only makes me laugh. I've seen worse than that, I want to tell her, I don't scare so easily, not these days. You could probably get an axe murderer in here wielding his weapon and I wouldn't flinch. The old me, the fat sad little me that I was in my young life, she was scared of everything. Everything.

Jenny comes later, after school like she usually does.

I hear there was a problem, Mum, she says, a problem with the soup.

Soup, I try to say.

For a moment I've forgotten and I have no idea what she's talking about.

I forget where I am and think of soup, trickling down the walls, hot soup tipped over my head. Trying to wash the pieces out of my hair later.

No, I try to say, no no.

It's OK Mum, it doesn't matter, Jenny says and I'm back in the room, remembering the drum roll and the spilled soup. It's such a relief to know that no one threw it at me, I'm not in danger, it's all OK. I start to cry.

Mum I'll tell them, Jenny says, I'll tell them you don't like it, don't worry, it's OK.

She looks worried but I can't stop crying.

I don't like it here, it's all wrong. No one can understand me and I can feel the prickly feeling again, that tingle as though I'm being watched. I think it's the man in the room across the corridor, I'm sure it is. I can't tell Jenny, it would upset her but I'm sure I can see him out of the corner of my eye. He probably just sits there, watching, I wouldn't be surprised.

Can I come home with you, I want to say to Jenny, I don't like it here.

I can't get anything out now except stupid crying, but I'm sure she understands me. She looks away.

Please, I try to say, and I hate myself for doing it. I know she can't look after me, not with the toilet in her house being upstairs and anyway there's her ex-husband, she shares the house with him, I can't go there. I know all of that but I don't seem to be able to stop myself.

Let's go for a little walk, she says, let's get out of this room and take in the sights. I'm on the back foot, pardon the pun, I can't really say no. I'm sitting in my special chair that pushes me up and out at the flick of a control button, then it's touch and go getting to the wheelchair. She's a strong one though, my Jenny, and I make the transfer without too much folderol.

32

Round the Cape of Good Hope? she says and it makes me laugh a little, out of politeness.

She's right, it is good to get out of the room. It crowds in on me, that place, squashes me down until I can't get my breath. I used to feel like that in the little flat in Pimlico when Jenny was a baby, but I'd forgotten it until recently. He's got his door shut, the man across the way, maybe he shut it when he saw me coming. She pushes me down the corridors past closed doors or worse, open doors with glimpses of old people's lives in them. Televisions blaring, little stick legs on beds or dangling from chairs.

They're not like people, I try to say, they're an alien race of stick people. Sick sticks.

Ssh Mum, she says. I know she'd find it funny if I could just explain it to her, I'd love to see a twinkle in her eye.

Come to the dining room, she says, just take a look, it's really pretty with flowers and fairy lights and everything. There will be a tree at Christmas, I bet it's a big one, she says as if the sole aim of my life so far was to get to a dining room with a big Christmas tree. I don't bother to answer. To be honest, the struggle isn't worth it, even for Jenny. My words are on the ration, that's the thing, and to be used sparingly like eye drops.

Come on, she says, cheer up, I hate to see you like this, you're usually such a happy person.

I am? I think, really? I try to show her what I'm thinking by raising my eyebrows. I think it works on one side of my face. Jenny bursts out laughing.

Oh Mum, she says and she bends down to hug me in my chair. It doesn't feel right. I'm supposed to be bigger than her, that's how it goes with kids. Anything else is like dogs walking on their hind legs, or elephants playing cards. I try to tell her that but I think the only word she catches is elephant. She looks worried.

We sit there for a while, at one of the round tables in the dining room. Neither of us knows what to say to the other. She's right, they have made an effort to make it look pretty. Soft lighting, big windows looking out on to the grass, more like an upmarket old-fashioned hotel than a nursing home.

Who's paying for this? I want to say. Jenny has no idea what I'm talking about, so I make the sign for cash, rubbing my thumb against my fingers on my good hand. I don't want it to come out of her inheritance, that's what I want to tell her so I make a gesture to take in all the fancy lighting and the soft carpet that most of the residents can't walk on anyway.

Pish, she says, don't think about it, everything is fine.

How are you going to get away from that stupid oik of an ex-husband if I don't help you? I want to say. I make the gesture of a walking stick, and a little wobble. I put my finger over my lip and under my nose like a moustache.

Ah, Jenny says, you're talking about the walking stick again.

Yes I am I try to say, my movements getting a tad frantic. It's a walking stick I own, you see, it's in my wardrobe, it was definitely used by Charlie Chaplin and it should be worth something. I got it at an auction.

Hush now, she says, don't worry, I know where it is, the stick. Let's do a jigsaw.

I can tell that she's a really good teacher. The kind of teacher who is loved by the children, but never promoted. Different from me, softer and kinder. I hate jigsaws, always have, but for once I think I ought to do something to please her rather than myself. And it's calming, it really is. Looking at pieces, seeing whether they fit in, for a moment there's no room for any of the ghosts who usually patrol my head. The jigsaw picture is of sweets and chocolates from the sixties and seventies, and my mouth is watering like a burst pipe in seconds. Opal Fruits and Bar Noir, KitKats with the real silver paper, Butter Snap and Aztec. All jostling for position on the table in front of us. It's like it used to be, just the two of us only this time I'm the infant and Jenny gets to be the adult.

I've made a will, I try to say. I thinks she gets the word, will. I lodged it with Cate who lives next door but one, I want to say, you know, the woman with the black car and the brown dog. I notice that even in the words I don't say I've been reduced to describing things by their colours. Cate, I could have tried, the woman whose husband died of oesophageal cancer two years ago last summer. As if I will ever attempt the word oesophageal again.

Don't talk about wills, Mum, Jenny says, talk about Crunchies instead and she holds up the missing piece of

Crunchie wrapper like a trophy. We both laugh and she reminds me that on a Friday we always used to have a Crunchie bar to celebrate the weekend. I'm struck by remorse and I can't explain why. Was that enough, I want to ask, is that a happy enough memory to keep you going?

The fun goes out of the jigsaw for a moment and I try to sulk quietly. I have surrounded myself with the mundane, I think, and you are the unfortunate byproduct. I refuse to comment on the piece of Cadbury's fudge she holds up. She's hurt, I can tell she's hurt, and I didn't mean to upset her.

Only joking, I try to say.

I attempt to fit a piece of Galaxy bar into the jigsaw but my arm does that trick again of being out of control and swinging and the whole thing tumbles to the floor. All the pieces, upside down, all the progress we'd made, gone.

Sorry, I say, arm. I can't see how anyone could understand, it's just a shout.

That's OK, she says, you couldn't help it, it's only a jigsaw, don't worry.

But I liked it I think, I liked it and before I know where I am I'm sobbing like a baby again, crying as if my last hope had just died.

It's OK, it's OK, Jenny says, we can do it again, and she hugs me and I don't like it but I've made so much fuss now that even I can see I will just have to bloody well put up with it. Just a jigsaw, just a jigsaw, she says in my ear, and I remember a time when I said similar things to her, it's just a woolly rabbit, it'll be OK, never mind.

I push her away. No point making a drama out of a crisis, that's what I'd say if I could. I've always had a thing about clichés, tried not to use them too much but these days they speak for me. Least said soonest mended, that one works, too.

I try to rub my eye with my good hand and it's then that I see him. Like rubbing a lamp to make a genie appear, my eye rub has produced a man over in a shadowy corner that I hadn't noticed before. I think he's the man who has been watching me, I'm not sure. From the room across the corridor. There's something familiar about the tilt of his head.

Is everything OK? he asks, anything I can do?

Jenny replies to him civilly and they exchange a few words about the weather and the flower decorations, that kind of thing, and all the time there's something playing at the back of my mind. I know that voice, I think, I know that person with his head tilted just so, as if he has a list of questions in his pocket to ask the world.

Mum, you're shaking, says Jenny, let's get you back to bed. Did you see that nice man I was talking to? He seemed really friendly, don't you be flirting with him now.

I try to pull myself together. This is important, I think, this is no time to go to pieces. Think, May, think. It's like an egg and spoon race in my brain when I try to think in a straight line. A slippery egg and spoon race through mud, with a gigantic egg and a tiny spoon. The harder I run at it, the more it slips off. What was it about the man? Why did he seem so familiar?

Before we're even halfway along the corridor to my room I've forgotten the exact shape of the tilt of his head, and the way he looked at me doesn't feel so bad. I'm an old woman, you see, and I've started thinking about toasted cheese sandwiches and chocolate instead. I can't even keep the thread of my unease. It's still there, in the background. It's like one of those tiny figures in the distance in a painting by that chap, is it Lowry, I try to say his name to Jenny. I can see it, I know it's there, but I can't actually make out the shape. She doesn't understand me this time, I can see that.

She stops pushing me along the corridor and she bends down close and says, what's that Mum? Say it again. I catch sight of the lines around her eyes, close up they seem very prominent. Did I do that, I wonder. I put my hand up to try to stroke them away, it's an instinct but I can't control my arm at the best of times and this is the worst of times so I knock Jenny and she's bending anyway so I catch her off guard and she falls.

I'm so so sorry, I try to say, I was only, I just wanted to, I'm sorry.

It's OK Mum, she says, but I can hear she's fighting tears.

I wouldn't ever want to hurt you, I try but the egg has slipped off the spoon and into my mouth somehow and the words sound even more like rubbish than usual, even to me. Like the chorus of a bad pop song, over and over again with no meaning.

I have a sudden memory of Jenny learning to speak.

She was such an earnest little thing. She tried so hard, as if someone had set her homework and she was going to be tested on it the next day. We had the TV on and it was Saturday afternoon, I remember. The presenter was reading the football scores. Liverpool one, Manchester United two, he said and every damn score he announced, she copied, with the exact same inflection in her voice and concentrating so hard on getting the shape of her mouth right. These days I would have videoed her I suppose, stuck it on Facebook for everyone to admire. Back then I just watched and marvelled and thought, I'm going to make sure things are OK for this child, I am going to keep her safe. Look at her now. Lined and lonely on the floor.

OK, I say, and my voice is suddenly clearer than it was by far. Go, I say. It's as near as I can get. What I want to say is, it's OK, you don't have to visit me here any more. Go off, travel the world, have a baby, rob a bank. Have some fun. I can't say it, only go, but I can see that she has understood anyway.

Mum, she says, getting up and brushing herself down, don't be daft, I'm alright, you didn't mean to, everything's fine.

I'm too tired now or I'd tell her that everything isn't fine, and that something today has made me think of danger, I'm not sure what it is, and that she would be better off away from whatever it is that I'm too knackered to remember.

Go, I whisper again as we get back into my room.

She rings the bell for the carers to help me get into bed,

it's too late for sitting in the chair now. I need to lie down and the tiredness is like a massive weight on my head. Go away, I don't want to see you any more, I think. She understands that one, and there are tears in her eyes.

I'm saying it for you, I think, I've always tried to do what's best for you, I'm not going to stop now.

I could come back tomorrow, she says, let you know how 5B managed their poems about autumn.

I want that more than anything, but there's danger somewhere and I can't remember where but there's something about a tilt of the head and a smiling face that terrifies me and the least I can do is keep her away.

I'm tired, I try to say as the night duty carer helps me into the hoist, and I am, I'm tired, she must see that. Stay away, I think, let me rest, bloody Crunchie bars.

Don't worry, the carer says. I think it's Mary, the nice Irish one. Don't worry, she says, she doesn't mean it like it sounds, it's the brain injury talking. Why don't you just stay at home for a day or two so that you can catch a rest as well? That way, when you come back everything will be like shiny new again. She'll be pleased as punch to see you.

I keep my head hanging down, don't look up or she might see I'm crying.

What was it, I remember thinking just before I went to sleep, what was the danger? Tilt of the head, that's the echo back, tilt of the head, rhyming with dead.

CHAPTER FOUR

October 1977
Hull

May looked at her reflection in the department store window and smiled. She didn't have a long mirror at home, and she couldn't help being surprised every time she saw how big she was. She had worked hard to stay slim, and in that time her life had changed beyond recognition. Husband, baby, a whole life that had been waiting for her. She hoped she hadn't jinxed things by getting fat, even though it was for a good cause, even though she was pregnant. May didn't know any other pregnant women, so she wasn't sure whether she was unusually big, but she thought she might be. She was the kind of huge that made perfect strangers at bus stops smile at her, or feel entitled to stroke her pregnant stomach as if it belonged to them. May felt like a massive insect full of eggs. It was difficult to believe that there was only one baby in there.

'Looking good,' May heard someone say. She realised

that the woman was speaking to her. She turned from her reflection.

'Oh gosh, yes, I'm sorry, just can't quite get over myself, you know?'

The other woman laughed and May noticed that she was pregnant too, but smaller.

'You too,' May said, 'welcome to the club!'

'Literally,' said the other woman.

She looked younger than May, taller and with a more graceful bump.

'I like your bump,' May said. 'Sorry, I didn't mean to be rude. No offence meant.'

'None taken,' the woman said. 'In fact I think from now on I will only allow comments on my bump from women, and specifically, women who are more pregnant than me. It's a good rule.'

May laughed. It must be lovely, she thought, to be as confident as that, to be able to make jokes with complete strangers.

'I'm Helen,' the woman said. 'Pleased to meet someone else who might be as bonkers as I am. Do you ever wonder why you're doing this?' Helen pointed to her pregnant stomach.

May laughed. 'Only about every five minutes,' she said. 'I mean, don't get me wrong, I'm happy and all that but...' May's voice tailed off as she wondered if she had spoken out of turn. She looked down towards where her big feet would be if she could see through her stomach. Typical, she

42

thought. I've been longing to talk to someone else who's pregnant, and when I do I mess it up. No one likes a moaner.

'Hey,' said Helen, 'maybe we should stick together. Safety in numbers and all that. I know how you feel. I think it's normal, in fact I'm sure it is, I read it in a book!'

May felt as though she wanted to cry. Pregnancy hormones, she thought.

'Have you got much ready for your little one?' May asked. 'Only it's difficult to know how much we're going to need, isn't it? Some books say twenty babygros, others say twelve.'

Helen threw back her head and laughed.

'Twenty!' she said. 'I reckon these books are funded by the babygro industry. Mine will be wearing nighties anyway, I've made them myself.'

'Oh, me too,' said May and the two women smiled at each other. May thought how lovely Helen was. She was dark skinned, possibly Asian, with long black curly hair. Even pregnant, she shone out as something rare in the litter-flying grime of Hull city centre. Beautiful, like a lizard from a beach landscape or a fire in the distance. May blushed at her silliness for thinking such things.

'You really do suit being pregnant,' May said.

Helen laughed. 'Well I'm never going to be pregnant again,' she said, 'so maybe I should have a photograph taken. I haven't got any pictures, and I can promise you, this little one is going to have absolutely no brothers or sisters.'

'A dog?' said May. 'I was thinking, for mine, maybe a dog might be company for her.'

'For her?' said Helen, raising her eyebrows. 'So you think you know the sex then? Have you done that wedding ring test, where you loop the ring on a hair from your head and dangle it over your belly to see which way it swings?'

'I have not,' said May, 'and if you're asking me that, I know you're not the rational woman I thought you were a moment ago. Sometimes I think she's a girl and I say her, sometimes a boy. Today she's Amelia or Rose.'

They both laughed, and May felt an unfamiliar warmth, a sense of camaraderie.

'I'd ask if you want to come for a cup of coffee, in Binns,' Helen said, 'but coffee is out of my budget right now.'

May was happy that the hike in coffee prices had not just affected her. She had been so lonely recently, she had started to believe that everyone else was still swilling coffee like they used to, and that she was the only one who had had to give it up.

'Tea it is then,' said May.

May was excited. She hadn't realised how much she needed someone to talk to, and Helen was the best company May had met in a long time. The only company.

'I should tell you,' Helen said as they sat down in the department store cafe, 'I'm a lone mum, I'm on my own with this one, a single mother, I think that's what the papers say.'

May wondered for a brief moment what that would be like.

'You're brave,' she said, 'I don't know how I'd manage without Alain.'

'I guess you're one of the lucky ones,' Helen said. 'A good man and a straightforward life, well done you.'

Helen sounded as if she meant it, as if she really was pleased for May. May felt embarrassed at her good fortune.

'Maybe I can help,' May said. 'You know, when your little one is born. Many hands make light work and all that stuff.'

Anything, she thought, I'll do anything to have a friend.

'Ha,' said Helen, 'tell me that again when you've had that baby. Have you ever looked after a baby?'

'I babysat for the vicar's little boy when I was a teenager,' May said. As soon as she had said it, she realised how silly she sounded. As if looking after someone else's child for a few hours would be any kind of preparation. And vicar – how prim did that make her sound?

'I mean…' she said and both women exploded with laughter.

'I'll know where to come for advice if this lump of a baby has any spiritual queries,' Helen said, 'seeing as you might have a direct line.'

'Oh my goodness,' said May, 'I'm not, I mean I don't know why I said that, but please don't think I'm some kind of religious nutcase.'

'Just because you said the word "vicar?"' Helen said. 'Don't worry, I think I'll let you off.'

May liked Helen more and more. Humour, she thought,

she'd been missing that recently. And closeness to another woman. She wondered if it would be rude to ask Helen about her baby's dad. What must it be like, she wondered as she stirred her tea, how did she manage the loneliness?

'I feel like we've been friends for a while,' Helen said. 'Isn't that weird?'

'No,' said May, 'it isn't weird, I feel it too. Maybe meeting when you're very pregnant is like meeting in wartime or something.'

May hoped that she didn't sound too ridiculous. Why had she thought of wartime? She was pregnant and happy, wasn't she?

'Exactly,' said Helen. 'When the bombs and the babies start flying, it's time for us women to stick together.'

There was an awkward silence as May tried to think what to say next. She didn't want to scare Helen away by being too needy, and she wasn't quite sure why it was all so important.

'We're moving soon,' May said, 'to Bangor. My husband has a job there.'

'Bangor?' said Helen. 'It's lovely there, I went for a university interview, gorgeous. You don't sound too happy about it though, surely you're not going to pine for the mean streets of Hull?'

May laughed. She couldn't trust herself to speak for a moment. She had no idea, none at all, why she felt so low. It must be a pregnancy thing, she thought. It was ridiculous to be so pleased to talk to someone else, ridiculous.

'We went there last week,' May said, 'and stayed in a nice hotel and everything. I didn't get to see the flat because I didn't feel well, but Alain did and he said it's lovely. Huge grounds and everything, it goes with the job.'

Helen stirred her cold tea.

'Sounds lovely,' she said. 'Maybe me and Baby Lump here will be able to come to stay.'

'Oh yes,' said May, 'that would be amazing.'

May noticed that Helen seemed less bouncy.

'Are you OK?' she said.

'Yes, sorry, I'm fine,' said Helen, 'only I feel lonely, that's all, and hearing about your plans, I'm just worried. What if I can't do this on my own?'

May realised how thoughtless she had been. Typical May, she thought, thinking about yourself instead of other people.

'I'm so sorry,' she said, 'I haven't even asked about you. Is he involved, your baby's dad? Is he going to help you?'

Helen looked around as though she might find an answer written on the wall, or out of the window. May wished she could kick herself for being so thoughtless.

'That's a story for another day,' Helen said. 'Don't worry about me, I'm fine, I've got a politics degree and it would take more than a tiny baby and a stupid man to stop me. I'm going to be a writer. I've been on my own for about a month now and it's just fabulous. Honestly, I'm hard up but there's the dole, and the landlord at the local pub gives me the odd shift, cash in hand. No one tells me what to watch on TV, or what to eat. I never have to worry about anyone else, May. Imagine that.'

May found that she couldn't imagine that, not quite. It didn't seem possible.

May thought about that later, when she was back home. Neither of the women had telephones, so she and Helen had exchanged addresses but May wasn't at all sure whether they would be able to meet again. Binns cafe, they had said, they would both try to get to Binns cafe on Friday mornings if they could.

'It'll be fine for me,' Helen had said. 'Fire, flood and pestilence permitting, I'll be here.' It was May who might have the difficulty, but she couldn't explain that to herself, let alone Helen. Still, even if they never met again, May thought that it had been wonderful to talk to another woman.

May put on the dress Alain liked and spent the afternoon cooking. A celebration meal, she thought, a Bangor special. She pushed Helen to the back of her mind, thinking that she would ponder it over later, when she was in bed. May didn't know where Alain was, but he'd talked a lot recently about going for interviews at schools, just to get the lie of the land. He hated it when May asked lots of questions, so she had no idea why he would go for interviews when he already had a job. May guessed he wanted to have a backup plan, in case anything went wrong. He was always so careful. He wanted everything to be definite, and who could blame him? If the Welsh Film Board would just contact them, to confirm starting dates and so on, May was sure Alain would feel much more secure.

May could tell from the slam of the door as Alain came in that things had not gone to plan.

'Hi, darling,' May called. 'How did it go? Would you like a cuppa?'

'No thanks,' he said. 'Not in the mood.'

May wondered if it was something she had done. She checked the mugs on the mug tree but they were OK, all pointing in the same direction. Alain was so tidy, he could get really upset when she just threw them on any old way. May pushed her hair back with her arm. Alain did not seem his usual self at all. He picked up his knitting from the table, shook his head and put it down again.

'Leave the cooking, May, turn it off. We need to talk.'

'But I…' May said. But I've been cooking for an hour, she wanted to say, it's a meal you like, and I haven't been eating recently, I was looking forward to it too. It will be horrible heated up later.

She looked at Alain's face. I'm so selfish, she thought, fancy thinking about myself and my fat stomach when he is so worried.

'OK,' she said, 'let's go upstairs to the living room. The students are in but they're up in their attic, with their music. It's more comfortable upstairs and I've been standing for a while.'

'No,' said Alain. 'I'd like to talk down here. I'm fed up with wondering whether they're listening to me every time I say anything.'

'OK,' said May. She felt wrong-footed somehow, as if she had been caught out.

'While we're talking about stuff that annoys us,' said Alain, 'maybe we should talk food.'

Are we, thought May, is that what we're doing? Where did this come from? May didn't want Alain to know how upset she was, it would make her seem so childish.

'OK, fire away,' she said, trying to sound amused.

'I don't want to be rude,' Alain said, 'but could we eat something that isn't from the bloody Paupers Cookbook? If I eat another recipe made with cheap cuts of meat and tinned soup I think I'll be sick, honestly.'

May tried to smile. She should have known, she thought, she really should have known that her cooking was completely disgusting. She was trying to cook on the cheap, that was the thing, and May wasn't sure that Alain realised how hard up they were.

'I'm sorry,' she said, trying to keep her voice steady. 'Seems reasonable to me. I'll try some other stuff.'

'I think it's better if I take over, don't you? Leave you more time for whatever it is you do in the daytime.'

May felt stung.

'Al,' she said, 'Al, don't be like this, I'm sorry about the surplus of mince, honest I am, but you're not going to have time to cook when you're working.'

'And that's another thing,' Alain said, 'the job, it didn't work out.'

'The Welsh Film Board?' said May. 'Oh Al, I'm so sorry, you must be upset.' She moved towards Alain, instinctively wanting to comfort him, reassure him that she still cared about him. Alain stepped back, held his arms out as if to ward May off.

'No need to get maudlin,' Alain said, 'no point talking about it, these things happen. They lost their funding, that's all there is to it. I'm back in the market for a teaching job and that's that. I'm sure one will come up.'

But what about the flat, May wanted to say, what about the money I paid for the hotel when we went to Bangor? They said they were going to refund it; will they still do that? And if not, how will we cope? She didn't say anything. It wasn't the right time. Alain's face was set, he looked hard, like a person she hardly knew.

'We'll be OK, Al,' she said. 'We have each other, and the baby.'

It was the best she could come up with, but as soon as May had said it she knew it was the wrong thing. Alain looked at her in a way that made her shiver. She put her hands on her stomach as if she needed to protect the baby.

'Really?' Al said. 'You're sure of that, are you?'

May concentrated hard on trying not to cry. It's just those pregnancy hormones making things seem worse, she thought, it's all fine, just a little setback, that's all. Everyone has moods. Count to ten, don't say anything, keep your breathing even.

May could feel the tension in the room uncoil. It's getting better, she told herself, see, it was just a blip. Alain smiled and reached out to touch her arm.

'Hey,' he said, 'don't look so worried, it's all OK, something else will come along. I didn't mean to upset you.'

May felt as though the world had righted itself again, as though a comet that had been hurtling towards her, hurtling towards them, had changed course at the last moment. Perhaps it was all in my imagination, she thought, I'm ridiculous.

The students who shared their house came downstairs that evening. Alain usually liked to stay as far away from them as he could, but that evening he went out of his way to play the host. He cooked scrambled eggs for all of them and they sat together in the dining room.

'Isn't this lovely?' Alain said, beaming round the table. 'We should do this more often.' He balanced the plates up his arms like a waiter and brought them to the table.

'Ta da,' he said. 'Look at that, I've still got it.' Alain did a little twirl and sang, 'I did it my way.'

May caught a look between the two students. They obviously found him funny. May felt protective of him, annoyed with them for being so immature. They didn't like him, that much was obvious, and he had tried so hard, it wasn't fair. What did they know? They were both practically still teenagers. Both with long hair parted in the middle, and both hardly able to keep their hands off each other for long enough to eat the meal Alain had prepared. May felt so angry with them that she forgot how much she hated scrambled eggs, forgot how the gloopiness usually made her heave. Alain must have forgotten that too, she thought, hardly surprising when he had so much to think about.

May looked up from her plate and saw that the male student, Steve, was mimicking Alain's expansive hand gestures. Ruth, the young woman, convulsed with laughter and covered her mouth with her hand to keep her food in. May looked at Alain and saw that this time there was no doubt that Alain had seen it. He looked crestfallen and May's heart went out to him.

'I'm feeling tired, Al,' she said. 'It's been lovely, eating together, but maybe Steve and Ruth have got work they need to be getting on with. We don't want to keep them.'

'Ah, May is feeling tired,' Alain said. 'So we must all do as she says, eh, you two?'

He winked at the students. They shuffled awkwardly, hilarity forgotten. They were clearly almost as embarrassed as May.

'I only meant...' she said before tailing off.

'And there you have it, ladies and gentlemen,' Alain said. 'She only meant, and we her humble slaves can do nothing but obey.'

He lit a cigarette, picked up May's hand and kissed it.

'Your servant, ma'am,' he said, bending his knee to the floor with a dramatic flourish.

Alain laughed as though he had made a great joke and the students stood up. May stood still, trying to resolve what had just happened. Was he mocking her? Surely not, surely that was her being insensitive again, not getting it. He meant well, he loved her.

'Let us do the washing up before we go,' Ruth said. 'Come on, Steve, roll your sleeves up.'

'No need, no need at all, it was our pleasure, wasn't it, May?' Alain said.

May nodded, not trusting herself to speak. The students went upstairs, but later, when May came down to get some water, she bumped into Ruth on the stairs. Ruth had a strange expression on her face and for a moment, May couldn't place it. She was back in bed and lying down before she realised what it was. Pity. She had seen the same expression on the faces of her mother's friends at the funeral. Poor May, they had said to each other, thinking that she wasn't listening. Poor May.

CHAPTER FIVE

November 2017
Lewisham

It's not quite as bad here as I thought it would be.

Don't get me wrong, it's not a holiday camp, not even a rubbish one like the place in Filey I took Jenny to once, but it's not Holloway Prison either. I've been getting out of my room more, that's what's made the difference. Socialising with the other residents, they call it. Like in prison. I can't actually talk to them, of course, they wouldn't understand me. We're in a different kind of prison here, I'd tell them if I could, imprisoned by our own bodies. They've ganged up on us, our bodies, and got their own back for all those years of abuse. That strikes me as very funny and I decide to practise saying it, in case I get a chance. Timing, that's the key, if you're going to make a joke you have to make it at the exact right time to get them laughing. I might have enjoyed being a comedian, only my life wasn't very funny and anyway I didn't think of it till recently. It's a bit late now.

We had a meeting the other day, all the residents in the dining hall. What a sorry looking lot. Missing legs, arms that wouldn't move, bent spines, heads that couldn't look up. If you scrapped us all for body parts you'd be hard put to make one decent whole one. Anyway, one of the carers, ('call me Siobhan', if you please. I would if I knew how to say it, I want to say), one of the carers says, we want to hear from you guys.

Guys, I thought, aren't we mostly gals? I don't understand why the young ones aren't protesting more about that. In my day it was 'man'. Everyone said 'man', as if it meant woman as well, and we all said, don't call me man, I'm a woman.

She said, guys, we need to hear from you about what you want to do, recreation wise. Cocaine, I tried to say, that's a recreational drug, but they can't understand me, even on a good day, so I can say anything I damn well please.

Knitting, one of them said, a knitting circle. That's not much good for me, one of the old men said, last time I looked I had a pair, and he looked down at his lap. As if real men couldn't knit. I get a picture then, little knitted animals lined up and it makes me feel tearful. How dare he say that. I can't believe this is the level of ignorance I have to live with, I thought, me, me who could recite the opening chapter of *Pride and Prejudice* if only my mouth would work properly. Knitting, I'd say if I could, I'd like to learn to knit. I was always too clumsy, back then. Two left fists and neither of them fit for purpose, that's what Alain said the time he tried to teach me.

What about something that suits everyone, Siobhan says, what about bingo? She gets a bit of a cheer for that one, but there are groans as well and I'm happy to groan along with the best of them. Ooh, she says, that's controversial, I like a bit of controversy. Bingo it is.

What about a letter writing circle for Amnesty International, I think, and I'd say it if I could. I wish I'd done more of that sort of thing in my life, made a difference for someone. I feel like I understand more about being locked up now that I'm in here. I wish someone would write a letter asking for my release. Free the Lewisham One, that's what I'd write on my wall if I could.

What about dancing, one of the young carers says, I've seen this research that says it's good for, good for. She tails off, as if we're going to be surprised at her calling us old people or people with brain injuries or whatever thing she was going to say. As if we didn't know what we were.

One of the old chaps gets up. He's tiny and neatly dressed. He goes to the front, bows and starts twirling round, bending and swaying as if he's at a Saturday night shindig. He stops after a while, he's coughing too much to go on. He's not bad actually, quite a sense of rhythm and we all clap when he's finished and he bows. You can see that Siobhan is getting a little bit cross.

Dancing, she says, well I'll put that on my list.

Pub quiz says someone else, a woman on the next table to me. That's a bloody good idea, I think, that could be fun. It's nearly Christmas, says someone else, let's have a card making workshop. Let's not and say we did, I think but Siobhan, she loves that idea. She actually claps so I guess it's going to happen pretty soon. I suppose it will be worth sticking some glittery trees on some folded paper so that I can get out of that damned room. I can send a card to Jenny, maybe cheer her up a little.

I'm thinking that the meeting is over, that someone will come and wheel me back, when one of the really old ones speaks up. Singing, she says, we could have a sing-song. She points at the piano over in the corner of the dining room. I hadn't noticed it until then. Nearly everyone likes that suggestion. They're all chatting away and I can hear a snatch or two of a tune. Everyone wants to say what their favourite is. Of course, most of them are much older than me. The Beatles, I want to say, Billie Holliday, Eric Clapton, Elvis Costello, what about some decent jazz. Leila, I think and the old riff plays in my head as if I have headphones. Da da dee dee da da da, la la la la la. 'May You Never', I want to say, my theme tune. But no one can understand me, so I keep quiet and listen to the sad old voices warbling about bluebirds and Dover or Tipperary. Surely we're too young for that, I think, even the oldest of us?

My my, Siobhan says, that's got you all going, I can see that you would all love a sing-song. Only thing is, we need to find some songs you can all sing, ones we all have in common.

Good luck with that, I'm thinking, but then this old one pipes up from the back. She's got a loud voice, not usual in here where everyone is aquiver and speaking like they're worried they might interrupt someone from dying. She sounds like a head teacher or a politician. What have we all got in common, she says, what's a thing that we all learned at our mother's knee? You have to be careful with that kind of language in a place like this, I'd like to tell her, a mention of the word 'mother' and the word 'knee' in one sentence and they'll all go stark staring bonkers. They do too, there's a dabbing of tissues at the corners of eyes, a sniffing and a sighing and a shuffling.

I don't know, says Siobhan, and she's speaking for me too for once. What have we got in common, she asks.

Nursery rhymes, says the loud old one, we all know our nursery rhymes and they're very relaxing. I don't know who for, I'd shout if I could. I wouldn't care who heard, who got upset. It's the worst idea I ever heard. I can't think of any way to convey quite what a bad idea I think it is. Bloody nursery rhymes? As if we weren't infantilised enough already, grown women and men – you wouldn't believe it if you hadn't seen it with your own two eyes. I'm expecting everyone to think like I do, to be horrified and shouting and telling the loud voiced one what she could do with her idea. I want them to rise up, to get some dignity in here but they're nodding. They're a bunch of those nodding head dogs from the back windows of cars, nod nod nod. What a good idea, I hear one of them say, and some old woman on my table starts humming baa baa black sheep. I try to arrange my hand so I can give her the finger but she doesn't notice. I look up and catch the eye of a woman on the next table. She's grinning, and she mimes a little clap, so I try a bow but it may have looked more like a lurch.

I've noticed the woman on the next table before, and to be honest, I've been thinking that she looks like the most interesting one in here. It's her hair, that's the thing. She stands out in a sea of shampoo and set lookalikes. They're all grey and white and tidy and short. I'm not knocking it, I am too but she's different, this woman. She's old, maybe around my age, maybe even older, it's hard to tell, but she's got dreadlocks that reach halfway down her back. She's pretty too, pretty for an old one, and I wonder how on earth she's ended up here. I'd say she had a look of my lovely Helen, same confidence in her own skin. There's a spirited look I remember Helen having, that's the other similarity. A let the world go hang itself look, a don't bother me with your nonsense look. I can see it now on the woman at the next table. They're both their own person, that's the thing. Some days I still miss Helen. I smile over at the woman on the next table. I hope she comes over, I think, she's not in a wheelchair, she must be able to walk. I hope she comes over at the end when it's mingling time.

There's a bit more talk about knitting and playing cards

but I've lost interest now. I'm thinking about the way she looked at me and smiled, as if we were the only two people in here who would understand what nonsense it all was. I try to look interested in it all, just in case she's watching me. I try not to look at her but I can't help sneaking a peek from time to time, I'm only human. She tilts her head in a way that makes me think of someone else but I can't remember who.

Just at the end, when it's all being wrapped up and the carers have come forward to disperse us, take us to our various perches and give us a cup of something and a biscuit, they bring in another old chap. He's in a wheelchair and he's a bit slumped so I don't recognise him at first but when I look again I realise that it's the old man from the room across the corridor from mine. He's changed. He looks like his head won't stay up but there's still something about him, I don't know what, that gives me the absolute creeps. I've got a feeling that I'd like to go over there and slap him, which surprises me because I'm not often the slapping kind. Especially someone who looks so poorly. Bill couldn't come to the meeting, his carer says, Bill's been having his physio, what did we miss. She says it in that sarky way, you can tell she's only saying it to get attention from the other staff. There's a clucking of ladies, the ambulant ones, and one of them even gets up and goes to fiddle with Bill's blanket.

I don't like the look of him, that's the only way I can say it. Something wrong, something amiss, and I was enjoying myself, he's one of those people who spoils things, I can tell that. I take my eyes off him, the poorly spoiler man, and look back at my new nearly friend on the next table. She looks at me, looks over at him and makes an, aww face, a shorthand face for, oh, look at him poor fellow. I make the face back, or a version of it anyway. One side of my face still doesn't move, so I'm surprised that she can interpret it but she does, and when the meeting breaks up she comes over to me, not him.

Hallo, hallo, she says, I haven't seen you around much in here.

I point in the direction of my room, to show her I mainly stayed there until recently and, strange as it sounds, I think she can understand me.

I don't blame you, she says, this lot would drive you to drink.

We both laugh as if she had said something much funnier.

Nursery rhymes, would you believe it, she says, and I want to jump out of my chair. It's so exciting, having a conversation with someone new. If I could manage a word or two I'd be over the moon.

She doesn't seem to notice, she just trundles on as if it's absolutely normal, talking to someone who jerks and points and doesn't say anything recognisable. I suppose it is in here. I can tell she's educated. She's got a lovely way with words.

I'm sure they're not trying to diminish us, she says that,

and something about no malice aforethought. I could listen to her all day but I don't want her to think I'm one of those vegetables, not like the others. I work and work on my tongue and the shapes, that's what the speech and language therapist told me, concentrate on the shapes before you open your mouth, feel what you're going to say. I miss the last things she's saying to me because I'm trying so hard and then it comes out, pops out like my mouth has turned into one of those guns that shoots little pieces of cork.

Proust, I say, and I make a pantomime of reading and point to myself to show her that I've read Proust, I'm not like the others. I can see that she is nearly as surprised as I am.

Well done, she says, that's more than I have.

I'm relieved at that, because it's a lie, I actually never read Proust so I'm pleased that she won't be trying to talk to me about the plot. It's the kind of thing I would like to have done, that's all. I used to say it when I was young as well, and it's got me quite a lot of admiration, as well as dropping me into some sticky situations. I tune back in to what she's saying.

Poor chap, I hear her say, and she's talking about the chap in the wheelchair who just came in.

He was walking about only last week, she says, he's had a nasty bout of pneumonia.

I bet he's faking, I want to say. It's lucky I can't. What kind of a heartless bitch would she think I am? Only I mean it, his kind, they lie and they cheat and they are crammed full of fakery. I can tell from his eyes. He's looking over at us now and she's preening a bit, my new friend. It would be fun, like being at a Saturday night dance with a mate, if it wasn't him she was preening for. He looks bad, that's all I know. He looks like the smell that hits you when you open a packet of chicken that's way past its sell by date, sour and familiar.

My name's Jackie, she says, bunching some strands of her dreadlocks up on top of her head and looping them so that they stay there. What room number are you, Miss Proust Reader?

I hold up three fingers on my left hand, twice.

Thirty-three, she says, quick as a flash.

I mime a little clap. I'm still worrying about the stupid Proust thing. I try to be more normal.

May, I try to say, pointing at my chest. I don't think she understands because she leans over to read the label on my wheelchair.

May, she says, lovely name.

I want to tell her I was born on the day the war ended.

Bye-bye, she says, is it OK if I pop round later? I'm getting tired, all this excitement, I need to go for a lie down.

She does look tired, too, bone tired. It happened quite suddenly. One minute she's chatting away as if she shouldn't really be in a place like this, the next she's like one of those wind up record players when it's wound down. Speaking more and more slowly. It's excruciating to watch.

I make a shooing motion to show her that I want her

to go back to her room. She looks old, suddenly, maybe even older than me.

Thank you, she says, as if I've given her something. Thank you, Miss Room 33 Proust lover.

I feel sorry for the stupidity of my lie. It's not like I haven't read other books, I could easily have talked about them instead if I wanted to show off. Or I could have asked her something about herself, that would have been even better. If she gives me another chance, I think, I'll act like the perfect friend. I'll act like someone that anyone would be proud to know.

Everyone is dispersing now, there's a carer helping Jackie, offering an arm, and Agnita comes over to me.

Time to go, she says, shall I escort Madame to her room?

She's smiling but I know she thinks I'm stuck up. It's a thing people have always thought about me, Alain pointed it out first, only it's worse now that I can't talk. It makes everything I do more important than it needs to be, as though I'm always showing off. I try to think of a jokey way to show her I'm nice underneath. I don't know why, but my filters seem to have rusted over so instead of sifting through what I might do and choosing, I do the first thing that comes into my head. I make a cap doffing movement with my good hand. Agnita doesn't look amused.

I'm sure there's no need for that, she says, I'm trying my best.

So am I, I think, so am I, only I don't get to go home afterwards like you do. Maybe it's not so good to fraternise,

I think, maybe I was right first time, better to stay in my room and refuse to speak to anyone. Safer.

So she wheels me off, turning the chair round first so I'm facing the correct door. I hate it when they do that, suddenly turn you round without warning. It's like being on one of those rides at the funfair, the ones that spin you round and round.

Oi, I say. It comes out well, so I can't help being pleased, even though I hadn't intended to say anything.

Oh, Agnita says, pardon me m'lady, I'm sure I didn't mean any disrespect.

She doffs an imaginary cap too, in an exaggerated way. I can see her in the big mirror that hangs over the door. She doesn't do it for me because she doesn't realise that I can see her, that's how I know it's not a joke. She does it for the other staff and I can see quite a few of them giggling away as if it's the funniest thing.

I'm embarrassed and sorry for myself. It's a horrible feeling, being laughed at, and it doesn't help to know that it's quite justified. I'll keep myself to myself from now on, I think, speak to no one and then no one has anything to poke fun at. Probably Jackie won't want to be my friend anyway. I slump a little in my chair. It's been a tiring morning, a mixed bag, and I just want to be back in my room.

Most of the others have left the dining room now. I'm still here because Agnita has stopped to talk to Sammy, one of the other carers. Sammy is pushing the poorly man, the one from the room opposite and they're so engrossed in their conversation, Sammy and Agnita, that our chairs end up next to each other. Me and the poorly man, side by side like we are in a ski lift or commuting on the 7.19 train from the suburbs. I've still got my head down. I've had enough socialising for one day, and I think the best form of defence is to keep on slumping, talk to no one. He smells a bit funny. He smells of old man.

Hello, he says and it makes me jump.

He's covered in blankets and nearly as slumped as I am. I wasn't expecting him to talk. His voice is croaky, like he doesn't use it much and it needs oiling.

I try to look as uninterested as I can. There's something about him, I'm not sure what. Something that upsets me.

I think I'm in the room opposite you, he says in his rusty voice, we're neighbours. I've been unwell but I'm getting better and I hope we can be friends.

It's familiar to me, that voice, I almost recognise it. Best to keep quiet, I think, best not to say anything at all. There's danger in him, I can smell it and I can hear it and I can see it. He might look like a poor old chap with his blankets and his white hands clasped on top of the blankets like a baby but I know something else about him, I'm not sure what yet but I know something, that's for sure.

Drop by for a cuppa, he says, I don't get many visitors.

I bet you don't, I think. It's so hard not being able to say anything, and I feel so odd and there's something wrong and before I've thought it through I lean over the side of my wheelchair and mime spitting on the floor.

I suddenly realise Agnita is watching. There's a shocked silence and then she says, May, that's not kind, poor Bill, why don't you say sorry to him?

She's got a nasty streak, this one, Agnita says to the other carer, the one she was chatting to.

I know, says the other one, as if I couldn't hear anything.

You want to watch her arm as well, someone says, she's got a powerful left hook.

That's not me, I think, I don't recognise myself, that's not fair, I'm not like that. It's cruel, I can't even defend myself. I hate being talked about as if I'm not here, and I hate unfairness and people being mean, and I start crying even though I don't want to.

Oh, now we've got the crybaby act says Agnita, I think it's Bill that should be crying, not you.

We normally get on OK, Agnita and I, she's one of the nicer ones and this is too harsh, too unfair. I can feel the tears plopping down my face like a child and I wonder how long it would take me to die if I stopped eating anything at all. It's then that he speaks, this Bill character, this poor old man who everyone seems to adore.

It's OK, honestly, he says, leave her alone, she doesn't mean it. Look we're still pals, everything is fine. And he puts his pale old wrinkly old arm over towards me as if to shake hands.

Isn't that sweet, Agnita says but I look up at him and because of the position of our wheelchairs, no one else can see him and he's grinning, it's not a good grin, it's a grin that says hahaha got you now and I think I know that grin. I just need to concentrate, remember where from.

CHAPTER SIX

November 1977
Hull

May couldn't imagine life before the weekly meetings with Helen. Helen understood her, accepted her for who she was.

'I'm so glad to see you,' May said on the third visit to the department store cafe. 'I feel stronger now that I have you to talk to, less stupid. It's because you're in the same boat, or a similar boat or something, you know what I'm talking about. That's it, I think; either that or the fact that you never pick me up on the stupid things I say.'

'May,' said Helen, 'where's all this talk of stupid coming from? You're not stupid at all, and it's a horrible word. I think you're strong, and clever.'

'Yes, and maybe that waiter over there is Lord Lucan,' May said.

'I suppose he does have a bit of a look about him,' Helen said.

Both women laughed uneasily.

'A look of what?' May said. 'A look that he could have murdered his nanny, tried to murder his wife? Is it that easy to see?'

Helen stared into her tea.

'Aren't most men capable of it, if they're pushed, I mean?' she said.

'No!' May said. 'Certainly not my Alain, anyway. Do you know, he can't even bear to hurt wasps, he collects them in a glass or a jar and puts them outside, he doesn't like killing anything at all.'

Helen didn't say anything, and May could see there was something wrong.

'Never mind Lord Lucan,' she said, 'there's something wrong, I can see it, and I'm here if you want to talk.'

May felt like the most useless friend ever. She had hoped that she could talk to Helen today about the terrible business with the Welsh Film Board, but she could see that Helen had her own demons, and she should have realised that more quickly. Alain's right, May thought, I'm rubbish at empathising. I have Alain at home, and Helen hasn't got anyone, and I'm still putting myself first.

'It's probably nothing,' Helen said, 'and I hope it's OK for me to go on about it, but I'm worried. I think Frank has been hanging around. My ex, daddy dearest. I haven't actually seen him, but, oh, I don't know, it could be my hormonal brain playing tricks on me, I'm not sure. Only there seem to be little clues all the time, tiny things. So small that I'm never sure if I'm just imagining them. Flyers in the hallway of my flats, for a pizza place we went to together. But thousands of flyers, and yes, they could have been dumped, before you say it. But it's a coincidence, you have to admit. And there's also the flat itself.'

'What?' said May. 'Has he got into the flat? Surely not, Helen, oh no. How? What do you mean?'

'It's honestly probably nothing,' Helen said, 'and I'll scare both of us if I keep going on about it.'

'Don't worry about me,' said May, 'I'm not the one who has to live with it. It's you I'm worried about. And, for the record, I've always been a scaredy cat, my mum used to say I was frightened of my own shadow. You're much braver than me, honestly.'

May shifted in her chair. The truth was, the idea of her brave, strong friend Helen being terrified was terrifying all by itself, whatever the reason.

'It would be great to talk it through,' said Helen, 'because the thing is, I might be wrong, it might be my imagination playing tricks on me, I don't know. All I know is, I've got a strong feeling, a really strong feeling, that Frank has been in the flat. More than a head feeling, it's a sort of gut feeling. Sometimes I think he leaves these stupid clues. One dead flower in the middle of the table, the book I've been reading moved from the side of my bed and put back on the bookcase, or once, in the fridge. That kind of silly stuff.'

'But that could be something you've done and then forgotten, you know, pregnancy amnesia, that kind of thing. I left my purse on my pillow a couple of days ago, then went out to buy milk.'

'I thought that too,' said Helen, 'right up until the dead flower. That was yesterday. It was a red rose. May, you either have roses in your home or you don't, and I didn't, there was nowhere it could have come from.'

'How could he get in?' May asked. 'And are you sure, about the rose, that you hadn't had some and forgotten to throw them away or something?'

'I didn't have a rose in the place, I'm sure of it. And I've been thinking about how he could have got in, when he'd given me back his key. In fact I've been thinking about little else. I've got a vague memory of getting a new one cut for him, months ago when I was first pregnant. He'd lost his. Now I'm thinking, either that was a big fat lie and he never really lost it, or maybe he's found it again. Either way, it doesn't really matter, I'm in trouble.'

'Oh Helen, that's terrible, I'm so sorry. You could come to mine, only...'

'Hey,' said Helen, 'that's fine, I didn't mean that, I hadn't even thought of it. You're living in a shared house with a baby due any day, I didn't mean that. I could still be wrong, anyway.'

'Where will you go, if he turns up again?'

'I'll go to that hostel for battered wives, the one in the town centre. I went there the other day and spoke to someone. I'll be fine, don't worry. Let's talk about something else, this is creeping me out. What's new for you?'

'Ha,' said May, 'there's only one story in my particular town.'

'Let me guess, does it begin with Welsh and end with Board?'

May laughed despite her anxiety.

'How do you do that?' she said. 'How do you make me laugh even when I'm worried? It's a gift. You should market it.'

'I could be a comedian,' Helen said. 'Can women be comedians?'

'They bloody well ought to be. OK, I'll tell you what happened, at the risk of ruining the moment. The police called round last week, and apparently it's a crime, writing a cheque when you know you have no money in the bank. It's called, obtaining pecuniary advantage by deceptive means.'

May shuddered as she remembered it. There had been two policemen, just like in the movies, and they both seemed impossibly huge. One of them had been kinder than the other. He seemed embarrassed that they had to go through the whole sorry process, charging her, arranging an appointment for her to come to the station, all that. The other one seemed to revel in it.

'Have you got a husband?' he asked. 'Only if my missus was out running up bills she couldn't pay when she was up the duff I'd have something to say.'

He's out, May had thought. He's out like he always is when I need him, and what's more I'm glad he's out because I couldn't cope with him being here. They didn't stay long, the policemen, just long enough to make May feel as though the whole house had been contaminated.

'I guess that little one in there,' the smug policeman said, pointing to May's stomach, 'that little sprog will put an end to your shenanigans. Either that or you'll train him to pick pockets.'

They both found this hilarious, but May felt angry enough to break walls with her bare hands. She wished that she could explain to Helen how odd her life had become.

'But the Welsh Film Board,' Helen said. 'Did you show them the letter that said they would reimburse you if you stayed in any hotel in Bangor? Surely that changes things?'

'I'm afraid not. I can't find it. I've looked everywhere. I was sure I put it in my tray on my dressing table. I'm quite organised about stuff like that, you have to be if you live in a shared house. Alain says I probably threw it away, you know, in a forgetful pregnancy moment, but I didn't, I'm sure of it.'

'I believe you,' said Helen. 'So what happened next?'

'Well I told them about the letter, obviously I did, but they just laughed and said a crime was a crime was a crime and that I had to have an official caution. Helen, it was terrible, I had to go to the police station for it and everyone was looking at me.'

'Did you go on your own?'

May nodded.

'You're bonkers, I would have come with you. And Alain, why wasn't he there?'

May flushed. 'He really doesn't cope well with the police,' she said. 'Honestly, I can see the way you're looking at me but it's true, he's quite sensitive.'

Helen snorted. 'And you?' she said. 'Aren't you a bit sensitive too? Did you even tell him, May?'

May hadn't told him, but she could see now how stupid that seemed.

'I'm going to,' she said, 'I'm definitely going to but I've got to wait for the right moment.'

My life has turned into a series of 'waiting for the right moments', she thought.

'Alain is quite, erm, stressed at the moment. He's finding it hard, all this waiting for the baby and not having a job that he thought he had and all that.'

May had thought that Helen might dismiss her worries but she seemed to understand straight away. She looked at May, really looked at her, and May squirmed, unable to meet Helen's eyes.

'Hey, it's not your fault. I know what you're going through, honestly.'

But mine isn't a complete baddy like yours, May thought. Mine can knit, mine can sing, mine can talk about poetry.

'I'm not saying Alain is as bad as Frank, not at all,' Helen said, as if she could read May's thoughts, 'but I can see that you're not at ease, May, that's the thing. You're not comfortable, or relaxed, and I'm still old-fashioned enough to think that those are things women ought to be, when they're, what's the common term for our condition?'

'Up the duff,' May said, thinking of the policeman, and the speckles of white foam at the corners of his mouth.

'Let's drink to that,' Helen said and they clinked their teacups.

May wanted to change tack, talk about Helen's problems. She felt that she had monopolised the conversation and she wanted to make absolutely sure that her friend was safe, but a sudden fierce cramping pain made her unable to think about anything else. This can't be it, May thought, not here in Binns cafe with my friend. It felt like a stomach cramp, as though she had eaten something bad.

'Helen,' she said, 'I think there's something wrong. My stomach. It really hurts.'

Helen put her hand on May's.

'Do you think you might be having a baby?' she asked, and as May looked up she saw the twinkle in her friend's eye.

No, May thought, no, this isn't how I planned it. I've got no idea where Alain is.

'I can't start without Alain,' she said.

Helen laughed. 'Did anyone ever explain to you that giving birth is not like having a meal in a restaurant? You can't book it for a convenient time. Hang on here and I'll go to the phone box across the road in the station and ring the hospital, nothing will happen for a while, trust me, I've read every book there is. I'll come with you, if you'd like.'

May thought that she would like that very much. It would have been lovely to have Helen by her side, gentle and encouraging. Another pain bit into her and May wondered what on earth she was thinking. Alain had longed for this moment, prepared for it, read about it, and had a phone installed in the flat with the last of the money her mother had left her. The phone. That was what she needed to do.

'Please can you go to the phone box and ring the hospital *and* Alain?' May said. 'Tell him to meet me there? You could say we just met. Don't get me wrong, I'd love it if you could be there. Women's lib and all that. But blimey, Helen, he's even read the book. He's desperate to be there. Ow,' she broke off as the pain crunched through her. 'It hurts, I've always been a coward. Take no notice, don't let me scare you.'

May gave Helen a slip of paper with the phone number on it. Helen squeezed May's hand and took off for the phone box, leaving May sitting at the table. The contraction tapered off and May put her hand on her bump, surprised at how hard and solid it felt, and how fast things seemed to be going. All the books had talked about gentle contractions at the beginning, time to get in tune with your body, easing your way into labour and things like that. This was more like a sudden onset thunderstorm. May didn't feel ready.

She was crying when Helen returned.

'I'm not sure I'm ready for this right now,' May said. 'Sorry, sorry, did you get through to Alain?'

Helen gave May a tissue and patted her hand.

'I did, and there's nothing to apologise for, nothing to worry about, my friend. We can talk about everything later,' Helen said. 'You make notes and tell me how it goes. You've got a job to do now, and you'll be fine, I promise. I'll be thinking of you.'

I'm not like you, May was thinking, even as her body screeched into gear, flexing muscles she hadn't known she had, I'm not on my own, I'm so lucky. Alain isn't like Frank, he's just having a difficult time. My situation isn't as bad, I'm not like you. I'm not a battered wife or anything, I've read articles about them and my Alain is an angel.

'It's all fine,' she said, hoping that Helen would understand. 'Alain will be here any minute, I know he will. He's an amazing man, so funny, so clever. He's a sensitive man. He knits. Oh,' May put her head on the table, trying to remember the breathing she had learned from her book, 'oh, this bloody hurts.'

'Maybe it would help if you stop worrying about Alain. Just concentrate, woman, you can do it.'

When May tried to put the events that followed in order later, she wasn't sure what went where. There was an ambulance, and a stretcher, and a solicitous manager offering free teas for a month, and Helen giggling at that.

'You're quite safe,' May remembered Helen saying, 'she's not going to be battering down the doors begging for a cuppa for a while, I think she's going to be busy, don't you?'

The manager blushed. 'A year,' he said, 'a year, I meant a year, have free teas for a year, and have a lovely day.'

Even May managed to laugh at that as the ambulance men wheeled her out of the restaurant and into the lift. She was sure that she could walk but they wouldn't let her. Nowhere in the books had it said that things would go this quickly. May wished that she could meet the authors of the books and punch them.

May didn't see Helen go. One minute she was there, the next she had gone, taking her comfortable, calming presence with her. May felt very alone.

It seemed ages before Alain came. May lay in the hard hospital bed and watched the clock on the wall move from afternoon to evening. The pain became a part of her, an extra limb, and she became so used to it that she forgot from time to time why it was happening.

When Alain arrived, May was surprised to find that she felt fairly indifferent, too busy with her body to be thrilled. He bent to kiss her and she registered a smell of the outside, of life beyond the walls of this small room. A combination of fried food, unwashed skin and traffic fumes, and she wondered if he always smelled like that.

'Hey,' he said, 'darling, I'm sorry it took me so long to get here. There was traffic, and this old woman had dropped her shopping and I had to help her pick it up, there was no one else around, I'm sorry.'

May felt as though the pain had washed her clean, cleared her mind. She wondered which part, if any, of what Alain had just said was true.

'Does it hurt much?' Alain said, holding her hand and rubbing it.

Stupid question of the century, May thought.

'Not now you're here,' she said. She wondered if he would be able to tell that she didn't mean it.

'My brave darling,' he said. May thought that he sounded just as insincere as she did, as though they were both reciting lines from different scripts. She pulled her hand back and decided to be more honest. Maybe then they'd feel more like a team.

'You should try it,' she said. 'Lie down on the floor and get someone to drive across your stomach with a steam roller, like they use to lay roads. Make sure they keep doing it, every few minutes. Should be a doddle.'

Alain smiled and rubbed her hand some more. May forced herself to smile. Stop the bloody hand rubbing, she thought, and resolved to tell Helen later how annoying she had found it. It would make her laugh. She could see from the way that Alain looked at her that he was expecting her to spare him by being quiet and stoic, and she knew that she had to try. It was important to get this right, she could remember that even though she was no longer sure why. She hadn't expected it to hurt so much. At the antenatal class they had told her to practise breathing while she twisted the flesh on her thigh and May was good at that, she could twist until her thigh was bruised, but this was way, way worse than a bruised thigh.

May had chosen to give birth in a small cottage hospital.

She had wanted an experience that was as natural as possible, minimum intervention like in the books, and she tried to remember that, concentrate on it, make it happen even though she was frightened.

'Keep going, honey,' Alain said, 'you're doing so well.'

Am I? May thought. Am I really? Do I have any choice?

'I'm glad you're here,' May said, 'I really am. Just us and our baby.'

She winced as another pain tore through her. Maybe it would hurt less if she could stop thinking so much, go with the flow.

'You're so brave, my darling,' said Alain.

He loves me, May thought, he loves me and I'm having a baby. It's OK, everything is OK. I can do this, come on, baby.

He held her hand again and bent towards her.

He sang the song they had listened to as they first made love, and May felt stronger for hearing it. So what if they had some little problems, she thought, he was here with her when it mattered. Another pain began, harsher this time, and May clung to Alain.

'No one said it would be like this,' she said. 'Why is it hurting so much? Do you think there's something wrong?'

'Here,' said Alain, 'let me put this cold cloth on your head. I'll tell you a story, if you like, about the animals in the Hundred Acre Wood. They all have babies too, you know, how do you think Piglet got born?'

May tried to relax, to go with the pains and listen to

Alain's voice, so calm and familiar. She couldn't concentrate on the content of what he was saying, and he obviously knew that, because once or twice she realised that he was repeating himself. It didn't matter, what was important was his tone, so soothing. He stopped whenever the pain got too bad, and pressed the cold flannel to her head. If she had been truthful, she didn't much like that, the feeling of wetness seemed a little too much to cope with, but May didn't say. She was grateful that he was there, by her side at this special time.

'Anything you're worried about, just tell me,' he said, 'we can be completely open with each other now. This is the time of our lives, May.'

The time of your life, maybe, May thought. You'd feel differently if you were being squeezed to death from the inside out by an alien creature. Another rogue thought to tell Helen. She waited until the next big pain was gone before speaking again.

'Really?' she said. 'Do you mean that? Only I never understood, about the Welsh Film Board, and why they didn't pay the money they promised, for the hotel.' May shouted the last word as another pain threatened to swallow her whole. There. She'd said it. Maybe it was the injection the midwife had given her, some kind of truth drug along with the pethidine.

'Hotels, money, what on earth are you talking about?' Alain said. 'Have you gone crazy? Do you want me to call someone?'

'No,' she said. 'It's the drugs, ignore me.' Not the time, she said to herself, not the time, not the time. It's all OK.

'I'm sorry,' she said.

May started to cry.

'Come on now, no need for waterworks,' the midwife said when she came in to check her progress. 'We're getting there, we're rolling along nicely. Bun's in the oven, almost cooked.' She laughed at her own joke. May held her hand out for a tissue and Alain handed it to her.

'I think it's just hard for her,' Alain said. 'We're new to all this.'

'Bless you,' the midwife said, 'what an understanding man you've got there, Mum. Don't you worry now, it'll all be over soon and you won't remember anything, you'll probably be back here next year having another one, you'll like this one so much.'

She went off, chuckling again at her own joke. May stared at Alain.

'Did she really say that?' she said. 'Tell me we're not doing this again next year.'

Alain laughed, and the sound was comforting. 'It's not that I don't want a football team of babies,' he said, 'not at all. But it isn't me who has to go through all this pain, darling, so I'm am hereby and forthwith handing any decisions about future members of our family to you.'

May would have liked to laugh but everything hurt too much. She couldn't believe that she had been fussing over money, hotel bills, all that stuff. What on earth did it matter when she had this helpful, kind, loving man by her side? The pain was terrible and getting worse, and she couldn't deal with it on her own.

'I've been rubbish recently,' Alain said. 'I want to be better to you, and to the baby, honestly I do. I don't blame you for asking about the job, I'm just so ashamed that it didn't work out, that I couldn't provide for you. I've been feeling so odd, I can't explain it. I'm going to try harder, I promise I am.'

'It's OK,' said May. Her voice seemed to come from a long way away.

She raised her arms above her head and hung on to the bars of her bed head. It helped for a few seconds.

'May,' said Alain. For the first time, he sounded worried. 'May, are you alright? Shall I get the midwife back in?'

Alain started to cry. May watched, but found it difficult to connect now that she had arrived at a place where terrible, excruciating physical pain had suddenly become completely normal. She steeled herself and, with an enormous effort, reached out and took his hand. For a while it was just the two of them, concentrating and working together. May pushed all of her other concerns to the back of her mind.

'I couldn't do this without you,' she said.

We're a team, she thought, together. Only once she thought she saw boredom in his face, but the next time she looked it was gone. May thought she might have imagined it.

'Come on now, darling,' he said as the pains got closer and closer together, 'you can do this.'

May realised that the midwife had come back in to the room.

'Is everyone alright?' she asked. 'Let's have a look at you now. Goodness me you've moved on a fair bit, and hardly any noise at all. You're a quiet one I must say.'

May felt grateful for the praise. See, she wanted to say, see, I'm doing this OK after all.

'I think she's amazing,' Alain said, 'I'd be terrified.'

Alain stroked May's hair.

'Now you're the kind of dad I like,' said the midwife. 'My name's Julie, and I've been doing this job for more than twenty years, and I know a nice dad when I see one. You've a good one there, dear, no need to worry. I bet he'll even change a nappy if you ask him nicely.'

The midwife smiled at Alain as if she had made the most enormous joke. He smiled back at her as if the two of them were playing cards together, a team on a winning streak. Before the next wave of pain May just had time to wonder why he hadn't spoken up, told the midwife that they were going to share things.

'You mark my words, lovey,' the midwife said to May while she was checking her pulse, 'this one is one of the good guys, think yourself lucky. There's lots of ladies in your position would give anything to have a nice gentleman like this dancing attendance on them. I'll look in again in a few minutes.'

'She fancies you,' May said as soon as she had gone.

'Who wouldn't?' Alain said, bowing to the corners of the room before sitting back down next to May's bed. 'Seriously, don't be daft. Are you OK? Not bothered by her old-fashioned nonsense?'

Everything upsets me, May thought. This is what it's like to be crazy. She concentrated on dealing with the pain and stopped speaking.

'I forgot to say,' the midwife said, putting her head back round the door, 'press the buzzer if you need me. And be nice to your poor husband. It's hard for men too, you know.'

Alain laughed. It's not funny any more, May thought. I can't laugh, don't expect me to. She turned her head to the wall.

'I'm sorry,' Alain said, 'I'm sorry, I wasn't dismissing what you're going through, I just wanted to lighten up a little, I'm sorry.'

May hadn't got enough energy to tell him that it was OK, so she squeezed his hand instead.

'Promise me we'll be happy,' Alain said, 'just us and this little one.' He put his hand on May's stomach. 'We can be happy, can't we? You won't ever leave me.'

It's me that needs comforting right now, May thought. Leave? Where on earth would I go? For a moment, just a flash, she had a picture of her and Helen, side by side with their buggies, bringing up the children together as siblings.

'Of course I'm not leaving, said May. 'I'm busy trying to have this baby.'

Of such requests are dreams shattered, she thought, the words dropping into her head like raisins into flour. Was that a quotation? She couldn't remember where from, and she didn't know why she had thought it. She should be grateful. Grateful for this kind, handsome, man, father of her beloved surprise baby, her connection with the world of couples and homes and pushchairs and breastfeeding. Not all saviours come with a clean slate, she thought, and the thought calmed her.

They sat together in the quiet little hospital all day and into the night. May stopped looking at the clock and tried instead to listen to her body and the baby, as she had been practising. It proved to be incredibly difficult, and more painful than anything she had ever known, and when the pains were at their height and the room was full of people rushing and fussing and unwrapping instruments and asking her to sign things that she couldn't read, then she was more than glad of Alain. Then she hung on to him and he shushed her and cried with her and promised all sorts of things. There were more injections for the pain and May tried to tell Alain that the pain was just the same, only her ability to shout about it was affected. He seemed to understand, and he was a comfort. Poor Helen, May thought, having to go through this on her own. Thank goodness she had Alain.

The baby was pulled from her in a crescendo of shouting and yelling and gasping and bleeding.

'Give me my glasses,' May tried to say. 'I can't see who

it is.' But they didn't understand what she was saying and this and the absence of pain struck her suddenly as extremely funny.

Alain was sobbing openly and May wasn't sure why.

'Anyone would think someone had died,' she said.

The stares of the medical professionals showed her that this, at least, had been clearly understood.

'Would you like to hold your little girl?' the midwife said, bearing down on her with an impossibly small bundle in a pink blanket.

'Girl?' said May. 'Girl? Oh no, oh no, a girl, I'm not sure I'm up to this.'

The midwife stood poised holding the baby, not sure what to do.

'Darling,' said Alain, 'darling, a little girl, that's exactly what we wanted. It's just the drugs talking. Could I?'

He held his hands out and the midwife placed the baby in them.

'Hello, sweetheart,' he crooned to the baby. 'You've got a beautiful mummy, and you are the most beautiful baby in the world. You're going to be a doctor, or a prime minister or just the happiest person ever.'

'See?' said the midwife. 'I told you he was a good 'un, your fella.'

May watched it all, feeling as if she'd been cut loose from normal feeling somewhere along the line.

'What a good 'un,' she repeated. 'Could someone please give me my glasses so that I can join in with this?'

Or shall I just get the bus home, she thought, and leave you lot to marvel over each other?

The midwife frowned. 'No need to get upset,' she said. 'Keep your energy for the next eighteen years. You're going to need it. Your mummy thinks the hard part is over,' she said to the baby 'but you've got news for her, haven't you?'

Alain stood up and placed the baby in May's arms, and as May took her and held her she felt a rush of love just like the one the books had predicted. What the books hadn't prepared her for was the rush of terror that followed.

'I'll look after you', she whispered into the baby's perfect ear.

CHAPTER SEVEN

December 2017
Lewisham

I have never liked Christmas.

It's a nasty spiteful time of year and I try to keep away from it. I always have. It was different when Jenny was little, I think I might have had some fun then. I remember waking up to find her shaking me, holding out a sock I had stuffed with nonsense and pretty things for her to ooh and aah over. I remember pulling her into my bed and us being together and happy, just the two of us. It's a cloudy memory, not a clear one. I don't get it out much because there are always other memories that come to crowd it out, pushing and shoving each other to the front as if there's a prize for being first.

Here's a paper hat for you to wear, Agnita says, we're having a party.

She claps her hands together as if it's the most exciting thing she can think of, sitting round with a group of coffin dodgers reminiscing about their long ago happy memories that they are probably making up anyway. They're probably lying, I try to say but I think only the 'lie' bit comes out. Agnita looks puzzled. No lie, she says, it really is party.

Duh, I want to say. Like the kids do, when someone doesn't get what they're trying to say. Duh, you don't even know what I'm saying, but what comes out is a load of nonsense in a sing-song tone, it's all I can manage.

Carols, she says, do you want to sing the carols and then she's off and it's all silent night only in Dutch or German or something. I used to speak German, I want to tell her. I was quite good at it, A grade at A-level. I didn't mean my arm to jerk out, I wasn't even thinking about Hitler, I don't know why she got so upset. It was nothing like a Nazi salute. Obviously a bit of a spasm or something, probably I've been sitting too long in one position and whose fault is that? Not mine, I'm not one of the carers who's supposed to check on how the poor old people are sitting, that's for sure. I'd jump off a bridge rather than work here.

Anyway, I know Agnita speaks Dutch not bloody German and it wasn't a Nazi salute but it's obviously a sensitive thing for her.

I am from the Dutch West Indies, she says, and I think, big news.

I shrug my shoulders but I don't mean I don't care, I'm just trying for sarcasm because that is the most dignified thing I can muster right now. It seems like everything I do is misinterpreted.

I'm not sure if you even deserve a hat and a Christmas party, Agnita says, and I want to tell her that's fine with me but she doesn't understand. I'm not having a good day.

Here, she says and she tries to fit this stupid gold hat on my head, a small cone shaped hat.

I can do it, I try to say but that causes quite an amount of spit and I can see her wipe her hands when she thinks I'm not looking, as if she had touched something disgusting like rat pee, not just my ordinary spit that won't stay in my mouth.

I've got some sympathy about the spit thing, only I don't want her to know that. I used to hate the bodily fluids associated with teaching. Children with mucus pouring from their noses or wiped on their sleeves. I almost wish I had been kinder now that I'm like them, but I guess the fact is no one likes a spitter, young or old.

But I can't wear the hat. There's something cruel about expecting old women with wrinkled faces to wear hats that look like witches' hats.

No, I say, no, and I give a big heave and a push so that she gets exactly what I'm saying.

Well OK, she says, only all the others will be wearing them and I can't believe you want to be the odd one out.

You'd better believe it, I think, because it's true. I smile and she gives me what they used to call a sideways look and I think, maybe she heard what I thought.

*

The dining room is a scene from hell. A medieval tableau of despair, complete with the obligatory smell of cabbage and disinfectant.

Happy Christmas, call the ones who can talk. Isn't this lovely? I hear one of them say.

No it's not, I say, but it's just a growl.

Agnita puts my wheelchair at a table full of the usual no hopers. I look around for Jackie but she's not here yet.

Hallo, says an old woman whose skin looks like some kind of science fiction fruit, haven't they done this nicely? Aren't they good to us? She goes on as if I was agreeing with her. I try to stare her out, we used to do that at school and I was good at it. Fat girls are often good at unpopular sports. She doesn't notice at all, just goes on trilling and nodding her head like someone's pet budgie. I think there will be mince pies later, she says, and maybe some games, oh I can't wait.

I decide to talk anyway, whether I can be understood or not. I should think there would be bloody mince pies, I say, after dressing us up like silly arses and interrupting our afternoons. It's just a load of spitty nonsense by the time the words get out of my mouth but I feel better for saying them.

There are two others at my table apart from Ms Budgie. A very fat woman with a small line of saliva dribbling down from the corner of her mouth and a tiny old man, like one of those shrunken heads they used to have in history books only shrunken all over. I think he's the one

94

who did the impromptu dance the other night when they talked about activities. He is wearing a small sparkling trilby hat, and it seems oddly fitting. If he could understand me I'd ask him if he could tap dance too.

Ladies and gentlemen, he keeps saying, ladles and jelly spoons. He seems happy though, smiling and clicking his fingers to a tune only he can hear.

Hello, says the fat woman, have you been here before? They've done it nicely, haven't they? She nods towards the tree in the corner, and then sweeps with her hand to take in the paper chains and tinsel draped around the room. I'd like to get into a chat with her about religion and the insidious way it creeps into our lives in the guise of naked consumerism but I growl instead. It has much the same effect.

The last twenty years or so I have ignored Christmas completely. Jenny always asks me over but I don't go. Now that I can't go any more, even if I wanted to, I can't help wondering what it might have been like. Donations to charity, that's all she ever wants so I'm sure it wouldn't be a barrel of laughs.

Oh, thank you for this Oxfam goat, I imagine her saying, here's some money towards a drainage ditch. The thought of it makes me laugh, and I'm spluttering lukewarm tea all over the place. My tablemates look away. I hate the bloody tea in this place. They give it to me in a plastic beaker with a lid, the kind you give to toddlers. I could manage a proper cup, I know I could, I'd just need a bit of guidance at the elbow but they haven't got any time for that. It makes me cross, the bloody beaker and I try to fling it on to the floor. It's not my fault that it hits Ms Budgie and it's certainly not my fault that the lid comes off on impact. They should make them screw on tighter, we're old and helpless and we need proper equipment.

Oh dear, oh dear, oh dear, Ms Budgie trills. She sounds like one of those talking dolls that Jenny used to want. Oh dear, oh dear, oh dear, my best dress too. Look at my best dress, oh dear, oh dear, oh dear.

I wish with all my heart that I could make myself understood. Never mind the heart to hearts with my daughter, the only thing I'd want to say right now is, oh my gosh, I never, ever would have realised that was your best dress. It's true, I wouldn't have. It's like a cliché dress, a dress they would use to dress a generic dowdy old woman. Navy crimplene, or whatever they use instead of crimplene these days. I hate her dress with a vengeance and suddenly I'm glad about the tea. I wish I hadn't drunk any of it so that more of it could have splashed down her front. She's crying now, and the staff are all over her and looking at me with narrowed eyes.

It wasn't her fault, Ms Budgie says, she didn't mean to. Oh dear, I don't want to spoil Christmas, oh dear, I'll be fine.

She dabs at her heaving bosom with serviettes patterned with holly.

Don't you worry, she trills over to me, don't you worry,

it wasn't your fault, I'm always a bit emotional in the festive season. Brings up a lot for us oldies, doesn't it dear?

She holds the serviette to her face and a couple of members of staff pat her in a reassuring way, throwing evil looks in my direction. I wish I had a dog to stroke or something to soften my edges a little. Like Richard Nixon in that TV interview. Sorry, I try to say, not that I really do feel sorry or anything but it seems like the right thing to do. I remember why the navy crimplene dress seems familiar. I think I had one a bit like it in my fat days, before Alain. Poor me, I think, poor me wearing that sort of stuff when I was young and pretty. Prettyish. I can't help it, the thought makes me sad and I start crying. I'm discreet about it, the old tears rolling down the face business, nothing dramatic. I'm not like Ms Budgie, I'm not looking for any attention, I can't help it, that's all.

I have to decide fairly quickly whether to ask for a tissue or let the snot run down my face. I can't quite reach the serviettes. I'm sniffing like a hound and trying to decide when I feel a tiny tap on my arm.

There you are, my dear, he says and it's the tiny sparkly man, holding out a Santa serviette in his shrunken hand. It's more like a dainty claw than a hand but I'm very grateful.

Ssh, I try to say to him, just to let him know that it's our secret, my tears, but ssh is one of the things I shouldn't even attempt. I spray him with spit and he wipes his lapels without looking horrified.

The staff are too busy with Ms Budgie to notice. I'm elated to have got away with it. Crying in public is a top hobby here and it's not one I want to join in with.

Keep away from the s words, dear, Mr Sparkly Hat says in a quiet voice. Don't annoy them, and try to get your nearest and dearest to bring you in some spirits. Brandy, whisky, doesn't matter what. We all have our dreams, my dear.

I can't help laughing, and of course that makes the staff still comforting Ms Budgie turn and look at me as if I have just drowned a bucketful of puppies. It's Kelly with the complicated hair and Abi with the purple streak and neither of them have ever liked me.

I'm not laughing at her, I say, it's him, he's funny and I point to Mr Sparkly Hat but he's looking off into the distance at the other end of the room. Glazed, that's how he looks, glazed as a carrot. They don't understand what I'm saying.

Fancy trying to put the blame on Trevor, I hear one of them say, and the other one, Abi, speaks directly to me and says, now, now, now, I don't think it was Trevor that threw the cup, do you?

Don't be cross with her, says Ms Budgie, still dabbing at her breasts, she can't help it, my mother went like that at the end, doolally, she's probably unhappy inside too.

Aw, Kelly says, patting her complex hair as though it was a pet, aw listen to you. You're a saint, d'you hear me? Isn't she a saint, Ab?

She's a saint, Abi agrees and they both turn and look at me to make sure I've heard. There are times when not being able to talk doesn't stop a person from trying and this is one of them.

I'm not fucking unhappy inside, I'm fucking unhappy outside and it's your fucking fault, I shout at Ms Budgie. She flutters her hands but it's clear she has no idea what I'm saying. No one does but they can tell I'm angry.

I'm sorry almost straight away. I mean, I do know it's not her actual fault but part of me still feels that she shouldn't be such a sanctimonious bitch if she wants to avoid the slings and arrows of this miserable world.

Abi and Kelly give each other a look.

I'll do it, Abi says and she pulls my wheelchair back from the table more roughly than she needs to. She whirls it round and I get the old fairground feeling for a moment, then she pushes me over into the corner by the doors. She bends down, purple streak flopping over her eyes. Close up it's clear that her eyebrows are completely drawn in, there's nothing underneath at all. Maybe the purple hair is a wig, maybe she's had cancer or something. I'm deciding to be nice on account of the possible cancer when she bends over and talks right in my face.

Right, she says, I've just about had enough. Poor Mary, tea all down her best frock. What would the world be like if we all had our tantrums whenever things didn't go the right way, huh?

She looks at me as if she is really asking a question,

which is ridiculous because she knows I can't talk. I point to my mouth with my good hand to remind her.

Oh I know all about that, she says, waving a dismissive hand, but some of us can see through you all the same.

That's not fair, I want to shout, but I don't because there is absolutely no point. How dare she speak to me like that? As if I want to be in here any more than she wants to be looking after me. Less in fact, at least she gets paid for it. I count to ten to try to calm myself down but it doesn't work, the unfairness of it, being told off by someone young enough to be my granddaughter. Someone with no eyebrows and a purple streak, it's not fair. And I can't stop them then, the tears that burst out like I've been holding them back for days, which I mostly have. Once I start, I can't stop. OK, there's no need for the waterworks, Abi says, come on now, it's not that bad. Let's go back and join in the fun with the others, she says, we'll say no more about it.

Silly little bitch, as if that would make me feel happier. I wonder if they have to have any qualifications at all to work here. I guess not, but even thinking that doesn't cheer me up in any way at all. It's like a switch has been thrown, and I can't stop crying. I haven't cried like this for a long time. It's baby crying, abandoned crying, the sort you do when someone dies or when there's no hope. Locked in a prison cell in a foreign country, that sort of crying. As I get into the rhythm of it I find it easy, simple, something I learned how to do long ago. I picture myself with a baby in my arms, locked out of my house, crying like this. I see Christmas decorations from long ago in a room I had decorated in brown and yellow, and a baby in one of those canvas chairs on a wire frame. I'm crying like this then, too, only I'm in such a bother right now that I can't quite remember why.

Abi is squatting down next to my wheelchair. Come on, she says, I didn't mean to upset you like this. She's holding out another tissue and I take it and hold it over my face but it won't stop. I'm heaving like I'm going to throw up and Kelly has come over now, one of her plaits is coming slightly undone but she's still wearing a hairband with a pair of furry antlers attached.

Come on, she says, Abi didn't mean, and then Abi chimes in and says, Kell, I didn't, I was just saying.

I give some kind of regal wave to show that I have forgiven the poor fools, and that in fact there are much sadder things in my life than them and their drawn on eyebrows. My sobs are slowing down but I'm in that stage, I remember this too from long ago, that stage where if someone said something, anything, that could set me off, I'd go right back into extreme crying again, nought to sixty in a fraction of a second.

Would you like some water, one of them says. I think it was Kelly. Shall I get you a mince pie?

Do they teach you any people skills at all, I want to ask, or did you perhaps complete your scanty training in a kennels? This strikes me as funny, really funny so I'm off again only this time it's laughter which should cheer them up only I don't think they can tell the difference.

They're both standing there looking all concerned and shuffling from one foot to the other. They're looking round a lot too, and I guess that they don't want to be told off by whoever is in charge of this zoo, and that means I've got the upper hand for once. I let them push me back into the room. Let's join the party, they say and although it's the most pathetic party I've ever been to, for some reason I want to be there, I want to be with people, even these wrinkled old half-dead ones.

We go back to the table and Ms Budgie is full of smiles.

Oh, she says, I was hoping you'd come back, I've saved you a mince pie. Mary. I must remember to call her Mary in my head and stop with the budgie stuff, just in case there's a miracle and I can suddenly talk again and all that comes out is nonsense. I incline my head, channelling a royal personage again. It's getting to be a habit. I try to look grateful for the mince pie, although it's definitely shop bought and the pastry is as dry as everything else around here, Mary included. I make a nice face though, or at least a lopsided version of a nice face, and it's then that Jackie comes over.

Hi she says, as if we were at a real party, maybe a cocktail party or a reception on a cruise ship. Isn't this nice? And she sweeps her arms round to take in the whole sorry scene but suddenly she's right, it is nice, it's like she's turned a light on to it or something.

Hello Mary, she says, how's that hip? Hip? It never occurred to me that Mary had a hip, not a hip that needed asking after. I listen in, trying to look concerned. Gives me a bit of gyp, she says, mainly in the mornings. Gyppy hip, says Trevor, the tiny sparkly man on the other side of the table, hippy gyp. We all laugh although I for one am not sure why.

Sit next to me, I'm thinking. There are two empty chairs, one between me and Mary and one between Trevor and the extremely fat woman. I think she is called Pam-Pam only I would never say the second Pam even if I could talk, it's a ridiculous name for a woman who is not only grown but overgrown. Sit next to me Jackie. I must be going backwards, winding back like an old movie because I do the visualisation thing, like I used to do at a disco, say, if I wanted someone to ask me to dance. You have to imagine it happening, will them to do what you want them to do, concentrate and visualise. Sit next to me Jackie. Go on go on. It works this time because she does, she sits next to me and I almost clap.

What was going on over there with you and Abi and Kelly? Jackie says, I was on my way back from physio, that's why I'm a bit late to the party, I think I saw you crying, she says.

It's a bad day for the words today. It's a bad day for the words every day. They're stuck in my throat and a growl is all I can manage. I can't imagine how I said the Proust thing the other day, and I'm furious that I used such a precious resource to say something so stupid. In the end I settle for a nonchalant wave, to give the impression that whatever happened in the corner with the carers, it really wasn't important. I want to imply that I could use words if I wanted to, I just can't be bothered to waste them on something so trivial.

I obviously don't get my point across, because Jackie says, next time, I'll bring a notebook and pencil, and you can write it down.

It's a stupid idea, because my arms aren't completely reliable, well, the left one isn't too bad but I never could write with my left hand. It's a kind thought though, and I'm worried that it will reduce me to tears again so I think of something pleasant. That's what I used to tell Jenny to do, think of something nice and you'll go to sleep quickety split. I don't know what was nice for Jenny to think of. I should have asked her then, and maybe I would have been able to borrow it now. Poor Jenny. Lumpy Jenny with her ink-stained fingers. Jenny at thirteen, asking what happened to her dad. Jenny at fifteen, staying home on Saturday nights with me. I told her to go out and have fun but she didn't want to.

I'm miles away with all this, thinking how great it would be to have a second chance. I look up, thinking I can meet Jackie's eyes properly now that I know I'm not going to cry but he's there again, like a bad penny. The man called Bill. The one in the wheelchair who everyone seems to love.

Hello, he says, and he's wheeling his own chair this

time, wearing those pretentious fingerless gloves. Mind if I join you?

Oh Bill, trills Mary, oh Bill it's so so lovely to see you looking so well. Do you know, she says to the rest of us, do you know that Bill is the youngest of all of us, just a baby really. And he's going to go home soon, when he's well enough, isn't that lovely?

She claps her hands and Jackie joins in and even Trevor claps a little. I keep my hands where they are and so does my chubby table mate. Solidarity, I want to say to her but I think it's more that she has no idea of what's going on.

Does anyone mind, says Bill, if I steal Jackie away for a moment? Just a moment? I want to show her something, we'll be right back.

It's weird because he's talking about Jackie but he's looking at me, and I feel like we're connected by something but I still don't know what. He's bald, completely bald so maybe I knew him with hair, without his tortoiseshell glasses, I don't know. But I don't want Jackie to go off with him.

Stay here, I try to say but I can see that she hasn't understood. Stay here, I try again, I'll look after you. I put everything I've got into it but I can hear what comes out. It's an urgent growl, that's all it is. The kind of growl a polar bear might make if someone went for her cub.

I'll be back, she says, I won't be long.

CHAPTER EIGHT

December 1977
Hull

May's world shifted focus as quickly as a conjuring trick.

'It's terrifying and wonderful at the same time,' she said to Helen, 'and, so you know, it's all true what they say in the books, every word. I love having her, but I do miss her being inside, part of me, my bump.'

It was their first meeting since Jenny's birth, and May had been looking forward to it. The manager and all the staff had been over to congratulate May.

Helen cradled Jenny over her own bump.

'I can't believe I'm going to have one of these,' she said. 'I've been so worried about you. How's it going with his lordship? Is he feeling all that stuff they talk about in the magazines, you know, nose pushed out of joint and all that?'

'No,' said May, 'and that's the amazing thing. He absolutely dotes on Jenny, seems to love being a dad. He's been really helpful, washing nappies, making me endless cups of tea when I'm breastfeeding, all that sort of stuff. He even gets up with me for the night feeds and tells me stories so I don't drop off with Jenny attached. He's amazing.'

There's another part of the story, May thought, don't ask me anything else about him. I don't want to jinx it, I can't explain.

'It sounds great,' Helen said. 'I'm jealous. I can't wait to have mine, even though I haven't got a wonderful Alain to help me. Tell me though, honey bunch, I can hear something in your tone that worries me – is it really so marvellous at home? If it is, you'll be one of the first new mums I've ever met with no complaints.'

Relief washed over May like a summer shower.

'Is that right?' she said. 'Do other new mums feel a bit, you know, lost? Only I've never met any, not close up and personal. I thought everyone was screamingly happy. And Alain, well, he's mostly very helpful, on the whole.'

For goodness sake, May told herself, what's wrong with you? Stop it, Helen doesn't want to hear all this. It's fine, just hormones, stop it.

'Sorry,' she said, 'don't take any notice of me, I'm fine, it's all fine, I guess it's just like starting a new job, it takes you a while to learn the ropes, doesn't it?'

'I don't mind,' Helen said. 'I just want to help, that's all. You don't look happy, I can tell that something is a bit off-key. I'm sure it's normal. I'll probably be bawling my eyes out when it's my turn and then you'll have to look after me. I'm pleased that things are going well for you on the whole, honest I am. Maybe that's the most a person can ask for with a brand new tiny person to care for. Can I just ask though, what happened to all that stuff about the job with the Welsh Film Board and the caution and the money? Did Alain explain? Did the letter ever turn up?'

May could feel herself droop. She had known that Helen would bring the whole mess up again. In a way she welcomed it. After all, she would have to face it at some time. It felt better when she didn't have to actually say anything out loud, that was all.

'We haven't really had time to talk about it. It's too late now anyway, as far as the law is concerned I definitely did commit a crime and the caution stands. Who would have known that writing a cheque on an empty bank account could be so serious? It's going to be on my record and everything, I keep thinking about it. I'm not sure how it will pan out when I want to get a job.'

'Don't you think you should talk about it with Alain?' Helen said. 'Sort it out together? It doesn't seem fair that you've been dumped with it all.'

'Ah,' said May, 'I'm not sure that's a good idea. I haven't said anything yet, not with Jenny and Christmas and every-thing. I'm going to talk to him about it afterwards. What's the point of upsetting him? No point in both of us getting stressed out. It's done now. The thing is, I know he's really upset about the job. He hates that there's no chance of moving to Wales now. I can understand that he doesn't want to hear about it any more, doesn't want me to mention it. It's hard for him, we're back to looking for somewhere to live, we can't stay in a shared student house much longer.'

'But why would you get a police caution when you had the letter saying you'd be refunded?' Helen asked. 'And where on earth has the letter gone? Can't you ask the Welsh Film Board to send it again? Surely Alain will help you, give you the address? And if they don't send it again, he can speak up for you, explain what happened, that you had a letter but lost it. It's not fair otherwise.'

You think I don't know that? May thought. She had a sudden memory of telling her mother something wasn't fair, maybe something about those damn multicoloured biros she had wanted so much. Life isn't fair, her mother had said, you'd probably better get used to it.

'Honestly, I'm fine, don't worry, please leave it,' May said. 'Let's talk about you. Have you had any practice contractions yet?'

Their talk was stilted after that. May tried hard, for Helen's sake, but they both knew that something wasn't right. It was like hearing some music, May thought, where one instrument was slightly out of tune. She was upset on the way home from the meeting. She didn't want to think about why she couldn't bear to ask Alain for help. Why she wanted to keep the lid on the can of worms and seal it up tightly. She had been looking forward to talking to Helen, and she had wanted so much to paint a good picture, make herself look less like a stupid victim, concentrate on the marvel that was Jenny rather than the bloody job and the police thing. May wished that Helen hadn't brought it up, but she couldn't blame her for it. She would have done the same in Helen's position. It was just that she had been desperate to show the baby off, and to have a little celebration for Christmas and for Jenny, but Helen's concern had made her realise that things at home were odd, off balance.

May leaned into the pram to make sure that Jenny was tucked in against the wind coming from the North Sea. Time out, she thought. I'm going to give myself some time out, just over Christmas. Relax with Jenny, not think about the difficult stuff. The new year, that was the time to think about it all. She had enough to think about for now with breastfeeding and nappy changing and, worse, the daily bath. They had taught her how to do it in the hospital, but May was not confident yet and she doubted that she ever would be.

Alain was out when she got back from the meeting with Helen, and the two students had gone home for the holidays. May prepared some food for later while Jenny slept, and then woke her with a kiss.

'Time for me to behave like a real mum,' May said to the baby. 'I'm going to give you a bath all by myself. That way, it'll be over and done with and both of us can relax for the rest of the day.'

Jenny looked at her mother and moved her mouth as if she would like to say something. May held her out so that they were face to face and kissed her. She was actually loving this baby business more than she had imagined. If she could just sort the other stuff out, she thought, that's all. She poured water into the baby bath and covered the baby in soap until she was too slippery to hold.

'Right,' she said, 'one soapy baby in the bath.'

May had read in one of her baby books that even if you don't feel confident, you should try to sound confident so that the baby isn't alarmed.

'Are you alarmed, baby frog?' she said. 'Are you scared that I'm going to drop you?'

'Yes, Mummy,' came a falsetto voice from outside the door.

May felt as if she had stepped off a pavement into space, or got into a car in a late-night car park only to find a man with a gun in the passenger seat. Don't let this be happening, she thought, please, not in front of Jenny.

'Alain?' she said. 'I didn't know you were in.'

'No,' he said, still speaking in the same strange falsetto, 'I don't suppose you did.'

'Come and give me a hand,' May said, trying again to keep her voice confident and normal, but knowing that this time she was not succeeding. 'I can't quite reach the towel.'

'Oh, the towel,' said Alain, this time using a deep, gruff voice.

May tried to breathe deeply, keep herself calm for Jenny, but she hated the scary voices, always had done and Alain knew it.

'Anything for the little lady,' Alain said with an American accent. 'Or should I say, the fat lady, yee ha.'

He whirled the towel round over his head and then hurled it like a lasso to the other side of the room.

'Oh sorry,' he said, normal voice this time. 'Sorry, I don't think you can reach it, can you? Oh God, how thoughtless I am. I expect you'll want to go and meet up with someone now, tell them how stupid and unhelpful I am, won't you?'

Alain made no attempt to reach the towel. May could feel herself starting to shake. Not now, she thought, not now we have a baby. That was never in the plan. She forced herself to speak calmly, for Jenny.

'Could you give us the towel?' she said. 'I can't get the hang of this slippery baby stuff. D'you know, I think I'm going to try to bath her another way tomorrow, a bit less soap can't hurt her, can it? It's not as if she's been down a mine or anything.'

Alain didn't get the towel, but at least the funny voices had stopped. He stood still, staring at her. May took a deep breath and then tucked the baby under her arm and moved slowly towards the towel. The wall of sound trick was going well, she thought, she'd better keep it up, as long as she could keep the shakes out of her voice.

'Some people say that baby soap isn't even good for babies at all,' she said. 'It washes all the natural oils off or something. I'm not sure, sounds a bit like hippy nonsense but on the other hand, I find this slippery stuff very difficult.'

May was nearly at the towel and she reached down with her left hand, keeping the baby tucked in to her right side. Alain whirled round and grabbed her left hand by the wrist.

'Are you saying,' he said, 'are you saying that I'm rubbish, that I can't even give you the towel when you ask for it?'

Jenny started to cry.

'See,' Alain said, 'she hates me, she thinks I'm rubbish too, she's cold and I didn't even give her the towel, what kind of a father am I? Who the fuck would do that?'

May was shaking all over by this time. It was part anger and part fear, but the anger was starting to win out. This is where I have to be careful, she thought, there's Jenny to think of, I could really mess up here. She wanted to run so badly that her feet started involuntarily twitching.

'Don't worry,' she said, 'Jenny's fine, the electric fire is on both bars and she's tucked in to me. Can I just get…'

May reached down and scooped the baby into the towel in an awkward one-handed movement.

'I didn't even help,' said Alain, hitting his forehead with his fists. 'I didn't even do anything and it's nearly Christmas.'

May held her breath. Yes, she thought, turn into Sorry Alain, Remorseful Alain. Get to the part where you cry and beat your breast, because hateful as that part is, it's safer for me and Jenny. There was even a chance that she could help him.

'Don't worry,' she said, keeping her voice level, 'I know you've been under a lot of strain. Why don't you go and make a cup of tea, I'll finish drying her and then I'll come through to the living room to feed her. We could watch something together, or read. Bit of peace away from the Christmas rush.'

May knew that she had said something wrong as soon as the words had left her mouth.

'Ah,' he said, standing a little too close to her, 'bit of peace is it now? That certainly wasn't what you wanted earlier today in Binns cafe, was it?'

So that's it, thought May, trying to push a vest on to Jenny with trembling hands, he knows I was out with Helen.

'No,' May said, 'it was crazy. Christmas shopping, huh? Who'd want it?'

Keep calm, don't act scared, that was the only hope May had. Act as if it was completely normal to go to town and meet a friend. Because it is normal, she thought, don't start thinking like a mad person just because Alain is behaving like one, it is normal and you'd better not forget it or you'll be as bad as he is.

Alain left the room.

'Tea,' he said, but there was no sound from the kitchen as May dressed Jenny in woolly tights and the little red velvet dress she had made her. No running water, no whistling kettle, no shouting.

'There,' May said to Jenny, breathing in her lovely soapy

clean smell, 'lovely Christmassy baby. I was going to save this dress for the actual day, but I think we all need a bit of Christmas cheer today.

'Look,' May called out as she went into the kitchen. 'Look who's got a new Christmas dress on, just to cheer up her daddy?'

There was a strange smell in the kitchen, which wasn't unusual. It was never terribly clean, and the student couple tended to cook odd things at odd times. They're away though, May thought before she realised what was happening. She looked closer. It was Alain. He was holding his index finger over the electric ring, so close that May could hear an occasional sizzle as the flesh caught.

May clung on to Jenny as if she might be able to help. She had to stop him. It was her fault he was so upset, it must be. She wasn't sure what else he might do, there were no rules that she understood. He had never gone this far before.

'Stop it,' May shouted. 'Alain, stop it now. It's OK, come on, stop hurting yourself, everything's OK.'

Alain took his finger away from the cooker and cradled it in to his chest. Look what I did, May thought, I am so, so sorry. She moved forward to comfort him and as she looked, May realised that perhaps he wasn't as badly burnt as she had thought. He must have waited until she appeared, she thought.

'It's not OK,' he sobbed, 'it will never be OK, will it? I'm rubbish, just rubbish, I couldn't even get you the goddamn towel and the baby was all slippery and cold and it's all my fault.'

May wrapped Jenny in her shawl and put her in the carrycot, which was standing in the doorway of the kitchen. She forced herself to talk in a steady voice. No sudden movements, she thought, keep it together, you'll be OK, concentrate.

'It's OK,' she said. 'Honestly, it will be alright, we'll be fine, we'll all be OK, look, Jenny's fine.' May pointed to Jenny, who had fallen asleep as soon as she was inside the carrycot. Sorry, Jenny, she thought, I'll pick you up and feed you in a minute, honest. She had no idea whether she was doing the right thing. May felt alone and lonely. She wished she could tell someone, ask their advice. She resolved to tell Helen everything, next time she had a chance, get some perspective on it. Try to find a way to stop being scared.

'Let me have a look at that finger,' she said. 'I think we have to run it under cold water. Otherwise you might have to go to casualty, get it dressed.'

'No,' Alain said, sounding heartbroken. 'No, I can't leave you and Jenny. What's happening to me, May, what's happening?'

May was trapped. She wanted to grab Jenny, run away, comfort Alain, tell him she loved him, lock the door between Alain and her baby, call the police, tell Alain she would always be there for him and hit him with something heavy. All of those things. Every single one. Especially hitting him with a heavy object. She had to protect Jenny first, May thought. Yet she knew she had to try harder to help poor Alain, that was her job too. To keep them both safe, she thought, wasn't that the bottom line?

Alain was still sobbing. May did not feel safe. Not yet, she thought, be careful. Too much sympathy and Alain would get suspicious, think that she didn't mean it. Too little and he might become either angry or suicidal, it was hard to know which. What May really wanted to do was pick Jenny up and feed her. Poor Jenny, poor little baby who had never asked to be part of this madness, who was surely too watchful already. It had been over four hours since she had been fed, the magic four-hour slot had been and gone, and even though she looked as if she was sleeping peacefully May wasn't sure what damage was being done by not giving her any milk.

Alain cradled his finger to his chest.

'I bought a present for Jenny today,' he said. 'A Christmas present. And for you. May, what's the matter with me? I was so thrown by the sight of you and that woman. I don't even know her.'

Alain put his head into his hands, carefully holding his hurt finger away from the others.

'She's my friend, Alain, is that not OK?' May said. 'Am I not allowed to have friends, girlfriends to chat to and talk baby stuff? I didn't tell you anything about her before because I know you get upset so easily, but it doesn't make sense, Al, does it?'

May felt very brave. It was as if the two of them together were making her stronger, the baby and Helen, a team.

'Come and sit with me in the living room. The others are out of the way. I'll feed Jenny and we can play Scrabble, I'll make a bandage for your finger, would that be good?'

'Yes,' said Alain, nodding. 'I really am sorry, May.'

'It's fine,' May said and for that moment it was. He was sorry, and he was a good dad, a good man underneath it all, and if she could just help him, be a fitting partner for him, he would get better. And Jenny needed a dad. Am I crazy, she wondered, thinking like this? Can things really get better? Could they stay like this? She filed the questions away to ponder on, and to ask Helen the next time she saw her.

'We could have gone for tea in Binns together,' Alain said. 'You didn't need to take Jenny to sit with a stranger. I would have come.'

Something in Alain's voice made May push away her thoughts of Jenny and Helen and look up. He was muttering something to himself and staring towards the cot where Jenny slept. May realised that she had relaxed too quickly, and that things could still go terribly wrong. There was danger in him still for Jenny, and she would be mad to think otherwise. How had she ever thought that he wouldn't threaten the welfare of this child he professed to love so much? She must have been crazy. She should have been more careful. May needed to think quickly.

'I was going to ask if you'd like to come, next time,'

May said. 'Helen is dying to meet you and they have some really nice cakes in there.'

'Cakes?' said Alain. 'Cakes? Since when have we had the money to afford cakes from a fancy cafe? Do you even realise that I haven't got a job yet? Did you even notice that the job at the Welsh Film Board, the one where I could have actually used my other language, Welsh, my special skill, did it even register with you that that chance has gone now?'

'I know,' said May. 'It's OK, the cakes were on the house because of Jenny; I know we're hard up.'

Welsh, she was thinking, why do you speak Welsh anyway when you come from Sevenoaks, nowhere near Wales? Why are there so many odd and weird things about you that I don't understand and am too afraid to ask?

'Everything I do is for you and Jenny,' Alain said. 'I think of you all the time. There isn't any me without you.'

He cried as he said the second part of the sentence, and covered his eyes, but May was sure that he had left a big enough gap between his fingers so that he could still see her.

May tried to work out whether she could get out, and if she did, where would she go? She couldn't bear to admit to anyone what was going on. No one would believe her. And everyone else she knew here was part of a student world, she couldn't tell them. There was Helen, but she had enough trouble without May turning up. More immediately, May was desperate to pick Jenny up and feed her. May's breasts felt hot and hard, and she was worried that if they got too full Jenny would find it difficult to latch on.

She sat down on the sofa and gestured to Alain to come and sit with her.

'It's OK,' she said, 'I'm here, I love you.'

Alain reached under the little table next to the sofa and pulled out a carrier bag. All May's muscles tensed despite her tiredness, coiled like an athlete on the starting block.

'Here,' Alain said, 'I'm a terrible person, a rubbish husband and father, I know all that. But I got this for Jenny even though I'm sure she doesn't want presents from such a no-hoper. No point waiting till Christmas.'

He reached into the carrier bag and May flinched. Thoughts of guns, knives and baseball bats raced through her mind as Alain pulled out a soft furry rabbit.

'Look,' he said, 'for Jenny.'

'Oh,' said May, 'she's lovely.'

'She?' said Alain. 'She? This rabbit is a boy rabbit, called Hitler.'

No, May thought, no, please. How could he turn something nice, a present for his baby, into something scary, a nightmare from a horror film? She knew she should keep quiet but she couldn't.

'That's ridiculous,' she said. 'Why would you say that? Why would we want Jenny to associate a cuddly rabbit with something evil and nasty?'

'Because it came from me, so it's a bad bunny. An evil bunny,' said Alain. 'Two sides of the same coin, like me. It will teach her a valuable lesson about trust.' He held the rabbit in front of his face and moved its head so that it seemed as if it was speaking. 'Good bunny,' Alain made the bunny do a little dance, 'and bad bunny.'

Alain made the bunny punch him in the face. His head smacked against the wall. Before May could duck, Alain jumped to his feet and swung the rabbit at May with his fist behind it. It hit her full on the side of the head and for a moment the hallway tilted. When she looked up, the rabbit was in front of her face, its paws rubbing its eyes as if it was sad. May held her hand to her face, too shocked to cry. This was the worst time yet. She moved her tongue round her teeth, trying to feel if any were loose. Come on, May, she said to herself, you can't pretend it isn't happening any more. Think of Jenny. Pull yourself together.

'Oh dear, oh dear, oh dear,' said Alain in a simpering little voice. 'Poor old Hitler Rabbit, can't get anything right.'

'Alain, stop it,' said May, trying to keep her voice steady. 'Just stop it now.'

He threw the rabbit to the side and stroked May's throbbing cheek.

'Can I hold Jenny?' he said. He shook his head as if he was shaking out the madness.

The options raced through May's head. Either she sat still, trusted him to calm down and cuddle his daughter properly, or she had to run, and run quickly. Both options had glaring deficiencies. May felt angry with the baby books she had read so carefully. She had been so thorough, as if she was studying for an exam. She could have given essay-style answers to questions about gestational diabetes or cleft palates but nowhere, nowhere in the books had they mentioned what to do when your husband hit you and gave the baby a rabbit called Hitler. She felt as though she couldn't get enough oxygen.

'Come on, Alain,' May said. 'Let's stop this. I'm sorry, I'll get her up, she needs feeding. Why don't you put the rabbit away so that Jenny gets a surprise at Christmas?' Does that sound sane, she thought, is that the right thing to say? Is there even a right thing to say? For a moment she felt so furious that she knew it would have been easy to kill Alain. I said sorry, she kept thinking, I said sorry, why would I do that? Why am I taking the blame?

'Forgive me,' said Alain. 'Help me, May.'

CHAPTER NINE

January 2018
Lewisham

The decorations come down today. Twelfth night. None in my room, not like some of them here. They act like kids, glittery with excitement. There's tinsel and holly everywhere in their rooms as if an edict had gone out that they had to use as much as possible, regardless of taste. I will say, though, it's been nice to look at the holly in the dining room. Or I would if I had a voice. Makes a person feel normal, holly.

I never went along with that twelfth night stuff. Take 'em down on Boxing Day, that was me. I remember Jenny begging one year, please keep them up Mummy, I love to see the tree when I come downstairs in the morning. It's like having a friend waiting to say hello to me in the living room, she said.

I told her straight, I said, friend or no friend, who has to hoover up the pine needles?

It's funny how people change as they get older. I'm thinking now, did I have to be so damn bossy? Could I not have left the bloody old tree up for a little while, like everyone else? I liked a bit of order, that was the thing, always that feeling that if I let things slip, I couldn't tell what would happen.

Jenny came last night and I tried to tell her I was sorry, about the tree. She claimed that she didn't understand, said we had nice Christmases, reminded me of some stuff I'd forgotten like the time we made real authentic cookies to hang but the lower ones were all nibbled away by mice. I think she was being kind. She brought chocolates, the ones wrapped in shiny paper that hang on the tree. The kind I never remembered to get for her when she was younger.

Here you are, she said, I brought you these, off our tree at home. They always taste more Christmassy than other chocolate, I think it's because they've been well hung. It's OK, I tried to say, I'm off chocolate and I'm off Christmas too but I started coughing and that was that. I haven't got a cough, not really but I do have trouble swallowing my saliva sometimes and that can make a person cough like a steam train.

I've brought you an iPad, she said, extra present. I was thinking that you'd be able to manage it, you only need to touch it and we'd be able to talk, you could watch TV and read on it and everything. I could show you my classroom.

I had a look.

Touch it like this, she kept saying, this is the password, this is where the BBC is, this is where my photos are.

Too much, I would have said if I could, take it away, I don't want to learn anything new, it makes my head hurt. I could see she was upset but just looking at the thing in its nice bright red case made me nervous, like it was a test I had to take that I hadn't revised for.

She left soon after that but this morning I started thinking about it and what I think is, I would not like to use the iPad ever again but I would like to eat one of those tree chocolates. I would like to see if it tastes of Jenny's house, and Jenny's life, and I would like to imagine it hanging there where it could see her and hear her talking. It will be strange to have something going through my intestines that has been with Jenny, I hope that doesn't sound too creepy.

So I sit up and reach forward for the tray that slots over my bed. I'm still in bed, they haven't come to get me dressed yet but I'm sure that's where Jenny put them last night so it should be fine. It's where everything important is kept, on a tray the width of a single bed, passport, photos, books, purse, everything. I have to rummage around a little, push a few things from one side to the other, knock my hairbrush on to the floor, that kind of thing. They're not there. I can remember them clearly, a Mickey Mouse, a Bart Simpson and a fat Santa with coffee cream in his tummy. I lean over as far as I can without falling out of bed but they're not on the floor either. I decide I need a systematic approach, so I take everything off the tray,

Christmas cards, wrapping paper, other chocolates I was given for Christmas, all the things that gather if you're a person who can't get to drawers and shelves. I try to pile it up on the bed but of course I'm in the bed myself, so every time I move there is a bit of slippage and things fall on the floor. I can't find the tree chocolates anywhere. I can't and I absolutely know they were there, they were there last night for goodness sake. It's not the kind of thing I would get wrong.

Of course Agnita comes in while I'm still looking and she sighs about all the stuff on the floor and I'm sorry, I'm really sorry, I know that her back hurts her in the morning and I'm not a mean-hearted person. Stay away from the s words said the little man in the sparkly hat and I have been trying but pardon is not the same as sorry, not at all. So I try to say sorry and I try to explain to Agnita but the only word that comes out is chocolate and she doesn't understand.

What do you mean, she says, what do you mean, you want chocolate? Are you not able to see all of these?

She holds up the Christmas gift chocolates, the tiny bitter ones in a beautiful box. They have ingredients whose names don't go with chocolate, like cardamom and black pepper. It's not those I want, I try to tell her. And then she offers me the Mozart balls, big mouthfuls of marzipan and hazelnut that I used to buy for Jenny for a joke and now she buys for me. Neither of us like them. It's a Christmas tradition, a habit.

You have them, I try to say to Agnita, you have them they need a good home and I try to push them towards her but my arm does the unexpected lunge thing again and it's more like throwing them at her.

Calm down, she says, calm down now there's no need to get angry like that and I'm not, I'm not angry like that or like anything else but I want the chocolates from Jenny's tree and they've gone. Of course somewhere along the way I forgot to be careful, forgot that I hadn't been to the toilet yet so I had an accident and although I've got plastic sheets I know that having an accident causes trouble. So I start crying.

It doesn't matter, Agnita says, that's what I'm here for, don't worry. It can't be what anyone is here for, I want to say, you deserve more than clearing up other people's messes. She's one of the kind ones. Really. And it's not possible for her to understand about the Christmas tree ornaments, I don't even understand it myself.

Kelly comes in then. It takes two of them to get me to the toilet, and then to strip the bed so that I can have clean sheets. I hope they don't think I'm not appreciative. I try to do a bow, to show I'm thankful, but I don't think anyone would recognise it.

Try and sit up, my dear, Agnita says and I wonder what it would be like to really be somebody's dear. I lift my head up and it's then that I see him. The man from the room opposite.

He's in the doorway of my room, and he's standing

up. Standing up! I thought he was in a wheelchair, he certainly was last time I saw him. Seems to be he's in and out of wheelchairs like other people are on and off buses. He needs to make up his mind. He waves at me, just a little wave of the fingers as if we were old friends. I don't know you at all, I would like to say, please don't do that. And who asked you to come in my room anyway, it's my private property as far as I'm aware.

He's clever though, because they couldn't see him. The carers, I mean. He kept an eye on which way they were facing, and seemed to know when to slide to the right and when to slide to the left as if it was a little dance they were all engaged in. As they moved first one way and then another to help me get from the bed to the chair, he followed their movements and leaned that way too, to keep himself out of their eyeline. I would have told them he was there but I couldn't get the words out.

By the time I'd been hoisted into my chair and washed down in the bathroom I was ready to go back to bed. So tired, I just wanted to sleep.

No bed for you, milady, Kelly says, we'd all like to have a little lie down mid-morning, wouldn't we?

She smiles at Agnita over the top of my head and adds, depending who with, of course.

Agnita chuckles and I miss my voice terribly. I'd like to join in, I think, not to say anything vitally important but just to have a bit of company. Something that isn't about whether I want a drink or a crap. A bit of banter, isn't that what we all want? I can't believe that I wasted all those years shutting my door and speaking to as few people as I could get away with. I could have had dinner parties, cooked spaghetti Bolognese and laughed with my guests about how obvious and retro my food was. I could have ordered in food from the Indian takeaway around the corner, it strikes me now that people wouldn't have minded. They might have been pleased to come and sit round my table just for the company.

I thought about it, of course I did. I used to clip recipes from the Sunday papers, look in my local supermarket to see if they stocked some of the more unusual ingredients. I even set dates sometimes and planned things, but I never quite had the courage to go through with it. So damn difficult to decide who to invite. So difficult to know how to be.

They go eventually, Kelly and Agnita, go off giggling to the next poor sucker. I'm left in my chair, feeling clean but battered, as if I've been for a bracing walk along a windswept cliff. I open a book and try to read. I'm rereading *Pride and Prejudice*, because I don't seem to be able to get the hang of anything new. The speech and language therapist thought it was best, so that my brain can get used to interpreting the written word on familiar territory, so to speak. Only I don't seem to be able to make it out. The words blur and swim, it might be the font or the letter size or something. Perhaps I should try the big print books. I remember the old ladies borrowing the big print books when I worked in the library. We all used to laugh because most of them seemed to be cowboy novels but the poor old ladies were stuck with them. It's not so funny now.

I'm thinking about cowboy novels and wondering if they have any women in them, cowgirls or love interest, it wouldn't matter which, when I see a movement over by the door frame. I'd forgotten all about his tricks earlier on but I remember straight away when I see him. I don't know if he's been there all the time, or if he has, why. He surely can't have been that desperate for a glimpse of flesh when my nightie rode up as I got in the hoist. Flesh on show is common as tinned peas in this place. St Barbara, patron saint of prisoners, miners and mathematicians. Specialising in lost causes, leave your dignity at the door. That should be the catchphrase. I start to chuckle at the thought of it written in neon over the door and I see that's got him interested.

What are you laughing at, he says. There's something familiar about his voice but then, don't all men sound pretty much the same? Not enough shades of difference, that's men. All wearing the same clothes as if they were a uniform, all doing the same things with their barbecues and their football.

Nothing, I say, I'm laughing at nothing but of course all he hears is a garbled mush.

I'm glad you can find something to laugh at in this place, he says, you've got to take your pleasure where you can.

Come in, I say, and I gesture it too so that he can understand. Keep your enemies close.

I don't mind if I do he says and he sidles round the door. Reminds me of a snake or something else cold blooded, the way he moves, but I guess it's because he's been ill.

I'm glad you're better, I want to say, just to be polite. I try to show him instead by smiling and pointing. It's not because I'm really glad, I'm not but I still remember the way people are supposed to speak to each other. And he does seem to be better, apart from an odd tic, a way of shaking his head every few minutes like a horse shaking off flies. It reminds me of something again. I feel like my memory has broken, short circuited or something. It keeps spluttering, recognising things I haven't seen before.

May, he says, reading the sign above my head, merry, merry May. I hold on to my call button with my good hand.

I knew a woman called May, he says, and he laughs. One of his front teeth snags slightly in front of the other in a way that would probably be corrected these days with braces. I knew someone else with that tooth snaggle, I think, and the feeling of dread builds a little higher in my stomach.

Chocolate? he says and he reaches in to his pocket and pulls out a Bart Simpson tree chocolate. I think that's mine, I want to say, but I can't so all he sees is a lunge, a grab for the chocolate that makes me look like a demented and greedy old woman.

Let me unwrap it for you, he says, open your mouth.

No, I say, hoping that he's joking. He couldn't really expect me to do that.

Go on, he says, go on, open up, there's a good girl. He's really serious, I don't know why, and it triggers something in me and I think, I've been here before, and I'm so scared I can't move. He unwraps it, takes off the foil that turns it into Bart Simpson and it's just a solid lump of chocolate.

Here we are, he says, pushing it towards my mouth, chocolate time. There's only one thing you can do when something soft is pushed at you like that, and that's open your mouth, however much you might not want to. I know that.

So that's what she sees, when she comes in, my new friend Jackie. I would have liked her to come across me reading one of the classics, or watching a documentary. This is mortifying.

Help, I try to say, this man has attacked me with a stolen Bart Simpson but I know how stupid it would sound. Besides, he's quicker than I am.

Hello, he says, May was wanting to have some chocolate, so I'm giving her this. He holds up the slightly mangled Bart. My niece brought it in but I reckon May wants it more than I do.

Oh, she says, like I knew she would, oh that's really nice of you. May, isn't it nice?

What can I do? I want her to be my friend and I can see

the glint in his eye, he knows he's got me. Such a familiar glint.

I do a kind of nod and try to swallow the lump that's broken off in my mouth but it's big and stale and my mouth is too dry. It makes me cough, then that makes me retch, and before you know it there's chocolate flying everywhere and I know I'm either going to have to have my clothes changed again or go around all day with brown stuff down my front.

Oh dear, says Jackie, oh dear can I help? She starts dabbing at me with a tissue but of course that makes it worse. He goes over to the sink, the man from the room opposite, and he rinses out a handkerchief. Don't worry, he says, tilting his head to one side, it's clean. He starts rubbing at the mess I've made of myself. I can't even open my mouth to say, it's OK, leave it. I want to, I'm embarrassed, but I know that if I do I'll end up spitting on his damn head.

Oh look at that, May, says Jackie, isn't he practical? The only thing to do is to smile and nod as he rubs away, breathing right in my face with his peppermint breath.

Oh isn't this lovely, says Jackie, just the three of us, it's not like being in a, in a, a place like this, is it? I am surprised that she can't even say the word nursing home. I didn't know she had a thing about it. To my mind she's sounding a tad shrill. I want him to go now, stop the rubbing and get his scary self as far away from me as he can. I want Jackie to be talking about how nice it is to be here with me, the two of us, not with him. I make a kind of shrugging movement so that he knows I want him to leave me alone.

I think that will do now, he says. He winks at me and then turns to look at Jackie and I bet he's winking at her too. I try to wink back at him, in a sarcastic way, but sarcasm is a high branch to reach for when you're on the ground with an eye that doesn't necessarily obey any commands.

Are you OK, he says, have you got something in your eye?

You bastard, I think, you knew that was a sarcastic wink. I flutter my hands at him in a no gesture and then I look over at Jackie. She's practically swooning at the sight of him. I need to work out how to take him down a peg or two. People like him shouldn't be allowed to swashbuckle around making everyone look at them. It's not right. I've been longing for a proper heart to heart with Jackie and now here she is in my room and it's no good, he's here too, larger than life and twice as ugly.

My friends and I used to have code words to use when we were out together, so that no one else would know what we were talking about. I wish I had a code I could use now, with Jackie, to tell her that I'd like to spend some time with her on her own. She probably wouldn't want to anyway.

Hey May, she says, as if she has read my poor old mangled brain, what about you and I have a game of cards? A bit of girl time.

I'm pleased, even though she says girl time instead of women's time. I smile a yes smile at Jackie. Who's to say it isn't a tiny bit good to think of myself as a girl? I don't feel any different in some ways.

I'll go then, he says, the lizard man from across the way. He's shaking his head again like there's a fly in his eye. It stirs something in my memory but then, what doesn't these days? The jingle of an advert, the taste of a good fruit, everything has extra meaning when you're old.

I'll leave you girls to it, he says, as if we might not have heard him the first time. I look at Jackie and I am expecting her to cave in, ask him to stay too. It's certainly what he wants. You can see that in his face as plain as plain can be. I almost do it myself, to save face for her, only I realise that he wouldn't understand what I was saying. I remember the Christmas chocolate then, and how nasty it was to have it pushed into my mouth. I'm glad she's standing firm. Go Jackie, go Jackie I think, silently willing her on to stand firm but trying to look nonchalant.

I'll be lonely, he says.

She's a kind hearted one, Jackie, and I think, oh no, he's going to persuade her but she makes a move towards me and it's like that part at the end of a concert when you realise there aren't going to be any more encores, no matter how much you clap. I want to hug her but the best I can do is keep my hands strictly to myself so that I don't hit her or cause any damage.

Goodbye Bill, she says, see you at dinner. I'm not particularly happy that they're making arrangements for later. See you at dinner could mean all sorts of things. I probably won't eat dinner, I think, I'm not hungry.

He comes over to me then and it strikes me that if Jackie wasn't there I would find him quite frightening.

Here you are, he says, you can have these and he puts the Mickey Mouse tree chocolate and the fat Santa with a creamy belly on my tray. None for you, he says, winking at Jackie. I know there's no point at all saying that the chocolates were mine anyway. She wouldn't understand me and she wouldn't believe me if she did.

Oh that's not very nice she says, no chocolate for me then? Say thank you, May, you're honoured.

She's using the same silly voice she probably used when she was fifteen. All squeaky and girly. He looks at me over her head and I swear it's a victory look. Nothing as simple as a cat who got the cream. More like a predator who killed some poor unsuspecting animal on a wildlife documentary.

I change my mind about the card game.

CHAPTER TEN

January 1978
Hull and Pimlico

After weeks of searching, Alain decided his chances of getting a job would be higher if they moved to London, where the work was. May managed to get a flat in Pimlico from the housing organisation that had housed her mother, and the move happened so fast that she hardly had time to pack.

'A new start,' said Alain. 'We'll leave this godforsaken place behind and go quietly in the night, leaving them all wondering where we are. Just us, a family, no more shared housing. Everything will be peachy from now on.'

Really, May thought, are you sure? She wanted to be sure. She wanted to love the idea of a fresh start, of leaving Hull and being in London again, but she was terrified. The previous night May had watched Alain dancing Jenny round the house, our last waltz, he had called it. He was so gentle, so sweet with her. May felt ashamed of herself for being so negative. It was what they needed, she thought, a shake-up, things would change. Alain would change. He would be better. It would get them back on track. The family, that was what was important. Never mind that she would miss Helen. They could write.

May couldn't leave without saying goodbye to her so she told Alain she had to get some last minute shopping and took Jenny into town in her sling. Helen was already there when she got to the cafe.

'Sorry I'm late,' May said as soon as she sat down. 'I've been packing and there's so much to do. It's really going to happen, Helen, we're off to the bright lights. I won't even be there when you have that baby of yours, I'm so sorry.'

'Wow,' said Helen, 'two apologies in one sentence. I'm going to miss you too, May, who the hell is going to apologise to me when you're not here?'

May laughed. She leaned forward slightly, holding Jenny's head with her left hand as she reached for the sugar with her right. May's sleeve pulled back and the bruises on her wrist were clear to both women. May pulled her sleeve back down and Helen winced.

'Hey,' she said, 'let me see that.' Helen reached over and gently pulled back May's sleeve so that the bruises were visible again. She looked at them carefully.

'Right, I'm going to say what I see, OK? There's four together here, and one slightly to the side. That looks to me like a grab bruise, like someone grabbed you hard by the wrist, am I right?'

May bit her lip and stared at her tea.

'Look at me, May, please look, I'm your friend, remember?'

May couldn't look up. She felt ashamed that her friend had seen, and she also felt that she had let Alain down. He hadn't meant to hurt her but she knew Helen wouldn't believe that. May didn't really believe it herself a lot of the time.

'He didn't mean to,' she said. 'Things have been really difficult for him lately.'

May expected Helen to scoff, point out the obvious flaws in what she had said. Instead, there was silence and when May looked up she realised that Helen was crying.

'I'm so sorry this has happened to you,' Helen said, 'and I do understand. Look.' She pulled up her own right sleeve and May saw them there, a line of round scars, some more angry-looking than others, marching up Helen's arm and disappearing into her jumper.

'They're burn scars,' she said, 'and that's the kind of thing they move on to after the bruises. I bet if you took your clothes off right here, right now, in Binns cafe, I'd see loads of other bruises, am I right?'

May didn't say anything. Helen was right, May had looked in the mirror the night before and counted them, bruises on her legs, her arms, her torso, everywhere.

'I think it will change, when we move to London,' she said.

'Oh May, listen to yourself. They don't change, believe

me, I'm sure of this. A man who is capable of doing that to you when you've just had a baby, when you're so sweet and lovely, he'll do it again, why wouldn't he? He likes it, that's why.'

'No, he doesn't, honestly he doesn't. He gets really upset afterwards, really sorry, he cries, he even pulls out his own hair. It's just the pressure, the stress of how we've been living. He's a good man, honestly, he is.'

'They're all good men when they're not beating up their wives,' Helen said.

'Honestly, he is, he loves poetry, he sings, he knits little toys for Jenny.'

Tell her, May thought to herself, tell her that he cuts them up, sometimes, the little characters he knits for Jenny. Tell her about the rabbit.

May bit her lip, trying not to cry.

'I'm not having a go at you, I'm just worried, that's all. I know what you're going through. Is there nothing I can say to make you see that you're in danger? Please keep in touch. Can I at least come to see you in London and bring the baby?'

'First trip away for your little one,' May said. 'I'd be honoured.'

The two women spent the rest of their time together talking of babies and other non-contentious things but it was there in the background, the more difficult stuff. May wished she could talk about it more.

Helen rolled May's sleeve back gently when they said goodbye.

'Don't let this become your normal,' she said. 'You can always live with me. We'd manage. Bye-bye, Jenny Wren, see you soon.'

May felt confused and shaken but she knew she had to give Alain another chance. She would try harder, help him get things back on track. The trouble was, thought May on her way home, that she knew Helen was right. She knew she was in danger, she knew that it wasn't likely to improve just by changing the place that they lived in. But she couldn't stop thinking it was her fault. If she was different, more confident, less pushy, more loving, less needy, if she could only be a good wife, the right wife. If she could love him better, that was the bottom line, if she could love him the way other people loved people then she would be the one who saved him, who made things OK. He was a good man, she knew that, and that meant it must be her who had made him bad. It had to be worth one more push, for Jenny if not for herself, to see if there was anything she could do to make him feel better, to enable him to bring out the kindly, caring side that she knew was there.

'Look,' he said when she got home from meeting Helen. 'Look, I've made some curtains for our new front room. I worked on them last night when you were asleep, and this morning. I asked for the measurements and I thought I'd give it a go, I got that old hand sewing machine out of the cupboard.'

'I got that at a jumble sale,' said May. 'I didn't even think it was still going.'

'It wasn't,' said Alain. 'It wasn't but I took it to pieces and I fixed it and now I can make anything, I could make clothes for you and Jenny, I could sell made-to-measure curtains, everything.'

Alain's enthusiasm was infectious and May started to feel some of her anxiety drain away. Alain held out the curtains and May examined them.

'Fantastic,' she said, 'couldn't tell them from shop bought.'

'Are you sure?' Alain said. 'You're not just saying that?'

May thought how wrong Helen was about him. He didn't have any confidence, that was all. If she could keep remembering this, stop dwelling on the difficult stuff, there might be a chance.

That feeling lasted nearly all the way to London the next day on the train. Their belongings were following in a van.

'I can feel it, May,' Alain said as the train jogged through the flat snowy landscape. 'Things are going to be different, I promise. Give me your hand.'

May clutched Jenny to her with her left hand and reached out her right. Alain clasped it like a drowning man.

'I swear, I do solemnly swear, that from this day forward, our lives will be different. I will bring you nothing but joy, May, happiness and light and all that stuff.'

May squirmed in her seat. She wanted to encourage this new Alain if it was possible, but there was something about such raw openness that made her feel uncomfortable.

'And Jenny,' she said, 'let's not forget about Jenny. We need to bring her nothing but joy as well.'

Alain took his hand away. May knew that she had said the wrong thing.

'This is about us,' he said. 'I don't know why you bring Jenny into everything. She's fine, aren't you, my darling one?'

Alain reached into the bundle of baby that May was holding and touched Jenny's face. May stiffened. It had been difficult to get her to sleep, and May wasn't enough of an expert yet to be confident about the journey if Jenny was awake. She had planned for this moment all morning, keeping Jenny awake, moving her feed times, and it had worked but she would never sleep through this kind of touching and patting.

'What?' said Alain.

May felt as though he had heard her thoughts.

'Can't I even cuddle my own baby girl?' Alain said. He tossed his head back like a skittish horse.

May realised that she had been caught in one of those traps that had become all too familiar to her. She had to either resign herself to Jenny waking up and being fretful or push Alain away and precipitate a full-on confrontation.

'Here you are,' May said, passing the baby to Alain, 'you have her. I think she would like a daddy cuddle.'

Alain cooed and clucked over Jenny until she was fully awake and starting her pre-crying noise, and then he gave her back.

'She doesn't like me,' he said, 'she's always like that. She only wants you. I think you've spoiled her.'

'You can't spoil a two-month-old baby,' May said. She wasn't sure it was safe to be so vehement, but this was something she felt so strongly about that she couldn't keep quiet. 'All the modern research shows that that's a myth, something our mothers believed, but we know better now.'

'Modern research, huh?' said Alain. 'Look at the academic speaking now. Time for that doctorate, I guess. I'm just a loving daddy. Don't know nothing, me.'

He stared out of the window and May tried to think of something that would make up for what she had said, retrieve the day so that they could get to their new home without having a full scale row. It would be such a bad omen to start off like that. She jiggled Jenny a little, enough to disturb her from the sleep she was beginning to settle into.

'Oh look,' May said, 'she's not happy with me either. I think she doesn't like sleeping in the daylight. She needs a darkened room.'

'Well that's what I thought,' said Alain, 'that's why I made her those heavy curtains last night, they're on top of the stuff in the van. We'll have to get them up as soon as possible, good thing I thought of it.'

Goal, thought May, shame he's not always so easy to manipulate. May wondered if other mothers had to plan their words so carefully, keep themselves on guard at all times. She didn't think so. Her father had died when she was a child, so she hadn't ever witnessed a relationship between a man and a woman at close quarters. Perhaps it's what everyone does, she thought, perhaps that's what no one can ever say, they just learn to live with it. Or not, like Helen.

Alain seemed cheery as they unloaded the van and chose where to put their few belongings. The woman from the flat across the hallway came out and offered to help. May worried that the woman's offers of help would annoy Alain but he seemed to like her.

'I'm Joan,' she said as she hauled a box into their bare living room. 'Pleased to meet you.'

'Hi,' said Alain before May had a chance to speak. 'I'm Alain, and this here is baby Jenny, and this is my wife.'

My wife, thought May, no name of my own.

Alain and Joan were soon chatting as they unpacked. May didn't join in. She wanted to but couldn't think of anything bright or breezy enough to say. She had hoped so much that London would work out, but it didn't seem to be getting off to a great start. Alain seemed OK now, she thought as she fed Jenny in the middle of the boxes and bags, but what had happened on the train? Had she imagined it? Should she have stood up for herself? What would have been the worst that could happen? Was there part of her that wanted him to explode so that she could run away legitimately? Go and live with Helen? And if so, was it her own fault? The questions buzzed through May's mind like ticker tape until she thought that she might explode. You've got to stop this, she thought to herself, give this move, this family a proper chance. After all, look how much other people liked him. She carried Jenny through to the bedroom to settle her and listened to Alain and Joan chatting outside. May was almost drifting off when she heard her name mentioned.

'I don't know what's wrong with May,' Alain said to their new neighbour. 'You'd think she'd be happy, moving into our own home and all that.'

May was sitting on the floor in the little room that would be Jenny's. Alain must want her to hear, she realised. It was a tiny flat, he could hardly think she was somewhere else.

'It's probably just baby blues,' said Joan, and May felt like crying at the concern in her voice. 'It takes some women like that.'

'But she acts so strangely,' Alain said. 'Sometimes I, well, I think we'll leave it for now.'

Alain broke off quickly as May came out to the pavement outside the flat where they were taking the boxes off the van.

'I'm fine,' she said, 'absolutely fine, let me take some of this stuff indoors.'

Shit, she thought, I overstressed that. Far too much emphasis.

'So nice to meet a neighbour,' May said. 'Fresh starts can be daunting. It's nice to know someone nearby.'

May realised that Alain looked furious. She tried to think what it was that had upset him. He didn't speak again until Joan had gone.

'Did you have to do that?' he said. 'Make a show of yourself, tell her we don't have any friends?'

May tried to think what she should say to calm him down. She hadn't meant any harm, hadn't thought that what she had said had been contentious but she knew she had to make things OK or their first night would be ruined. The atmosphere had changed completely. Alain glared at her in a way that made her stomach lurch.

'I've got plenty of friends, you stupid woman. I don't want them around you, that's all,' Alain said as he threw Jenny's toys into her room.

'I just meant,' said May, 'we're new here, that's all.'

Shut up, May, she thought, stop talking, you're making it worse with every word you say.

There was a silence, and May tried to make a plan.

'Earth to May, Earth to May,' Alain said and May realised that she had been standing still, thinking, while Alain unpacked stuff around her.

'I'm sorry,' she said, 'I was just thinking how nice it is to be together here in London.'

A jar of peanut butter slipped out of Alain's hands and smashed on the hard kitchen floor. Alain tapped the ash from his cigarette onto the mess.

'Oh dear,' he said, staring at May. 'Oh May.'

May noticed that he was using his soft and soulful voice. The scary one. She was on her own, with a baby to protect. May had to think fast. She had to placate him.

'Why don't you have a sit down?' May said, keeping

her tone even. 'I can see the kettle in the corner of that box, and the tea bags have already been unpacked. I'll clean this up in a jiff with kitchen paper and then I'll get the dinner on. I've got all the ingredients ready to go, it won't take me long.'

May pretended to ignore the way that Alain was glowering at her.

'I'm sorry I upset you,' said May. 'I think we're going to be happy here, and I didn't mean to do anything, say anything, to jeopardise that. I love you, Alain.'

'Love?' he said. 'Love? Well I think you've shown your love by finding this marvellous flat, haven't you? We were nothing, we had nothing, and now we have all this.'

Alain swept his hands round in a grand gesture meant to show the flat. The poor dingy little flat, with its tiny windows and its three rooms plus a toilet, no bathroom.

'You'll feel better when you've had something to eat,' May said. She hoped it was true. If he didn't, she had run out of choices for the moment. It would be unbearable to try to trace old friends only to ask for help, and anyway she had lost touch with most people since she had married Alain.

Alain was quiet while May cooked. She was glad that she'd brought food ready to cook. If she thought back, Alain was often at his worst when he was hungry. May had read an article about the effects of low blood sugar, and it was possible, probable even, that this was part of Alain's problem.

It was nearly ready when Alain walked over to the stove and sniffed the pot. May held her breath.

'That mince is off,' he said. 'Are you trying to poison me?'

The air seemed to go very still, in the way that May had read about before an earthquake or a tornado. The mince was still bubbling, but more quietly now. May checked instinctively that Jenny was still asleep in her carrycot and reached out to stir it.

'Are you not listening to me?' Alain said. 'I said the mince is off. I can smell it, see, and you would be able to if you weren't so fucking stupid. Even your nose doesn't work properly, can you believe that?'

May stood with her spoon poised above the saucepan. She was hungry, and it had been smelling delicious, she was sure of that. Of course, it didn't smell so delicious any more. It was more like a pot pourri of hatred and terror, but she was still sure it hadn't gone bad. Don't act apologetic, she thought, that always makes him worse.

'You don't have to have any,' she said. 'It's a new recipe, but there's bread and some of that nice cheese we bought the other day if you prefer. I'm going to have some though, I don't think it's off, and if it is, oh well, I've got a cast-iron stomach after all those weeks of being pregnant.'

May attempted a small laugh, and lowered the wooden spoon into the saucepan. It was a good way to disguise the shaking of her hands. Keep going, she thought to herself, act confident, you're doing well.

'I can't believe you would do that,' Alain said. 'I can't believe even you would do that to me. Christ, you must hate me. Is it because of the Welsh Film Board? Do you think that doesn't upset me far more than it upsets you? You must be absolutely, bone-shakingly stupid if you think that for one tiny moment I'm going to let you get away with something so evil.'

May stopped stirring. She was used to Alain's twisted logic by now, but this was something else entirely.

'What?' she said. 'Get away with what?'

As soon as the words had left her mouth she tried to recall them. Come back, words, she thought, come back, let me not have fallen into another trap so quickly. Alain clearly saw that he had executed a winning move, and his expression became almost kind.

'Oh dear,' he said, stroking May's face as she stood frozen over the pot of mince. 'Oh dear, who's a stupid, stupid little girl?'

May put the wooden spoon into the mince and reached out her hand to turn off the gas. Damage limitation, too late for anything else, at least get away from the hot stuff. She remembered Alain's finger. She should have backed down sooner, she could see that clearly now, this big strong brave act was for fools.

'I'll tell you what I'm talking about, dear little sweet little stupid little May. I'm talking about this.'

He moved his hands as he spoke, down from her face

to her shoulder to her chest until they were resting on her stomach, still swollen from the birth. May stood still.

'This,' he said again. 'Have you even tried to lose weight? Were you planning on staying like this for ever?' He jabbed May's stomach with his fingers as he spoke. She held her stomach in and tried to step backwards, but she was right next to the cooker. It was a narrow kitchen, and to get away from him she would have to step round him. It wasn't going to happen. She had to work with what she had. May's fingers tightened on the wooden spoon.

As if he was reading her mind, Alain spoke. 'Give me that,' he said, 'the wooden spoon, hand it over. I'm worried you might hurt yourself with it, do you know why?'

May remained frozen, holding her stomach in and trying to think what the right thing to say or do might be, the safest path, the way to get out and away. Nothing seemed possible.

'I said, do you know why?' he said, jabbing her stomach again, harder this time so that she cried out.

'No,' she said. 'No I don't know why.'

She handed over the spoon, dripping with sauce.

'Because you're so fucking stupid you can't even be trusted with a wooden spoon,' he said.

He laughed as if he had said the wittiest thing ever. 'Do you get it?' he said. 'Or are you too stupid to even understand how stupid you are?'

He wiped the spoon as he spoke, round her face and over her clothes, dipping it in the saucepan now and again until she was totally smeared. May tried not to wince at the heat of it.

'This is the thing,' he said.

He spoke in a quiet, reasonable tone, as if he was explaining something in a friendly way.

'You're not going to poison me. I know your little tricks, you see, I'm one step ahead of you at all times, and you would be best advised not to ever forget it. You'd feed me the mince, and I'd eat it, like the fool you think I am, and bingo. You'd be able to keep her,' he pointed to the sleeping baby, 'all to yourself, mummy and baby. Am I right?' Alain stared at May. 'I said am I right?'

May tried to think. If she said yes, not only would she be admitting to something insane, but she would also be in terrible danger. If she said no, there was a chance that he would become even more angry. She decided to hedge.

'I don't know why you would think that,' she said. 'This is the same recipe we had last week, I thought that you would like it. Has something happened today to upset you? Is it the flat? I'm sorry if it's me.'

What am I doing? she thought. Standing here, exhausted from the move, asking him if he's OK, pretending to be reasonable. She was covered in tomato mince sauce, and she was terrified. This was not the new life in London, the quiet family life she had imagined. This was not the life that anybody sane would choose to live.

'Eat it,' he said. 'Stick your hand in there and eat it like the little piggy you are. Go on, eat it.'

'What do you mean?' May said. 'I only just turned the gas off, look, it's practically still bubbling, I can't put my hand in there.'

'Eat it,' he repeated, 'yum yum yum.' Alain thrust the wooden spoon at May's mouth.

'I've had enough,' she heard herself shout. She hadn't known that she was going to say it until she heard the words. 'Stop it, get out of my way, I need to have a wash. Leave me alone.'

She pushed past him, picked up Jenny and left the kitchen, propelled by the momentum of her own words. She ran into the toilet, the only room with a lock, and pushed the bolt home. Jenny was still asleep and May kissed her.

'I'm so sorry, Jenny,' she said. 'I'm going to sort this out, I promise.'

May was covered in dinner and trembling so hard she thought she might drop the baby. She wiped off the worst of the sauce and settled down on the floor to feed Jenny, crying, until she fell asleep.

May woke from a dream of hot babies covered in blood that looked like tomato sauce. Jenny was still snuggled in, suckling. It could only have been a few minutes. May scrubbed her face with toilet paper and cold water. The mince had crusted round her ears and hair, and it took a while. Her face was red and puffy. She looked at the bolt on the door. It was flimsy, but it had held. That must mean that he wasn't going to try to pursue her here for some reason. Think, May, think, she said to herself, what's he going to do next? Her only hope was to stay ahead of him. Jenny was OK, that was the main thing.

May looked at the window. It was tiny and high up. Even if she had a chair to climb on she wouldn't be able to reach it, and even if she could reach it what could she do? Throw a note into the street and hope it was picked up? No. If this was a film there would be someone standing out there, or else the police would storm the building, or…

May tried to pull herself together. This wasn't a film, it was her life, Jenny's life. She was hungry, cold and trapped in the toilet of her new home with a tiny baby. She stood up. She needed to be determined and dignified, that was the trick. She would walk out of the front door. It should be easy. It should be the easiest thing in the world, a woman leaving her house with her baby, it must happen every second of every day in every country. She walked over to the toilet door and listened. May's hand was on the door handle and she was about to leave when she heard a noise. Breathing. She could definitely hear breathing outside the door. She tried to still her own breathing to be sure. It was breathing, ragged, gaspy breathing as if someone had been running or crying. May's stomach lurched. She was trying to decide whether to speak, try to leave, or just settle back down on the floor when Alain spoke from the other side.

'May,' he said, 'my lovely May, my darling Jenny, what have I done?'

It could be a trick. She stepped back from the door. 'Alain?' she said.

'Thank God,' he said, 'thank God you're OK. May, I'm so, so sorry, I'm the sorriest man there ever was, sorrier than that even.'

May wasn't sure what to say. She didn't want to start another argument, that was definite, but she also didn't want to roll over and accept the apology as if it was something almost normal, as if he had broken a favourite cup or forgotten an anniversary.

'I need to come out of here, am I safe?' May asked. It was a pointless question. Of course he would say yes, whether she was or not, but the way he said it – that was what she had to be listening to. She had to make sure that it wasn't a trick.

'I would never, ever hurt you, my darling May,' Alain said. 'And I'm so, so terribly sorry. I heard today, before we left, that I didn't get the job I'd thought would be a cinch, the one I really wanted. I think it hurt me more than I realised. After the last time, too, with the Welsh Film Board. What can I do to show you how sorry I am? How can I ask you to forgive me? That I would hurt you, the precious mother of my precious child, defies belief.'

He sounded as though he meant it, and May decided to take a chance, but be ready to run if it was a trick. She slid back the bolt and left the toilet. As soon as she saw Alain's tear-stained face she knew she had been right. She felt an irrational surge of gratitude and sank to the floor next to him in the hallway, Jenny snuggled between them.

'Come on,' she said, 'it's OK.'

May pulled Alain's head on to her shoulder. She wondered how it was possible to fear and hate someone yet also to love them, to be grateful to them for the quiet times.

'It's not OK,' he said. 'I was unkind to you, and I don't know why.'

Unkind, May thought, unkind? Surely unkind was when you told someone you didn't like their new dress, or you teased them for listening to the top ten. Was it the right word for smearing a person with hot sauce on the first day in a new flat and then making them take refuge in a toilet with a little baby?

'I think there might be something wrong with me,' Alain said. 'I'm going to go to the doctor now we're down here, honestly. I think it might be something serious.'

Alain started to cry, sobs that tore at May's soft, exposed heart.

'Ssh,' she said, cradling his head. 'Ssh, it's OK, I'm here, don't cry.'

'I'm sorry, Jenny,' Alain whispered into the baby's ear, 'and I'm sorry to you too, May. I'm really going to try, from now on. No more nonsense.'

He looked at May with such a pleading look that she was torn for a moment. If she kept quiet, they were much more likely to have a good evening. But there was something about keeping quiet, about pretending that everything was OK, that damaged some part of her.

'It's more than nonsense, Al,' she said. 'Look at me.' May gestured to her hair and clothes, encrusted with sauce. 'We're a family now, we need to sort this out.'

'I don't know why, I don't know why,' Alain said. 'I just feel so angry all the time, it's not your fault, I'm so sorry.'

'Hey,' said May, 'it's OK, it's OK, I'm here.'

She knelt on the floor next to him and put her arm round him.

'It's OK,' she said, 'don't worry, I love you.'

Do I? May thought, do I really?

'I never knew my real mother,' Alain said. 'I think it's had more of an effect on me than I wanted to admit.'

This was news to May. She realised how little she knew about her husband, about the Alain that had existed before she met him. He'd never mentioned this before, in fact his mother had come to their wedding. Or so May had thought.

'Who was the woman who came to the wedding?' asked May. 'I thought she was your mum?'

'Oh I call her Mum,' said Alain. 'I always have, she's my father's wife. My father was the village doctor, in a village in Wales. That's why I chose Lampeter, when I went to university.'

At last, thought May, maybe we're getting somewhere.

'But my dad and his wife, my mum, couldn't have children, in fact she was a perpetual invalid who took to her bed. So he had an affair, with a woman from the village. I think she was his cleaning woman. The woman got pregnant, and Mum offered to bring up the baby, and that was me. But she never loved me, which is understandable in the circumstances. And it's just, just, sometimes when I see you with her, with Jenny, I just feel so jealous.'

It wasn't everything, May thought, and it possibly wasn't anything, but it was all she had. Only, the woman she had been introduced to at the wedding, she hadn't been a perpetual invalid. Had she got better? She didn't seem much like a doctor's wife either, but May thought that would be more difficult to tell. She decided to give him the benefit of the doubt. Anything else seemed wrong on their first night in their new home, and surely, surely she could have handled it better. May knew she was partly to blame.

'My darling,' she said, 'I'm so sorry, of course I love you too. We can make it OK.'

And she did want to make it OK, she really did. But it was so difficult to mean the words that she said. So difficult to stop the things that were niggling away at her, things she needed to think about, things that meant that she couldn't completely trust him. Stop obsessing over the details, May, she thought, just take in the wider picture, the little bits and pieces don't matter. But they do, another part of her thought, oh, they do.

'You don't believe me, do you?' Alain said, blowing his nose. 'I can feel it, there's a reluctance. You with your happy childhood, happy little fat girl with her lovely teacher mummy.'

May jumped back slightly as if she had been slapped.

'That's not fair,' she said. 'That's not fair at all. I do believe you. It's just, it's just I'm surprised, that's all. I'm genuinely surprised. I'm so sorry to hear it and I'm so sorry for you, and I'm going to try never to let you feel left out again.'

'But you believe me, don't you? Say you believe me, say it or I won't know. No one ever believed me when I was growing up, I was just the doctor's bastard son, none of the other kids wanted to be my friend.'

Where is he now, this doctor, May thought, where is he? There was something else as well, something niggling at the corners of her fuzzy baby brain.

May didn't get a chance to think it through properly until later, when she was sitting feeding Jenny in the quiet of the night. Alain had gone for a walk, to clear his head, he had said. May couldn't help worrying. He wasn't used to London like she was, and Pimlico had some very rough parts. It wasn't a place where people wandered around taking night-time strolls, but there was no telling him anything like that.

She listened to the baby's familiar sucking noises and tried to calm down so that the milk would keep flowing. Jenny had had enough interrupted feeds in her little lifetime. May tried to empty her head of everything except Jenny, just for a moment, and it was then that it came to her. The reason why she had been feeling so sceptical. Not only was Alain's mother the oddest doctor's wife she'd ever seen, a large, grubby woman with a cockney accent who had brought Jenny some stained nylon vests the only time she had seen her, but also there was the conversation they had had. May had been pregnant at the wedding, and she hadn't made any attempt to cover it up.

'Hope we're not going to have to deliver it here,' Alain's mum had said. 'I never even knew I was in labour with Al till his head popped out.'

May had managed to move the conversation quickly to something else, but she remembered it now. She could have been lying, obviously, but there was something about the way she said it that had a definite ring of truth to May. Why on earth would Alain pretend she was his adoptive mother?

'Oh Jenny,' May said into her daughter's fluffy head, 'we're in a pretty pickle.'

CHAPTER ELEVEN

February 2018
Lewisham

I have always liked February.

Jenny used to say, you're the only grown-up I know who still loves their birthday month, but it isn't that. I like it because no one else does. And because spring is hidden there with the hope of a better year to come. Not to mention that it's short, too, over quickly and payday just around the corner.

The months and the seasons merge into each other in this place. I haven't been here in spring and summer yet but I know nothing will change. They keep us all at the same temperature all year round, even now, in the snow. Like precious manuscripts, Jenny said. Bless her, nice try but more like a funeral parlour, I thought. So I know it's February from the calendar, and I could make a good guess from looking out of the window, but I can't feel it on my skin, and that seems like a loss. One of so many losses I can't keep count.

Jackie pops in most mornings. She drops in like we're neighbours in the real world, and for me that's something to wake up for. She can even understand me sometimes. I managed to explain to her with a lot of mime and expressions that I miss reading the most, and she said that she loves to read aloud. She offered to read to me so we're reading that one by Kazuo Ishiguro about the clones. She reads beautifully, she could get a job reading books aloud, she would honestly be great. I chose the book and I'm proud of it, it's a good story. It's set in a school for these people that aren't real people because they've been cloned, they don't have families or anything.

Seems just like here, I said to Jackie but that's three s's in a row right at the beginning of the sentence so I'm not sure she got it at all. It was good to say it, nonetheless.

Today is my birthday and I know Jackie doesn't know but I still feel excited when it gets to ten o'clock. Maybe she will have found out somehow, or maybe Jenny told her but that hasn't happened and she comes in her own sunny self as usual.

Good morning, good morning, the sun is coming back to join us after the winter hibernation, she says, in Finland they celebrate the return of the sun, did you know. Did I know, I think, of course I know, I know so many things I can't tell you. Just for a moment I envy her and her long sentences so much I have to breathe deeply and let it go, or I'll explode with longing. Breathe it out, that's the way, they're her sentences, not yours, May. Your own are living in your head at the moment and that's better than living nowhere at all.

I've been to Finland, I try to say and there's no s's in that, none at all but she still can't understand me. I went to Moomin land, it's on an island in the west of Finland. She gets part of that.

Moomins, Jackie says, I love the Moomins, they're from Finland that's right.

Do you know, she says, I don't think this place is too bad at all. It reminds me of when I was at university, living in a hall of residence. She looks shy when she says this, sort of letting her long dreadlocks fall in front of her face as if they could shield her. Some of the people are really OK when you get to know them, she says and I see her glance towards the room across the corridor from me where that man lives. Snaggle-tooth Bill, I think, and I make a grimace but she's away on a dream of her own.

Some people get out, she says to me, it doesn't have to be true that you never get out. She blushes and it suits her.

I'm going to get out, May, she says.

I'm surprised at that. I don't mean to start crying but there's a tear or two escaping even while I'm thinking, you silly woman, of course you're never going to get out of here, it's a myth, the only way out of here is in a box.

Oh don't cry May, she says and she gets a tissue from her cardigan pocket. I'll come back and see you, she says and we both know that is a lie in so many ways but it's still nice that she said it.

Not, I say, meaning that I'm not crying at all. I'm still trying with the dignity thing even though I'm wearing an adult nappy and talking like a fool.

I heard that, she says, clapping, I got that one clear as a bell. You're getting better May, soon you'll be able to take a turn reading the book out loud.

It isn't true, of course it isn't true, but it's nice of her to say it. You only got it because of the context, I want to say, you wouldn't have stood a chance if I'd said something more random. Or if I was having a bad day. No one can understand me then, even the thoughts inside my head are jumbled.

Why don't we practise, she says, we could go over a few words until you've got them, and then surprise everyone.

It's exciting and scary but I like it, I really want to do it. I imagine Jenny's astonishment when I ask her a question in words she can understand. I imagine talking to Agnita and the others so that they know there's more to me than bodily functions. I could be like that famous person who came back from a stroke, there could be inspirational radio programmes about me. This is turning out to be quite a birthday after all.

Yes please, I say, and there is spit to match my enthusiasm and my arm jerks along with the spit to show that it doesn't want to be left out.

Jackie laughs. I think that's a yes, she says, you're on,

we've got a deal. Let's show 'em. What's the first thing you want to say, what's the magic phrase we can work on?

It's funny but when she puts it like that I can't quite think what I want to say. Everything, that's what I want to say but that's not helpful and if there's one thing I want to be it's helpful.

How are you, I try, and I make my face look quizzical to give an extra clue.

I'm not sure, Jackie says, this isn't working too well, maybe we're running before we can walk, let's just relax and have fun, catch the words as they turn up.

Poem, I say, although I'm not sure it's what I want. Wouldn't fuck off and leave me alone be more useful? Most people would think so but not my Jackie. She's so positive it's bordering on insane most of the time.

Are you always this cheery, I try to ask and she says, whoa, let's start with something simple, whatever you said then just went whooshing past my head.

Poem, I say. I say it slow and clear and try to keep the spitting under control. Po-em.

Great idea, Jackie says, poetry, that would be so nice. Old ones like us, we learned a lot of that in school, didn't we? I don't think that kids today do so much. Too busy reaching targets.

I nod to show I agree. It's a proper grown-up conversation, and I think I'd agree with whatever she said.

I'm going to ask a question now, Jackie says, let's see if this works. Who is your favourite poet?

I close my eyes so that I can concentrate on my answer. Names of poets dart around my head like firework trails but I can't catch them, they're flashes of light that don't quite form into words. Normal after a stroke, apparently, but still maddening and scary. Think, May, I tell myself, who is that American woman? The one who wrote about death as if he was a person? I can almost get the quote but not quite, it's slipping away. I can't catch it.

She wrote about saying nothing, I know she did. About how sometimes saying nothing could be powerful. It's not powerful for me, Emily. I can think the words, I can imagine them, and then my mouth opens and a stream of vowels come out. It's unbearable. Why would anyone want to spend time with me?

Jackie looks blankly at me and my voweling growling so I think, let me listen to those wise words myself and stop trying to talk. I smile at Jackie to show her that it's not a hostile silence and she smiles back. It's like the sun coming out, her smile, worth anything to see it.

I'm going to find some funny poems, she says, there isn't much to laugh at in here but we can look further afield, that's the way.

She spends a moment or two looking at her phone and then just as quickly as that, reads me a poem about a teacher killing his whole class to teach them a lesson and she's right, it is funny, we laugh and laugh and I wish I could keep the poem, remember it to show Jenny. It might make her laugh, and it would show her that I was thinking of her too, I sometimes think she doesn't know how much I think of her when she isn't with me. I decide to keep saying nothing.

A name flashes into my head, lit up like the West End lights. Emily Dickinson, that's who it was I was trying to think of, and that name wouldn't have come to me if I hadn't kept quiet. I wish I could say it but instead I point to Jackie's phone, to show her that I'd like another poem. I can't believe she could just do that, find poems on her phone. Same age as me and using technology like that – I'd love to tell her how clever I think that is. I wonder if I should have tried harder with the iPad.

OK, OK, she says, maybe you can join in soon, help me out. Just say something when you can, to get the feel of the words.

In a minute, I say, holding up a finger to show her what I mean.

I get it, she says, in a minute, huh? We're cooking on gas. Listen to this, she says, and she reads me a poem about turkeys, be kind to your turkey this Christmas, and she reads it in a West Indian accent I haven't heard her use before and she stands up, she's moving around the room and saying that turkey poem like she is on a stage.

It's marvellous, bravo, I call at the end. Something like bravo, anyway and she takes a bow and we're both giggling like school girls when he walks in. Bill, the brazen one from across the way. Just walks in like he was invited, like I had issued an invitation to my room.

Did I hear Benjamin Zephaniah, he asks, that's always been one of my favourites.

Oh, Jackie says, I'm sorry, I didn't mean to disturb you.

Liar, I think, I bet you wanted to disturb him all the time. I bet you were only reading to me so that he would hear you. All my happiness has gone, vanished like a burst balloon. I remember with my whole body how it used to feel to be the one who didn't cop off, the one walking home alone or worse, tagging along behind a couple. I felt like that right up until I married Alain and plenty of times since.

I'm miles away but I realise that he's talking to me, Bill, trying to tell me something about what a good reading voice Jackie has, and how lucky I am that she is reading to me. I tune the words out and try to think where I saw that snaggle tooth last. He's embarrassed, not used to being ignored I guess, so he does that head shaking thing, as if he still has long hair he has to get out of his eyes. He stands there, head on one side as if he has questions in his pocket to ask the world.

Perhaps he was a teacher in a school I worked in, I think, or a parent or a caretaker. Maybe he worked in my local library, or waited tables in a wine bar I went to with colleagues. I raise the palm of my good hand in a questioning way.

Sorry, merry May, he says, I'm going to need a few more lessons from the lovely Jackie before I can understand you.

You liar, I think, you got that one, I'm sure you did.

Jackie wasn't looking but I'm damn sure Bill was.

May and I were working together, says Jackie, I'm really sorry Bill, we haven't finished yet.

Oho, he says, shaking his head, both my ladies playing hard to get.

That really makes me mad. Both my ladies indeed. One, he doesn't mean it, not at all, he's just after her and in the most shameless way possible. Two, I would never be one of his ladies, even if he held a gun to my head and three, she's worth ten of him. A hundred even. He can see that I'm getting mad and it amuses him, I can see the slight smile. If I wasn't in this chair, if my arm worked properly, I would thump him so hard. He looks quite scrawny, I reckon I could easily get the better of him.

That's enough of that sort of nonsense thank you Bill, says Jackie, come on now, back to your room please or find something else to do. We're busy here.

Yes, I think, go on Jackie, you tell him, but when I look at her she's laughing, she didn't mean it at all, it's a kind of game between them. I'm a kind of game between them.

He does stand up and leave though, and that's a good result.

I'm sorry May, Jackie says, I didn't mean for our time to be interrupted.

It's not your fault, I try. Jackie listens close, her ear near to my mouth as I speak.

Nope, she says, sorry, I can't get it.

The morning is spoiled. It won't work any more, the funny poems won't be funny and Jackie won't be able to understand me and the whole thing is ruined. I'm trying not to cry. I don't want her to know I'm upset. I don't want her to think I'm a crazy old lady.

Oh I'm sorry, she says, I don't want you to be sad, we can do it again, I'll have a word with him.

No I say, and she gets that one, no, but the next bit is too complicated to say. Keep away from him he's dangerous, I want to say, there's something about him I can't explain. I don't think he's who he says he is, there's something about him. I try anyway but it's no good at all.

I'm sorry, Jackie says, I've got you all upset now and I didn't mean to. It must be so hard, not being able to make yourself understood, I'd hate it. I know, shall I just ask you yes and no questions?

I nod, mainly because I don't want her to be upset and think it's all her fault.

Are you normally a chatty person, she asks and I nod but that one has me thinking. Am I? I've lived alone a long time now, and got used to my own company, but back in the day I could talk the hind legs off a donkey, I'm sure I could. At work, with the kids, we'd talk all day.

Do you like cooking, she asks and I shake my head, no. She laughs and says, me neither. I start to feel more comfortable and at home, but I can't help glancing towards the door every couple of minutes in case he comes back.

Do you like classical music, she asks and I do another big shake of the head.

Rock music? she says and I nod.

Hey we've got lots in common she says and I feel a glow. I'm not being completely truthful here but I'm getting a chance to refashion myself in a way. Truth was I liked silence most of my life, preferred not to have anything spoiling it whenever possible, but I think I'll be different now. If I get another chance I'll play some of that noisy music Jenny used to like when she was a teenager and I'll play it with the volume turned up. There's no silence as big as the silence inside my head, that's how it feels.

We've established some favourite authors in common by the time they bring my lunch and Jackie heads off to the dining room. OK, I haven't been completely truthful and some of the authors we talked about are new to me but I'm going to read them if Jackie likes them. I'm going to read them and talk about them so that we've got even more in common just because it's so wonderful to have a friend. You're worth losing my voice for, I want to say to her but I remember that people do not always like it if a person goes overboard with admiration.

I think about the chatty person question all through lunch. You need something to think about at mealtimes here because the food is terrible. It's like someone has taken great care and attention to produce a menu that is as fattening as possible. They never miss a carb if they can possibly shoehorn one in. Today it's salad for lunch, which involves a large pile of plastic-tasting grated cheese and two pieces of bread and butter. I carefully pick out the tomatoes and the green bits and eat only them, thinking of how lovely Jackie manages to look in plain linen trousers and a thin jumper. Not February clothes at all but just right for this place, not like an old lady at all.

I'm still thinking about the chatty thing when Jenny turns up that evening.

Hi Mum, she says, happy birthday, how are you feeling today?

I realise that the reply I'm about to make is horrible. I want to say, how do you think I'm feeling? I don't know why that pops into my head. Have I always spoken to Jenny like that? I try to remember specific occasions and I think yes, maybe I have. Recently anyway.

Fine, thanks, I try, then I point at her to indicate that I'm asking how she is too.

She doesn't get it, but then she wouldn't be expecting me to ask after her, would she? If I needed any further confirmation I can see it on her face. She looks as baffled as usual.

Oh, she says, well done for giving it a go, that's nice, and look what I got for you. Jenny holds out a parcel, loosely wrapped. Of course it makes me start snivelling again, I think it's probably the medication they have me on. I've never been a crier.

Jenny looks like she is on safer ground now. Come on Mum, she says, it's your birthday. Here.

She pushes the parcel at me again and helps me to take it. She hasn't used any sticky tape, which is so thoughtful I nearly cry again. As if I care about things being wrapped up, I want to say, I'm happier being ignored. I pull at the paper and it's a nightdress, a pretty one with pink flowers.

And a Kindle, Jenny says, there's a Kindle in there that might be easier to read than paper books, it's lit up from the back, see? It's much easier than an iPad.

I am grateful, very grateful, and I wish I could tell her thank you. I put my hand on her arm instead, as gently as I can, and stare at her with a smile so that she will see how happy I am. Jenny looks away, she's never been so good at eye contact, and she fiddles with her coat and her gloves. I want to ask her if it's cold outside, so I cross my arms over my chest and try a questioning brrrr face.

It's a pointless question, because as I ask it Jenny takes off her padded coat and her scarf and her gloves and she rubs her fingers and hugs herself as if she can't believe she is really safe in the warmth of this place.

Yes, she says, it's freezing but I didn't have to wait long for the bus.

I picture her there, at the bus stop, all wrapped up and looking more like somebody's grandmother than somebody's daughter. How strange to have a middle-aged child that used to be a tiny baby.

Time, I say. I'm thinking of the tricks time plays on us all. Jenny leans in, determined to catch my mumblings.

No, she says, it really wasn't that long. She still thinks I am talking about her time at the bus stop. She is so sweet, so forgiving, how come I don't notice it more often?

I pull some faces, stretch out my cheeks and open my mouth wide. Jenny looks alarmed.

It's what actors do before going on stage, I think, facial warm up. I have no way of explaining this so I stop.

I remember the pad of paper they've been wanting me to use. It's worth a try. I anchor it with my useless right arm and gesture to Jenny to take the top off the pen for me.

When you were little, I write, the words appearing in a wobbly way as if I had been transported back to Year One, was I a chatty mum?

Oh, Jenny says, this is not what I was expecting. You sure know how to keep a girl on her toes, Mum. Let me think.

If you have to think, it's a no, I want to say. I keep quiet, let her think how to say whatever it is she's going to say.

You had a lot on your mind, Jenny says, I know I wasn't an easy child.

I feel ashamed. You were, I write, you were an easy child, who told you that you weren't. Even as I write it I know who told her. It was me of course, me who said things like, I don't know why you have to be so difficult. Poor little mousy little Jenny.

Of course the more upset I get, the more incoherent I become, and the more my writing slips and slides and my right arm won't hold the paper down. She doesn't get any of it as I apologise and tell her she was a dear, easy baby.

Don't get upset Mum, she says. She looks uneasy and I want to make her feel better so I try to calm down.

Breathe in through the nose, out through the mouth and concentrate on a point on the opposite wall.

I was thinking, says Jenny, maybe I could take you out soon, as soon as the weather improves. In your wheelchair.

I give her a look, trying to indicate that I'm too heavy.

I would manage, Jenny says, but about that, I was wondering, I mean, Dan and I are getting on much better now.

What, I write, playing for time.

There is always a problem when people get back with ex-partners, I've seen it all before. I have always been the friend who is happy to say bad things about the ex during the split, but then if things go differently and they want them back, it somehow becomes my fault.

Hilary, the deputy in the first school I worked in. She found out her husband had a stack of nasty porn hidden in the attic, and when she threw him out it was me she turned to. I suppose she thought that because I was a single mum I would understand, and I did. I told her everything she wanted to hear, agreed with everything she said about him. I told her things were OK on your own, and that she didn't need a man like him. It turned out that she did, though, and when they got back together three months later I was suddenly off the friends list without a trial. Literally, snubbed at the Christmas party, overlooked for a simple promotion I was more than due, and we never spoke again apart from in the course of our duties. I don't think she could look at me without seeing those poor girls in the pictures.

So Jenny and Dan. I try to arrange my face in a neutral way. A Swiss face, I think, because of Switzerland being neutral in the war.

Oh, I say, giving it two syllables to imply that I'm not sure whether it's a good thing.

Oh Mum, Jenny says, he's a nice guy, you know he's a nice guy really. And who wants to be alone when they get older.

Oh no, Jenny says, I didn't mean, it's just that, I'm sorry I wasn't thinking.

I wave to show I'm not offended. I'm feeling a mixture of disappointed and triumphant. Disappointed that she would go back with him, and that she would do it for such a banal reason, and triumphant because I always feel happy when things go wrong, especially when I've predicted it. I can't help it. It's a tiny triumph compared with how sorry I am.

I pat her arm to show it's all OK. I'm not sure if she notices. I point at the tissues on my tray.

What if it all happens again, Mum, Jenny says, I couldn't stand it.

I keep my mouth shut. It would never happen again, I want to say, no other woman, however naive, would ever look at him with anything but contempt, surely?

The truth is, Jenny's Dan is a spineless little creep of a man. He teaches philosophy to sixth formers and I always imagine that his classes must be the butt of jokes for long after students have left school and moved on. No one, and especially not Jenny, was prepared for him to have a liaison with one of his pupils, he just didn't seem the type. He works in a hardware shop now.

I'm busy thinking about how to play this one when Jackie pops her head round my door.

Bye, May, she says, bye-bye we're off to the cinema, maybe you can come next time, see you in the morning.

We? I think. We? Who the hell is she talking about? I know really, of course, I knew before he poked his stupid head round the door.

Bye-bye merry May, Bill says, sleep tight and don't let the monsters bite.

Bill, says Jackie as they walk away, it's not monsters.

Mum, says Jenny, that's what we used to say, isn't it?

I shrug my shoulders.

Yes, she says, we did, I remember. Everyone else said bedbugs.

She's right, I think, and the thought gives me a cold feeling.

CHAPTER TWELVE

February 1978
Pimlico

'London isn't paved with gold,' May wrote to Helen, 'but there's something magic going on. Alain's working, he's teaching infants. He's got a long-term supply job and he's a different person. Honest, I can hear you not believing me but it's true. He's happy, that's the difference, happy and fulfilled. He comes in at night and talks to me, really talks about the children, and what they've been doing, and if he has a problem, he asks me what I think he should do and we talk it over. So, no, I'm not using my teaching skills myself, I couldn't bear to leave Jenny in a nursery yet. But I'm using my brain, and honestly I'm so happy.'

May paused. Most of it was true, and the other part, the exaggerated part, that was because she wanted it to be true, so much. Alain really did seem a little better. Happier, more talkative, smiley and less angry. Much more open, sunny, all the things May loved about him out there on show every day. Well, nearly every day, but no one is happy all the time, May thought.

Jenny was thriving, and May had decorated the little flat with yellow walls and brown paintwork. She made sure that she was always finished for the day before Alain came home from work, so that he wouldn't feel pressured into helping.

'I'd better go now,' May wrote. 'Alain will be home soon and I'm making that casserole with bacon and white sauce. Don't worry, I'm not turning into a Stepford Wife! It's just that with a baby, routine is more important than it used to be. You'll find out any day now, as soon as that baby stops dithering and decides to join us!'

May put down her pen and looked over at Jenny in her cot. She was still asleep, and May knew that she would pay for that later. If May's mother was here, she would probably have suggested that May picked Jenny up and woke her so that she would sleep later, but May wasn't sure. It seemed such a shame to disturb her. She hadn't expected that there would be so much compromise involved in child rearing, so many small daily negotiations. She hadn't expected that she would miss her mother so much.

May decided to make dinner a real treat, to show Alain how happy she was that things were going so well. She wouldn't eat much herself, just move it round her plate a little. He was right about the extra weight she had put on with Jenny, it was slow to shift. She had to show him that she supported him, that was the important thing. After all, if he had a physical problem like diabetes or appendicitis it would be easy to sympathise, and that wasn't fair. Just because whatever ailed Alain was hidden, a psychological problem, that didn't mean that she should abandon him, whatever Helen said. May knew that she should try harder, help him more. He was such a good person underneath.

May had asked her health visitor for advice a couple of weeks ago after a very frightening argument with Alain about E.M. Forster. She hadn't told the health visitor what the argument was about, because it sounded ridiculous, but she had tried to explain what life was like living under these conditions. The health visitor, a cheery young man with red hair, had suggested that Alain might be allergic to caffeine. May had reservations about the possibility of being allergic to such an everyday substance but the man had assured her that there was a great deal of research about exactly that going on at the moment. Alain had been in an abject, apologetic mood that night, and May had managed to explain to him that caffeine could be the problem.

'Yes,' Alain had said, 'yes, I'm sure that's it. I drink loads of coffee, all day. Oh God wouldn't it be marvellous if I could stop? Help me, May.'

May didn't want to feel suspicious, but he had latched onto her suggestion so quickly that she felt winded.

'It's just an idea,' she said.

Alain had taken both May's hands in his and looked into her eyes.

'We'll beat this together, May, we'll sort this out for ever, I swear. Just don't buy any tea or coffee and I'll keep away from it when I'm out of the house too.'

May thought there was something slightly unfair about this, and that on her own at home with a small baby tea was as necessary as air, but she kept quiet. It had to be worth a try, despite her reservations.

It had been ten days now with no tea or coffee in the house and things were going well. At least they were doing something, May thought, and all the time they were taking action they were acknowledging that there was a problem. In fact they had joked that May was finding it much more difficult than Alain.

'I know you're doing this for me, and I know it's hard for you,' Alain had said the previous night. 'No one has ever done anything for me before, not something like this that proves they really care. I want you to know that I appreciate it with every part of my soul. Talk is cheap, so I'm not going to say that everything will be plain sailing from here, because it might not be, but I'm going to try, darling wife, I know we can get through this together.'

May loved that phrase, 'darling wife'. It sounded so special, unique, as if nobody before her had ever been addressed that way. Alain had been gentle in bed after-wards, making love to her like he had done in the early days. None of the rougher stuff he had seemed to prefer recently.

'Look,' Alain had said, 'no coffee, no coffee at all. I'm caffeine free.'

He had lifted Jenny into the air as he said it, spun her round and round. Careful, May had wanted to say, don't drop her, she doesn't like it, she's just had a feed.

'Clap for us, Mummy,' Alain had said and May clapped. Even though she could see Jenny's lip wobble, even though Jenny was seeking out eye contact with her and there was definitely panic in her sweet little eyes, May had clapped.

'We had family fun last night,' May wrote to Helen once the casserole was in the oven. 'Alain is really bonding with Jenny now.'

She sat back and looked at the sentence she had just written, and at the rest of the letter. It's what people do, she reasoned to herself, no one tells the whole thing exactly like it is, friends spare each other the grim details. It's not the same as lying. Jenny started to cry and May folded the half-written letter, tucked it into a copy of *1984* on the bookshelf and picked her up.

'Maybe I'm being stupid,' she said to Jenny. 'Maybe it's all OK now that he's given up coffee. Maybe everyone has these sorts of niggles when they're trying to live together. Maybe I'm just a bad person and if I was better, he'd be OK. Maybe it's me, Jenny, did you ever think of that? Maybe if I left him we'd both be better off.'

Jenny stared back with her milky blue eyes. May felt as though she had hit on a desperately important truth. That's it, she thought, if things go wrong again I've got to get out, leave him not just for me and Jenny but, even more importantly, for Alain's sake. There's something in me that seems to make him mad, it's my fault and if I leave, he'll be able to be the proper, kindly, intelligent man that he really is, underneath. The other thing, the thing that May couldn't admit even to herself, was that this new caffeine-free Alain who was so pleased with himself at beating his addiction, this healthy happy version of her husband that she was so proud of, well, didn't he seem just a little bit drunk, most of the time? He swore that he never touched a drop and certainly they didn't have enough money to buy any. But he swayed like a drunk, he giggled like a drunk, he snored like a drunk and more than once he had repeated himself. If she thought back, it had happened before. Not at the very beginning, she hadn't noticed it then, but when she was pregnant, there had been a couple of times then. A couple of times when she had thought he seemed drunk. She had always pushed the thought away, assumed that she was being ridiculous.

May forced herself to think of the other night. The other night when he had rolled his sleeves up to help with Jenny's bath, and although May had tried hard to reason it away, hadn't she seen marks on his arms that he couldn't explain? He had said they were the scars of a skin infection like acne when he was a teenager, but did that make any sense at all? May had tried to ask him more about it but he had pulled his sleeves down and left the room.

'I can't bear to talk about it,' he had said later. 'I'm so embarrassed.'

May never felt able to ask. If Alain was in a good mood,

she wanted to keep it that way, and if he wasn't, she didn't dare. Nothing made sense.

May pushed the thought to the back of her mind and set the table for dinner, Jenny balanced on her hip. She paused for a moment before setting out the glasses and the beer she had bought for a treat. Surely she was being stupid, she thought. Letting her imagination run riot. He was happy, that was all. Happy, not drunk.

May fussed with the table. She put a small pot plant she had bought as a moving-in present in the middle, on a beer mat. If tonight doesn't work out, she thought, if anything goes wrong, I'll pack a bag for Jenny and me and we'll leave. The thought went round and round her head until she wished she could push it away.

May could always tell how Alain was feeling by the way he opened the door. If things were bad, he opened it in an angry way, as if a monster had entered the house and was looking for someone to kill. The door hit the wall as he pushed it, and his footsteps were heavy with misery. Tonight, however, the door opened in a normal way and Alain almost danced in.

'Where are my favourite girls?' he called. 'I'm home, I'm home, I can't wait to see you.'

Jenny jumped a little in May's arms when she saw her father. May decided that she was pleased to see him, and that to think anything else would be ludicrous and a prime example of the fact that she thought way too much, looking for problems when there weren't any.

'Here we are,' May called.

Alain came into the living room whistling a Rolling Stones song and danced May and the baby round the living room. May tried not to smell his breath just in case she found something but she didn't, he smelt of herbs and peppermint.

'You're looking at the teacher of the year,' Alain said. 'You know that boy in my class I was telling you about, the one who wouldn't settle and kept crying?'

May nodded.

'Well I got him to join in today, and guess what? He did a picture of me and wrote, "my teacher", underneath it. It's the first time he's done anything like that, I didn't even know that he could write. I sent him to show the Head and she was really pleased as well and she said I've got a way with me. May, it was amazing.'

'That's wonderful,' May said and it was, it really was wonderful, only she kept thinking, that poor little boy, he doesn't know, he doesn't know what you're really like. She couldn't stop herself. Shame on you, she thought, he's a good man with a problem and you should be more caring, then he might be OK.

'We were right to move to London, May,' Alain said, 'things are going to be so much better.'

May realised that Alain had tears in his eyes. Come on, she thought, stop being such a spoilsport, join in, celebrate with him, for goodness sake.

'Yes,' she said, 'I'm sure you're right.'

It was a lacklustre response, she knew that. Something that a tired parent might say to an enthusiastic child, not a partner's response, not a proper wife's. May knew it and she knew that Alain knew it as well. Her stomach clenched. If he hit her now, she thought, she had only herself to blame. If she was such a misery that she couldn't even celebrate success, be pleased for him about the little things, then she didn't deserve any better. May kept her head down and waited for what was coming.

Nothing happened, and when May looked up again she realised that Alain was crying, holding Jenny close to him and sobbing into her little neck.

'Here,' he said, holding her out to May, 'you take her, I don't even deserve to hold her. I know what I've done, May, and I know how badly I've treated you, both of you. I could say I'll never do it again, and I want to say that but I don't know. I'm not myself, May, it's like I'm possessed or something. It isn't me, you've got to see that.'

May felt as though she had been thrust onto the stage in the middle of a play she didn't have a script for. If she said the wrong thing, it could all start again. She put her free hand to the patch on her head where Alain had pulled some hair out during the E.M. Forster argument. There were little tufts coming through, short and prickly. Alain dropped to his knees.

'Forgive me, May,' he said. 'Forgive me, Jenny, I'm the sorriest guy in all of London town.'

May was frozen for what seemed like ages but was

probably only a couple of seconds. Come on, she said to herself, he's making an effort, do something.

'It's OK,' she said, 'don't worry, I know you didn't mean it. Come on, I've made dinner, that casserole you liked, we'll be OK.'

She could see that he was slightly disappointed, and that he had expected more, a hearts and flowers speech full of forgiveness and plans, but May knew that she couldn't do it.

'Maybe in time,' she tried to explain, 'I'll be different, I feel so numb at the moment.'

'I know, darling, I get it. Baby blues, right? I've been reading up on it. Lots of women get them, it's perfectly natural, don't feel bad. We'll face it together, whatever happens.'

May gave him back the baby, who was watching the adults speaking as if she was at a tennis match. He would be safe with Jenny, she was sure, safer than she felt at the moment. May's hands shook as she took the casserole out of the oven. She felt overwhelmed with anger in a way that she couldn't remember feeling before, as if the core of her was made of white-hot steely fury that was radiating out to every part of her body. Baby blues, she thought, fucking baby blues. So that's the way it's going to go, is it, everything her fault? A quick sorry for all the pain and the fear and the anguish, the smashed up house and the sadness of broken dreams? The bruises on her legs and her poor sore ribs and Jenny flinching and the sleepless nights? Just a quick sorry, that was all?

She spooned the mixture on to the plates, all thoughts of special dinner and celebrations gone, all sympathy for him gone. Breathe, she thought, just breathe, calm down. May knew that if she didn't get herself under control it would start again and there would be no doubt at all this time, it would be her fault. She thought about the transcendental meditation course she had started and ditched, and tried to steady her breathing. In, out, in out, come on, May, she thought. She was concentrating so hard that a hand on her shoulder made her jump. She spun round.

'Where's Jenny?' she said. 'I mean, is she OK?'

That would do it, she thought, one thing Alain hates is me constantly putting Jenny first, and then I go and say something stupid like that.

'She's fine,' Alain said, massaging May's shoulders. 'I popped her in her bouncy chair with her giraffe and she's as happy as anything. It's you I'm worried about. You seem so strung out and jumpy. Is it me, merry May? Have I made you like this? I can't bear to think that it's my fault, I just can't bear it.'

May felt as if she might explode. She wanted to rage at him, hurt him, tear him to pieces, but she wanted to accept the comfort he offered as well. Without thinking, she put her hand directly on the casserole dish and screamed as the palm of her hand registered the pain.

'Oh darling,' said Alain, 'come, put it in the sink, let me run the tap, it'll be OK, keep breathing, the pain will go off in a minute, come on, brave girl.'

He walked her across the tiny kitchen, locked together as if they were dancing, and put her hand under cold running water.

'I'm sorry,' May said. 'I'm so sorry I didn't mean to, I just...'

'Ssh,' said Alain. 'I'm here, I'm with you, it's OK. There's no need to say sorry, remember that dreadful film? "Love means never having to say you're sorry"?'

'That was a ghastly film,' said May.

The pain was easing as she held her hand under the water. I'm acting like him, she thought, it's fucking contagious.

'I don't know,' she said. 'I didn't mean to do it, but I can't bear how things are, Alain, I can't do it any more, it's got to change.'

Alain's eyes overflowed with tears as he held her hand gently under the water.

'There's nothing I can say,' he said. 'I'm screwed up somewhere and I want to be different, I want to be different so much. For you and Jenny. I want to be the kind of husband and dad you can both be proud of. Hang on.'

Alain went into the living room and started fumbling through his pockets.

'Here,' he said, holding out a small box. 'I know it's not your birthday yet but it's close, and you need these more today than you will next week. Go on, open it.'

May didn't want to take her poor burnt hand out of the water, but Alain seemed so eager. She patted it dry on a tea towel and took the box. Inside were the most beautiful earrings, gold, and shaped like a circle with a cross, the symbol for woman.

Alain got down on one knee.

'We're already married, I know I can't ask you that again,' he said, 'but I would like to ask you this: would you please stay married to me? Would you give me another chance and try to stick with me while I clean up my act?'

May felt sick. It was as if he had read her mind, she thought. He knew. He could see her thoughts attached to a huge pendulum, swinging between leaving and staying. Each side of the argument seemed so clear. Of course she should leave; he was dangerous, a liar and a bully. Of course she should stay; he was the father of her child, a loving partner and a sweet, thoughtful companion. May looked again at the earrings.

'How the fuck can you have the audacity to wear a feminist symbol if you stay chained to this wife beater?' May could hear exactly what Helen would say. But Jenny, she thought, what would Jenny say? May could imagine trying to explain to Jenny why she hadn't stayed with her dad when she was a teenager. May's hand was beginning to throb again.

'Here,' said Alain, 'I'll run a bowl of cold water for you, you just go and sit down with your hand in it, completely submerged. I'll get the dinner out. I'll feed Jenny too, if you've still got one of those bottles of expressed milk. You take it easy. You look a bit green.'

May did as she was told. It wasn't just the pain in her

hand, she thought, and it wasn't just the muddle she was in, not knowing what to think. She really did feel sick.

'I think I might have eaten something dodgy,' May said. 'I really do feel sick, I don't want any dinner, just eat yours.'

'Oh darling,' said Alain, bringing his plate of food through to the living room and scooping up Jenny with his other hand as if he had been practising the move for years. 'I'm going to look after you now, properly. Hey, do you think you might be pregnant? You know how you were with Jenny, sick as a dog. Wouldn't that be marvellous, darling?'

Marvellous? thought May. What the hell would be marvellous about having two children with only a year between them? The sleepless nights, the sore breasts, the lack of freedom. He was wrong, she thought, definitely wrong. Everyone said you couldn't get pregnant when you were breastfeeding, everyone.

'I'm sure it's just the bit of ham I ate while I was cooking,' May said. 'It probably wasn't cooked through. I'm fine, you eat, give me Jenny and I'll feed her. Thank you for the earrings, they're lovely.'

Alain bowed. 'Whatever the lady wants,' he said. 'Sorry, I mean, "the woman", obviously I do.'

Later that night, while Alain was asleep, May got out the letter she had been writing to Helen.

'Help, Helen,' she wrote, 'I think I might be up the bloody duff again and I can't face it. I want to leave him but he's being so nice, and I'm so tired, and I feel like I'm playing that party game where you're blindfolded and then you get spun round and round and round and you have to point to the door. I can't point to the door, Helen, I don't know where it bloody is and I certainly don't know how to walk through it. He can be so nice, Helen, that's the thing, he's not all bad, and if I can just love him enough then maybe we have a chance. I hated growing up without a dad, I don't want that for Jenny, I wish you were here and we could talk properly. All my love to you and the nearly-born, sorry for bending your ear.'

May put the letter into an envelope and sealed it up. She felt better for letting off steam but worried that she should have been more loyal to Alain, and less dramatic about the chance of another pregnancy. May got out the earrings to have another look at them. This time she pulled out the satiny inside of the box that was holding the earrings. Underneath was a slip of paper she hadn't noticed before. 'Darling Sue,' it said, just that, in Alain's neat, schoolteacher's writing.

CHAPTER THIRTEEN

March 2018
Lewisham

We're going out shopping today, and I'm excited.

Stupid old woman to be excited, but I am, I'm so excited that I couldn't sleep last night. I never tell them when I can't sleep because they give me those pills, the ones that knock you out. It's my secret. They come in every morning asking how I slept and I give them a thumbs up with my good hand, regardless. Some things have to be private. I can't give them everything.

So my night-times are my own, and I lie here thinking about things. About Jenny and the times we used to have. I can recall all the books and stories I used to read to her, word for word. The one about the little boy whose cuddly dog accidentally gets given to the school fair, I've been thinking about that one. I think it has a happy ending, I think he gets the dog back, but it strikes me now as an outlandishly sad story to tell to a small person. Hey, you might as well say, hey this is the score, bad things are going to happen to you, in fact they probably have happened already while you were watching the damn mobile hanging on your cot. Everything you love is vulnerable, baby, so you'd better harden your heart.

That's what I tried to explain to Jenny, there's no sugar coating. When I can talk I'm going to say that again, along with a few other things. I've got an agenda written on my notepad. I can't write much, it's too tiring and anyway I wouldn't want anyone reading the private stuff, so I write it in code. I'm fantastic at keeping things covered up, I always have been.

So shopping. I haven't always liked shopping. When I was a young woman I was haunted by my own body, consumed with hatred for it. I wanted to wear what the other girls wore but everything looked wrong on me. All my clothes bulged and puffed and heaved as if they were hoping I'd take them off and they could find someone else to wear them. Then I got thin and met Alain and for a while I was the prettiest girl I could be but it didn't last, and it didn't do me any good at all. So I gave up and I spent quite a few years, the Jenny rearing years, looking as though I was in mourning. Black shapeless shifts, long grey skirts, flat lace-up shoes. I dressed like that right up until I got ill, now I think of it. Just didn't care. So what it is that makes me long for flowers now, I don't know, but I'd love to wear something pretty. Not too gaudy, just a sprig of flowers here and there to brighten it up. Red flowers, old-fashioned ones, vintage flowers. I've no idea why I long for that but I do, I think of it often and when I wrote it down for Jenny she seemed thrilled. I think she was pleased to have a plan.

I've seen something like that, she said, they've got a top like that in a shop in Lewisham.

I point to my old tracksuit bottoms and flap my hand to show her they wouldn't match.

Nonsense, she says, those tracky bottoms could do with lightening up, or lifting, or whatever it is they call it these days.

She knows I hate them. I'd give anything to wear a skirt again but when you need hoisting to go to the loo and all that undignified stuff, it's better to take the easy option.

Jackie is lucky. She's my age, but naturally slim and with a good clothes sense. Plain understated stuff, that's what she wears, all natural colours like stone and turquoise. It's a pleasure just to watch her walk in.

Why are you in here, I wrote down for her on my pad the other night. I know it sounded rude but I couldn't help it, it just burst out of me. I mean, I know she's my age, but she would surely be able to manage on her own, outside. She doesn't need any help with eating or washing or any of the other stuff they have to do for me. She's like a spring chicken. I wrote that on my pad, I wrote, spring chicken and then I pointed at her with my good hand so she'd know what I meant.

That got a laugh out of her. Spring chicken, she said,

did you ever hear anything so silly. Look at this, she said and she squeezed her eyes shut so that I could see the wrinkles on her forehead. I just laughed. Wrinkles are nothing, I wanted to say but it tires me, writing on the pad, so I save it for the important things.

I need to be in here just as much as you do, May, she said, I get too sad on my own, that's the thing, I can't be trusted.

Oh, I thought. Sad means mad, in here, in this looking-glass world where the old people are. It had never occurred to me that she was a mad one. I always thought you could spot the mad ones a mile off but it seems I have been wrong on that, as on nearly everything else.

Don't worry, she said as if she had read my head, don't worry I'm not stark staring bonkers, it's just sometimes I can't stop crying.

Seems sensible to me, I wanted to say but I wrote it instead. I wrote 'sensible' and she nodded, thank you.

She's coming out shopping with us. Me, my friend and my daughter, what could be better. I've got the kind of excitement that you get at Christmas when you're five and I suddenly want to go back, take more pleasure in small things, take more pleasure in Jenny. Some of the teachers I used to work with would have been glad of a shopping trip, I know they would. We could have done that.

Jenny arrives in a burst of frosty air. She's got a gleam about her that might mean recent sex, and I shudder at the thought of that Dan with his hands so limp on her lovely matronly body.

Mum, she says, are you ready for an adventure. I used to say that to her when we were going out, and I want to cry now that she has remembered it for me, but crying is not in the spirit of this day so I laugh instead. I say laugh, but I am as aware as anyone else in the room that it's a cackle at best, a witch's cauldron noise. I can't remember what my real laugh was like but it wasn't this, I'm sure of that. I make a mental note not to laugh when we're out. I don't want to embarrass anyone.

Jackie comes in and I have a moment of pure envy that takes me back to my teens. She's got a coat on, I haven't seen it before but it's purple and gathered from just below the bust, more like a dress than a coat. That's a lovely coat, says Jenny, and Jackie does a little twirl of acknowledgment. I'll buy you one like that, Jenny, I want to say, there's room for a bit of purple in your life. Jenny favours navy, sensible padded coats that will last.

They get on well, Jackie and Jenny, I can hear them chatting about this and that as they push me into the cab. I think at other times I might have been jealous, but I'm busy calculating how long it's been since I saw the outside world. I can't work it out at all.

Bye-bye, says Kelly, her hair on top of her head this morning like a fat doughnut, don't do anything I wouldn't do.

For a moment I wish so hard that I could speak that I have to close my eyes and let things pass. Well one thing I wouldn't do is puff my hair like a sausage pie and pile it on my head, I would have said. I think Jenny and Jackie would have laughed.

So unfortunate Dan's career ended rather abruptly, I hear Jenny say to Jackie in the cab. Abruptly my arse, I'd say if I could, he had his hands where he shouldn't and that equals the sack in any job. Jenny looks at me as if she's frightened I will say something but I'm too busy looking at the trees. There are trees everywhere, still wintery looking but I bet if I could get up close I'd see little buds and signs of spring.

Jackie is quiet, nodding and making the odd comment as Jenny chats, and I think, how nice this is to stay quiet and listen to a good friend talking to my child. How lovely to have that trust. I wonder what child rearing would have been like in the early days, if I had sat around the table drinking tea or wine with friends while Jenny played with the other children. Helen flashes into my mind, Helen and her baby son Sebastian. He was a cherub of a baby, a fat little prince with an early smile. I don't usually think of them, it's too painful. Maybe Jenny and Seb will get married, we used to say, maybe we'll be grandparents together. I wish we were grandparents, Helen and I, together or separately, it wouldn't matter. A stake in the future, that's what it is to have a grandchild. A reason to care.

So we're going to try again, Jenny says, see if we can really make a go of it. She's talking to Jackie, but it's me she wants to tell, I'm sure of it. I push Helen and Sebastian away and make a thumbs up sign, solidarity.

We even thought we might try for a baby, she says, blushing like a teenager, how would you like that, Mum? A baby, I want to say, and I want to say it so much that I have a go, and nothing comes out but a gurgle. You're forty, I think, is that safe? Is it advisable? I realise I was right about the glow I saw on her earlier. They're trying already, I'm sure of it and I'm all in a dither. Part of me wants to whoop with joy, jump out of my wheelchair and dance about, and the other half wants, just for a moment, to tear Jenny's hair out and slap some sense into her. Why now, that part of me would say, why now when I can't hold her or feed her or take her out for walks or read her a story? What kind of cruel punishment is this to dream up? Like nailing a thirsty man to a tree and drinking water in front of him, wasn't that an old form of torture?

Oh Jenny, says Jackie, and she gives me a sharpish look as if to say, don't spoil it for her, oh Jenny, that's lovely news, that's happy news, I know you're not counting any chickens yet but it's still news to make a person smile. I marvel at how she knows the right thing to say on any occasion. Reminds me of Helen.

As she wheels me out of the cab Jackie whispers in my ear, I know, I know, she says, but try to be pleased for her, it means a lot. She gives my shoulder a squeeze. I'm so happy I could burst, honest I am. I smile my lopsided smile and I decide that I won't say anything about Dan, no warnings or anything. At least for today. Today is a good day. I wonder if this is what it's like to have two people bringing up a child, if it's always a kindly conspiracy that warms the heart. How nice that must be, to have two of you thinking round any problems, two of you working out what to do. That time when Jenny was bullied in Year 6 and I was at my wits' end. If I had known someone like Jackie then, I think, I could have talked it through, made a reasoned decision. It would have been so nice to know that I wasn't the only one who had her best interests at heart.

Where to first Mum, Jenny says, it's your trip. Jackie and I are your servants.

She winks at Jackie and they both laugh. I don't know what to say. I haven't been shopping in so long, and I don't know when I last went into the centre of Lewisham. There isn't much point when you're on your own. There are so many memories buried in unexpected places. I always thought that I hadn't put down a single root, but it's not true. London belongs to everyone, that's the thing, it's a communal project, but there are still personal pockets of memory scattered about that can trip a person up. I can't help claiming some. That street corner over there, opposite the station, that's where Jenny and I waited for a cab when we had been Christmas shopping. My heart was breaking, I wish I had managed to be happier. That run-down department store there, I used to avoid that because it reminded me of Binns, my meeting point with Helen, the nearest to grand that Hull had. I point to it and make a drinking sign with my good hand.

They both laugh.

Coffee already, says Jenny, sounds like a good idea to me. You know there isn't a coffee shop in the department store any more don't you?

I raise my hand to show that of course I know, but in truth I had forgotten, and I was expecting it still to be there on the fourth floor with the tablecloths and everything, like it was in Hull when Helen and I used to go. I think it was waitress service but I'm not sure, sometimes I remember things from books or films and think that they are my own memories.

Let's go to Costa, says Jackie, it's good for wheelchairs. I know this sounds odd but I had to look round, see who was in a wheelchair. I forgot it was me.

I don't like those kinds of places, big chains. I don't like my coffee in a paper bucket but I don't say anything. This is a nice day, I'm thinking, a day out, a day away from that place. The only thing is, the more the day wears on, the more fun we have going to shops and trying on clothes and eating little pastries they would never serve in the gravy boat, the more I don't want to go back. I don't think they notice. Isn't there some way I could live with Jenny, I'm thinking, I wouldn't be any trouble but I would, I know I would. I'd be the most trouble ever.

Cheer up Mum, Jenny says, aren't you having a nice time?

Yes I am, I am I want to say but I nod vigorously instead.

Only I hate to see you looking sad, she says, and she bends down and gives me a kiss, like I used to do to her when she was in her pushchair. She should have had a sibling to share the load of me, but I can't think about that. This is a happy day.

Did you never have kids, Jackie? Jenny asks her and it's as if she can read my mind. I've always wondered that. I would have asked before now if I could but it seems a stark thing to write down just in case there's a sad story. Most things are sad stories by the time you get to our age.

No, says Jackie, no I tried, and I even had IVF in the early days, but it didn't work. I did have a little dog, she says, and she looks as if she might get all tearful. Come on Jenny, I think, change the subject, don't make her sad.

Hey, says Jenny, see that sign? There's a pop up art gallery. Shall we go? Jackie and I smile a grown-up smile at each other, a smile that says, ah, look at the young ones trying so hard, see how kind they are to us old ladies. I'll share Jenny with you if you want, I think, you can co-parent a forty-year-old with me. The idea makes me laugh so much. I can't help myself.

What's funny about a pop up art gallery, Jenny says but that makes me laugh all the more and then Jackie joins in and Jenny starts to look quite grumpy.

Aw, sorry darling, says Jackie, you mustn't take any notice of us old ladies, we're a bit highly strung. She puts her arm round Jenny and I can see Jenny is melting and it's all going to be alright. I manage to get my notepad out of the pocket of my jacket and write 'lovely day' on it and show it to Jenny and she sings this song about didn't we have a lovely day and Jackie seems to know it too so she joins in. People are looking at us but we don't care.

We don't make it to the gallery, but we go to all the shops and I've got a flowery top to take back to the gravy boat. It's too pretty to wear in there, I'd rather wear it in the real world but that might have to wait. I'm feeling a flash of hope, thinking that maybe I won't have to stay there for ever. Maybe we could get a house together, me and Jackie and Jenny, maybe that could work. If it was anything like today, we would have some laughs at least.

I'm glad though, when Jenny says it's time to go back. I'm feeling tired, and I can see that Jackie is too. Plus I need to get sorted out in the toilet department, and that's not something that can happen in a public lavatory. We pile into a cab again only this time we're comfortable with silence. No polite conversation. We're like a proper group of friends on the way home after an outing.

I'm thinking it will be sad later when Jenny goes, but I'll still have Jackie. Maybe she will read to me again, some more poetry or a short story. I don't like to ask her while Jenny is still here in case it looks as though I'm planning to be rid of her.

That was fun, Mum, Jenny says, we should have done more stuff like this.

Jackie looks out of the window as if she's fascinated by Lewisham Way.

We can, I write on the little notepad, soon.

Oh Mum, Jenny says, you're a love.

For once I'm pleased I can't speak. I have no idea what to say. A love. What a thing to be called. What a happy thing to happen, what an unusual thing to say to a grumpy old woman in a wheelchair. I flap my good hand at Jenny, as if to say, go on with your nonsense but she just laughs. My lovely mum, she says and I break into a sweat, I've had enough of this stuff now. Also there's Jackie. I would hate for her to feel that she's being left out, like we're forming some kind of club without her just because we're related or something. I give Jenny a meaningful look, and then I look at Jackie, so that she realises what I'm trying to tell her. I see a quick understanding flash across her face.

So Jackie, Jenny says, what are you and my mum going to get up to later, when I'm not keeping an eye on you any more? Midnight feasts, drinking after lights out?

I know she means well but I wish she wouldn't try so hard. It sounds patronising, I don't want Jackie to be offended. I look over and Jackie smiles, I can see that she understands.

That's for us to know, she says, and she gives me the biggest grin. I don't think I have been a grinner before now but I decide there and then that I'm going to practise it. It cheers people up, makes them think of happy stuff.

Let's have a quick look at what we've bought, Jenny says, I always used to love looking at a new thing on the way home, still in its bag.

Did you, I think, did you ever tell me that? I expect

I would have brushed it away. Yes, yes, no time for that sort of nonsense. That's the sort of thing I would have said. So I go along with her, try to look excited about the purchases, to make up for all the times I didn't join in when she was growing up. Jenny has bought a long tunic to wear with trousers, about as boring an item of clothing as could be but we enthuse. Jackie has a flowing kimono style robe in bright colours, and I have my flowery top, big bold red flowers on a black background. I used to have a dress a little like it in the eighties, although I never wore it much. I'd like to wear my new top every day.

It's raining by the time we get back and the glitter has washed off the day. Jenny sees me back into my room, explaining all the time that she is going to cook something special for Dan tonight, she's got some sea bream or something. I wish she could stay longer. He is not a person who deserves a special effort, I'd like to tell her. Chargrilling, if you please. If you ask me, it's Dan who ought to be chargrilled.

So we're sorted and sitting in my room drinking tea, me and Jackie.

Your Jenny is great, she says, so funny and full of life.

Really, I think, gosh that's not what I would have said at all. For once I'm glad my words have gone.

It must have been fun, bringing her up, Jackie says, what happened to her dad?

I put my hand to my head, as if I've got a sudden pain. It's the best I can do, but actually my head does hurt as soon as I do it, no lie. Of course she didn't expect me to reply anyway, she was just making conversation. I shouldn't take things so seriously.

It's OK, she says, I was going anyway, I'll see you later, you rest.

No, I want to shout, don't leave me, what about the sisterhood, what about the fun we've had, what about the midnight feast, please don't go. I nod and raise my hand in a small wave.

I'm going out with Bill, she says, in an hour or two, I need to have a quick nap before I get ready. I can't burn the candle at both ends like I used to.

I'm shocked. I feel as though I have been punched in the gut, and hard.

Have a nice time, I write on my pad.

CHAPTER FOURTEEN

March 1978
Pimlico

'Why don't you wear those earrings?' Alain asked. 'I thought you liked them. Special present for a special person. They're exactly my merry May, I thought when I saw them, understated and pretty, like my woman.'

Like Sue, do you mean? May thought. Is she a feminist too? I don't think so. May had wanted to ask about Sue so many times but she was terrified of what might happen. He had been attentive recently, more like his old self, and May hated to think it might be because he was seeing someone else. She knew what Helen would say. What anyone would say, to be honest, anyone with a brain could see that things were dodgy. He went out for a walk every night, that wasn't normal for a start. And a couple of times he'd stayed out all night, even with a class to teach in the morning.

'I'm fascinated by these city streets,' he'd said but that

had to be the stupidest lie May had ever heard. Or maybe I'm just a jealous bitch, May thought, maybe he does love walking the city streets, maybe it wasn't his writing on the little slip of paper. Surely his letters were more stylish, less flourish? The 'g' on 'darling' as well, the tail was far too long. Maybe someone else had bought them then returned them because they'd fallen out with Sue, there could be a hundred different explanations.

May decided to worry about it later. There was so much else to think about. He loved her, wasn't that the main thing? And he had told her when they met how much he hated clingy women. He was in such a good mood right now, he hadn't got into a rage for days. School had finished for Easter and Alain really seemed to be enjoying his time at home. He had even stayed home the last few nights, instead of wandering. You're history, Sue, if you ever existed, May thought. Things were definitely getting better, and the best thing was to ignore the pointless doubts that sprang up from time to time. She only had to look out of the window to see that in the dismal wet streets of London there was a hint of warmer weather to come. At home, Jenny had become a small smiley person who tried hard to sit independently, and May could make her laugh just by pretending to sneeze.

Alain had been more settled, that was the best thing. May had almost begun to believe that the slip of paper in the earring box was legitimate, the maker's dedication to his wife, perhaps, or something that had found its way in there during the manufacturing process. Not Alain's writing at all. That was what she told herself at nights, when she lay awake next to Alain thinking of all the Sues she had ever known or heard of. There couldn't be anyone else, could there?

May felt tense, as if she was ready at all times to fight for her life or run for it. She thought this might be an inbuilt characteristic she owned, like red hair or reckless-ness. An overdeveloped flight or fight mechanism. There was probably an evolutionary reason for it, a period in history when it would have come in handy, only right now it wasn't helping her at all and she knew that she needed to calm down.

'I think I'll wear them this weekend,' May said. 'I've been saving them for a special occasion. And I can't quite fit into my jeans so I've got to wear something else nice.'

'Of course,' said Alain, 'the visit of the famous Helen. I will be banished to the cold streets to atone for my sins. I confess, I confess, I've got a penis. Do you think she will like it if that's the first thing I say to her?'

May was horrified at the thought, but knew it was best to try to pretend she found his comments funny and light-hearted. Any sign of weakness and he would be ready to pounce. She wanted Helen's visit to be as good as possible, especially since she had had such a hard time recently.

'She'd find it funny, I expect, she's a funny sort of person. But she may have lost her sense of humour temporarily, Seb's birth sounds like it was pretty traumatic,' May said.

'Honestly, don't look so worried,' said Alain. 'I'm not going to say anything I shouldn't. It'll be nice to meet your friend, lovely to have a chat with someone else who's got a little one like we have. I'll be good, I promise.'

May forced herself to laugh. She wondered whether she should go to the doctor, get some of the antidepressants she had read about in magazines, or maybe some tranquillisers. She didn't want to feel like a humourless bitch, she really didn't, it was just that she couldn't stop thinking about Sue, and more or less nothing made her laugh any more, even if she could see the humour behind it, analyse it in a technical way.

Helen arrived on Good Friday afternoon. May left Jenny with Alain and went alone to the station to meet her. She felt sick with anxiety. I wish I'd never suggested that Helen could come to stay with us, she thought, what have I got to offer someone who is feeling so down? What if Alain starts acting up, or worse, what if he is violent in front of her? Oh God, what have I done? The screechy, repetitive lyrics of 'Wuthering Heights' were playing on repeat in May's head, over and over until she thought she would scream. It's a mistake, she thought, it's all a terrible mistake.

By the time Helen appeared, looking fresh and unruffled in jeans and a denim jacket and wearing her new baby in a sling, May was ready to run away.

'Helen,' she said and she grabbed her hand. 'Helen, I'm so pleased to see you, you have no idea. Hello, Seb.' May kissed the baby's little head, nestling under Helen's chin. 'Hello, both of you.'

'Wow,' said Helen, holding May's hands and leaning back to look at her properly. 'Wow, that's a greeting worth leaving Hull for. No, I tell a lie. Anything is worth leaving Hull for. I'd leave Hull for twenty-five new pence and it would still be a bargain. Look at you, the trendy London mum.'

May blushed. She didn't look trendy, she knew she was no good at that, but she had made an effort. Washed her hair, plaited it, and put on a granny dress she had bought from a jumble sale.

'I apologise in advance,' she said, 'for Alain and his smoking. I hope he behaves himself.'

Why did I say that, she thought, why was that the first thing out of my mouth?

'And of course, welcome to London. It's so good to see you here.'

'You've got to remember that young Seb here, he's never been out of Hull before. He's not used to the noise and the bright lights. You'll have to excuse him. Maybe Jenny can have a word with him.'

May wanted to cry. She had forgotten what good-natured humour felt like, humour with no additional edge intended to upset or humiliate. 'I truly am so pleased to see you,' she said. 'You have no idea. I wish I could have been there for you, when this bad baby boy was giving you so much trouble.'

'Ha,' said Helen, 'trouble, you have no idea. He's going to have to be nice to me for the rest of his life if he wants any pocket money, if he wants to go on school trips, if he wants to eat anything other than gruel. And speaking of a life soaked in misery, I really cannot believe you are going to do it again. Seb is definitely an only child for ever, let me tell you; if he wants a brother or a sister we will definitely get a dog.'

'Was it really that bad?' May asked.

'It was terrible,' Helen said, standing still in the middle of the busy station concourse and looking directly into May's eyes. 'It was torture, just like real torture, and I was on my own. I could feel it when they gave me a caesarean, even though they told me I couldn't. And it hurt like hell. But I'm on my holidays now, and I've nearly forgiven this poor little chap because I love him to pieces, and I'm pleased to see you. That's my news. How's things down here?'

'Oh Helen,' said May, 'I'm so sorry for you, going through all that. They're worth it, though, the babies, aren't they?'

May had a terrible feeling that she was going to cry. It's not your turn, she said to herself, for God's sake let someone else be centre stage and stop being an attention-grabbing bitch. Don't talk about Sue, whoever she is. Concentrate.

'Hey,' said Helen, 'it's OK, I'm here, tell me, catch me up, what's been going on? I don't get much of a clue from your letters, you know.'

'I know,' said May. 'I'm a terrible letter writer. Sometimes I think I write how I want things to be, not how they really are.'

'Do we have to go straight home?' said Helen. 'Seb had a massive feed on the train, all the way from Goole to Grantham. He'll be quiet a bit longer, we could go for a cup of tea. Will Jenny be alright with Alain?'

May wanted to tell her that Jenny had never been left alone with her father before, that she always found an excuse to take her wherever she was going, that she had a slightly creepy feeling. Not that Alain would hurt her, he wouldn't, but that he would whisper things in her ear, and that they would drip into Jenny's consciousness somehow and harm would be done.

'Yes,' May said, 'she'll be fine. He adores her.'

May looked down at her feet.

'Hey, this is me,' Helen said. 'I know what it's like, remember? If you can't look me in the eye that's not good.'

May pinched her left wrist with her right hand.

'I'm sorry,' she said. 'I'm not used to being with someone like you. I haven't really caught up with my old friends down here yet, and it's harder to make new ones than I thought it would be. Let's get that cup of tea.'

'So Frank tried to come and see the baby, when we were still in hospital,' Helen said as they walked. 'He was shouting and screaming about fathers' rights, I could hear him from my bed.'

For a moment May felt too overwhelmed to speak. She imagined the scene, and how frightened and alone Helen must have felt.

'I wish I'd been there,' May said. 'I'm so sorry you had to go through that.'

'I'm glad you weren't,' Helen said. 'Honestly, I wouldn't wish him on anyone. He's scary, May, and the less he's in my life the better. And Seb, Seb won't be like him. I'm sure of that. I'll bring him up differently.'

'Of course you will,' May said, 'you're going to do a brilliant job.'

The two women ordered tea in a dingy little Italian cafe just outside the station. May tried to relax but the feeling of dread wouldn't shift.

'So what happened, exactly?' May asked. 'With Frank?' She wasn't sure whether Helen would want to talk about it but she had to know, she couldn't leave it.

'I'd asked the nurses not to let him in and they were as good as gold. "She's got to rest," they said at first, and then when he came back the next day they said, "she doesn't want to see you", just said it straight out. They even called the police and the police spoke to him and he went away, but I've been getting phone calls with heavy breathing and sometimes I think I can see him at the end of the road when I look out of the window. I'm so glad I'm here.'

Helen looked round the dingy cafe and smiled.

'Don't get me wrong,' Helen said, 'if he can calm down, act like a human being, I'd love him to see Seb. Kids need dads, don't they? Just not bad ones.'

'Not bad ones at all,' May said. 'You did the right thing.

You're so brave. And for the record, I'm really pleased that you're here too.'

I'm going to look after her, May thought. I won't let her be on her own with it all any more.

'Let's talk about something else before we all start crying again. What about this little one,' Helen said, pointing to May's slightly swollen stomach. 'Don't tell me it was planned. Two babies in a year? How on earth are you going to manage?'

'Thirteen months actually,' said May, 'no need to exaggerate. No, of course it wasn't planned, but some people say it's good to get it over with quickly, then you can bring them up together. I'll manage, it'll be OK. How much harder can two children be than one?'

May looked at Helen as she said the last part and neither of them could keep a straight face. They laughed so hard that the old lady behind the counter came over to check everything was OK.

'We're fine, thanks,' said Helen, 'only my friend here thinks that two babies may be as easy as one. What do you think?'

'*Mamma mia*,' said the woman, 'you see this white hair?' She pointed at her head. 'This white hair, I get from babies, not from cafe and coffee and tea and sandwich. *Mamma mia*.'

She ran a hand gently over May's dark hair, and went back to the counter, tutting.

'Great,' said May quietly, 'thanks for the vote of confidence, oh ancient one.'

'That's the thing with us girls,' said Helen, 'we tell it like it is. Are you going to take me home to meet this super stud of yours? What's wrong with condoms anyway? Never mind the stuff they say about breastfeeding, you can't believe everything you hear, you know.'

'Alain doesn't like them,' May said.

She knew how pathetic that sounded but this was Helen, her friend, and she had waited so long to have someone to talk to, someone who would allow her to tell the truth, put things straight in her own head.

Helen put her hand over May's.

'It's OK, May, I'm on your side,' she said. 'I'm not having a go at you, or being difficult. I just want to help. It's like seeing someone caught in a sticky spider's web, you can't get them out unless you're prepared to get your own hands dirty. And the person in the web has to realise they're caught.'

May laughed, even though she was feeling bad.

'That might be the worst metaphor I've ever heard,' May said, 'but I take the point.'

'Listen, mate, the way my brain feels now, that was a bloody stroke of genius,' Helen said. 'But seriously, do I need to know anything before I meet Alain? Subjects to avoid, ways to butter him up, that kind of thing?'

May stood still and tried to think. Everything seemed fraught. If she suggested that Helen ignored any particular subjects, say, women's lib, babies, earrings, women called Sue, school, anything that could cause an argument, then

Alain was perfectly capable of making an argument out of something else, if he was in the mood. On the other hand, there had to be some no-go areas or it would be terrifying.

'I can't think,' May said. 'Honestly I'm not sure.'

'I get it, friend,' Helen said. 'Keep away from anything controversial and we'll have our own chats later.'

'Thank you, thank you,' said May, a great wash of relief breaking over her head and dripping down her body. 'I've been longing to talk to you. I knew you'd understand.'

Seb was protesting loudly by the time they reached the little flat, and Helen sat in a chair to feed him.

'Hi, Alain, hi, Jenny,' she said. 'Sorry about this but if I don't do it straight away he'll get agitated and then we'll never get any peace.'

Alain sat in the chair opposite Helen. Jenny was on his lap and May thought he looked like the perfect dad.

'Can I get you anything? Cup of tea? You need to keep your fluid levels up when you're breastfeeding, we've found that, haven't we, love?'

May was taken aback for a moment by his niceness, his conspiratorial tone. Of course, it was for Helen's benefit, but she loved it anyway and wished it could happen more often. Also, the breastfeeding comment was a surprise. They had never, as far as she could remember, had a conversation about keeping fluid levels up. It just hadn't happened, she was sure it hadn't. And another thing, was she being really mad and unreasonable, or was he positively gawping at Helen's breast?

'I'll make some tea,' she said.

They had agreed to relax the no-caffeine rule for the weekend in honour of Helen's visit.

'Did my wife tell you I can't take caffeine in any form?' Alain said. 'I've got many allergies. What we don't realise, in this world, is that everything is connected to everything else. Do you know what I mean?'

Alain leaned over so that he was uncomfortably close to Helen, who shrank back in her seat.

'Good strong suck,' he said, 'he'll be supping pints in no time.'

'I hope not,' said Helen.

May was mortified. Alain was behaving oddly, and it looked set to get worse. She had worried that Alain would be brusque, or removed, but this leering slobbering stranger was not something she had planned for. She stood in the kitchen making tea with shaking hands and tried to run through her options. Could she confront him about his behaviour in front of Helen? She would be safe enough while Helen was here, but terrified about what would happen when she left. And there was Helen herself, her special friend who was managing on her own to look after a baby after a difficult birth. Was it fair to get her involved?

'Is there a problem with that tea?' Alain shouted. 'Only Helen here, she's wondering why you're taking so long. I don't think she likes being left alone with me.'

'Alain,' said May, no longer able to pretend it wasn't happening, 'come on, this is our first visitor, be nice.'

She put the teas on the table and reached to take Jenny.

'Let me give you a break,' she said. 'You've had this one for ages, she must be driving you mad.'

'Nice,' said Alain. 'Nice? I *was* being nice, wasn't I, Helen? I was joking, that's what you don't get. I mean,' he turned to Helen, 'if I said to you, my wife doesn't understand me, you'd know it was a joke, right? But May here, bless her, she was born without the humour gland or whatever it is that makes us know when a thing is funny. She just ain't got one, have you, merry May?'

He stood up and kissed May's cheek.

'Bye, girls – sorry – women, naughty me for getting it wrong. See you later.'

Alain pulled on a coat and left, blowing a kiss over his shoulder. May stood holding Jenny, trying hard not to cry. She was burning with embarrassment and shame and had no idea what to do.

'That's Seb finished for at least half an hour,' said Helen, tucking her clothes back round her and sitting him up. 'Now we have to work out what we're going to do about you.'

May found it difficult to believe the matter-of-fact way that Helen spoke. No recriminations, no anger, nothing but concern.

'I'm so sorry,' May said. 'I didn't think, I don't know why, I just thought it wouldn't be like that.'

'That's what's worrying me,' said Helen. 'Did you even notice how much he put you down? Or how much he was staring at my breasts when I was feeding Seb? Or, more to the point, did you realise just how drunk he was?'

'Drunk?' said May. 'I don't think he was actually drunk, that's just how he is.'

'OK, maybe not just drunk. But you know that peppermint smell on his breath?'

'He loves polo mints,' said May, feeling stupid even as she said it.

'I'm sure he does, and so do most people with a drink problem. That's not the only thing though. How long has he had those marks on his arms?' Helen asked.

May felt rooted to the spot.

'Marks?' she said. 'Ah, erm, those marks, well, he said that he had a kind of skin infection on his arms when he was younger, like acne.'

'Like acne?' said Helen, and as she said it May could hear how ridiculous it sounded.

'Yes, I know, and that's not all.' May explained about the earrings, and Sue.

Helen looked at her. 'Another woman is one thing, May, and it's terrible, I know it is, but let's establish some priorities. His sleeves rolled up a little, when he was playing with Jenny. May, I don't know enough about it but I think they might be drug marks, maybe where he's injected something, I'm not sure.'

May wished she could put her hands over her ears like a child, drown out what Helen was saying. It wasn't anything she hadn't thought herself, that was the thing, but she had decided that she must be wrong, chosen to ignore it. If she admitted it to herself then everything would have to change, and May was frightened.

'Not necessarily,' said May. 'I mean, I know you mean it, you're not being sensational or anything, it's just that, well, you've seen the size of this flat. I would have seen something, spotted something. Drink and drugs, he would have to hide them somewhere, wouldn't he? I'd notice, wouldn't I?' May went to the window, lifted the curtain and looked out. 'Sorry,' she said. 'Sorry, I can hear how pathetic I sound. I don't want to be like this, I'm not sure, I think it's hormones or something, I just don't know what to do.'

'Come with me,' Helen said. 'Come back to Hull with me, we'll manage. We can share childcare, help each other out, cook together, honestly it'll be fun. And it will be safe. Believe me, I'm not trying to rock any boats, but this rickety old canoe? It's rocking so hard already all I want to do is offer you a lifebelt.'

'I'm not sure,' said May, 'I want to, I'm so fed up with living like this, honestly I can't begin to tell you. I'm scared all the time, scared and lonely. I'm sure he's seeing someone else. I lie awake at nights wondering how to manage. I cry at sad adverts on TV, but I can't tell anyone or do anything because I really do think it might be my fault. I mean he's told me, Helen, straight out, he's told me that he never used to be like this, that it's me who makes him behave like he does.'

It was such a relief to have finally told someone that May started to cry, and Jenny joined in.

Helen wrapped Seb in a shawl. He was sleeping now, and she laid him gently in the armchair before taking Jenny from May and cradling her with a rocking motion that calmed her.

'It's not your fault, May. I'm sorry, I don't want to say this in the wrong way, but you're a victim, not a criminal. He is as responsible for his behaviour as you or I. And I don't think people change, May, I don't think they do. Everything I've read makes me think that Alain will still be dishing out psychological cruelty when he's an old man, and if you're with him he'll still be thumping you. Is that what you want?'

May was crying too hard to speak. She couldn't believe that Helen's longed-for visit had disintegrated so quickly. That the paper-thin backdrop she had constructed so carefully had been torn down.

'I'm so sorry,' she said.

'Look, I'm not trying to push you,' said Helen, 'but I'll bet you haven't even told me all of it, have you? And you haven't got any relatives to go to, have you?' May shook her head.

'I don't mean you have to come with me. I mean I'd love it but I'd be really happy if you would go anywhere, anywhere that's not here. How long have we got until he comes back?'

'I don't know,' said May. 'I know this sounds weird but

he says he loves to walk through London streets in the dark, when no one is about. I don't know what he does. Who he's seeing. A couple of times he's been gone all night. Sometimes though, sometimes he comes back a bit shaken up, says he's been beaten up. Once he had a black eye that kept him off school for two days.'

'Do you realise,' Helen said, looking at May over the top of Jenny's head, 'do you realise that this is most definitely *not normal*? That this isn't how other people live? That you deserve better?'

May knew that Helen was right. She shook with nerves as she got out a small case from under the bed while Helen looked after the babies.

'We can't take everything,' Helen said. 'Just bring a couple of changes of clothes for you, and a few more for Jenny. We can sort everything else out. Bring your passport and contact lens stuff, don't worry about books, my place is like a bookshop. Or toys, Jenny can share Seb's.'

May rushed around, her heart pounding. She couldn't stop to think, or she would start worrying about something else, and she had no time for that. She knew this was her big chance, and that she owed it to Jenny to leave right now. She was scooping up underwear when the phone rang.

'Don't answer it,' said Helen. 'Leave it, let's just go.'

May wanted to do as Helen said, she really did. She could see the new life waiting for her, she could almost taste it. She knew that Helen was tired and scared, and she felt disgusted with herself for involving her friend in all this. She let the phone ring.

'You know how grateful I am, don't you?' said May. 'I can't think what would have happened if you hadn't come to stay. I'm sorry about your holiday, I really am.'

'You know, I'm not even surprised,' said Helen, 'and you certainly don't need to apologise. I had a feeling, reading between the lines in your letters. And I'm happy to help, for goodness sake, just get a move on.'

The phone rang again. May knew that she would have to answer it this time.

'I've got to, Helen,' May said. 'It might be important, I can't go without answering it.'

Helen sat down with both babies cradled in her arms.

'Hi,' May said. 'Yes I am, is he there? Can I speak to him?'

Helen rocked the babies gently and May wished for a moment that someone could comfort her like that. She listened as the person at the other end spoke.

'Thank you,' she said when they had finished. 'Give him my love and tell him I'm on my way.'

She put the receiver down without looking at Helen.

'It's Alain,' May said. 'I don't believe this.'

She sat on the arm of the chair as if her legs had suddenly buckled.

'What, May? What about Alain? Don't get fooled again, honestly, I'm sorry but you can't trust him.'

May looked at Helen.

'No,' she said, 'it wasn't actually Alain. It was the hospital, St Thomas's Hospital. He's been badly hurt, Helen, they couldn't give me details but they said I should go as soon as possible.'

'Nothing's changed,' said Helen, 'you can still leave with me.'

Both women knew that wasn't true.

CHAPTER FIFTEEN

April 2018
Lewisham

Jackie's been out with Bill a few times recently.

Out of the nursing home and into the big wide world, no kidding. I don't know what she sees in him, I swear I don't. He's a greasy snaggle-toothed oik, that's what I want to tell her but I don't. He came in here yesterday, bold as brass.

Have you seen my screwdriver, he said, I want to mend that kettle.

What kettle, I wanted to say but I think even if I could have got my words out I wouldn't have said anything. He makes me feel scared, so terrified my bowels turn to water. It's his face. It's his face and the way he walks and everything else about him, if I'm honest.

I know you, don't I, he says and comes right up to me and peers into my face, so close I could have kissed him. I'd rather bite him on the nose but I'm stuck here so I had to sit it out. I could even smell his breath, it was horrible. Sewer breath, I wonder that someone as refined and lovely as Jackie can give him so much as a second glance.

He went out then, muttering about kettles and screwdrivers, and I realised I was shaking. I couldn't eat my cheese salad when they brought it in.

Are you alright, May, Agnita said, you normally like your salad. I looked at her but it wasn't a question I could answer with a nod or a shake of the head. Do you want your pad, she said, but I shook my head then. I've got a growing unease about the man across the corridor, I would like to have written, I think I know him and he scares me. Why would he come in here looking for a damn screwdriver, what kettle is he talking about. Just the thought of so many words makes me want to go to bed for a nap so I point to my tummy instead to indicate that I'm full. It's the only answer I can manage.

We'll have to keep an eye on that, says Agnita as if I'm a skinny frail child who's in danger of fading away.

I spent a couple of hours trying to draw little screwdrivers over a whole page of my jotter. There are a lot of straight lines in a screwdriver, you wouldn't believe how difficult they are. On a bad day I can hardly make a mark, but this was a good day and I think they ended up looking pretty good. They were even cute, some of them. I was thinking I could add two tiny legs at the bottom and a face where the handle bulges out and maybe write some adventures for them. It would be therapy, the sort of thing the occupational therapist would love, even if the results weren't clear to anyone but me. It was one of the things I loved best when I was a teacher, making up stories for the children. Stories like Alain used to tell. You should put them in a book and sell them, people used to say but it's not as easy as that. You need to show them to someone outside school, for starters. I was thinking about that when Jackie came in smelling of lavender and freshly ironed cotton.

What are you drawing, she says, ooh look they're really good, I can't believe you can do that with one hand. Are they screwdrivers? Why screwdrivers?

Your beau, I write, quick as a flash. Jackie looks a bit embarrassed. I would too if it was me, to tell the truth. It's always more dignified not to have a partner than to have a crazy one, a stupid one or a bad one. That's a thing a lot of women don't learn until they're old, and sometimes not even then.

Oh, she says, oh Bill, he's not very well at the moment. I can't help myself, I point to the side of my head like we used to when we were kids, to indicate that someone had a screw loose. The thought of loose screws and him looking for a screwdriver makes me laugh and I can see Jackie is a bit shocked.

He scared me, I write, and it's the longest thing I've written in ages. The screwdrivers were easier. My hand feels like it's going to drop off.

Oh poor May, says Jackie, you mustn't be scared. He

sometimes thinks he's at home, and that he has jobs he has to do. Was he looking for a screwdriver?

I nod.

Oh, poor you, poor him, he's asleep now, but when he wakes up I'll tell him off. He has this bladder infection and it's making him a bit bonkers, he doesn't know where he is half the time.

I have to think then, should I try to explain that I think he's familiar, and that I feel as though he could be dangerous, or should I go along with her? It's so long since I've had a friend I don't know what to do. I don't think for long. I'd be lonely here without Jackie. Poor Bill, I write and then I let the pad slide to the floor, as if my hand is so disgusted with what I've written that it can't hold on any more. Jackie doesn't notice.

I knew you would understand, she says, thank you so much for being lovely and understanding. The staff don't really approve of friendships between the sexes and neither of us has anyone to tell, outside of these four walls, so it makes all the difference to have a friend on our side.

Steady on, I want to say, hang on a minute, I didn't sign up as number one cheerleader and founding member of the fan club. Jackie hugs me though, and she smells so fresh, I can't help wanting her to be happy.

So this morning when she came again I tried to look interested when she started talking about Bill, but not too interested. The single worst thing about being in my situation is, you can't change the conversation. Makes me realise how many times in my life I've turned the talk back to me, me, me, made people pay attention to whatever it was I wanted to say. It's a skill but I've lost it.

Let me tell you about how I met Bill, she says, as if she's doing me a great favour. She looks all excited as she says it, as if it's the best secret in the world. I'm split in two. Part of me wants to enjoy the girlie chat and give Jackie the gratification she wants, after all she's been good to me and she deserves that. Then there's my mean part, my evil sarcastic twin. She just wants to say, let me guess, did he come into your room looking for a screwdriver, by any chance? Just thinking it makes me chuckle so I'm relieved I can't speak. Jackie sees the smile and claps her hands.

I knew you'd want to hear, she says, it's so good to tell people things sometimes, isn't it. Her face clouds over.

Oh, she says, I didn't mean, it must be awful for you, I'm so sorry, dumb head, that's me.

I'm trying to shrug to show her that I don't mind and I find I really don't mind, in some ways I'm communicating more with her without words than I have done in years of talking to myself. She's not looking at me though, she's staring at the floor and saying, dumb head, dumb head and hitting herself with a closed fist on the side of her head. I don't want to press my emergency buzzer, if the staff come they'll take her away, back to her own room and she wouldn't want to be on her own, I know that. I reach out with my good hand but I can't quite get to her so I slap my hand on the tray over my chair instead.

I'm surprised, it's quite a good slap and several things go flying. My glass with the water in it, some polo mints Jenny brought in, a magazine I don't want to look at given to me by some visiting do gooder. I've caused quite a stir. Enough for Jackie to stop and look up as if she's waking up from some kind of trance.

Oh, she says, sorry, shall I help you tidy up. I nod and curse that I can't say more, but at least while she's picking stuff up and wiping things down she isn't hurting herself and it looks as if she's calmer now.

I don't know what happened there, she says when she's finished tidying and fussing.

She looks at me like she wants me to help her make sense of the whole thing so I shrug my shoulders and blow her a kiss. It has to be enough.

It isn't a very exciting story, she says, me and Bill. Well, exciting for me but I don't tell it well. I've never been good at explaining things. It was just, I used to talk to him when he was so ill, you might not remember but he was really poorly, just after you first came here. I used to chat to him and no one thought he would get better but then he did, against the odds and he said it was me that gave him something to live for. Isn't that sweet?

I nod, of course I nod and I smile as well, but in my real self I'm doing that thing the kids do, where they stick their fingers down their throats and pretend to vomit. Come on, I think, wake up and smell the sewer breath, that man is a bad man. He makes me think of death and dying and evil clowns in gutters and the smell of the water in a vase when you've forgotten to empty the flowers and gone away for a month or two. He stirs me, that's the best way to put it, he stirs me up and down and round until I'm not sure who I am.

But Jackie looks happy. She could be about fourteen, I'm not joking, there's a freshness about her that takes me back to when Jenny was a teenager. It wasn't boys with her, that came later but she would get that look on her face when she was explaining something that she cared about, a science project or an interesting fact about whales. Jackie's got that look right now.

Oh May, she says, and she clasps her hands together in excitement. She's wearing an old-fashioned dress today, with lots of tiny covered buttons going from the waist to the neck. Honestly, if Charlotte Brontë saw her she would put her straight in a book.

Oh May, I know it's going to be fine, when he gets over this silly bug. The other night, we went to a restaurant in the city centre and he gave me a rose, there was a woman selling them. A red rose, have you ever heard anything so romantic.

I'd like to laugh, and shake her, both at the same time. Not the old red rose trick, I'd say if I could, surely you didn't get caught out by that, not at our age.

You probably think I'm silly, she says as if she can read me, but he caught my heart with that, he really did. I haven't known many nice men, May, I've had a different sort of past to a lot of people. I bet you had a lovely husband, and it must have been fun bringing up Jenny, she's such a sweet young woman. I bet you went for days out to the seaside and had pizza on Fridays and everything.

Oh, I miss my voice. I grab my jotter and line it up so that I can write without it sliding. Which bit do I write? Do I tell her that Jenny and I had all that eventually, the seaside and the pizza but we had it just with the two of us, so I was never sure if it counted? Or do I let that one go and tell her the important stuff?

Red rose not enough, I write. I wish I could tell her more, tell her about Frank and his arms full of roses. Roses he left lying around to scare Helen. May, I remember her saying, you either have roses in your flat or you don't, and I know I didn't have any there. He must have got in, somehow. Oh yes, I know all about men who enjoy grand gestures. Earrings, I think, next thing you know he'll be giving you earrings. I try to say, Sue, but it gets stuck. I haven't thought of her for years and I don't want to now.

Oh, Jackie says now, and she looks as if she might cry, oh I can see you're not convinced, do you think he might not love me, I hadn't thought of that. She looks downcast, sad as a teenager with a broken heart. I'm torn. Do I make her feel better or go with the gritty realism? One thing's for sure, I'm glad Helen helped me to understand about Alain. I wish someone had warned me off completely, right at the beginning. That would have been a helpful thing to do. True I wouldn't have Jenny, but maybe I'd have a different Jenny and I wouldn't know what I'd lost.

There's a knock at the door and it's Mr Sparkly Hat. He's not wearing the hat, of course, but somehow the ghost of it is always there. Happy Monday ladies, he says and it's as if someone turned the light on in Jackie's eyes.

Why thank you sir, she says, and were you wanting anything in particular, because this young lady and I were just having a girlie chat.

Something a gentleman never does is intrude, says Mr S.H. I learned that at my mother's knee. I was merely dropping in to say hello to one lady, but it seems I have two on my hands and that's too much even for Trevor. I'll be off.

He bows towards me and bows towards Jackie. I'm sorry to see him go and before I've thought it through I say one of my garbled words. Sentences really but it all comes out as one wedge of nonsense. I haven't done it much lately, I've given up. I realised that no one knows what the hell I'm talking about but he's different, Trevor, Mr Sparkly Hat, he sometimes gets it.

I'll go and get a chair, he says, and disappears off down the corridor to get a chair from the day room.

What was that about, says Jackie, what did you say, and did he really understand it. She looks rattled, and I feel sorry for her. I didn't mean her to feel left out or hurt. I don't know why I invited him in to be honest, maybe because he looked so lonely standing there. I know what it's like to be the one standing on the edge. It must have taken a lot to bring him to my door. It hasn't happened before.

I shrug at Jackie and reach for her hand, and she doesn't stay cross for long. More of an audience for the Jackie and Bill story I think, only not in a nasty way. It's just that now I can't speak to people, put myself into every conversation, I can see more of the dark and light and grey shades of what they are saying. It's given me a different view. I can see behind the scenes of conversations, that's how I think of it.

Sure enough, when Trevor comes back from the day room lugging a chair that seems to be bigger than he is, Jackie offers him a glass of water and helps him arrange the chair in the best position.

Isn't this nice, she says, if only Bill was here too. The most marvellous thing happens then, I catch Trevor's eye and he winks, just a quick wink but unmistakeable nonetheless. He thinks it's funny too, the whole geriatric romance thing, and for once I can see the humour instead of just being scared of Bill. I'd like to tell him, I'd like to explain to Trevor about Bill, and how he is familiar and sinister but I don't know why. I need to do it when Jackie's not here.

So how did you understand what May was saying, Jackie asks, I mean I'm her best friend in here, I see her all the time and I can't do it.

She looks upset, so I pat her hand to say never mind but really I'm very interested in what Trevor is going to say.

It's a long story, girls, but I had a partner, oh, a true love, let's call a spade a spade. A lovely, lovely man, my best friend and my love. Trevor shakes his head in a sad way and I wish Jackie had never asked him. It seems to be too difficult for him to get the information out.

OK, I'm going to tell this quickly, like pulling off a plaster. You ready, he says. Jackie and I nod.

There's not much to tell, my lovely Michael, he had a stroke, complication of a terrible illness, you know the name of the illness I think. I don't like to say the name out loud even now. It struck him young, this evil thing, it took all of our best young men. He was twenty-five when he had the stroke, and he died when he was twenty-nine. Never got to thirty but if you'd seen him, you wouldn't have known that. So this is the second time around for me, second time of living with oldies, even though I was young last time. If that makes any sense.

Trevor looks at us to see if we understand. Jackie is crying a little but I'm not, I owe it to Trevor and Michael to put a brave face on things. As brave as I can, anyway. It's a challenge to think of what I can do in response but I have to do something. I settle for a sad shrug and a bit of wobbly eye contact.

Yes, he says, I know that shrug, thank you, May. And can we bloody move on now please, we don't need another minute of maudlin. Do either of you lovely respectable ladies like a bet, now and again? Because I have here in my pocket just by chance, you understand, a pack of the finest Moomin playing cards, direct from Finland. And also, but let's leave chance out of this one, I've practised hard, I happen to be a kind of genius, brilliant at poker. No excuses, May, it's a game you can play with one hand.

This day is getting better and better. Maybe there will be some sad news about Bill before bedtime.

CHAPTER SIXTEEN

April 1978
Pimlico

At first May preferred the convalescent Alain to the original, despite his demands and his constant cigarettes. He was quiet but good company, someone to share the fun of Jenny with, someone to talk to. Wherever he'd been going to before, whoever he'd been seeing, it wasn't happening any more. May tried to put Sue out of her mind. Alain was hers, it must have been a mistake. He stayed home and May was as happy as she could expect to be. There was hardly a trace of the usual anger, in fact Alain seemed to be more loving and grateful than she had ever seen him.

'It's as if some of the bad stuff has been beaten out of him,' May wrote in a letter to Helen. 'As if he's come to his senses or something. Honestly, Helen, you wouldn't recognise him.'

It was only when May was alone at night, watching Jenny sleep, that she allowed herself to think of what might have been. Only then could she imagine how it might have felt to escape, to feel safe.

Helen didn't write back. She'd only written once since she went back to Hull while Alain was in hospital. She was sad about what had happened but pragmatic, and accepting of May's decision to stay.

'I get it, May, honestly I do, I understand why you feel the need to help him. He's Jenny's dad after all and I know you care about him. But this still isn't normal, that's all I can say. The way you live is horrible and you deserve better. You'd be OK on your own, May, I promise you would. You're a strong woman. Anyway, enough of all that. You know what I think. In other news, Seb cries all the time, do you think he could be getting a tooth this early? And don't forget, I've got a couch and a spare cot and you're welcome here any time. Just turn up, that's all, no need to book in advance. And if you're worrying about Frank, well, I have seen him hanging around a couple of times but I've decided he's harmless. If he was going to do anything he'd have done it by now.'

That letter had arrived a couple of weeks ago now, and May hadn't heard anything since. She'd tried to ring, but Helen's new phone was either out of order or cut off. May reread the parts of the letter about Frank again and again, looking for clues. Maybe they'd made it up, she thought, and that was why Helen was too busy to call. May wished she could speak to her, make sure that she was OK, check with her own eyes and ears. The silence felt so strange.

She wanted to talk to her friend, explain that things were better and then she wanted Helen to laugh in her face. She wanted Helen to say again that things weren't normal, that she was fooling herself. She wanted the truth. She would need help if she was going to leave, she knew that. The big thing, the thing she had started to realise was, each day that Alain got better, she became a little more scared. Just tiny steps at first, nothing too glaring, but by the end of the third week she had no time to worry about Helen, and she no longer wanted to spend time with Alain chatting about Jenny. May needed every scrap of her concentration just to get through each day. It was as if the temperature had plummeted. Alain hobbled from room to room in the tiny flat like a caged bear.

'God, your life is boring,' Alain said.

It was the first time he had got dressed properly since his accident, whatever that was. May still didn't know and she didn't dare to ask. Alain had told her that he didn't want to talk about it right from the start, and May had not been brave enough to push things. Alain's right arm and left leg were still in plaster so it had taken ages to get him dressed and May had had to cut some of his clothes to get them on him. His ribs were strapped up too, and he moved slowly and with great care. He lowered himself into the armchair as May knelt on the floor. She was setting up towers of plastic bricks for Jenny, and helping her to knock them down. She felt winded by the injustice.

'Hey,' she said, trying to keep her voice light. 'Hey, don't knock it till you've tried it, pardon the pun. Our Jenny is a great demolition girl, aren't you, Jen?'

'And where did the bricks come from?' Alain said.

May realised with a sinking heart where this was going.

'Well, Helen gave them to her, you know that. Jenny loves those bricks more than anything.' She hoped her voice wasn't wobbling.

'Helen gave them to her,' Alain mocked in a ridiculous falsetto voice. 'Helen, Helen, Helen.'

May realised that Alain was between her and Jenny and the door. She tried to think clearly and rationally.

'Would you like some of that dandelion coffee stuff?' she asked.

'I really wouldn't,' Alain said. 'It tastes like shit, you know that and I know that. Complete shit. I'd like some of the proper stuff, the stuff you drank with Helen. I think I deserve that after what I've been through.'

May built the tower again for Jenny, to give herself time to think.

'You told me to hide it away, Alain, and never to tell you where it was, don't you remember?'

'Look,' Alain said, 'just because I go along with your nonsense and your insanity sometimes, it doesn't mean I'm willing to all the time.'

He spoke in a gentle voice, as if May was a child in his class struggling to get to grips with addition.

'You've had your fun,' he said, 'made an idiot out of me for long enough, and now I'd like to get back to normal, please. I'd be very grateful if you and your big feet would go and make me a cup of coffee, while I play with my daughter. I'd do it myself, but I can't.'

Alain gestured towards his arm.

May felt frozen to the spot. She didn't want to leave Jenny with him, and she certainly didn't want to run the risk of giving him any coffee.

'I threw it away,' she said. 'I decided it would be too much of a temptation for me, having it in the house. I've been feeling so much more healthy since I've stopped drinking it. Some people think it might be bad for the baby as well, in the breastmilk, so I just don't want to risk it. Sorry.'

May bent to adjust Jenny's cardigan. She felt sick with anxiety, not sure how he would react to what she'd said. She listened out for his breathing, often a sign. When he was really upset and going into a bad phase, he tended to pant a little, breathe through his mouth.

Alain stood up, holding on to the mantelpiece to steady himself.

'I'd like a cup of coffee,' he said. 'I'd like a cup of coffee and I'd like it now. I do not believe that you threw it away, so you'd better start thinking. I've had enough to put up with over the last few weeks, and it's thanks to you that I'm in this state, so the least you can do is get me a cup of fucking coffee.'

Alain's voice rose on the last two words, and no longer sounded as though he was explaining something to a child.

May crashed through the various stages of mounting terror as he spoke until she got to the end stage, the one where she was unable to think clearly. Think of the soldiers, she tried to tell herself. She had read an article about soldiers in Vietnam being revved up by speeches just like the one Alain had just given. Their officers would rant at them about how rubbish they were and accuse them of things they didn't understand, like hating the American flag, until when they were finally given the order to kill they didn't question it.

May stood up.

'Hey,' she said, 'don't order me around. I'm happy to get your coffee, if you're sure you want it. I'm just trying to help, that's all.'

There was a silence as May went into the kitchen. Her hands were shaking so much it was hard to get the coffee down from the Christmas biscuit tin on top of the cupboard. She went through what Alain had said again and again in her head, and one thing stood out above everything. Don't mention it, she thought, think of Jenny, don't say anything, but before the thought had even been processed, May found herself calling out.

'I'm making your coffee,' she called. 'I can see it's very important to you so I'm doing it, but then Jenny and I are going out. She has an appointment at the baby clinic. But I need to ask, Al, why on earth is it my fault you're in that state? What the hell did I do?'

Stupid woman, she thought to herself as she poured

the boiling water, stupid, silly, dangerous woman. Do you not realise how alone you are? Couldn't you have kept quiet? No, the other part of her shouted, no I bloody well couldn't, it's not fair, how can I be blamed for his accident? I've been so kind to him while he's been unwell.

Alain appeared in the doorway of the tiny galley kitchen. Well done, May thought, you and your big mouth. Now you can't get to Jenny and you're stuck in two square feet with a lunatic and a boiling kettle. Nice.

'So,' said Alain, 'finally you're interested in what happened to me. What a wife. Three weeks, is it? Three weeks and a couple of days? And you've never asked?'

'I did,' said May, 'of course I did, and you told me you'd been beaten up and you didn't want to talk about it, so I haven't said anything else.'

She was stung with the unfairness of it. May would have liked to know every single thing, all the wheres, whys and hows, but she had left it because Alain had told her to.

'Ah, but why, merry May, why was I out walking the dangerous streets of London at a time when everyone else was home with their families? I'll tell you why. Because that fucking stupid woman was in my house, whispering in my wife's ear, turning even my baby against me, that's why.'

Alain stood back as if he had scored a winning goal and was just waiting for May to recognise and acknowledge it.

'But,' May said, 'but that's ridiculous. You didn't have to go out, Alain, you know you didn't.'

May knew she shouldn't speak, knew she would make

things worse, but she couldn't help herself. She kept her back to the kettle so that Alain wouldn't be able to reach it. He was wobbly on his crutches and she had to hope that would be enough for her to be able to get out. She had to say something to defend Helen, the only friend she had.

'Helen was pleased to meet you,' May said in a faltering voice.

'Was she, merry May? Was she really?' Alain produced a letter from his pocket with his good hand. May's heart sank as she recognised the familiar handwriting. It was the letter Helen had written when she went back to Hull, the only one to have arrived in recent weeks.

'Give that to me,' May said, reaching out to make a grab for it. 'That's mine.' May had hidden it in her underwear drawer, and she was angry with herself that she hadn't realised that Alain had been in there looking for clues, or evidence, or whatever he might consider it to be.

Alain wobbled a little and righted himself.

'I'm going to read it to you,' he said, 'or bits of it anyway, I'm not so interested in that fat miserable baby and his teeth. I'm going to read it because her attitude towards me, which I could see right from the start, will explain how I came to be walking in east London, the dangerous part by the river, when I could have been at home with my family.'

May tried to work out whether she would be able to get past him standing in the doorway, whether she could push him and barge through. On the one hand he was wobbly on his leg, which should make it easy, but on the other he was angry, and when he was angry he was even more unpredictable than usual. She stayed still.

'Listen to this bit,' Alain said, holding the letter aloft as if it was a scroll. '"This isn't normal, that's all I want to say, the way you live is horrible and you deserve better." Who the hell does she think she fucking is? What's so horrible about living with your loving husband? I'll tell you why she said that, she's jealous, that's all. She can't get a man, so she's jealous that you have. She's probably a lesbian.'

'Oh Alain,' said May. Keep quiet, her inner voice was screaming, don't upset him, this is dangerous. She couldn't listen to it. There wasn't time. 'Oh Alain, that's a ridiculous thing to say. How could you use "lesbian" as a term of abuse? That's not what you believe, I know it's not. And she isn't anyway, she's just worried about me. I'm trying to help you, but you must realise as well that we don't live like other people.'

May wished she hadn't said anything, had held her tongue and looked meekly at the floor. This was going to be a bad day, the sort of day they hadn't had for a while. Maybe she could save the situation, she thought, maybe she could get to Jenny, wrap her in a shawl, get her out of the door and away, it wasn't too cold outside. If they got out and stayed out it might give Alain time to calm down. As if Jenny was in league with her, May heard a small wail from the next room. Alain smiled, and May recognised the calculating look in his eyes.

'So, merry May, do you want to show me how devoted

you are to your daughter by defeating the scary one-legged monster so that you can swoop her up?' Alain said.

'Don't be silly,' May said, trying to sound confident and to put a no-nonsense approach into her speech, 'you're not one legged and you're not a monster. I'm going to pick Jenny up, she doesn't like being on the floor for too long. You're going to let me through and we'll all go on as normal.'

As soon as she had said it, May knew that she had used the wrong word.

'Normal?' shouted Alain. 'Normal? This isn't normal, she says, Helen the bitch from Hull or hell, this isn't fucking normal. What's not normal about a married couple and a baby living together, huh?'

Alain waved the letter in the air as if it was proving his point for him. He pushed May back towards the sink.

'Get off me, Alain,' May said, trying to keep her voice calm. 'Get off me and let me go and get Jenny. Then we can all get on with our day. I'm sorry that Helen's letter upset you but look, I haven't gone to live with her, have I? I'm still here with you and we're trying to work something out and it will all be alright but now please let me go to pick up Jenny.'

One good push, she was thinking, one good push and he'll fall over, he can't balance on one leg and there isn't enough room in the kitchen for him to angle his crutch for maximum stability. Come on, May, come on, just push him, punch him, whatever it takes.

'Pah,' said Alain suddenly, 'do you think I've got nothing better to do with my time than grapple with a stupid fat bitch in a kitchen? This may be your idea of a good time, honey, but it's sure not mine. I am fed up with getting caught and dragged into your head games, you twisted bitch.'

May tried to translate what Alain had just said. It was possible that he was aware she would get the better of him if things turned any more physical, and so he was backing out, but it was never worthwhile to try to second guess him.

'OK,' May said, 'let's stop.'

She tried to walk past Alain to the door to reach Jenny, but he held his crutch out to block her path.

'Just fucking no. Stay here,' he said.

May stood where she was as he made his way into the living room, where Jenny was wailing sadly to herself.

'You can't pick her up safely, let me help,' she said, but Alain slammed the door to the kitchen shut.

May heard Jenny stop crying as Alain grabbed her with his one good arm, and then start again as he hobbled into her bedroom. May heard the springs of the cot shift as Alain put her in, and then full-blown howling. Jenny still slept in their room with them, and her little bedroom wasn't even ready. There was a mattress in the cot, but nothing much else, and Jenny had never spent more than a couple of minutes in there. May opened the kitchen door in time to see Alain shut and lock Jenny's bedroom. He pocketed the key.

'Would you like to come and get the key, merry May?' he said, backing away across the room. 'Listen, she's crying, wouldn't you like to be the big hero mummy and rescue her?'

'Don't be ridiculous, Alain,' May said, making an enormous effort to keep her voice level. 'She's just a little baby, she's scared, and she's hardly spent any time in that room. There aren't any toys in the cot or anything.'

'Ridiculous?' Alain said. 'My dearest, merriest May, who's being ridiculous?'

May noticed that Alain's speech sounded slightly slurred, like the ghost of a cartoon drunk. She told herself not to be silly. His teeth at the front were crooked, that was all, and sometimes his words tripped over themselves, especially when he was upset.

'Life is hard,' Alain said, 'and the sooner my daughter learns that the better. She's got nothing to be scared of. I don't want her ending up like you, frightened of her own shadow.'

May had no idea what to do. Every path seemed fraught with difficulty. It was tempting to try physical force, but she found it very difficult. It could be conditioning, she thought, or it could be the fact that she was so very bad at anything physical. She couldn't swim or drive or ride a bike, and she certainly had no idea how to start knocking out full grown men, even if they were injured. On the other hand, she could hear Jenny's mounting terror at being shut in an unfamiliar place and she knew she had to act.

'Alain,' she said. 'Alain, listen to her. It doesn't have to be like this. Give me the key and I'll go and get her and we can talk.'

Alain stared at May as if he had no idea what she was saying. He didn't move at all. I could get the key, May thought, I could just reach in there and pick it out. It seemed so terrifying to act in any way that she stood still too. They faced each other and stared and May suddenly thought, one of us is going to die here. She might have been right too, she thought afterwards, but the doorbell rang. The sound seemed to wake Alain up from some kind of sleepwalking, some kind of trance and he limped off to open the door, throwing May the key to the little bedroom first.

It was Joan, their neighbour at the door. May could hear her cheery, normal-sounding voice. She unlocked the bedroom door with shaking hands and grabbed Jenny out of her cot. May held her tight.

'One day,' she whispered into Jenny's tiny ear as her sobs gave way to baby sniffles, 'one day I'll explain all this to you, I promise.'

Joan's voice sounded like a blast of normality from a world May didn't belong to any more, and it made her want to cry.

'Hi,' Joan said. 'I saw that you'd been in the wars and brought some scones I made, they're still warm.'

There was an awkward silence as Alain stared at her, saying nothing. May pushed through, holding a sniffing Jenny.

'Hi,' Joan said. 'Is everything OK?'

'I've got things to do,' Alain said.

He hobbled back into the living room.

'I'm sorry,' May said, 'he doesn't mean to be rude.'

'Are you OK?' Joan asked again and May realised that she must have heard something, that the scones were a front. Tell her, she thought, walk right out of the door and go with her, make sure you and Jenny are safe. She couldn't speak. He'll be OK now, she thought, the dangerous part was over. May stood as if rooted to the spot, staring at Joan.

'Really,' said Joan, 'are you alright? You don't look well. Can I help?'

Alain appeared in the doorway.

'We're fine,' Alain said. 'Thank you for the scones.'

He pushed past the two women and left the flat.

'Don't wait up for me,' he called over his shoulder.

'Can I come in?' Joan said in the kindest voice May had heard for ages.

They went into the living room and sat down. May's brain was spinning. She was grateful to Joan for saving the day, but so embarrassed that she had seen a glimpse of the life May was living. May looked at her. Joan was wearing faded jeans that fitted her perfectly and a striped skinny rib jumper. No milk stains, no rude and dangerous husband in tow. How could May explain? Where were her words when she wanted them?

Come on, May thought, tell her. Let her help you. She

wants to, you can see that, she wants to and she's right there, waiting. Just say something.

'Erm,' said May, 'things aren't going very well.'

'I'm listening,' Joan said, 'go on.'

May was deciding how best to explain things when she caught sight of something moving outside the window. Joan was facing into the room so she couldn't see, but from where May was standing she could see Alain. The flat was on the ground floor, and the front room window faced the street. He stood to the side of the window, and he was shaking his head. As May looked at him Alain shook his head slowly, and mimed zipping his mouth shut. He pointed at Joan, and put two fingers to the side of his head like a pretend gun. He then knocked on the window and waved to May and Joan, in full vision now and blowing kisses.

'It's nothing,' May said. 'Just hormones I guess. I'm pregnant, so it's all a bit, you know, but I'm fine.'

'Are you sure?' Joan said. 'Only I'm not being nosy or anything but if I can do anything, I'm just here.'

May felt furious with Alain. This woman was nice, kind, and she was a neighbour. She could have been a friend, just a normal, ordinary friend like other people had. Instead, May knew that she couldn't confide in her, couldn't be friendly. It would inflame the situation even more, possibly putting Joan at risk as well. She felt so ashamed. Alain's pantomime outside the window had been very clear. It was not a risk May felt she could take.

However well-intentioned Joan was, however much May wanted to tell her, she absolutely couldn't, that was clear.

'It's OK, honest,' May said. 'No problem.'

May could see that Joan didn't believe her. She was not surprised. This has absolutely got to stop, she thought, I cannot go on like this.

As soon as Joan left May strapped Jenny into her buggy and went off to buy a ticket to Hull.

CHAPTER SEVENTEEN

May 2018
Lewisham

I know I shouldn't like Tuesdays but I do, I can't help it. Tuesday is craft day, and the Do Good Lady comes to my room to play at helping the sick and giving hope to the hopeless.

I wouldn't talk to her the first few times. I just lay there and stared at the wall or the ceiling but she kept on chatting to me as if I was joining in. I'll say one thing for her, she's got some stamina. She talked to me about all sorts of things, politics, stuff in the news, the lot. It's put her in an odd position really, I know all about her family and her opinions and everything but she doesn't know anything about me, only what they've told her here. Obstinate old woman, they probably said, not a lot going on up top.

I feel sorry for her. I sat in my chair and watched what she was doing and one thing I liked about her, she wasn't condescending. She didn't talk to me like I was a mad old woman, even when I acted like one.

It's nice being here with you, she said last week, kind of restful. I've got some stuff to make cards if you'd like, or if you don't fancy it, I'll just sit here and knit.

Look, she said and she held up her needles with a nearly finished stripy sock on them, look I'm making some socks, I thought they'd be difficult with the heel and everything but it's quite easy, as long as you remember to count. No good getting distracted.

I indicated with my hand that I was fine with her knitting her sock and we sat like that for an hour or two. It was quite pleasant. I've always liked watching people knit. She told me about her eldest boy, and how he has a problem with the drugs they sell these days, even though he's a clever boy and could easily go to university. He's jealous of his sister, though, a sister two years younger than him who can't help being good at everything. She dances, and sings, plays the cello, and gets top grades for everything. You'd think that would be a good thing but my Do Good Lady, she says each new award her daughter wins or exam she passes just makes her think of Patrick, the brother. They're one of those annoying families who think it's cute to share the same initial so my lady is called Penny and her children are Patrick and Poppy. I have not asked what her husband is called because I don't care, although I would be interested to know if she has one or not.

So today I'm up and ready for her when she comes. I've written a sentence for her on my pad, I did it yesterday when I was feeling strong.

Some people complete their education later, it says, it can work better that way. It took me ages to write because yesterday was not a good day, and it's shaky. I hope she can read it. It isn't everything I want to say but it's a start. I wait when she comes in, wait while she takes off her raincoat and dries her hair with one of the paper towels from the bathroom.

It's raining cats and dogs, she says, isn't that the oddest thing, when we say that. She looks at me so I nod, but I'm thinking that actually there are much odder things that we say.

Wouldn't it be lovely if it was true, she says, if lovely fluffy puppies and kittens were falling from the sky, and all you had to do was catch them. Of course, she says, there would have to be soft stuff down everywhere to break their fall, mattresses and that bouncy flooring they have in playgrounds these days.

I can see she needs to chat a little, get something out of her system so I nod and try to look sympathetic.

But more importantly, she says, never mind me going on about puppies and kittens, more importantly how are you. Have you had a good week?

I make a hand movement that's supposed to mean, so-so, and she laughs.

I guess that's pretty good for being stuck in here, she says, I wouldn't like it, I'm sure.

It's weird but when she says that I start to feel protective of the damn place, the damn gravy boat, I feel like maybe it's OK for the inmates to say how crap it is but not for outsiders who just come by when they feel like it. I'm not having that. I turn to another page in my jotter and write, it's OK, but when she takes it to see what I've written she sees the page before, where I wrote about it being fine to complete education later.

Oh, she says, and her eyes are all watery, oh did you mean that for me, about Patrick, that's so kind of you. And you're right, of course you are, except he's gone missing now, he's been away for a week, the police aren't interested because he's been in touch, told me he's OK. Lots of young people like to challenge their parents, the police said, he'll be back when he's ready. I'm sure they're right, of course they are, but I worry, I can't help it.

I nod like mad, show her I'm listening. I can't do much else. I never had any problems with Jenny, she was a good girl but I can imagine how hard it is if they go off the rails. I think Alain had a stormy adolescence but then again I never knew whether anything he said was true.

We had a row, she says, still crying into her knitting. It's another stripy sock, only in sombre colours this time to match her mood. He was smoking in the house and I asked him not to because of Poppy, she gets asthma. Only I didn't say that because it would drive him mad, I said that I couldn't bear the smell in the house.

That's reasonable, I think, smoke in the house is dreadful. I make a whatever gesture with my hand and Penny picks up what I mean.

That's the thing, she says, and she looks really agitated, he caught me once, having a sneaky fag on the garden step, I couldn't go right out because it was raining. This was quite a few years ago, he was about eleven.

I'm sorry, I said to him, I thought you were upstairs. Do you know what he said to me then? He said, it's OK Mum, it doesn't bother me at all. Such a lovely lad, he was.

Oh dear, I think, the two things are not at all the same. I reach for my pad but my good hand isn't behaving itself at all well today and I can't manage. I want to write something like, don't beat yourself up, something like that but I have to settle for a small squeeze of her hand instead.

Oh listen to me, I'm a silly woman, she says, he'll be fine, much worse things happen, look at you not complaining that you're stuck in here.

She lowers her voice when she says 'stuck in here' and looks towards the door and then smiles at me and it feels like a little club, just the two of us. I wonder if I can tell her what's bugging me. I've got a wish to talk to someone, share things, and it's so strong it's making me feel crazy. It's making me feel homesick, that's how strong my desire to share my troubles is. I'm not sure where I'm homesick for, certainly not that lonely little house I've been living in, or the poky flat in Pimlico or even my childhood home. Homesick for a feeling, that's more like it, the feeling of talking to someone, someone who cares, and being listened to.

You want to tell me something, don't you, Penny says. Let me hold the pad steady.

I appreciate that. It's nice of her. Even if it doesn't work it's nice that she is trying.

Let's see if it makes it easier if I hold it steady and keep your bad arm out of the way, like this, she says.

She pushes her chair as near to mine as she can get, and leans across me so that she can anchor the pad.

Go on, she says, give it a try now.

I can smell her shampoo and it smells like pot pourri. The stuff I used to put in little dishes at Christmas. I used to use shampoo that smelled like green apples, I think, and the thought makes me sad. I get the pen in my hand in the right position and I think I'm going to write about Penny's lad, how she shouldn't beat herself up. Or about her shampoo smelling nice. And then I think of it, just like that. I could tell her. I could tell her about Bill, and then it would be someone else's responsibility.

I'm worried about the man in the room opposite, I could write, I think he may be my ex-husband and I'm scared of him.

Oh, she might say, let me help you with that. I want to do it so much that I even make myself write, I'm, to start it off and then I think, nice one May. Not only would he know I was onto him but also there's a fighting chance that I'd end up in a real loony bin instead of this bloody gravy boat. I'm tired, I write. I drop the pen and slump back a little.

OK, says Penny, are you sure that's all? Only I thought, for a moment.

I nod like crazy but I don't think she's completely fooled.

Anything that's worrying you, she says I hope you know you can tell me. For a moment I think I'm going to cry. She sounds like my Helen, that's the thing. A kind person and we know what happens to them.

I grab the pen back and write, what do you come here for. I feel sorry then, I never meant to be mean to her so I make big lines through what I've written. Big lines that scratch and tear the paper, until my writing underneath can hardly be seen.

It's OK May, Penny says, it's OK you don't need to do that. Look, I'll do it for you. She takes the pad and tears off the top sheet, the one I had been trying to cover up and she tears it into little pieces.

There, she says, all done.

I open out my palm in a gesture that is supposed to show her that I feel desperately lonely, that I don't know what to do, and I think she gets it.

I can tell there's something wrong, May, and if you ever want to tell me, that's great, but if not, I promise I'll keep an eye out for you, when I can.

I can't look her in the eye, I just can't, so I stare at my stupid hands. I need more than that, I think, in fact I need a miracle.

Shall we make some cards, she says, I've brought my crafty bag, look.

She empties her bag all over my bed and there's card and little cut out shapes and glitter and all the things that would thrill a small child. I want to shout at her, tell her that I've got serious worries and all she can do is show me this nonsense but I look at her face as she's laying things out.

You bitch, May, I think, you absolute bitch. What do you expect her to bring, a crochet hook? She doesn't know, she can't know that I was handy once, even the word makes me laugh now but I was. I learned to sew and make things and every time there was a fancy dress parade at school Jenny had the best costume. I manage to meet her eye and I give a thumbs up. It'll be worth it for the chat, I think, and it will take my mind off Bill.

As if I'd conjured it up by thinking about him, there's a knock on the door. Jackie's head pokes round first and she says, hi Penny, hi May, can we come and join the party?

I don't know, says Penny, looking worried, it's May's room.

I'm pleased to see Jackie so I gesture for her to come in and then I realise Trevor is with her and my old heart is glad. I attempt a smile.

Very crafty, me, says Trevor, I once made seventeen feather boas for a pride parade in London.

Wow, says Penny, they're difficult to do, getting all the feathers attached. Trevor looks as pleased as punch.

Just call me nimble fingers, he says and he's off to get chairs for everyone. I like the feeling of togetherness as my room fills up. Jackie and Trevor are rifling through the contents of Penny's bag and exclaiming over the pretty colours like small children. I can't quite join in but I'm happy they're there and Penny gives me a wink over their bent heads so it's all OK.

I know, says Trevor clapping his hands, let's make a collage together, of how we're feeling. I've got just the thing.

He rushes out and comes back with a large piece of white cardboard.

Don't ask any questions, he says, it was legally obtained. I will do the sticking and everyone can take it in turns to choose a piece.

May is at a disadvantage, says Penny.

I'm so pleased that she has thought of me that my eyes tear up a little. I make a hand gesture that's supposed to mean, you guys go on, I'll just watch but none of them are happy with that. They're so sweet, all of them, that they start gathering up bits and scraps and clearing off my tray so that they can put them on there for me to choose.

You go first May, it's your room, it's only fair, says Jackie. She leans over and gives me a little kiss on the top of my miserable old head. How come I was on my own for so long, I want to say, I could have had friends like you coming round for tea, I could have made a cake.

We're here now, says Trevor as if he understands, go on, choose.

They all look excited so I look down at the scraps on my tray. Glittery stuff, pretty red net, wiggly lines of binding, little pictures of dogs and chickens and cats. I shuffle it about a bit with my hand and there underneath is a piece of material, brushed cotton, pink flowers on a dark green background. I made a little dress in fabric just like that for Jenny when she was little, I remember it as clearly as if I'd just put my needle down. I sewed it by hand and halfway through something happened, but I can't think about that now. I hold it up.

That's lovely, isn't it, Penny says, I made a dress out of that, a maternity dress.

I bet you lot would just shove it on anywhere, says Trevor, thank God I'm here.

He scrunches it artfully into a corner of the cardboard and all of us are laughing like mad when there's another knock on the door. I freeze and look at Penny but she's still smiling and I feel safe until he puts his smarmy little head round. Bill. I suppose I should have known that if Jackie has fun, he'll want to join right in. He was always like that, I think, killjoy.

Anyone mind if I join the fun, he says and just like that, the atmosphere changes. I remember that, how the atmosphere could change the minute he walked in. I've never met another person like it. As if he was made of ice and cooled everything down, made it seem like winter, it's difficult to explain.

Oh lovely, says Jackie, clapping her hands, the more the merrier, don't you think.

My hand is itching to draw a screwdriver. A menacing one this time, a big old dangerous old screwdriver, a screwdriver that could get him right in the eye.

I don't think I make any noise but perhaps I'm wrong because I look up and everyone is looking at me. Trevor and Penny look concerned and Jackie looks very worried. Stop it, I think to myself, don't make a fuss, you're safe here, he can't get you. I manage a shrug. The other thing I'm thinking is, keep your enemies close. Isn't it better to be aware of what's going on at all times? To know where he is?

The only one who doesn't seem to notice the atmosphere is Bill. I know your true name, I think, and then I laugh because who's to say which of his names are real? Could be he was Bill all along.

Trevor explains to him what we're doing. I can tell from the glaze in his eye that Bill doesn't really understand it but he watches as we all choose pieces in turn. Jackie goes for something sparkly and Penny chooses a dried flower and then looks all coy and won't say why. Trevor has a feather, of course, and he holds it to his lips for a moment before he sticks it on. I've got quite good at lip reading now that I can't talk, I think it's because I concentrate more, and I see him say, my darling, to the feather.

It would be a perfect afternoon if he wasn't here, the man of many names, the man I've met so many times before. It's his turn next and I have another spiteful thought about screwdrivers but then he chooses and it makes me gasp. It's a piece of material shaped a little like a heart, and I'm immediately back in the art class at teacher training college.

Cut out a shape and pass it to the person next to you, the lecturer said. I don't remember the point of the exercise but I remember this, Alain cut out a red heart and passed it to me. We hadn't met or spoken at that point although I'd noticed him of course, all the women had. I was so surprised I actually looked over my shoulder, I couldn't believe the heart was for me. We went to bed for the first time that night, and Jenny was conceived three months later.

I look over at Bill and he's smiling, grinning really. For Jackie, he says as he puts the heart in the middle of the collage. But it's me he's looking at, I'm sure it is.

CHAPTER EIGHTEEN

May 1978
Pimlico

May left on the last day of her name month. The days were getting longer and even in the middle of London birds could be heard announcing the season. Weed flowers sprouted between paving stones and Jenny didn't need so much dressing and wrapping. Life became softer, more manageable. A good time to go, May thought.

May had been struggling with her decision for days. She should have gone as soon as she bought the ticket, she knew that. She knew that a brave, sensible woman would not have been able to stand another minute but it didn't help to know that. It just made her hate herself more, feel more ashamed of her inability to act.

You're pathetic, she told herself, fancy putting your own daughter at risk.

'I just need time,' May wrote to Helen in one of the letters she didn't send. 'I need to come to terms with the enormity of what I'm doing.' She knew this wasn't completely true.

'Let's face it,' May said to baby Jenny, 'I've been hoping that things would change. Giving your daddy another chance, really, only he doesn't know that.'

If anything, Alain's behaviour had got worse. He had written a list of what he called 'May's Stupidity', and stuck it on the wall over the sink.

'It's for your own good, May,' he said. 'You must see that. If you want to live a normal life, and if you want Jenny to live a normal life, we've got to address some of these things.'

May hated the list, but she was too scared to take it down. The first item he had written was, 'reading crap family sagas like a stupid old woman'.

May had argued at first, said that it was light reading for when she was up in the night feeding Jenny, and that it did no harm, but Alain had been so scathing that even without being hit or hurt at all she had thrown several books away, including one she hadn't finished reading.

'It's OK to read what you like, baby,' May whispered to Jenny when Alain was out. 'Comics, Famous Five, the lot.'

There were four other items on the list. Not frying the onions before cooking them, that was one, obsessing over the baby, making a ghastly chewing noise when eating apples, and not understanding that moth infestations are serious.

May had her small bag packed and waiting under her

bed. She loved to think of it sitting there when she lay down each night, holding her clothes like a helpful friend. She had put a layer of Jenny's old baby clothes on the top so that if Alain ever did find it, he would assume that was all it contained. The open ticket had been much more troublesome to hide. It was small, but so was the flat and places to hide things were in incredibly short supply. May had finally decided on a bag of sanitary towels, and she had cut a slit in one of them and poked the ticket in.

May might have gone on waiting for ever if things had not come to a head. Alain was feeling better and stronger, and he'd been out for most of the day. He had told May that he was visiting his school, but she doubted it. He would be going back to work soon, and it didn't make sense to go in before that. To be honest, she didn't much care where he had gone. Worries about Sue seemed like something from another life. Her world had shrunk to this flat and this baby plus the new one she was growing inside. She felt sick and scared all the time, and her mind was a whirl of pros and cons until she felt torn in half. As soon as May decided to leave she would remember how sweet Alain could be sometimes, how much he loved Jenny. As soon as May decided to stay she could only remember the cruelty and the terror. It was impossible.

If only Helen would get in touch things might be easier. There had been no letter, no phone call, nothing. May couldn't believe that Helen was still angry with her but each day without contact made May less sure, more scared.

She decided that if she wanted to leave Alain she would have to go up to Hull and explain that she really had left him this time, throw herself on Helen's mercy and make a new life. It was a terrifying thought.

May was chopping onions when Alain came in.

'My darling,' he called as soon as he was inside the flat, 'darling May, merry May, I've been thinking about you.'

He swept into the kitchen, smiling. May felt confused. He had stormed out this morning after trumping up an argument about the milk, which he said had gone bad. She hadn't been expecting this at all. Her stomach felt as though the baby had grown to full term overnight and was doing a somersault.

'I've been thinking,' Alain said, 'what we need is a holiday, a few days away somewhere pretty. Cornwall or Devon, somewhere like that. Sea, sand, tinkling masts, the whole thing. I know, I know, you're going to say we don't have enough money and it's true, but I've got a plan, there's someone at work I loaned money to and he's going to pay it back.'

Keep cool, May thought to herself, don't get pulled in, imagine a holiday if things went wrong, imagine being somewhere lovely by the sea with Alain when all the other families were having a happy time, imagine being the only one who was scared, and bullied, and hurt.

'We don't need this stupid thing for a start,' Alain said, tearing down the list of May's stupidity on the wall over the sink. 'I'm so sorry, I don't know why I did that. It was cruel, wasn't it?'

May wasn't sure what to say. Yes, it was cruel, she wanted to say, anyone in the entire world would agree it was cruel. It could be a trick though, Alain getting her to let her guard down so that he could get even more angry. This sort of thing had happened before. May shrugged her shoulders and just like that, it was over, any idea she might have had that things could change. I'll always be like this, she thought, this is my future, hunched over the sink pretending things don't matter when they do, frightened of what's going to happen next, flinching at loud noises.

May put her knife down.

'I'm tired,' she said. 'I'm tired and I'm sick. I don't want to chop onions and I don't want to have anything to do with dinner. I'm going to put Jenny to bed and then I'm going myself, sorry.'

Something in the way she said it made Alain stop and look at her. He's really looking, May thought. She had a sudden moment of terror that he would be able to see into her head, see the ticket and the plan and the happy life she had hidden there. Just in case, May forced all thoughts of tomorrow out of her head and concentrated instead on thinking about the material she had bought to make a little dress for Jenny. It was dark green brushed cotton with a pink flower, very unusual for a baby dress, and May loved it. She was making the dress by hand, and she imagined showing Helen and sewing together in the evenings when the babies were asleep.

'A life where we can live in peace,' May whispered to Jenny while she was changing her nappy. 'A life of pink, fluffy stuff where no one shouts.'

Jenny gurgled as if she understood.

'I'm sorry,' Alain said as he slid into bed next to her, 'I really am. There's some dinner left if you want to warm it up. You should eat, you know.'

May kept very still and willed her breathing to slow down. She was ready to leave, she wanted to go, and having a heart-to-heart chat, or worse, sex, would not help in any way.

'I know you're not asleep,' Alain said, 'and I don't blame you for ignoring me, I'd ignore me too if I was you. I know you've got no reason to believe me either when I say I really want a fresh start, but I do, I do, and I'll show you how much, I promise I will.'

May was totally confused. She had been ready to go, she knew she should leave, but it was strange not to have heard from Helen, and maybe, just maybe Alain did really mean it this time. People could change, she believed that. Even murderers who had committed terrible crimes were worthy of redemption sometimes.

It might have worked, she thought later, she might have stayed if Jenny hadn't woken up. But Jenny was a creature of habit, and she started to cry at about two a.m., her usual time for a top-up. May leaned over and picked her up out of her cot and into bed.

'Here we are, my little poppet,' May said as she pushed

a nipple towards Jenny's mouth. I'm such an expert, May thought, I could do this in my sleep now. She was sore from the pregnancy hormones, but proud to have persevered with breastfeeding. Jenny made little grunting noises as she suckled.

'Shut that baby up,' said Alain, his voice full of sleep and venom. 'It sounds like a pig.'

May was shocked. Alain had never said anything like that before out of nowhere. Usually he was remote but sweet to Jenny unless they were in the middle of an argument.

'Al, she's just snuffling,' May said. 'Her little nose gets all squashed when she's feeding, she can't help it.'

Al leapt out of bed and came round to May's side.

'Oh can't she,' he said and his voice sounded like a snarl. May shrank back against the propped pillows, pulling Jenny close to her. She tried to think straight, but all she could think of was the fact that she was only wearing a nightdress, and how vulnerable that made her feel.

'Well I'll fucking leave then, if I'm asking so much of everyone.'

Yes, May thought, go, please go, please.

Alain threw his jacket on and stormed out of the front door. Jenny let go of May's breast in surprise at the sound and began to wail. May realised she had been holding her breath.

'It's OK, little one,' said May, rocking her, 'we're really going to see Auntie Helen, it's going to happen.'

The silence Alain left behind screamed at May like a warning bell.

The train seemed bigger and noisier than May remembered. She felt uneasy, and looked over her shoulder every few seconds to make sure that they weren't being followed. Alain hadn't come back before they left and May felt lucky that, for once, he had played right into her hands and things were going smoothly.

The train ride started well. No one leapt on at the last minute to stop the train, and Jenny slept. May was able to watch the flat green countryside slip away from the windows. Fields, trees, canals, everything looked so fresh and hopeful.

'Going away, are you?' said the woman opposite May.

May had been constructing a letter in her head, a letter to Alain that would explain everything, make him understand who she was and why she had to go.

'I'm sorry?' she said and the woman opposite repeated herself. She was clearly desperate for a conversation.

'Only it seems a bit funny, you travelling such a long way on your own with a little one,' the woman opposite said. She had the flat accent with twisted vowel sounds that showed she was heading home to Hull.

'Does it?' said May. 'Really?'

The woman opposite was about the age May's mother would have been. She wore a shapeless dress the colour of mud with a dark green cardigan thrown over the top.

'My hubby would have paddled my backside if I had gone missing on my own with a baby,' she said.

'Gone missing?' May said. 'What on earth are you talking about?'

She hadn't meant to reply but the woman's words were so surprising she couldn't help it.

'Oh, you're being met at the other end, are you?' the woman said.

There was a glint in the woman's eye that indicated that she didn't believe May. May was furious.

'Yes, actually,' May said, 'yes I am being met.'

'I'll help you off the train, if you'd like, it's a lot on your own, the pushchair and everything.'

What is this, May thought, some kind of secret agent working for Alain? Calm down, calm down, she told herself, she's just a nosy old woman and there's nothing spooky in it at all. She would have been the same with anyone, it's a coincidence.

'My name's Pet,' the woman said, 'only I'm not a dog or cat or even a tortoise.'

The woman sat back in her seat, clearly hugely pleased with her joke. I wonder how many times she's said that, May thought.

'If you want to go to the toilet,' Pet said, 'I'll hold that baby, any time. Oh yes. I've raised three of 'em, big brutes they are now. I've just been to see one of 'em in London. No, there's not much you can tell me about littluns, I reckon I know it all, the lot.'

May contemplated moving to another carriage but the train was busy and she couldn't face dragging the loaded pushchair along the corridor, or worse, having to come back and sit down in the seat she had just left if there were no empty ones. She got out her writing pad instead, and wrote to Helen. It was a crazy thing to do when she would be seeing Helen so soon but May had two reasons. Firstly she needed to clear her thoughts and May had always done that best by writing things down. Once she set things down on paper she could look at them in a different way. The other reason was that the Pet woman who had taken such a shine to her was beginning to seem creepy, really creepy.

'Can I give the little one some chocolate?' Pet said as May set up her pad in a position to her right, between herself and the window so that it couldn't be overlooked.

'No,' May said, more loudly than she had intended. The other occupants of the carriage, two men in suits, looked away.

'I mean,' May said, 'I haven't given her sugar, not yet, I think it's bad for her teeth.'

Pet burst out laughing. 'Now I've heard it all,' she said. 'She hasn't even got any teeth. Poor little mite.'

'Dear Helen,' wrote May, 'I'm on my way to see you so this is a ridiculous letter and I'll probably throw it away when I get to Hull. There's a mad woman sitting next to me who wants to feed Jenny chocolate. I don't know why but she made me think of you and how angry you would be if someone tried to do that to Seb – I swear I sounded like you when I told her no! You've taught me to stick up for myself, and I'm so grateful for that. I still can't believe I've left him but I have, and it feels so good, this is the beginning of a whole new life. I won't stay with you for long, I don't want to cramp you, it's just until I get on my feet. I'll get a flat round the corner and a teaching job nearby and oh gosh, that sounds like I'm going to crowd you but I'm not, honest I'm not, it will be such fun with the babies growing up together. Almost like on a kibbutz.

I'm worried, Helen, about why I haven't heard from you for so long. I hope you're not too fed up with me for not leaving Alain sooner, I wasn't quite ready and I know I waited too long, I know it now but I was scared. I still am really, I'm scared of Alain and I'm scared of the unknown. I'm even scared of the mad woman in my carriage! So I hope that you're OK, and I haven't really got a backup plan if you don't want to see me. I'm confident, honestly, that we will be OK.'

May folded the letter up and pushed it to the bottom of her bag as the train approached Hull. She managed to dodge the offers of help from Pet and instead pushed the buggy down the long platform and into the cavernous station. It was strange, May had only been away in London for four months and yet it felt much longer. Everything seemed odd, out of place, full of echoes, as if she was recovering from a serious illness. May filed it all away to share with Helen.

There was a row of cream-coloured phone boxes

against the far wall of the station and May wished that she could ring her mother. The urge was so strong that May even rehearsed the number in her head, her mum's old number. She would have known what to do, she would have anchored May and Jenny. May missed her more in that moment than she had done since she died.

'It's just us, kid,' May said to the sleeping Jenny, careful not to wake her. 'This is me, pulling myself together right now, and everything is going to be just fine, I promise.'

May couldn't face trying to get the pushchair on the bus so she walked along the straight, wide avenues until she got to Helen's flat. It was the top floor of a terraced house and May had been there several times. It looked wrong as May approached it and it took her a minute to work out why. The curtains were closed, that was it. Helen wasn't fanatically tidy, but there was no way she would have the curtains closed on a sunny afternoon. May felt a lurch of unease.

May rang the bell for the upstairs flat, still expecting Helen to open the window and drop the keys down, despite the closed curtains. The front door to the communal hall-way opened and for a second, just a second, May thought it was Helen. It wasn't, it was her downstairs neighbour. May had met her before, she and Helen had found her curtain-twitching surveillance of the neighbourhood quite touching. She was kindly, Helen had explained, just lonely and under occupied.

'What are you doing here?' the neighbour said. 'Ringing on Helen's door?'

'I'm a friend of hers,' May said, 'we met before, a few months ago, do you remember?'

'You'd better come in,' said the neighbour. 'Leave the pram in the hallway.'

She sounded abrupt, not at all how May remembered her. The unease that had followed May from London increased. May parked the pushchair, picked up the sleeping Jenny and followed the neighbour into her living room with a growing sense of dread. She was trying to think of the neighbour's name, which was much easier than trying to think of what might be wrong.

'It's Margaret, isn't it?' May said as the name came to her. 'I've come to stay with Helen for a while. Helen and Seb.'

'Oh,' said Margaret.

She jumped a little as she said it, and May wondered what on earth was wrong with her. I'll ask Helen, she thought, poor woman, maybe we can help her.

'Sit down,' Margaret said. 'Would you like a cup of tea?'

'No thank you,' said May, 'we're fine, we just want to pop up and see Helen.'

May could see that Helen's neighbour was struggling with tears.

'Are you OK? Shall I go and get Helen? Is there something wrong?'

Margaret stared at her.

'You don't know,' she said in a quiet voice, almost a whisper.

'I don't know what you're talking about, but I'll go and get Helen, maybe she can help.' May stood up, but before she could go any further, Margaret spoke again.

'No, don't go up there, please don't. Sit down, let me tell you.'

That was enough. May sat. She knew what Margaret was going to say before she said it, there couldn't be anything else.

'I'm afraid she's gone,' Margaret said. 'She passed away, I can hardly believe it myself. Gone.'

She shook her head as if she was trying to shake off a wasp. May felt a surge of unreasonable anger at her, before the sadness hit. That was why she hadn't replied, why May hadn't heard from her, how could she have doubted her lovely friend?

'What do you mean?' she asked. 'How, when?' May felt as though the world was spinning in the wrong direction. All this time she had been thinking just of herself, worrying, fussing, not wondering about Helen at all.

'It's not for me to say, but she was killed. Stabbed. A lot of people seem to think that it might have been her ex, Seb's dad. He's gone missing, so my money's on him. Either way, someone was waiting for her when she got home with Seb three weeks ago. I was out, I was at my local history group, and I'm so sorry I wasn't here. There was quite a tussle, you see, quite a tussle indeed and if I had been here I might have stopped it.'

'It wasn't your fault. Don't blame yourself,' said May

on automatic pilot. 'Of course it was him, it has to be him, who else could it be?'

I could have stopped it, she thought, I knew what he was, how scared she was of him. I could have kept her in London, I could have been less preoccupied with my own troubles. May held Jenny tight. She knew which question she had to ask next but she dreaded the answer. Without planning to, she put her hands over Jenny's ears so that she couldn't hear any of this.

'What about Seb?' said May. 'Where's the baby?'

Margaret started to cry.

'I guess it wasn't on the news down in London, not important enough. Oh dear, oh dear, I'm afraid he died too. That's why they think it was the ex, although it doesn't make sense. Who would kill their own child? There were roses in the flat, roses on the floor, on the beds, roses everywhere. They were both stabbed, that poor little baby and his mum. I just want to move now. I can't stay here. Would you like to stay with me tonight?'

May couldn't think of anything she would like less. She wanted to get away as fast as she could. Take Jenny and run, again. She couldn't stop thinking about where it had happened, and how, and whether they had suffered. She stood up.

'No!' May said. 'No, sorry, I can't.'

'Where are you going to go then?' Margaret asked. 'Have you got somewhere else to go? Other friends? Do you think your other friends might have any clues, did they know her?'

'I'm sorry,' she said. 'I don't know anyone who could help. We didn't really have any friends in common, I mean, I haven't really got any friends here. Except Helen.'

'Don't go,' said Margaret. 'I've been so scared since it happened, it's not right, that little baby.'

May felt trapped. She absolutely had to leave. She felt as though she couldn't breathe, as though she was being strangled. Helen, lovely Helen, fat little Seb. Stabbed. A knife, what kind of knife? Where on Seb's new little body?

'I've got to go,' May said. 'I'm so sorry. I really am. I know Helen thought a lot of you. Thank you so much for telling me, I've got to go, goodbye.'

May stumbled out into the hallway. Was this where he had stood? Was this where he was when she first saw him? Was this the door he left from, blood maybe still on his hands?

May put Jenny into the buggy as she felt the house close in on her. She couldn't bear to stay a moment longer. Visions of Seb's perfect body ran around her head, along with the terrible thought – who died first? Did Helen see her dear little baby stabbed and bleeding? Or did he kill Helen first and then go for Seb when he started to cry?

Oh Helen, she thought, oh Helen I wish I'd come up sooner. I wish I'd been with you, I would have been able to ring the police or punch him on the nose or stand in front of you and Seb. There would have been two of us to fight him off. I'm sorry I was so busy thinking about myself that I didn't notice the danger you were in. You told me you often saw him hanging around near the flat, I didn't listen.

And what if he's nearby now? May thought, looking up and down the road. What if he knows I'm her friend? She tucked the blankets more tightly round Jenny and set off back to the station.

There was no choice, she thought as she walked. No one to go to here, not enough money to stay in a hotel, choices running out. May would have to go back to London. Alain's not like this, she thought, thank goodness he's better than this. He's got a real problem, sorry, Helen, but we're not the same, you and I, we're not.

We're different.

CHAPTER NINETEEN

June 2018
Lewisham

I keep my door shut now. All the time, not just when I want a nap or when the carers are giving me a wash. All the time. Shut the door, please, I have to make it understood to every damn one of them, pointing at the door and indicating a slam and then doing this ridiculous thing I seem to have started of putting my hands together and bending my head slightly like a geisha girl, to show people I am grateful for whatever tiny task they've done for me. I can't even quite get my hands together, it's more like I'm high fiving myself to be honest, but at least people seem to understand what I mean. More or less.

What on earth for, Agnita said, the first time I asked her to shut my door. It's good to be sociable, come on, it's nice to make friends. Oh I wished for my lost words at that moment, I really did, although I can't help thinking that there wouldn't have been anything I could say that would have convinced her. I growled a bit instead, and did my pointing and slamming thing again. On a bad day it's the nearest I get to communication.

I know what you want, she said, there's no point doing it all again, that's not the problem. It's just we're all friends here, aren't we, and this business of shutting people out or keeping people in, that's not the way we make a happy home, is it?

If I'd known it was a happy home you wanted, I thought, I could have maybe slit my throat instead of coming here. Childish, I know. I was quite cross, upset really, and I may have knocked a couple of things onto the floor, I don't remember. Oh, I know Agnita was angry, I know I'm not her favourite or anything but she doesn't know, does she? She doesn't know about Bill or whatever he says he's called. She doesn't know about any of his little games, and I can't tell her, all I can do is look out for myself. Take care of number one, that's what I've been reduced to. It's me he's after. Even my Do Good Lady seems to have deserted me, she hasn't been in for ages.

Thank goodness for Trevor. He's the only bright thing around here sometimes, especially when Jackie is busy with you know who. He came in last night, knocked on the door with such a sweet knock.

I wanted to see how my favourite girl is, he said, although he sounded a bit breathless and he hadn't got a good colour. Only it's been a couple of days and I'm pining a bit, he said and he made a silly face, all moon eyed and lovelorn.

I thought about what it might have been like if we were friends earlier in my life, when I was still a walking, chatting person. Would we have got on? I think so. I think I would have liked to talk to him about Jenny, when she was younger, and problems at school, that sort of thing. I bet he would have made me laugh. Maybe I could have helped him too.

Let me show you a trick, he said last night, did I tell you I used to be in the Magic Circle? I forgot about Bill and everything else for a moment. I love tricks, always have. I guess that's why I've been tricked before, I thought and then I pushed the thought away. Don't spoil it, May.

Trevor pulled his hand out with a flourish from behind his back. He was holding a banana. See this, he said, one ordinary banana, straight from somewhere warm, they don't grow here dear, they've got more sense. It was a rehearsed patter, I could tell it was, and I wondered whether he used to be on stage. I made a mental note to ask him later.

Would you like a slice, he said and I nodded because that's what he wanted me to do. He held it up close to my face and I could see it was just a banana, nothing special, and then he peeled it, right in front of me and it was all in slices. No kidding, a banana that's sliced before being peeled. I don't know how that works but I was thrilled, I loved it and I clapped with my good hand against my leg. Bravo, I wanted to shout, encore. I wished that Jackie would drop by so that she could see it too.

He bowed. He loves bowing, Trevor, I've noticed that

before. Bows at the drop of a hat. He stood there after that, looked a bit confused, then he started coughing so he turned on his heel, snappy like a soldier, saluted and left the room.

I was in a good mood after that, a really good mood. What's not to enjoy about a banana that's sliced but not peeled? I was still thinking about it when that man came in here, Bill, not long after Trevor left. It was late, I know that because the televisions had gone quiet. All day you can hear them, the TVs up and down the corridor, turned up to the max because we're all a bit deaf. All of them tuned in to different channels. I've got used to it, it's a bit of company, but it's a nice stretchy out comfortable feeling when the sounds stop.

Jackie didn't come round at all yesterday evening, she was out with him I think, at a film or something. She often goes straight to bed when she comes in after a night out so I didn't think anything of it when she didn't come to say goodnight.

In fact I thought it was her for a moment, I was looking down at an article in the newspaper about nuclear weapons and I was glad of an excuse to stop reading so I looked up with a smile, wanting to tell her about the banana. I was going to shrug my shoulders to make a pantomime of the fact that she needn't have come to see me but I was grateful that she had. Oh, I remember thinking, maybe we can have some hot chocolate if one of the nice carers is on duty. Maybe we can stay up chatting and she can tell me the plot of the film and all that. It happens sometimes.

So I looked up but it was Bill. He was right there in front of me and that wasn't what I was expecting so I wiped the smile off my face as quick as that game. The one where you pass your hand back and forth in front of your face and every time it goes past you change your expression, smile, frown, eyes shut, eyes open, that kind of thing. I was aiming for steely, I didn't want to give away how scared he makes me. So I just stared at him.

Oh, he said, not so keen to talk to me now your little friend isn't here. I knew a woman like you once, he said and he grinned, grinned like it was the funniest thing. She wasn't old like you, she was young, well younger anyway and even a bit pretty in the right light but she thought she knew the lot. Everything. There was nothing she didn't know, and that can get on a person's nerves, do you know what I'm saying?

I looked towards the door, hoping one of the staff might be passing by but he saw me, caught the look and maybe he could read my mind, like he always could.

There's no point expecting anyone to hear you, he said, they're all down the other end of the corridor putting Manny back to bed. This is the quiet end, nothing happens here, they won't be back for a while. So you and me can have a chat, can't we, a chat that's been overdue. We've got lots to talk about haven't we?

Screwdriver, I tried to say but of all the words that are difficult to say in the whole world, screwdriver is probably one of the worst. I didn't even know why I wanted to say it. Bring him down a peg or two I guess, remind him that he's just a confused old man now, whatever else he might have been one day.

Oh dear, he said, you're a poor dribbling old thing, aren't you?

He was right, I was dribbling, it was the effort of trying to get the words out. That's what made me dribble but I hate that he noticed. Hate that he homed straight in on it. He was always good at working out whatever it was that would upset me the most, he had a feel for it.

He got this dirty old tissue from his pocket and he held it right by my mouth. I tried not to breathe so that I wouldn't breathe in his horrible germs but he held it there for so long I had to and it was repulsive. Grim. I nearly threw up.

Ah, he said, just trying to help my dear.

He tilted his head.

I was sure of it then.

He looks different of course, time plays all sorts of tricks on a person. Look at me, you'd never for a moment peg me as the soft young woman with the pretty hair and the quiet voice. Even his face shape seems to have changed, got longer somehow, as if he'd been dangled by the head until his chin dropped, but that's age for you. There's not one of us ends up the way we began, no matter what the film stars try to do. The wicked twinkle in his eye though, and the nastiness of his smile, not to mention the snaggly half twist of his front teeth. That's my evidence.

I had to see him off. I might be old and dumb in every

sense of the word, but I'm not a victim. Not now. I picked up the little scissors the Do Good Lady had left behind. I didn't do anything with them. I just stared. It made my eyes water but I stared at him, steady and fierce. I know who you are, I said through my eyes, I know exactly who you are and you don't frighten me. The words seemed to echo in my brain, deep and booming. He must have been able to pick them up, he must have.

Oh, he said after a minute or two of my killer stare, oh if you're going to be like that. I just thought you might like some company, that's all.

I didn't move, kept on with the staring.

Come on mate, he said and I could tell that he was getting really uncomfortable, come on, let's be nice to each other, I knew someone like you once, come on.

I kept on staring, and I allowed myself a slight curl of the lip as well, to show that I found him beneath contempt. I could remember so many things, so many times when he hurt me or was vile to me or said terrible things about poor Helen and Jenny. I can't believe that he could just sit there, talking to me as if everything was OK, as if we might have a cup of tea and a laugh together.

I breathed deep like the speech and language therapist showed me and I formed the word in my head before I let it out.

Al, I said, then I tried again. Alain, I said. I spat the word at him and I watched to see his reaction and I was right, I was sure I was right because he flinched and his eyes shut for a moment. It wasn't only because I was holding the nail scissors.

I don't know, he said, I don't know what you're trying to say. Do you want your notepad? Maybe I can get your notepad, I've seen you use that when you're with my Jackie or with the nurses, maybe that's the thing.

Some people might think that was a harmless thing to say, but those people do not know my Alain like I know him. Even if he says his name is Bill now I know how he works, and he was trying to get close to things that matter to me, my personal things on my tray. He'd cut them up, I know he would. Anything that I love, that's what he wants to spoil, he was always the same.

No I shouted, nail scissors held aloft. Just the usual grunting piggy noise came out. It stopped him in his tracks, he looked startled. A bit scared, even, although I could hardly believe that. He wasn't frightened of anything back when I knew him. You could have taken a bolt cutter to his fingers and he would have laughed in your face, that's the man I remember.

Stop, I yelled, or a mangled version of stop but I think the intent was fairly clear.

I'm not, he said, I didn't and he started to look scared, but he still had his hands in my private stuff on my tray, my notebook and my purse and my photographs and a postcard that Jenny sent me the other day, so I had to keep shouting.

Get off, get off, I said, or my version of it anyway. He

started to cry then, honestly he did, big tears like an old wrinkled up baby. I was hoping one of the staff would hear him and come by so I dropped the scissors. I thought I might be able to press charges or something, accuse him of breaking and entering and rifling through personal stuff but no one came and he seemed to pull himself together.

Don't you shout at me, he said, coming back over to where I was sitting, I don't expect that kind of treatment and I don't like it.

Just like my Al, I thought, crying one minute, begging forgiveness and full of the sorryness of the world for himself and then bam. Back to frightening little old ladies and speaking in a scary voice like someone from a horror movie. Bill scrunched his face up then, right up as if someone had asked him to pull the scariest face he could. Twisted it right out of shape and I knew I was right.

Don't fuck with me, he breathed into my face. It was really quiet, as though someone might have been listening.

Don't screw things up for me, he said again but the word screw, seemed to trigger something for him and he untwisted his face.

He left soon after that. Just stayed long enough to pick up a few things from my tray, and from the shelf opposite my bed. He picked them up and put them down again, like he was looking for something, then he shook his head and looked at me in a different way. As if he wasn't sure who I was, as if he'd been invited to a party but couldn't remember the name of the host. I think I caught the word screwdriver as he left but I'm not sure, and even if I did, even if he'd gone back to being a crazy old man, who's to say that it wasn't an act. He was always good at acting, Alain, he should have been on the stage.

As soon as he'd gone I'd tried to think of a plan. Jackie, that's who I was worried about. Jackie, with her sadness and her linen trousers, no one was going to look out for her if I didn't.

*

I've been up all night, thinking. They came to put me to bed after a while, said they were sorry but Manny had been unwell. As if I cared. I'm not even sure who Manny is.

No bed, I wrote on the pad, things to do. I caught them raising their painted eyebrows to each other then, Abi and Agnita, as if the idea that I might have anything to do at all was so ridiculous they wanted to laugh. I breathed evenly, in, out, in, out, staring at a point on the opposite wall and eventually they left.

We're not going to force you into bed, dear, they said, but we'll be down the hallway when you're ready. Give us a buzz and we'll come and help you as soon as we can.

I signed thank you even though they probably don't know any sign language. And I sat up all night, and now I know what I have to do. No messing around, no pulling back, I've got to tell Jackie, I've got to save her.

Hi, she says as she breezes in after breakfast, aren't you going to eat your toast? It's sitting there in front of me, two soggy slices covered in something that looks like butter but isn't. I wave my hand at it and wrinkle my nose as if it smells bad and she laughs, my Jackie, it really isn't that funny but she laughs anyway because she is a most loyal friend. One good turn deserves another, I think, and I motion for my notepad but before she notices what I'm doing she is dancing, yes, literally dancing from one foot to the other, she's so excited to tell me something.

I motion to her to sit down, take the weight off but she's so excited I don't think she can stay still.

Oh, she says, oh May I never thought, I mean I hoped but I didn't think it would necessarily happen, oh I'm going to miss you, of course I am but you only get one life, don't you? Only one chance at happiness and all that.

If I could speak, I would slap a cliché order on her, demand that she starts talking to me in normal language but that's a hard concept to get across in sign and she doesn't seem to have the concentration to be able to wait for me to write anything down. I don't blame her. It takes me a while on the best of days.

Let me start at the beginning, she says, like in the song. You know, don't you, that Bill and I have been getting along well, we've been going out, we're kind of special friends.

I nod, but I want to say, yes, when he can find his damned screwdriver, when he remembers who you are.

Well, she says, we talk a lot, me and Bill. There's not much else to do here is there? So we talk about everything, hopes, plans, you know.

Yes, I think, I know, because it's the kind of talk we used to have. Me and you. Jackie doesn't seem to remember that.

We even talk about what we would do if we could get out of here, where we would live and that sort of thing. Moon dreaming, Bill calls it. Anyone can dream, can't they?

Jackie looks at me with shining eyes as if what she is telling me is the most exciting thing ever. Even if my voice miraculously returned I wouldn't join in with this drivel, I think, I'd still want to vomit at the idea of moon dreaming. So I stare at her and she claps her hands and says, we're going to be able to do it, May. We're leaving here, Bill has come into some money and we are going to get out of here and get a place and have carers coming in and everything, don't look sad, you can come and visit us if you like, maybe you can even stay the night…

Her voice tails off and I feel like the meanest friend ever. But honestly, how stupid is she? People our age don't 'come into money'. We're the ones who leave it to other people. There's a scam going on somewhere and she's going to be terribly hurt, I can sense it and I know I'm right. I grab my pad.

Are you sure, I write and then, when?

Oh May, she says, of course I'm sure, I'll miss you and Trevor and everyone here but imagine being in my own little home again, making a cup of tea and calling to ask someone else if they'd like a biscuit with it.

I'm sorry, she says then, that was about as tactless as a person can get, wasn't it, I didn't mean to upset you, it's just, well, I was hoping you'd be happy for me, I haven't had a very lucky life but maybe this, this happy bit at the end, maybe this will make up for all of the other stuff.

I run through the things I could tell her, to see which one fits. Don't go, he's not who he says he is, I used to be married to him and he's dangerous. That's the straightforward version but it doesn't take a genius to work out that she would probably think it was sour grapes. I should have told her before, when I first suspected it was him. I could have included her in all my speculations and then it wouldn't come as a terrible shock but I didn't, of course I didn't, because of my damn words. My words have gone and it doesn't matter how much I need them, they won't come back.

I stare at her and I don't know how to arrange my face. Happy, sad, indifferent, anxious, interested. Even if I could pinpoint the name of the emotion I couldn't get it to show on my face.

Come on, Jackie says, be pleased for me, I'm happy, I'm in love, come on.

She does a little hop and a skip and takes my face in her hands and kisses me square on my dribbly old lips.

Would you be my maid of honour, she asks and for a moment the words resonate and I'm in a normal world, where people get married and have celebrations and there's dancing and cake and clothes bought specially for the occasion. There's a snap in my head like an old-fashioned flash camera and I see myself, out of the wheelchair and dancing with Jackie in a marquee. There's bunting, women in high heels and men in ill-fitting suits with flowers in their buttonholes. It's the wedding I never had and for just that one moment, I want it so much for Jackie that I almost forget.

Almost.

I look up and he's there, in the doorway, leaning and lounging and looking pleased with himself. He looks as though he has won the lottery, or robbed an old lady of her pension.

You've heard my news then, he says. His news indeed. As if Jackie was nothing to do with it.

I look at her and she doesn't seem to be bothered by what he has said. She's linking her arm through his and grinning like it's everyone's birthday. She turns to him and gives him a kiss and it hurts much more than I was expecting it to. I expect she's forgotten that she just kissed me, that would be the last thing she would be thinking of.

I look at him and he's smirking at me. Perhaps he only took up with Jackie to get at me, I wouldn't be surprised. Nothing he does would surprise me. He raises one eyebrow in my direction. Jackie can't see, she's snuggled into his shoulder, but there's no mistaking it.

I grab my notepad. Don't do it Jackie, I write, I know stuff. I'm exhausted then, and I meant for only Jackie to see it but he picks it up and I can't stop him and he reads it out in a voice that's pretending to be kind. I know that voice, I think, that voice that speaks one thing and means another. I know that voice and I start to scream, I can't help it.

Jenny came in this morning. They gave me something to make me sleep and I slept all night but I knew I was asleep, if that makes sense. I was aware.

Fancy spoiling your friend's big news like that, Agnita said, I remember that and then it was like being underwater, or watching wedding after wedding that I hadn't been invited to.

Are you better, Mum, asks Jenny. She's holding my hand and she looks so worried. I nod.

It's probably just the surprise of it, she says, I heard about Jackie getting married and moving out and I thought that must be such a shame for you. Very sad.

I look at her and I can see she means it. She really does understand, my funny, straight-laced Jenny and I feel so lucky to have her and so guilty not to have realised that, all at the same time. I'll be alright, I think, I'll be alright as long as I have Jenny. Poor Jackie, with no one to look out for her. I'm going to have to help her, I think, it's down to me, it really is.

I'm concentrating so hard on what I can do to help Jackie that I don't hear Jenny at first.

Good news, she's saying, something about good news and I assume it's something to do with her job and try to make my face look right. A promotion? Head of year perhaps? I'm trying to think what it is she's said when I hear something else.

I know it's late, and I'm old by their terms anyway but the midwife says there's no reason why the baby shouldn't be absolutely fine, lots of women choose to have them later these days.

I look at her, lost for an expression or a sound that would help. A baby. A grandchild. A small person with a smattering of my genes as well as the ones from the rubbish grandfather and the dodgy dad.

Someone to keep safe, someone to watch out for, I think. For a moment I'm back in the heat of that summer, holding Jenny, trying to get her out of the flat. My arms flap a little, as if I've lost something.

I thought you'd be pleased, Jenny says and she sounds so hesitant, so worried. I try to raise my arm up in a victory salute, an attempt to punch the air. Jenny laughs.

Careful Mum, she says, we have to keep you fit so that you can welcome your grandchild.

As long as he doesn't find out, I think, as long as we really can keep the baby safe.

CHAPTER TWENTY

May 1978
Pimlico

May got off the train at Kings Cross and went to stand by the ticket barrier. It was the place where she had met Helen when she had come to visit. If I close my eyes, she thought, if I count to a hundred, maybe the last twenty-four hours will be a mistake; maybe Helen will appear and say 'surprise', or launch straight into a tale of how badly Seb has been sleeping. She was here, May thought, right here, where I'm standing, how could she be dead? It seemed impossible. I'm so sorry, Helen, May thought. Sorry I didn't come running when you didn't answer my letter, sorry I didn't leave with you in March, sorry you're gone and I'll never see you again, sorry about lovely little Seb.

'Are you OK, love?'

May looked up and realised that she was crying, and that Jenny was too, and a couple of concerned women had stopped to help.

'Thanks,' she said. 'I'm fine.'

May bent down, kissed Jenny and moved away. I've crossed a line, she thought, I've become a person who knows something terrible. Who knows that the world is terrible.

May longed for a familiar face. She rang Alain from a phone box. There was no answer. May wondered for a moment whether he was with Sue, and the image of them together, laughing, maybe talking about her and how stupid she was, hit her like a fighter's punch. I need to talk to Helen about it, she thought and then remembered and dug her nails in to her palms to stop herself from crying out. If only her mother was still alive. If only she had a safe place that she could go to. Friends. She thought for a moment about the hostels for battered wives she had read about. Surely they were for women in much worse situations? They would probably laugh at the kind of arguments she and Alain had. Arguments over literature or cooking or answers on *Mastermind*, that wasn't what they were set up for.

'Enough of this,' she whispered to the hiccoughing, sleepy Jenny. 'Don't worry, I'll look after you.'

It was time to stop acting like a victim, May thought. Helen's death had to have a meaning and maybe that was it. May could change things. It was the very last thing she could do for Helen. May needed to be the person Helen had believed she could be, the person Helen had been. She would sort things out for herself, talk to Alain, explain how she felt, ask him to leave for a few days so that she could plan. It would be so much less inflammatory than disappearing, more adult. She refused to drag anyone else into the mess she had made of her life. She didn't want to tell anyone about Helen, or Seb, or even the stupid earrings. None of it. It had to be better, she thought, even though she realised that she was not thinking straight, it still had to be better for her and Jenny to be in their own home. Alain isn't like Frank, she thought over and over like a mantra, he isn't like Frank, he isn't like him.

She thought of how he had been the night before, before he turned nasty, how he had been so kind to her. She tried not to think of the other Alain, the one who had snarled at Jenny. After all, she reasoned, he was tired, he was unwell after his injury, she knew she had been difficult to live with, it wasn't as unreasonable as it looked at first glance.

Helen would have understood, she thought, Helen would have known that I have to go back, I have to make a go of it. Later, May would realise that she was wrong, wrong, wrong. She would wonder what on earth she had been thinking of, why she had chosen to walk back, no, run back, to a situation every bit as dangerous as the one her friend had been in, the one that had got her friend killed. It didn't make any sense, but at the time May's homing instinct was so strong that she had to follow it. Home, she thought, pushing everything else away, Seb's little hands, Helen's terror, just get home, May, and you'll be OK.

It will be safer, she kept thinking, safer with him than

without him. I'm sorry, Helen, I'm so sorry but if you had stayed with your man, if you hadn't left, you might be alive now. And Seb, May stuffed her hand into her mouth to keep from crying out loud at the thought of Seb, his sweet little face, his long piano playing-fingers. Anything would have been worthwhile if it meant keeping him safe, she was sure Helen would have agreed with that.

May moved fast, heaving the buggy on and off trains and up and down stairs like superwoman. She was sweating with terror by the time she managed to drag Jenny back across London to their flat. Every footstep behind her sounded like Alain, every voice in the street could be him. He'd find her if she left, she realised, he'd find her just like Frank had found Helen. Got to make it OK, got to make it OK, she mumbled as she ran, aware that she looked like a crazy woman but not able to do anything about it.

May turned the key in the lock of the outside door to the hallway. She listened hard outside her own front door. No music, no TV. Her hand shook as she turned the second lock.

'Hello,' she called, 'Alain?'

There was no answer.

May opened the door and manoeuvred Jenny, the buggy and her bag into the small front room. It seemed impossible that nothing had changed since this morning but there it was, her unwashed teacup, a bib of Jenny's on the sofa and the sun still shining through the grubby windows. May crept in. She took in every detail of the tiny flat like a cop in a movie. She checked in cupboards, behind doors and curtains, under the bedclothes, even in the fridge. No sign of Alain. It looked as though he hadn't been back at all, although May couldn't allow herself to hope.

On the alert, she said to herself, I have to be ready. It could be a trap, of course, he was completely capable of making sure that the flat looked as though he hadn't been there at all. Was the cup really in the same position, she thought, and did I leave Jenny's bib at that end of the sofa or on the arm, at the other end?

She had no idea, but by now her breasts were sore and swollen and Jenny was sobbing as if she knew that her little friend had died. May quickly tucked her suitcase back under the bed and sat down to feed the baby.

'It's OK, Jenny, we'll be fine,' she said as Jenny sucked with breathless little gasps.

The enormity of what May had done began to hit her as she relaxed. She had brought Jenny back into the most dangerous place possible. May thought of all the horror movies she had seen where the characters went into the cellar, or the woods, or wherever was the most frightening place. This is why they do it, she thought, this is why, because it's safer to keep your enemy, your danger, in plain sight. Safer to know they're in the next room than to wonder all the time whether they're outside, or round the corner, or waiting behind a door.

I'll move, she thought, I'll finish this feed and I'll go.

*

May woke to the sound of the front door opening. It was dark outside, so it had to be past nine o'clock.

'Hello,' Alain said, 'where's my girls? All safe and sound, back in the nest?'

Alain picked up his guitar and strummed the opening chords of 'May You Never'.

He knows, May thought, somehow he knows. Why would he say that otherwise? Alain swept into the bedroom, smelling of night-time London and beer. May forced herself to smile, and not to turn away.

'Hiya,' she said in a quiet voice. 'Jenny's just gone off, I'm knackered. Couldn't manage supper, sorry.'

'Oh I wasn't expecting any supper,' Alain said. 'Not with you so poorly and everything. Don't worry, I'm just glad to see the two of you all present and correct.'

'Where else would we be?' said May. 'This is our home.'

She knew it was a dangerous thing to say, but May felt that she needed to know where she stood, and how much Alain knew.

'It is, it is,' said Alain, bending down to kiss Jenny, 'and terrible things happen to little girls who get lost.'

What the hell, thought May, if he knows, how, and more importantly, what?

'So, how was your day?' Alain said. 'What have my girls been up to?'

'Oh you know,' said May, 'usual stuff, nothing exciting. Round the block and up the wall, you know the kind of thing. I was sick three times before breakfast but I've been OK since.'

It was a gamble, May knew it was a high risk strategy but she didn't really have any choice. She could either confess that she had tried to run away and plunge herself and Jenny into danger or she could try and bluff it out, wait until she had clearer evidence that he knew what she had been up to.

'Maybe now the weather is better,' Alain said, 'we could start taking Jenny out a bit, you know, further afield. Show her there's something outside central London. Maybe go on a train or something, to the seaside.'

May felt as though her face was on fire. He knows, she thought, he must know, why would he say it otherwise? It could be a coincidence, the rational part of her brain said, it's not an unusual thing to say in the summer. Keep going, May urged herself, keep going but try to be nearer to the door.

She stood up and stretched.

'I'm tired,' she said. 'I'm going to tidy up the bedroom. There are clothes on the bed, I haven't put the washing away yet.'

May moved towards the living room door, aiming for nonchalance.

'There's a direct train to Brighton from Victoria,' she said. 'Maybe we could take Jenny there, when this sickness wears off a bit.'

'Brighton,' Alain said, rubbing his chin. 'The south coast.

I suppose that makes sense. It's just, whenever I have the chance, I prefer going north, don't you?'

Don't panic, May thought, it's all still perfectly normal. Travelling north, that's all he's talking about, nothing more, keep calm.

'What seasides did you used to go to, when you were a little boy?' May asked. 'You know, if you went for a day out. Mum and I used to go to Broadstairs or Margate usually.'

As soon as May had said it she knew it was a mistake. Alain never said much at all about his childhood, but he was clear that it was a closed subject.

'So,' Alain said, 'because lucky little merry little May had some lovely days at the seaside, everyone else must have done too? Let me make sure I've got this right. What a glorious world we'd be living in if we were all as happy and lucky as merry merry May.'

May was stung.

'I didn't mean it like that,' she said. 'I wasn't trying to, I didn't mean to upset you.'

'I'm sure you didn't,' Alain said. 'You just can't help it, can you? Thrusting your happy life, your normal life, in front of everyone's nose like a lucky charm. I try to suggest an outing, an outing together, the three of us being a family, and that's just not good enough, is it? Oh no, nothing's good enough for you unless you can be making someone else unhappy.'

May moved a tiny bit nearer the door. The difficulty

was, Jenny was still asleep in her buggy near the kitchen. May would be able to get herself out, no problem, but getting out with Jenny would be much more difficult. The unfairness of what Alain was saying burned but she couldn't help thinking that if he had known about Hull and her escape then it would have been his main focus. Probably. The trouble with Alain was, it was extremely difficult to second-guess him.

'Sneaking to the door, are you?' Alain said. 'Don't think I don't see what you're doing. Don't think I don't know your damn plans. Always sneaking off somewhere, packing your little bags and making your stupid plans. Your stupidity almost amuses me, that's the funny thing. That's a quote, by the way, I think it's from Scott Fitzgerald, only that wouldn't matter to you, would it? If a writer isn't lesbian you don't really have much time for them, do you? And why is that? Could it be anything to do with Helen, precious Helen, Helen and the choir of angels that sing behind her head because she's so bloody perfect?'

OK, May thought, try to think straight. He seems to know, he's made enough references now, it seems the most logical thing to assume that he knows, otherwise why the choir of angels?

Alain got up out of his chair and moved towards May.

'So,' he said and May immediately stopped wondering what he knew. It doesn't matter what he knows, she thought as he slapped her face, first one way and then the other like a cartoon villain. It doesn't matter what he knows, she thought as he punched her, full in the face this time so that May could hear a bone in her nose shatter as her head hit the wall, it doesn't matter because he was always going to do this anyway.

'It's not because of me,' May shouted as she hit the floor. 'It's you, not me.'

Her voice sounded disgustingly nasal.

She knew she should keep quiet, take it in silence, try not to enrage him any further. May knew this because she'd done it before, begged for forgiveness, accepted a beating without arguing. It made things shorter, made Alain lose interest in what he was doing more quickly. But what she lost, May knew, what she lost and could never get back was her dignity. Both times she had adopted the passive approach May had felt sick afterwards at her own complicity.

Not any more. This is for Helen, she thought as she managed to get hold of Alain's leg with one hand. He was wearing shorts and May's nails were longer than usual. She dug them in as hard as she could and then a little bit harder, for Helen.

'Fuck off, bitch,' said Alain, shaking his foot to try to get her off. 'That's my bad leg. It's only just out of plaster.' May clung on, feeling her nails go through skin, feeling something wet on her fingertips, on her hands, knowing that the leg was weak, knowing that this was her only chance. Alain's attempts to move became increasingly frantic until he reached down, slapped May's head again and again and she had to let go, scraping her nails down his leg as hard as she could on the way.

'Ow,' said Alain. 'Ow, ow, you hurt me.' He hopped away from May towards the door, for all the world as though he had been attacked out of the blue.

'It's bleeding,' he said, holding his leg. 'Look what you've done.'

May stared at Alain's scratched leg from her vantage point on the floor. It was white and skinny from the weeks in plaster. They were only small scratches, but he was right, they were deep, there was blood, big beads of it travelling down towards the carpet. May knew that if she studied the scratches more carefully, she would see that the marks left by her nails were crescent shaped. She felt proud, as if she had made something clever like a coat for a baby or a dress, and she wished that she could take a photograph.

Alain stumbled to the kitchen and May took a quick inventory. Definitely a broken nose and quite a large amount of blood but nothing to be done, no point taking her nose to hospital. May knew that she had never been a beauty, but she had liked her nose. She put one hand up to touch it in apology. May's face felt sore everywhere, and there was an empty sound in her ears, as if she had just left a loud rock concert. Arms and legs OK, but there was a strange throbbing deep inside her that didn't feel right.

Get up, she thought to herself, this is your chance, grab the baby and leg it, go to the place for battered wives, or ring an old friend. The thought felt urgent, but May was unable to follow it. Get up, get up, she thought, quick, go on, do it now. No matter how urgent the voice became, May stayed exactly where she was. On the floor, semi-curled, waiting for the throbbing to go away.

'It's still bleeding,' Alain shouted from the kitchen. 'You've hurt me, May.'

May heard him but she couldn't completely understand. He didn't sound threatening or angry at all, more like a little boy who is puzzled about why the grown-ups are angry with him.

'May,' he said, 'have we got any antiseptic?'

'Hang on,' May said.

It was a clever thing to say, she thought. It would keep him wherever he was for another moment, and she would have time to, time to… May was puzzled. She couldn't remember what it was she had to do, before she got up. Something, she thought, something important. The baby, that was it, Jenny. May knew that she had to find Jenny and keep her safe, get her away. A small amount of urgency crept back into May's head and she tried to sit up. Her head and her nose and her neck were hurting but the worst thing was the giddiness. Dizzy like a carousel, she whispered. She thought it might be a line from a song. There was a song a few years ago about dizzy, an old pop song and May tried to remember how it went.

She sang to herself in a whisper and then it struck her how very funny that was, that she would have remembered a song she hadn't even liked and yet she couldn't remember why she was on the floor, or what she was supposed to do next.

'May, look, my leg,' said Alain and then he was standing over her and she remembered, she wasn't safe and there was a baby somewhere and she was supposed to get out. May started to scream. A feeble scream, an underwater scream but it seemed to scare Alain anyway.

'May,' he said. 'May, stop it, Jenny's asleep, you'll wake her up. May, stop screaming, what's the matter? It's me should be crying, look at my leg.'

Alain squatted down by May.

'Come on,' he said. 'Everyone has rows.'

His voice was conspiratorial.

'Stop crying, stop making that noise. I'm sorry if I was a bit rough but you really hurt my leg, you know.'

May breathed through her mouth and tried to stop screaming. She could smell danger. When Alain went quiet and irrational, it was never a good sign. He wants me to feel safe, she thought, he wants me to feel safe and then something worse will happen. Jenny. Jenny. May remembered Jenny through the haze of her poor battered head and put her hands on the floor to brace herself for standing. There was something wrong. She couldn't seem to balance herself properly, and her hands didn't appear to be able to bear her weight.

'Stop messing about, May,' said Alain. 'I've said I'm sorry. I said it. I'm sorry. There, I've said it again, what more do you want me to do?'

May could hear a note of panic in his voice. She wasn't sure why. The floor under her legs felt wet and May put her hand down to see what it was, thinking that maybe if she cleared up that mystery, she would be able to get up, get Jenny, see what was happening. Anything that would make her feel a little clearer, less muddled, would be good. May held her fingers up to her face.

It was blood. Sticky, smelly blood.

'May,' said Alain. May could hear the catch in his voice. 'May, you're bleeding, why are you bleeding? I didn't do anything, did I? You hurt my leg but I didn't do anything.'

'I'm bleeding,' May said. 'I think I'm losing the baby.'

CHAPTER TWENTY-ONE

June 2018
Lewisham

It's hot.

Jackie hasn't gone yet.

There are snags about moving in to their new flat in the warden assisted block, something like that. I'm grabbing hold of as many moments with her as I can, but our relationship hasn't been the same. We don't have the easy chats that we used to. She tries, my lovely Jackie, to be fair on her she tries very hard. It's me that's the problem. I want to tell her about Bill, tell her what I know but I can't seem to get it out. My hand has been too shaky to write and it's hard to point to danger when you don't have any words.

She talks to me, my Jackie, she talks about everything under the sun except for the wedding stuff, the important stuff, the things I know are uppermost in her mind. I get hold of the pad and manage to write, beware, danger, but they're very wobbly, my words. I'm not sure that she can read them. She looks at me with pity, I hate that, and she says she's fine.

I gesture that I want the pad again and I manage to write, not Bill. I'm trying to tell her that he's not who he says he is, that's what I want her to know, but of course she doesn't understand.

I write maid of h and I scribble it out, scribble so hard the paper tears. I need to show her that I can't collude, maybe that will make a difference.

Oh May, she says, I want you to be happy for me, I'm happy, please don't spoil it. I understand if you don't want to be there. He's old and he's all sorts of things but he's a good man, May, you don't know him like I do. He's funny, and he's clever. I never had a chance before.

And you don't stand a chance now, I think. He'll chew you up and spit you out and what good will your velvet curtains do you then?

I think I growl a little, it's easy to do that when I'm trying to talk, I can't help it. I growl and she cries. She looks young when she cries, like a young girl.

Oh what's the matter, sweetie, Abi says, May, you haven't been upsetting our summer bride, have you?

She gives me a really nasty look but with Jackie she's all tissues and kindness.

Go and have a lie down in your room, lovey, she says, May will be fine without you. I'm here now.

Jackie kisses me goodbye but she's sniffing, and I know

I've upset her. Upset her without even telling her the truth, it's unbearable.

I try not to cry out when Abi does my hair, pulling and twisting it into some kind of old lady ponytail.

Jackie is having pink extensions for the wedding, Abi says, no point in you being Mrs Jealousy now.

Bill looks in briefly while Abi is doing my hair. He's always popping in these days, even though I've tried to beg them to keep him away. It's as if the more I don't want him here the more he wants to come. Like a cat, he is, a sneaky nasty little creeping cat.

She's going off on one, Abi says, come and help me, Kelly. I can't cope when she goes all crazy.

I wasn't, I think, I was just laughing, that's not fair. I try not to cry. They don't like that either. It's always known as waterworks in here, never tears or sadness or crying, just waterworks. As if we were all on some giant Monopoly board. Waterworks. I used to like to buy up the utilities. No one else wanted them, that was the thing.

The only person here who can help me is Trevor. He understands about love and loss, he gets how I feel about Jackie and he understands me better than anyone. I didn't want to tell him about Bill being Alain. I didn't want to over burden him but I've got no choice now. Someone has to help me. I know he's a fragile little chap and the last thing I want to do is frighten him, but I have to tell someone else. I know he can't do anything, no one can unless Jackie knows and believes me. But someone needs to know.

He's there when they've finished doing my hair. Trevor, not Bill. I was looking down, trying not to cry when Abi scraped my hair back, and when I looked back up he was there.

Trevor, Abi says, well look who's come to see us.

He hasn't come to see you, I think, he's bloody well come to see me.

Always a pleasure, Abs, always a delight, Trevor says and he winks at me. I'm so relieved I nearly start blubbing again. Everything makes me cry these days. Trevor manages to make me feel dignified, as if he can see through to the old May underneath, the real person. He might be able to help.

He pats my hand. We'll have a chat in a minute dear, he says and for just a moment I think – let him come, the scary one. Let Bill poke his stupid ugly head round my door. I'm safe. It's how I used to feel with Helen, poor Helen.

They leave, finally, the carers. There's a whole lot of laughing and hilarity about what Trevor and I might get up to, when they've gone.

Don't you two do anything I wouldn't do, that sort of thing. They wouldn't say it if he wasn't gay, I'm sure they wouldn't.

I'd like to say I'm sorry but I can't so I do a kind of growly shrug. Trevor gets it immediately.

It's not your fault, dearie, he says, I've never been one to blame all the heteros. Some of my best friends are straight, he says and it makes him laugh a lot even though I can tell it's a well-worn joke.

So what's going on, my May, he says. He picks up my hand, the bad one, the one that stays in a claw, and he kisses it.

I don't like to see you like this, he says, you look very worried.

I shrug to show him I can't explain.

Well that's not good enough, he says, that won't do at all. Remember I've got experience in all this getting old stuff, I've been here before. Try to say the words, look my ears are out on stalks already. He points at his ears and it's true, they really do stick out and I can't help laughing.

That's better, he says, that's the May I like to see. When my Michael was, well, when he was at his worst, I used to think that if I made him laugh once a day I was doing OK. It wasn't always easy, he says and his face clouds over like there's a storm coming. Storm warning face, I'd like to say but that would be far too difficult. Trevor coughs that painful sounding cough again.

Michael, I say without thinking too much about it. It comes out well. Really well, and Trevor claps his hands and jumps up.

Oh listen to her, he says, as if there's a whole audience of people waiting by my bed, isn't she great, isn't she marvellous? I am so honoured that you said his name, Trevor says and I'm worried for a moment that he's going to cry. His eyes are definitely as sparkly as the hat he was wearing that first day.

If Michael was here, he says, he'd be very proud.

He sits there waiting, breathless from the coughing. It's like it used to be with the kids in my class, when they were sitting in the book corner waiting for a story. All expectant and looking up at you as if the story might just be the best thing they ever heard.

I shrug again. I'm over-using my shrugs but they seem to explain me best.

Go on, he says, I'm ready, give it a go, what have you got to lose?

I can't just sit there staring and I really do want to tell him so I open my mouth again to see what might come out. I suddenly remember all those years ago, wanting to tell someone about Earring Sue and not having the words. I try harder.

Jackie, I say.

No, he says, I didn't get that one, I don't know what you're saying.

I'm not sure if he's lying.

He looks sad though, sad and sorry for me.

You can't save the world, May, he says, talk to me about something nice.

No, I think, if I can't depend on you to help me, I don't want to say anything at all.

I'm sorry, May, he says, I'm sorry.

Jenny, I say. I didn't know I was going to say it until

I did. I wanted to talk about Jackie, only about Jackie, but I'm not sure if he wants to hear. I owe him, and to be honest I'm happy to stop worrying about her, even if it's only for a moment.

To me my 'Jenny' sounds like that dog they had on the TV, the one they taught to say, sausages, only it didn't sound like sausages it was just a grunt. I think I was right because he looks puzzled too, he clearly isn't sure what I said.

OK, he says, I'm going to guess, let me guess. Is it a person? I nod for yes.

I know it's not Jackie, he says, that's off limits, isn't it? Is it a person who lives here, he says and I shake my head.

Is it your daughter, he says and I nod so hard I wonder if my head might come loose and fly across the room.

What about your lovely daughter, he says, is she alright.

I nod again, and I point to my stomach with my good hand, then I make a cradling motion.

Oh my God, you're going to be a granny, he says, as if it is the most magnificent and unexpected thing, which I suppose it is.

You don't look old enough, he says and then he looks at me as if he's shocked at what he just said.

Don't worry, I want to say, it was a reflex, nothing more, I know you didn't mean it one way or the other. I sort through my repertoire of actions and decide the nearest match is a variation on the shrug, but with a smile and an open hand extended. I think he gets it.

I love babies, do you? Trevor says.

It's funny, I've been thinking about babies a lot since Jenny gave me her news but when Trevor says that I get a sudden picture of Jenny as a baby, as if I've only just understood. Jenny in the bath, Jenny in her little brown and yellow striped babygro, looking like a fat little wasp. Jenny when she had just been born, and she looked at me with those big worried eyes as if she wasn't sure whether this world was a place she wanted to stay in. Jenny and Seb leaning into each other on the sofa so that we could take a photo, that time Helen came to stay in the little flat in Pimlico. He was nearly as big as her, but she looked so much more grown up. Three months makes such a difference at that age.

Hey, hey, says Trevor, don't get upset, look, here's a tissue.

He makes a clumsy attempt to wipe my face. It's such a kind thing, touching an old person like me with my disgusting bits and pieces.

Maybe they'll call it Trevor, he says.

It's an attempt to lighten the atmosphere and I'm very grateful. And it's funny as well, the thought of Jenny choosing a name like Trevor.

Go on, he says, tell me what names they're thinking of, see if I can understand you.

OK, I say before I've even realised that I'm saying it.

Fortitude, I say. It's a hard word to say and a hard word to guess so I'm not surprised when Trevor looks dumbfounded.

Sugarhead? he says, sausages? Am I anywhere near?

We'll have to stop this, I think, the mention of sausages was too much, I'm going to have a little accident. He hands me my writing pad and I write it down, Fortitude. I show him. One thing about Trevor, he can do a good reaction.

He looks from me to the pad and back again, opening and closing his mouth like a fish. I'm not sure why, but it hadn't struck me until then just how funny the name was. Fortitude. I'd been so busy trying to accept Jenny's choice without comment or opinion that I'd forgotten to notice what a damn silly name it was.

Fortitude, Trevor says again and then he starts to laugh and I can't help joining in. He laughs hard, slapping his thighs and throwing his head back – the whole works. Every time he comes up for air he gasps, Fortitude, and collapses again. He's right, it's a ridiculous name, poor little baby.

You're a one, May, I can't believe you told me that with a straight face, he says finally. I'm assuming that's the name if they have a boy, right?

I shake my head. Both, I try to say.

That sets him off again. Poor little love, he says, tell me she won't go through with it.

Time for another shrug, just the right response this time. I really don't know if she'll go through with it, I have no idea, really, who my grown up daughter is, or what makes her tick. I wonder if other parents feel the same, or whether most mums would know for sure what their grown up children would do next.

Ah bless her, Trevor says, I bet it'll be different when she has the little one in her arms. She'll think differently then. She'll probably call it the most normal name in the world, Doris or Doug or something.

I nod. I think he's probably right.

Wise, I try to say. I tap my head at the same time to show what I mean.

Oh we're all wise as we get older dear, Trevor says, I think I would have made a good father. I wouldn't have minded at all whether it was a girl or a boy. I would have called it Arthur or Bella I think. Maybe Matilda, like in that film.

I nod to show that I think they are lovely names.

Did you want a boy, dear? Trevor asks.

I have to think for a moment, to try to give him an honest answer. I enjoyed the little lads in my class, but a boy in the house? I wasn't sure. I grab the pad with my good hand. Boys need a man, I wrote. I can't understand why I can write so much more clearly when Trevor is with me. He's a calming influence.

True, says Trevor, very true my dear. So why didn't you have a man? They're not too rare, except for in here, he says.

I'm trying to think quickly, but I can feel the old cogs turning too slowly. I'll never get a better chance to explain to him what's happened in my life. I look at him, sitting there so expectantly, as if he's going to be told a story. He thinks it's all in the past, the bad stuff, he doesn't know that there's bad stuff aplenty waiting in here, in this nursing home. Do I really want to drag him into it, I think. He's been through a lot, and the last thing he needs is to have his nose rubbed in the nastiness and violence that is Bill, aka Alain.

It's alright, he says as if he can read my thoughts, you don't have to protect me, I can see that maternal look all over your face. I'm a big boy, you know.

We both laugh. He's tiny, Trevor, but somehow he's convinced me that I can talk to him, he's got a big heart and that's what matters. In fact in my mind he's a towering giant of a man and I wish I could tell him.

You're big to me, I write then I blush like a fourteen year old.

Ooh, Trevor says. He claps his hands, ooh that's the nicest thing almost ever. Give us a kiss, my Mayflower.

He leans in and kisses me on the cheek and I wish for a moment that I was wearing nice earrings, ones that belonged to me and perfume, expensive stuff with a classy smell. I don't even have nice soap any more, just the anti-bacterial stuff that smells of operating theatres. I motion for him to give me my writing pad back.

Beware Bill, I write.

He starts to laugh, as if I've written a joke but when he looks at my face he can't help realising that I'm very serious.

He's alright, Trevor says, nutty as an Easter cake but harmless, surely?

323

I shake my head as vehemently as I can, and make a sign with my hands that I think means finished.

OK, OK, I can see you're serious, May, tell me more.

I'm in trouble, I write but that's not the right thing, that's not what I meant to write and it's nearly too late because my hand is feeling tired, it's like a dead weight. I try to write again but all I write is, Bill.

OK, OK, let me guess a bit, give you a break, says Trevor and it's as though all the laughter has gone from his voice. I'm sorry to be the one that made the laughter go away and that makes me even more angry.

You don't want him to marry your lovely friend and lurch off into the sunset? Trevor says. He coughs.

I write, more.

What can it be, merry May, let me have a proper think. I've watched a lot of detective films on TV and I should be good at this.

I think as hard and as quickly as my poor old brain will allow me to. I've probably got half a dozen words left in my hand, less if they're long ones. I need to use them sparingly and carefully in order to give Trevor the maximum information. He deserves that.

I steady the writing pad and flex my fingers. They don't move much.

It's OK, May, says Trevor, don't worry on my account.

I nearly stop then, give up altogether. It would be so nice not to have to worry about it any more. I think for a moment of the lists of stupid on the walls, on every wall by the end, every damn thing I'd done or said inscribed there for me to look at every day. I couldn't invite anyone in. He wouldn't let me take them down.

You need these lists, silly May, Alain had said, to stop you from being stupid next time.

I realise that Trevor is speaking to me.

Earth to May, earth to May, he says, trying to lighten the atmosphere, honest you don't have to tell me anything else if you don't want to. We can talk about music or books or dancing, happy smiley things.

He sounds breathless, as if he's been running. I smile my lopsided smile at him and I have to hope that it's enough to explain that I'd like to do as he suggests but I have to share, I've got to tell him, someone other than me has to know.

Bill = my ex, danger J.

That's all I manage and I'm sweating by the end, I need to lie down.

Trevor looks at it and his eyes widen. I always said he was good at reactions.

No, he says, no, really?

I nod as vigorously as I can manage.

True, I say, or something that sounds enough like true to get my point across.

So you're worried about Jackie, he says, sounding out the words slowly so that I can hear the thought process, and a little bit worried about yourself too?

I nod again. I'm just like the other old people, a little

nodding dog from the back of a car. Nodding because they can't help it.

Oh, Trevor says, oh maybe we should tell her, tell Jackie.

I'm so grateful that he believes me, just like that, no subsidiary questions asked, that I start to cry. Bloody stupid old people's tears.

There there, he says, it's OK, I won't let him hurt you. He wants to say more but that cough comes back.

It's no good, we both know that.

He can't help me now.

CHAPTER TWENTY-TWO

June 1978
Pimlico

It didn't happen the first night May bled, or the second or third. She bled on and off for another couple of weeks before she miscarried.

They carried her on a stretcher out of the flat and through a slice of warm night into the ambulance. May could think only of Jenny, and she lifted her head to see her, hoping she was asleep. There was an ambulance ride and then the lovely doctor, looking like a student with her long curly hair and her ankle-length skirt. May wasn't even sure that she was a real doctor until she gave her the news about the baby, that the baby was definitely gone. May waited for the sadness but all she could feel was guilt, terrible searing guilt.

'I didn't want another baby, not really,' May said to the doctor. 'I had enough to do with one, I'm not very good at this mothering thing, I'm not sure I could have coped with two. But I didn't want her to die, I didn't, honest.'

'Of course you didn't,' said the doctor. 'You would have managed just fine. You look like the coping type to me.'

May thought about those words often in the days to come. She wondered if the doctor had meant it. The coping type. It was a lovely thing to say, even if the doctor had only said it to be kind.

'Is there anything you want to tell me?' the doctor said. 'Only I'm not happy about the bruises all over your body, some of them old and some of them new. And you've got a black eye, are you even aware of that?'

May hadn't been aware of that but she touched her eye now and could feel how sore it was.

'No,' she said, 'no, but I'm always falling over things. I've got big feet. I'm very clumsy.'

May knew that the doctor didn't believe her but she didn't have the energy to be more creative. She was too tired.

'There's a place,' the doctor said, 'where you could be safe. There's a woman who has set up a safe space for women like you, a place where you can go and live with your children and be safe.'

'Battered wives,' May said. 'I've read about that. That's not me, honestly.'

It wasn't a lie, she thought, not really. Those other women she had read about, they were different from her. It's not snobbery, May wanted to explain, please don't think that. The doctor looked at her so kindly that May wished she could tell her what she was thinking.

I'm not saying I'm different because I've been beaten for saying that *The Great Gatsby* seemed shallow, she thought, or because he once hit me over the head with a heavy second-hand volume of Proust. That's not it at all. The men who beat them were cruel and violent and May felt so, so sorry for them but it wasn't the same as her situation at all. Her Alain was different. He didn't mean it, he didn't want to hurt her, it was just that she was so difficult, so hard to live with. He hated hurting her, he always cried afterwards. He'd read Germaine Greer, he knitted small dolls.

'Your nose,' the doctor said, 'was that broken recently?'

May felt sorry for the doctor. She was young, and worried in case she said the wrong thing. It was obvious, May could see it in the way the doctor nibbled her thumbnail and flicked some invisible dust from her cheek. May wished that she could tell her she was right. She imagined what she might say, and how pleased the doctor would be that she could help, even what the hostel might be like. Full of lovely women like Helen, perhaps, babies like Jenny and Seb.

A thought pushed at the back of May's head. Her daughter. Her Jenny. What about Jenny? Didn't Jenny deserve some peace? It wasn't her fault that she had an idiot for a mother. She could have had a happy mother with a bunch of children and a kindly husband, May thought. There might have been a gentle dog and trips to the seaside where she could lie on a rug kicking her legs. Poor Jenny.

Poor Jenny with May for a mother and Alain for a father, born into a world of fear and shouting. Poor Jenny who had learned to be frightened before she understood what it meant.

The doctor was waiting, looking at May with compassion, giving her time to think it through and change her mind. May was tempted. She could almost hear the chattering and the laughter of the other woman as they cooked supper together while the babies crawled around their feet. She wanted to say yes, please help me. She wanted to give the responsibility for her miserable life to someone else, she knew they couldn't make a worse job of it than she had. May was so close to saying yes that her mouth had opened to say the word when she looked up and saw him standing outside the door of her single room.

She looked at the clock. Four o'clock, visiting time and there was Alain, prompt and smiling at the window. The doctor looked in the same direction as May.

'Look,' she said in a whisper so quiet that May had to strain to hear it, 'you don't have to have any visitors you don't want, you know, I can send him away. I have doctor superpowers.'

She pointed to her stethoscope and smiled, and May loved her for making a little joke in such a dark place.

It was tempting, so tempting. Go on, May told herself, say something. Tell her. She looked up at the window. Alain had a crocodile hand puppet, and he was making it yawn and cry and clap, there in the window. To cheer me up, she thought, come on, May. He really isn't that bad. But Seb, a voice said, think of Seb. Think of Jenny, and how dangerous Alain could be if he was thwarted. The thought of the happy, cooking women disappeared, and instead she imagined the women frightened, hiding in their rooms because May's husband had found where they were. May had put them all in danger. It's my danger, she thought, it's all mine. I can't inflict it on anyone else. I got myself and my baby into this and I'll bloody well get us out.

'It's fine,' May said to the doctor. 'It's OK, honestly, it's not what you think, I'll be OK. I broke my nose years ago, playing hockey. We'll be OK.'

She tried to make her voice as hearty and believable as she could but it was clear that the doctor knew. She really knew.

The doctor looked at Alain outside the door and then back to May.

'Just ask for me if you want to talk again,' she said. 'Good luck.'

May felt bereft when the doctor left. She lay back on her pillows and stared at Alain.

'You poor darling,' he said, as the crocodile puppet on his hand held out a bunch of wilting flowers. 'Was it very painful?'

'Where have you been?' said May, brave now that she was in the hospital. He wouldn't hurt her here, there were people constantly walking up and down past her room and coming in to check on her.

'Only I thought you'd be right behind me in the ambulance, I thought you would bring Jenny. Is she OK?'

'That's a lot of thoughts for one person to have,' said Alain. 'I'm so sorry you were worried, darling. I couldn't get here straight away, I had to find someone to take Jenny and I wasn't sure, I tried a couple of people from school but they weren't in and then I thought of Joan, you know, in the flat across the hall. I had to wait for her to come home. Sorry about that, but I couldn't help it and I knew you were in good hands.'

May looked at him. There was something wrong with his story but she wasn't sure what. Sue, she thought, if my baby is with Sue, whoever she is, I will kill myself. She imagined Sue ignoring Jenny's cries or worse, and she tried to get out of bed.

Alain looked alarmed.

'What are you doing?' he said. 'Get back in, she's fine, Jenny is fine, I promise.'

'She's with Joan from upstairs, yes?' May said. 'Promise me, Alain, promise me.'

'Where's your merriness, May?' Alain said. 'Of course she's at Joan's. I said she was. Joan seemed quite pleased, actually.'

Alain looked at the ground like a child who had been caught out, and May wondered what else he hadn't told her.

'There's no baby, Al,' May said. 'It definitely happened this time. Jenny isn't going to be a big sister.' As she said it, May began to cry, and she realised that she was a lot sadder than she had realised. It was as though her emotions had undergone a local anaesthetic and the feeling was just starting to come back.

'Oh darling,' Alain said. He put the crocodile glove puppet neatly on May's bed, head turned to the side. 'I'm so sorry, I was looking forward to meeting her.'

'Him,' said May. 'It was a little boy, Al, a little brother for Jenny. They can tell that, you know, when you're this far along. Fourteen weeks at least, Al, past the danger stage.'

'A boy,' Al said, 'imagine that.'

'And past the danger stage, too,' May said again. 'What do you think happened?'

Alain wiped his eyes and stared at her.

'What do you mean?' he said. 'I know you've had a hard time, but I hope you're not implying what I think you might be implying. Be careful what you say, my love.'

A nurse bustled past the open doorway carrying a tray and May reckoned she was still OK. He can't do anything here, she thought.

'I can't pretend it isn't happening, Alain,' May said. 'I know you're a good person and you don't mean to hurt me but…' May trailed off as she saw the absolute indignation on Alain's face.

'Me,' he said, 'me hurt you? I don't know what you're talking about. Listen, May, you've had a nasty shock, a horrible experience and I get that, I really do. But I've been wondering, I've read some stuff about childhood trauma, and I'm wondering, do you think something bad happened in your childhood? Something that would make you, sort of, unable to function properly in adult relationships?'

May could feel the tears coming and she willed them back up her tear ducts to wherever they had come from. This was no time for weakness. She couldn't believe he had said that, that he had made it all her fault. It was outrageous. A tiny part of her stood back, watching what was going on. Of course, the tiny part of her said, what did you think he was going to do, roll over? Guys like him don't do that. Guys like him plan, and think, and make damn sure that no one catches them.

May pulled up her sleeve, and held her arm out towards him. There were three bruises on her forearm in three different shades varying from almost black to greenish yellow.

'What about this?' May said.

'Oh May,' Alain said, 'do you really want to do this now? What about this?'

Alain pulled up his right trouser leg and May gasped. It was where she had scratched him, but so much worse. He must have used a razor or a very sharp knife. There were cuts, gouges, some of them still oozing blood and some looking infected. There was no way she could have done this with just the nails on her hand.

'Do you need to see the injuries on my other leg?' Alain said. 'I'll show you if you want.'

May felt so tired. She had imagined Alain reacting in different ways but never this. He had won this round too, and she wanted to leave the fight.

'Only the thing is,' Alain said, 'I took a bit of advice,

you know, just to protect myself, and apparently this,' he pointed to his leg, 'this is enough to get me custody of Jenny, probably. If I thought it wasn't safe to leave her with you.' He smiled and reached for May's hand. 'It won't come to that, my darling, will it? I want us to live as a family, I'll help you with your anger.'

May lay back against the pillows. So this is how it goes, she thought. I grabbed my chance and he was ready, he's always going to win. I'm going to be frightened for ever.

'So put your bruises away, my dear,' said Alain, 'or I'll tell the nice doctor how you got them, and what you were trying to do to me when I managed to hold you off. You look pale. Are you delirious or something?'

May stared at him. She had nothing left to say. She could tell he was agitated. He kept looking towards the door and licking his lips as if his mouth was very dry.

'Look, love,' he said. He stood up and bent over to kiss May's head. She could smell something chemical and unpleasant. She shrank away from his touch.

'I won't tell anyone, May, you know I won't. I want you to be there for Jenny, you're her mum. I've had some problems, I won't deny that. And sometimes I've shouted a bit, thrown things about, I'm ashamed of all that. I never should have done it, not with darling baby Jenny there and everything. But I would never hurt you, May, you know that. I had to defend myself, my darling. I know sometimes you fall, you're clumsy, and you want someone to blame. And sorry, there's no easy way to say this, but

335

have you ever thought that a responsible mother would see someone? That your version of what's going on may be very real to you, I'm not denying that, very real, but maybe it's not what actually happened? I've been reading a lot about delayed childhood trauma and it's not uncommon, May, you're not on your own.'

Alain looked at May as if he had said something important, monumental even. She tried to understand what was going on. It didn't seem completely possible, but despite that she wasn't surprised.

'Self-harming, I think they call it. I've researched it, it's not that uncommon in cases like yours, honest. Apparently the first thing to do is to go to your GP and ask for a referral to a psychiatrist. May, think about it, you could get better, think how wonderful that would be?'

Alain grabbed May's hands and stared into her eyes as if he was rehearsing for a Disney movie. Any minute now, May thought, he'll be covered in tiny cartoon birds and there will be music in the background. The thought made her laugh, she couldn't help it. She pulled her hands back from his to cover her mouth.

'May,' Alain said, 'May stop it, you're hysterical. Shall I call the nurse? This is exactly the kind of behaviour I've been worrying about. Calm down.'

May stopped straight away. She felt as if a bucket of cold water had been tipped over her head. Of course. This was his plan, she had to make sure that she didn't play into his hands in any way.

'I'm sorry,' she said, 'it really isn't funny, I know that. But, Alain, you and I both know the truth. It isn't me, I didn't have a childhood trauma, and if you did, well we can work on that. But I'm tired, Al, leave me alone.'

'Exactly,' Al said, as if May had said something else altogether. 'Exactly, you can't even remember the trauma, that's how deeply ingrained it is. You need help, May.'

Alain stroked May's forearm where the bruises were. She flinched, and pulled her arm back.

'Go away, please, Al. Just go away and leave me alone. I'm sad, I'm ill, I just lost a baby but I'm not crazy. Just go.'

'Think about it, that's all I'm asking. Just think about it, I could help, all this,' Alain pointed to May's arm, 'all this could go away. We could be happy. We could have more babies, a football team of babies if you want. Just think about it.'

May thought that she must be going mad, she must be, it wasn't possible that he could talk with such passion and enthusiasm about their impossible future.

'Bye-bye,' Alain said, 'bye-bye, I'll go and get Jenny now. Don't worry,' his voice moved to a stage whisper, 'I won't tell anyone about this.' He tapped his trouser leg. 'It'll be our little secret,' he said.

There was more than a hint of triumph in his voice.

'One more thing,' Alain said when he got to the door. 'I don't want you to worry about Jenny at all. Not at all. If you're not well, if you're not up to looking after her, that's just fine by me. I can do it. I'll keep her safe, you needn't worry your head about that for one moment. I'll look after our little girl for you.'

May sat up in bed, wincing at the pain in her back.

'No,' she said, 'no, Al, I'm fine, I'll be out tomorrow, just leave her with Joan and tell her and I'll be fine to look after Jenny tomorrow. I'm OK, honestly.'

'Let's see how it goes,' said Alain.

His voice sounded thoughtful, even caring, but his mouth was grinning like a Halloween skull mask.

'Please,' May said.

Alain held up the crocodile glove puppet on his hand, wiggled his hands to make the puppet wave goodbye and left the room.

May sat still in bed, trying to control her breathing, trying not to gasp or cry out. She had to process what had happened. It was a declaration of war, that was obvious. He was challenging her to a fight over who would look after Jenny, now that their relationship was on the rocks. Any thoughts May might have had of rescuing Jenny, going off to start a new, safe life with her, she could forget them. He wasn't going to let it happen. May felt terrified. She was crying when the doctor put her head round the door.

'Do you mind if I come in?' she said. 'Only I heard some of that. Not eavesdropping or anything, just doing my job. He's got a loud voice.'

'No,' said May, 'come in, but there's nothing you can do, if that's what you were thinking.'

'May, I haven't met you before today, but I can tell

338

you something absolutely definitely. You didn't harm yourself, May. You have bruises – don't forget I've seen you undressed – you have bruises in places you couldn't possibly reach. And unless you want to tell me otherwise, I don't think you have any kind of balance problem. That means someone else did it to you, May, and I'm guessing it's your husband. Now not every doctor will agree with me, there's some really stuffy old ones in this profession. But if you want to prosecute, go to a safe place, I'll support you. Think about it, May.'

May felt too ashamed even to thank the doctor. She just wanted her to go, leave her alone, let her make a plan of her own. One that didn't involve persuading anyone that her husband beat her, that didn't involve people not believing her and ridiculing her story. He was so articulate. He had been to the same sort of school as the lawyers and the doctors and he could speak their language. Even with the help of the lovely junior doctor, May knew that she didn't stand a chance. Most people thought it was OK for a husband to hit his wife, and they certainly would once Alain talked about extreme provocation. If she lost, if she said all those things in a court so that everyone could hear how stupid she was, how pathetic, she might not even be allowed to keep her own baby, her own Jenny.

'It's OK,' May said to the doctor, 'it's OK, I don't need any help, thank you though. I'll be fine. I've got a plan.'

CHAPTER TWENTY-THREE

August 2018
Lewisham

It's hot in here, like a sauna or a front room full of family on Christmas Day.

I can't believe the radiators aren't on. I'd go and check them if I could. Maybe I can reach my hand out and check next time they wheel me past, make a complaint if they're on. I don't get to walk around much any more, I haven't got any mobility in this heat. My feet seem to have swollen to the size of clown's feet, I can't get them cool. I'm having trouble even feeding myself, all my movements seem to be bigger than I meant them to be. I can't believe I ever managed to draw those screwdrivers. Yesterday I knocked over three things, a jug of water, a glass of Ribena and a sandwich I was trying to pick up. It must be the heat. It's been hot for days now and the rabbits outside that I used to watch from my window are very still. They sit under the hedge and only come out in the evening, sometimes not even then. Hull never had summers like this.

Everyone in the gravy boat seems listless, as if things are too much bother. Spilt drinks stay spilt for hours and twice I've had an accident waiting for them to answer my buzzer and come to take me to the toilet. This nursing home is not built for heat.

Jenny is finding it hard. It's not surprising. She's almost forty-one, overweight and married to a borderline paedophile, what does she expect? He's not one of those, Mum, she always says, they got it wrong, honestly. I can't see how she can swallow that but it's not really my business and anyway, I should know better than anyone that a baby isn't necessarily fifty per cent made of its father. Or mother really, some babies are just themselves from the word go. I think Seb would have been like that. His own person.

Jenny came in to see me yesterday so I'm surprised to see her here again today.

You be careful, rest up a bit, that's what I'd like to tell her. Instead I make worried, clucking noises, smoothing the air with my good hand. I think she gets it.

I was just thinking about you, she said, in this heat. I thought maybe you could use a bit of company.

Hot, I manage to say.

I'm ridiculously pleased with myself.

Yes, she says, not hot by Mediterranean standards, but for Lewisham it's something else.

I point to her tummy and hope she'll understand that I'm worried about the baby.

Don't you worry about this one, she says, patting herself, she likes the warmth. Oh, and did I tell you, I'm not so sure about Fortitude any more, I mean Dan likes it, but I'm worried about her being called Tit, or Titty.

That would be the least of her problems, I'd say if I could. Instead I arrange my face into a quizzical expression.

Charity, Jenny says, Charity if she is a girl, and maybe Finch for a boy. Or Story for either. I like names that are also nouns, do you?

Knife, I think, fork, table, bottom, ladle, toilet. Where on earth do you stop once you start that stuff? I turn my face into a kind of interested non-committal vacuum.

Mum, Jenny says, now I'm pregnant I've been wondering about my dad. What he was like, if he was excited when I was coming, that sort of stuff. I have that picture of him, the one from just before he, you know, before it happened.

It's all a blur to me, that time, I think. It's not a lie, I can hardly remember a thing except the bad bits but this lovely dumpy grown child of mine does not need to hear that.

One thing I do remember, though, and I try to get it across to her.

Pooh, I say, Pooh. I push the other memory away, the headless, legless animals, the look in his eyes when he got hold of the scissors.

Oh, she says, you're talking about my knitted Pooh

animals. I'd forgotten them. He made them, didn't he. I always wondered where Eeyore went but I had the others. And the families, the sharks and the hedgehogs. Did he make them for me when I was a baby?

I nod. I'm glad I can't speak, glad I can't spoil it for her.

Oh it's so nice being able to talk about this stuff with you, Mum, I love it, Jenny says. There's a tear in my eye, and it's all I can do not to blubber. Waterworks. Jenny looks embarrassed and I think about how I can shift the mood.

Jackie, I try to say with a shrug, as if I'm only a little bit interested in whether Jenny has seen her or heard from her recently. Just a little bit, just making conversation. Something's up though, I can tell that straight away. She shifts in her chair. She's a big girl, my Jenny, a big girl with big feet. She can't shift gracefully so I can hardly miss it.

Jackie? she says. I can tell she's aiming for nonchalant, that she wants me to think that there's nothing up at all, and this makes me nervous. I nod, yes, Jackie.

Well I don't know, I'm not sure, I haven't seen her, Jenny says. She's fiddling with the clasp on her bag as if she has been given thirty seconds to fix it or the world will blow up. I stare. I'm sorry to do this, it's not that I want to make Jenny feel uncomfortable or anything but the thing is that I haven't seen her for a couple of days either, and that's unusual. I grab my pad.

Is she ill? I write, because that's what I've been thinking, that's what I've been worrying about.

No, no, I'm sure she's fine, Jenny says but she's not meeting my eye when she says it so I feel really weird and sweaty and I wonder if it's going to happen again, the stroke thing. I think it might have felt a little like this before.

Mum, says Jenny, are you OK, don't worry, let me get you some water, sit still.

That one makes me laugh. Sit still. As if.

Phew, she says, glad to see you're smiling. I thought you were having a funny turn then.

That makes me laugh as well, a funny turn, I imagine a comedian on the stage, taking a bow and turning around, saying, never mind me, dears, I'm having a funny turn. Trevor would like that, I think, he likes a laugh.

Jackie, Jenny says and I switch off the laughter as quick as a light switch. Jackie is erm, she's, well I'm sorry and I know you'll be sad but she's getting married today, at the register office, that's partly why I came, they haven't invited anyone, not any of the carers or anything, well maybe one to help Bill because he's not steady on his feet, you know that. They weren't leaving you out, she says, all sympathetic and nice, Jackie would have loved to invite you but it's Bill, he doesn't have any family and she didn't want him to feel different, you know how kind she is. They decided against the whole maid of honour thing, probably very sensible.

Today, I think, today of all days. Today, and she never even told me, didn't say a word. He is bloody different, I'll say he is, and he does have family, I think, he bloody does, I'm his bloody wife aren't I? Another thing, I told her I wouldn't go, she didn't leave me out. Get it right. There's no way I can explain this to Jenny, no way that won't upset her. No, I can't say anything, I think, I can't speak but I'll do something, I know that. I can't let it go. I imagine Jackie, her lovely locks torn out or hacked off with scissors. It doesn't make me happy and I remember reading somewhere, back in the days when we thought we'd invented feminism and that it was going to change everything, an article called, 'Don't blame your sisters', and I'm sorry. I'm really sorry and in my mind I reattach Jackie's locks, every single one of them and I apologise.

It's not your fault, I'd say to Jackie if she was here now, I'm sorry if I ever thought it was. It's him, Bill or Alain or whatever it is he's calling himself today. I wonder for a moment just how many names he's been through in his life. He probably answers to anything and everything, I wouldn't be surprised.

Mum, says Jenny, are you OK, would you like to play scrabble, I'm sorry if you're sad.

She deserves better, I think, that girl of mine, a better mum and certainly a better grandma for that little baby, Tree or Writing Desk or whatever it is they're going to call her. Or him. I make an attempt at a smile. Even if I could talk, I wouldn't tell Jenny all of it. There's so much she doesn't need to know. I mime at her that I'm tired, putting my head towards my shoulder like babies do when they want to sleep. She doesn't look too disappointed.

I hate scrabble anyway, it always reminds me of him, Alain, when we were young and Jenny was in her cot. Such a minefield it was. I trained myself to put down my second choice of words, always my second choice, so that my score wouldn't be too high. It didn't do to be competitive with him, always got him mad. I remember one time he accused me of 'closing off the board' as if that wasn't the aim of the game. He upturned the whole thing and made me eat one of the tiles. No more scrabble, Jenny.

Would you like to sleep, Mum, Jenny says, shall I leave you so that you can rest.

I'm torn. I'm a lonely old woman, I would like to shout, don't leave me here, all on my own. I don't, of course. Those kind of thoughts are always better kept inside.

You go, I try to say. It comes out more like, go, and I can see that Jenny is hurt but I can't help that, I can't explain it away or make it better. She'll have to manage on her own now.

She bends to kiss me and I get a pang, one of those feelings of sadness that come on suddenly, an emotional heart attack. If I wasn't so damn sensible I might mistake it for a premonition, it's that strong.

Jenny, I say into her neck. She seems to understand, she's very empathetic, my girl.

Mum, she says, it'll be alright, don't worry.

I'm a mess for a while after she's gone. Crying, snuffling, that sort of thing. I can't reach the tissues so I have to stop in the end or I'll have no sleeve left. I can't be doing that when Jackie will probably drop by in her wedding finery. I try to sort my hair out with one hand, tidy myself up as much as I can. She'll probably want a photo with me. I'm sure she will, seeing as I couldn't go. I don't want to let the side down too much, I've got to look respectable. I'm just wondering whether to ask the carers to change my top for the one I wore at Christmas, the glittery one, when there's a soft knock on the door and it's Trevor. I haven't seen him much since I told him what I told him. I thought maybe that when he went away and ruminated on it, he might have decided I was bonkers. I wouldn't blame him.

Hey, he says, my favourite girl, and as soon as I look at him I can see that he's been ill.

I haven't been too well, he says, I've got to have some bits and pieces done to my bits and pieces.

What, I say.

He understands that it's a wider question.

Well, he says, and he starts counting on his fingers.

I can see what he must have been like when he was a little lad.

One, I've got lots of fluid on my lungs, that's why I'm breathless all the time apparently, he says.

I can hear how breathless he is now.

I thought, he says, I thought it was because I'm just so excited all the time, that was why I couldn't get my breath, but apparently, would you believe it, he stops for a wheeze, apparently it's something to do with smoking for fifty years.

I try not to look too horrified but it's difficult. Trevor seems to have shrunk somehow, folded in on himself.

Who knew, he says in a jolly and raspy voice, who on earth knew that smoking was bad for you? I'm sure no one told me.

This makes him laugh so much that he starts coughing and can't get his breath. It's like a cough of death, a cough that starts somewhere in the body it should never be. I can't do anything, I have to sit and not watch and pretend everything is normal. When did it get this bad? How could I not have noticed?

Two, he says when he's finished coughing, two I need to have a little op to drain the fluid. Then they're going to test it to make sure it's nothing nasty. I suppose that's three.

I know I won't be able to get any words out so I hold my hand up instead in a kind of, what the hell, motion.

I may be dying, dear, Trevor says, but I'm damned well going to do it in a stylish way. Dying of Gauloises, would you Adam and Eve it? I thought smoking was a good hobby, kept me off the streets.

I can see in his eyes that he's putting on a brave show but he doesn't really mean any of it. He's frightened and I'd like to get out of this bloody chair and give him a hug but I can't. I think he knows.

Honest, don't worry about me, dear, he says, I've had a longer innings than most of my *compadres*. I've outlived nearly all of the clever ones, the pretty ones, the wild ones, I'm not going to complain that it's my time. I'm not going to have chemo, and go through all that indignity, ooh, none of that, dear. What on earth would happen if I lost my hair?

He smooths his hand over his head and I can't help laughing, because of course he hasn't got any hair, hardly a single one on his whole head.

Now, he says, let's talk about more important stuff. The fairy queen has married the wicked, wicked prince today, am I right?

I nod.

And we haven't managed to tell her, warn her off, in any way at all?

I shake my head.

Blimey, he says, we are in a pickle.

I adore that he says, we. I can manage anything with him, I think, anything at all.

Does she really need to know, he says through a cough.

I nod, trying to make it as emphatic as I can. Of course she needs to know, I want to say, he might hurt her.

OK, he says, is he really a bad 'un, May, only he looks a bit simple to me, a silly sad old man.

Another nod, so hard my neck hurts. I grab my pen and try to write, violent, only my hand won't work properly after the vio part. Trevor gets it anyway.

Well I've seen a lot of things, dear, he says, and one thing I know for certain is, leopards don't change their spots.

He looks so tired, Trevor, so tired and ill. I can see him squaring his shoulders, trying to make himself ready for the fray and I'm so sorry that I brought this into his life, sorry and angry with Bill for popping up again when I thought he was done with.

I'll do it, he says, I'll tell her, better late than never. It's got to be done. She comes to see me sometimes, when I'm not well, I'll make sure I'm in my room tomorrow and she'll come then. Don't worry. They're not going on a honeymoon or anything are they?

I shrug. I have no idea. My best friend, and I don't even know if she's going on a honeymoon. She should have told me. That's what friends are for.

Trevor starts coughing again and I feel guilty.

S'OK, I manage to say. I'm so surprised that it came out OK that I say it again, s'OK. I make a motion to go with it, a go away, be gone motion with my good hand. It comes out much wider than I intended and I knock over the water jug, which drenches Trevor's trousers on the way to the floor.

I shriek a bit, my nerves are jangled and I'm very sorry to have done that to Trevor but he says he's OK, says it doesn't matter but he has to go and change and I'm sorry to see him go. We haven't even made a proper plan yet.

Bye-bye dear, he says, I've got to go and change or people will think I didn't get to the little boys' room on time.

Agnita comes in then. We've never really got a great friendship going, me and Agnita. I try, no one can say I don't try, but she seems to be set against me in some ways. I don't think she likes me, and that's OK, no one can like everyone, can they? It's just that if you're stuck in here like I am and your only contact sometimes is your mentor friend, it's hard when that mentor friend thinks that you're a pile of shite. There really isn't any other way to put it.

Oh dear, she says, have we had another accident.

It's hard to think of what to say, especially when you can't speak. Best just to stay quiet, I think.

The thing about friends is, she says, we must be happy for our friends when they're happy. Envy is a terrible thing now May.

I'm puzzled for a moment and then I realise, she thinks I splashed the water on purpose because Jackie got married. The thought of it makes me laugh out loud. As if. If I wanted to protest, I think, you'd know all about it, so don't you worry your little head about that. There's nothing I can do though, I can't tell her she's wrong, or show her that I'm a nice person really or anything. All I can do is sit there and go limp, so that I don't help her in any way to clean up. I don't even lift my arm or my leg.

Jackie is happy, Agnita says in a sing-song voice, like she's telling me a fairy story. Don't you know that fairy stories have wicked trolls in them, I think. I think it so hard that I make a noise, a noise like a troll.

None of that now, Agnita says in her soft accent, you just be glad for her. She hasn't had an easy life.

I'm getting so angry here I could burst. Easy life. Who the hell has had an easy life, and what's that got to do with anything. I can see that I'll get no help at all from Agnita, even though she's supposed to be the person I can talk to. If I told Agnita that Jackie has actually got herself shackled to a bigamist, a wife batterer, a violent and unpredictable man she'd say, now now, no need for that sort of nonsense. I know she would.

He may not be George Clooney, Agnita says, but they're happy, and that's worth something at any time of life.

I'm more miserable than ever when Agnita has gone. At least I don't have to listen to her words of wisdom any more, all that stuff about how good friends are like rare pebbles on the beach or gold to a gold miner or something. She gets her metaphors mixed as well as having crap judgement about people, that's for sure. But sometimes having someone to talk to, even if they talk rubbish, is better than having no one to talk to at all. Especially if you can't talk.

I'm sitting on my own in my room, feeling hot and waiting for the sun to go down. And for Jackie to come to see me, maybe take some wedding day pictures together, girly ones without him in them at all. I can't settle and I get this feeling that something is going to happen, like the feeling in the air before a storm. Maybe that's it, I think, this is a storm warning, nothing more, and I look out of my window again at the rabbits.

When I turn back into the room he's there. Bill. Alain. The old man. The husband.

Hello, he says, did you hear my news.

I grope for my buzzer. It's usually round my neck but Agnita took it off when she was sorting me out and we both forgot to put it back. I can see it on the table over my bed. Bill can see it too.

Lovely news, he says, I've gone and got wed.

I don't say anything. I keep looking at the door as if that will make Jackie appear.

Never too late, he says, aren't you going to congratulate me.

There's a smirk on his face and a tilt to his head that I don't like. I recognise them, but I don't like them one bit.

I point to my mouth, shaking my head to remind him I can't speak but it's as if he never knew that.

Speak up, he says, I can't hear you. He's laughing as he says it and I can feel a familiar knot of fear, deep down where it always used to live. You can live most of your life thinking I'd gone, the fear thing says, but I was here all along, waiting for you. How do you like that?

I try to say, Jackie. In a questioning tone, keeping things light.

Sorry, he says, haven't got a clue what you're saying. Poor old dear. I probably shouldn't have come, but Jackie's tired and I thought you'd want to know our news. I'd have been in time to see your lovely daughter if I'd been a bit quicker, that's always a bonus, eh, even for an old married man.

I turn my head to the side. I can't bear him to speak of Jenny. He gets up out of his chair and starts walking towards me. I lean as far back as I can in my chair. It's the only thing I can do. There's an extra sense I developed years ago, when I needed it, and I feel it cranking up. It's the sense of knowing when someone is going to hurt me.

Of knowing when Alain was going to hurt me. I couldn't always avoid it, it wasn't even always best to try to avoid it, but knowing was better than not knowing. At least I could prepare, take deep breaths, make sure I guarded my teeth, that kind of thing.

He's coming towards me and it's slow, he's old, but there's also that slow motion thing that happens when you're very scared. Time slows right down. Not like this, I think, I don't want to die like this, sitting in a chair in a nursing home, unable to call for help or protect myself. I wet myself, I can feel the warmth. I shrink back and he lifts his left hand towards me and that's it. I reach out to push him away. Push him, that's all I want to do, one big shove and he'll be down on the floor where he belongs.

It doesn't work the first time, my arm only moves a little and he's saying something about the ring and he's so close I can smell his disgusting sewer breath and see his yellow old teeth. Snaggle teeth.

Get away from me, I try to say only of course it doesn't come out like anything recognisable.

My ring, he's saying, something about his ring but he's too close and I can't bear it and my arm comes out without me even asking it to, it pops out from my side like it's got a life of its own and he's small, he's weak, he goes down easily. If he'd been that frail when we were young, I think, my life might have been different. He's on the floor right in front of my chair and he's gasping like a silly fish, flopping around like one too. It's sad when you see a fish out of water and trying to get back in. No amount of flopping is going to help them. I just want him to stop it, stop the gasping and flopping so I act on instinct. My instincts are still quite fast but my body isn't so it takes me a little while to lift my foot high enough to stamp on his face. An old person's stamp, the stamp of a slipper not a shoe, but a stamp nonetheless.

If he was functioning properly, he'd have no problem pushing me off. No problem at all but he seems to be having some trouble breathing, and his hands are flapping and clawing at the air so I just keep my foot down, try and get him calm. I've got big feet, always have had so it's no trouble to cover his mouth and nose, keep him quiet.

He's making all sorts of noises but they're quiet noises, gurgles and grunts and that's good. When he quietens down, then I'll talk to him, explain that I know who he is, all of that. It's a familiar feeling, this, I'm not sure why.

We'll never be friends, I'll say, but we can at least avoid each other, stay away. You need to think about your behaviour, I'll say, like I used to with the kids at school. Just think about it. My foot seems to have gone into some kind of spasm now, I can't get it off his face even though he's quiet. Best just to wait.

There will be a carer along any minute.

CHAPTER TWENTY-FOUR

July 1978
Pimlico

Alain was kind to May while she was convalescing. Kind enough to unsettle her, make her wonder what was going to happen next, kind enough to frighten her. He brought cups of tea without being asked, looked after Jenny, and chatted like a normal person. She hadn't seen the scary Alain for ages, and she wondered all the time, night and day, when he was coming back.

'You look loads better now,' said Joan, 'do you feel it?'

Joan had dropped by for a cup of tea. May had seen her a couple of times in the last few days, and although they were not yet friends, she was glad of the company while Alain was out. He had said he was going jogging. He'd hardly been out on his own the whole summer so May didn't feel she could say anything, but the old fear of what he was doing and where he was only just below the surface and it didn't take long to emerge.

'I'm not sure,' May said. She was grateful for Joan's company, but she couldn't help thinking that she was the wrong person. It wasn't Joan's fault, but May wished above all that she could talk to Helen. Joan was nice, and well-meaning, but she didn't have a child and May was sure she would never have a violent partner. She wore clothes that were artfully simple, and she would never understand the fear that gripped May's stomach whenever Alain was in the room.

'He seems so nice, your Al,' said Joan. 'I wasn't sure at first, but I can see that he's really devoted to Jenny.'

May wished that Joan would leave, get up and go back to her tasteful flat and take her swirly grey skirt with her. Could Alain be having an affair with her? As well as Sue, whoever she was?

Or is that all a massive shoal of red herrings? May thought. Am I just taking my mind away from the real problem, the fear and the need to be on the alert at all times? She couldn't possibly tell Joan about the beatings and the way she was too scared to sleep sometimes. Or the fear, the terrible fear and the not knowing. Or even the earrings, the earrings with the slip of paper that had gone now, the slip of paper that she might have imagined, she was no longer sure.

May knew that she should talk to someone. She looked at Joan, and wished it could be an easy friendship, that they could talk about politics and music, men and babies. There was a price for staying silent, May knew that, but she also knew that some things were too terrible to say. Some truths changed everything. Some truths were too dangerous to let out.

'Yes,' May said, 'he's great. Hey, do you mind, I'm really tired. I think I'm going to rest now, have a sleep with Jenny.'

'Of course,' said Joan. 'Thanks for the tea. Let me know if there's anything, you know, if I can help. It'll all be good from here, I bet.'

'Yes,' said May.

She saw Joan to the door. I'm on my own here, she thought, just me and Jenny.

May had felt terribly weak when she first lost the baby. In the mornings it was as though her legs wouldn't hold her when she stepped out of bed. It was a frightening feeling, and she had been trying to get fit. Sometimes, while Alain had taken Jenny out for a walk leaving May to rest, she had done star jumps from a Jane Fonda fitness magazine, touched her toes and tried to carry heavy bags of clothes whilst jumping on and off the bed. She was definitely starting to feel stronger. Whatever came next, May thought, she would be more able to deal with it. She didn't want to be the frightened little rabbit any more. May even felt like provoking Alain sometimes, just to get the explosion out of the way. If it was going to come, she thought, it would be so much easier if she was ready for it.

Spookily though, Alain had continued to give almost no cause for alarm. Just sometimes, when Jenny cried for ages and wouldn't go to sleep, or when things didn't go his way, May could see a glint of anger that reminded her of what could happen. Just sometimes.

May was reading when Alain got back from his jog. He didn't look like a person who'd been running, May thought, in fact quite the reverse. He was wearing jeans, for a start, jeans and a T-shirt and he wasn't sweating or out of breath.

'Good run?' May said.

She tried to keep any hint of sarcasm out of her voice.

'Yes, marvellous,' Alain said. 'I went along by the river, it was gorgeous but a little too hot so I just walked back. In case you're wondering why I don't look sweaty.'

He grinned as he said it. He knows, May thought, he knows I'm on to him. In spite of the heat of the day May felt cold, suddenly. It's the moment in the horror film, she thought, I'm down in the cellar again and I've got no choice.

'Come here,' Alain said. 'Come and give me a cuddle, my little ice maiden. May-den, get it?'

May didn't want to go anywhere near him. He had that look, that smell of other, of bad, she couldn't explain it any other way. She wasn't safe. She could feel it.

'Jenny,' she said and made to move towards Jenny, who was sitting in her playpen sucking the leg of a squeaky giraffe.

Alain put a hand on May's arm and she stood still.

'She's fine,' he said, 'it's me that wants the cuddle.'

'It's still too soon,' May said, 'only four weeks since I lost the baby.'

'Oh I think it's been five, at least,' said Alain. 'Surely I've been a patient husband and a model father, surely there's a little bit of something in it for me.'

May tried to weigh things up in her head, but she was so scared she couldn't think straight. If she just gave in, had sex with him and pretended she liked it, would he stay OK, nice, friendly? Or would he turn on her anyway, become angry even though she had gone along with him? Maybe even because she had gone along with him, he was so difficult to predict.

May tried to arrange the pros and cons in columns in her head, but the words wouldn't stay still. They jumped around from one column to the other and all the time Alain was coming nearer to her, an evil villain look on his face.

'Come on, merry May, it's only me, your loving husband. Don't I deserve something for my troubles? Haven't I been a good dad and a lovely nurse while you were ill? Don't I deserve a bit of a reward?'

May felt trapped. She looked around to see if there was anything she could use, anything she could grab that might help to fend him off but there was nothing, a small pile of clean nappies and Jenny's sun hat, that was all. And Jenny in the playpen staring, staring.

'Alain,' said May, 'listen to me. I'm not ready, and Jenny is awake. It's a no.'

'May, merry May,' said Alain, 'I'm lonely. Do you want me to be lonely? Jenny won't mind. Jenny's OK.'

Alain put his arms around May and pulled her to him. Her face was against his shirt buttons. May tried to twist her head to the side so that she could breathe, and not to panic. It was difficult. She wanted to scream but even if she had had the breath for it, she guessed that it might excite Alain.

'Let me just get Jenny's giraffe,' May said, turning her head just enough for the words to come out. 'She'll cry otherwise and then we won't be able to have a cuddle at all.' She couldn't believe that she sounded so normal. If I stay, she thought, this will be my life forever, ducking and weaving, dodging and lying.

'Oh May,' said Alain, 'oh May, oh May, you don't get it, do you? You should be pleased that anyone fancies you, merry May, pleased that a real man wants to fuck you. You should be on your knees and begging me for it, my darling, don't you think that would be a good idea? Now?'

Alain pushed May's shoulders down towards the floor but she made herself keep standing. Come on, May, she thought, you can do it, keep fighting, don't let him do this. She was so scared that she could feel her legs shake.

'Hey,' she said, 'maybe later.'

She twisted and pulled and managed to break free. It was the element of surprise, she thought, it wouldn't necessarily work twice. Alain seemed almost shocked that she had fought back.

'Aww,' Alain said, 'my poor little frightened rabbit. Scared of her own husband. Big bad Alain. Don't worry, I can wait, poor little rabbit.'

Alain was furious, May could tell. She shivered, wondering what he might have in store for later.

'I'm going out,' he said, 'this place bores me, you bore me. Going out and don't wait up for me, I'll be very late. Very, very late.'

Alain poured the rest of his fizzy drink on to the carpet, right next to Jenny's playpen. 'Clean that up, could you?' he said. 'Jump to it, May.' He flicked the ash from his cigarette on to the sticky mess before grinding out his cigarette in it.

'Bye,' he called, 'get to it.'

Jenny pointed towards the mess from her playpen.

I'll get you, she thought, I'll get you if it's the last thing I do. I'll get you for me and I'll get you for Jenny. She could see that it would never change, that she would always be scared, that he would always be looking for new ways to hurt her, humiliate her, keep her under control. It was good to feel so clear, and May felt almost cleansed, free from the worry of having to treat him like a friend or a lover, free from worrying whether she was being unfair. She didn't have to decide any more. None of it mattered now. He could be a good father from now until the end of his life and it still wouldn't change anything. May stretched her arms up and laughed.

'The thing is,' she told Jenny later, speaking quietly so that Alain didn't wake up, 'the thing is that people mostly see what they want to see, believe what they want to believe. That's the thing you have to remember. That's what we've got to hope for now, that's going to be our only way out.'

Jenny smiled and said, 'ga.'

'Sssh,' May said, 'we'll be OK, I'll look after you, don't you worry.'

May put the sleepy baby back in her cot and got into bed, making sure to keep as far over to her own side as possible.

The weather stayed hot over the next few days and it suited May's mood. She felt as though she was living in a feverish state, not quite ill and not yet well, undecided about what to do and yet very, very determined that things would change as soon as possible. She tried to finish sewing Jenny's little green and pink dress but the material felt unbearably warm on her lap. Even reading seemed like too much of an effort. May listened to the new Bob Dylan album over and over again on the little portable record player, listening to the words and hoping to find an answer, a way forward, a plan. She knew she had to act soon, that every day she left the situation to stagnate was making things worse, but somehow she was stuck.

Alain was charming whenever he was home. He left the flat often, and always with an excuse that was difficult to argue with. May didn't want to argue anyway, she liked the time without him, was terrified whenever she heard his key in the lock. He knitted more, as if his life depended on it, Pooh animals and whole families of creatures, hedgehogs, otters, sharks and dogs, all of them with a mummy, a daddy and two babies. He built shelves in Jenny's room for them to sit on. May bided her time, knowing that she had to go but terrified of any change, anything that might upset the shaky peace. It was so difficult to make any kind of move. She had absorbed so much terror that she didn't dare to tilt him in any way, throw him off balance, in case the result was unbearable.

It took a phone call in the end, that was all. May had been out with Jenny, walking the streets of Pimlico and thinking. They had gone up as far as Sloane Square and along the King's Road for a while, looking in the windows of the shops. May loved the crazy punk fashions but didn't feel any envy, any longing to have them. She looked down at her old flared jeans and faded T-shirt and laughed. All I want, she thought, all I want is to be the most ordinary of ordinary mums. I want to wear shabby old clothes and save my money for Jenny to have violin lessons, and for us to have a week in a caravan in Devon each year. Most of all, I want her to be safe. I want neither of us ever to have to worry or be frightened. Ever.

Jenny woke with a smile and a stretch. May bent down and adjusted the seat so that she could sit up.

'Do you know what, little treasure?' May said to her. 'It really is going to be alright this time. I have such a great feeling. By the winter it's going to be just you and me, the two musketeers.'

Jenny giggled. May felt as if a cloud had lifted from inside her head. She pointed out dogs and trees and a police horse, seeing each individual thing as if it had just emerged after a rain storm.

We'll be OK, she kept thinking, it's down to me and I can do it and it will be worth it. No more, no more, no more. The whole of her life with Alain zipped past her on that walk, the courtship, such as it was, the tiny wedding with almost no guests, the shared house in Hull and the little Pimlico flat. All of the kindnesses and all of the fun times, all of the bad times. The bad, bad times. May felt as if gauzy cloaks had been removed from her eyes. None of the good stuff was worth it, that's what she realised. None of it was that good, nowhere near good enough for her daughter, and not even close to the life she had hoped for, even back in the days when she was fat and lonely and dreaming of a different life. She had still believed that she had some worth.

It's time for all this to stop, she thought, as soon as I can, I'm going to make some changes, big ones.

'Hello,' May called as she manoeuvred the buggy through the front door, 'we're home.'

May could hear Alain on the phone in the front room. She left Jenny in the buggy and went through, ready to talk, ready to explain why she was leaving, ready for anything. Anything apart from what she saw, which was Alain holding the phone tightly to his ear, so tightly it looked as if he was trying to push it through his head, holding the phone and twisting, crying even.

'No,' she heard him say, 'no, please.'

He turned and saw her and tried to loosen his posture immediately.

May saw fear and anger on his face, both fighting each other.

If I'd had an ounce of sense, she thought later, if I had been the teeniest bit sensible, I would have turned around and left. Just gone. Jenny was in her buggy, we didn't need to collect anything, we could have been at the women's aid hostel in half an hour and on the phone to a solicitor. May was never sure why she didn't do exactly that. Embarrassment? Loyalty? Love? Or just curiosity? May had wanted for so long to know what was going on, where the hell he went to, who he saw, and she knew that if she left now she might never know. She might live her whole life not knowing who she had married, or what had happened. May owed it to Jenny to find out.

'Who's that?' she said. 'Who are you talking to? Sue? What's going on?'

'Ssshhh,' Alain said.

His face was as pale as a dead man.

May turned back to the little hallway to get Jenny out of her buggy. She heard a crash as Alain slammed the phone back onto its receiver. Shit, she thought, what have I done? The momentum of the walk with Jenny and the resolution she had made to leave was still carrying her along, so it took May a moment or two to realise that the growling she could hear was coming from the living room. It was coming from Alain. Hard to believe, but he was actually growling. Growling like a mad dog, or a lion. May realised that this was real, not a growl for a game with Jenny. It was the growl of an angry grown man. There was only one thing to do. May knew she had to get the hell out, and quickly. She didn't have time to slip Jenny back into the buggy so she shifted it to the side and squeezed past in the narrow hallway, Jenny in her arms.

May almost made it to the door. She was reaching for the lock as Alain launched himself at her, smashing the buggy to the ground and out of his way.

'Give me that baby,' he screamed.

May wondered for a moment whether she could still get the door open before he got to her, get out into the hallway where someone else in the block might hear her.

'She's the daughter of the devil,' Alain shouted. 'Look at me, I'm the devil, you're scared, aren't you, scared of me.'

Alain threw back his head and laughed like a villain in a Victorian melodrama. His eyes were wild and he was sweating heavily. He gave off a smell so unpleasant it made May gag, a mixture of chemicals and spoiled food.

May couldn't speak. She tried to hold on to Jenny, keep her tucked in as close as she could to her own chest, both arms round her, tightly.

'Give me the baby,' Alain shouted. 'She's mine, she's mine, come to Daddy, little devil baby, come here.'

Alain pinched May's neck hard, twisting his fingers to try to make her let go of the baby, but May clung on. He grabbed her hair with his other hand and dragged her past the buggy and in to the living room.

'Alain, stop,' May said, trying to keep her voice calm. 'Whatever it is, let's talk about it. Jenny is scared, this is so bad for her, look.'

May gestured towards Jenny, who did indeed look shocked and scared.

'She's fine, aren't you, little dragon baby, devil baby, shall Daddy look for your horns?'

Alain grabbed her from May, judging the exact moment when May reduced her grip a little in order to right herself and get her balance as Alain pushed her. Jenny screamed an unbabylike scream and began to wail.

'Now, now,' Alain said, bouncing Jenny too hard so that she became breathless, 'you're alright with devil Daddy, let's see what Mummy does now.'

'Alain,' said May, 'give her to me. Go on, now. She's little, and she's scared, and she will remember this all her life, deep in her subconscious, unless you change things now.'

'Aha, subconscious is it now, devil baby, Mummy's been reading books, hasn't she?'

Alain stood in the middle of the living room, Jenny in his arms. She squirmed and held her arms out towards May, who had fallen into the armchair. May jumped up and Alain shoved her again, hard. She fell back into the chair.

'I'm sorry,' he said, 'she's got to go. End of the devil line. No more.'

He was swaying as he stood there and May realised that something was very wrong. Something more than rage, or a violent temper.

'Hey,' she said, 'Alain, sit down. Go on, sit down, you look like you're going to fall.'

It took every bit of strength May had to speak to him in a gentle tone, but he stopped shouting and stared at her for a moment so she thought that she was doing the right thing.

'Here,' she said, standing up, 'sit down here with Jenny and I'll make you a cup of tea.'

Alain sat down and tucked Jenny more comfortably onto his lap, so that she was sitting on his knee. He stared at May as if he had forgotten who she was, and what he wanted to say next.

'It's OK,' May said, 'just give me Jenny and then you'll be more comfortable.'

There was no response. Alain stayed exactly as he was, frozen in position, staring. May remembered an article she had read about hostages, after the American heiress had been captured. You were supposed to talk to your kidnapper quietly, never get angry, keep repeating things. Offer to help them.

'Shall I take her so that you can get comfortable?' May said.

Alain continued to stare at her, moving his mouth as if he was about to say something. No sound came out. He flinched and moved his hand to his shoulder as if something was hurting him there. May moved forward in time to grab Jenny before she toppled over. She scooped her up and put her in the playpen in the corner of the room. Alain didn't say anything. He didn't seem to be breathing, and his eyes were glassy, unfocused. His hands stayed in the same position, frozen as if Jenny was still there.

'May,' he said.

'Yes, Alain, what is it?' May said.

'May,' said Alain again.

May realised that he was sweating even more now, blinking as the sweat ran into his eyes. It was clear that there was something very wrong.

Be careful, she thought, it could be a trick. It didn't seem like a trick but May didn't underestimate his cleverness. It was just that she had never seen anyone look so ill, so suddenly. His face was grey and distorted, as if he was stretching it into the strangest positions he could think of.

'May,' he said again, 'May, help.'

He pointed towards the telephone. It seemed to be an enormous effort for him.

'We don't need anyone to help us, Al,' May said. 'Jenny's happy in her playpen, let's wait a minute, see how things go.'

Alain groaned and clutched his chest.

'Help,' he said again, his voice sounding much weaker this time. He scrabbled at the neck of his T-shirt, as if it was constricting him, and his face fell forward towards his knees.

'Oh dear,' said May, in the voice she would use in later life for speaking to exasperating pupils, 'somebody isn't sitting up nicely at all.'

It would only take a small push, she realised, just a little tiny shove and he would overbalance on to the floor. She stood still as he tumbled slowly from the chair until he lay curled, bottom in the air as if he was a toy that had been fixed at the knee and hip into a sitting position. He vomited a little and some trickled on to the carpet, just where May had scrubbed away the drink stain a few days earlier.

She touched him lightly with her foot, moved him on to his back so that the vomit would stay inside, keep the carpet clean.

'May,' said Alain again. It was more difficult to understand him now.

May hated him for asking her for help. What was she supposed to do? What was it he wanted? She tried to think back to earlier in the day, and the decisions she had made in the sunshine, with Jenny.

'Oh yes,' she said to Alain, who had started to shake in a very odd way, 'I forgot, I was going to say, I'm leaving. I'll find a better place to raise a child.'

'May,' Alain said again, for the last time.

He reached his hand towards her ankle and touched it, a flittery, light touch that she found unbearable.

'Get off,' she said, 'get off.'

She kicked him.

Not a hard kick, just enough to keep him away from

her, stop him from touching her again. Or getting up. In case he had been thinking of it.

He lay still. He had gone too far this time, May thought, this was a trick she hadn't seen before. Alain's mouth opened and shut several times as if he was going to say something and there was a gurgling noise deep in his throat.

'I don't like that,' she said. 'Stop it.'

Alain didn't seem to hear her. His mouth was opening even more widely now but she couldn't hear any breaths going in.

'Stop it,' May said.

I could put my foot, she thought, over his face. It would stop him from looking at me. Come on, she told herself as his eyes rolled back until all she could see was the white part.

'I'll go and get some milk,' May said to Alain, 'make you a cup of tea.'

The gurgling had almost stopped as May put Jenny in her pushchair and left the flat.

*

Much later, after Alain had been declared dead, the kindly ambulance man explained that there would have been nothing May could have done, even if she'd been there.

'I took the baby for a walk,' she said, 'he was fine when I left.'

The ambulance man said that she shouldn't blame herself and that there would be an autopsy because he was so young but that he could see from the needle marks on his arms that he was a drug user. He explained that heart attacks happen when people inject narcotics and offered to call someone to be with May.

'No thank you,' May had said, 'we'll be fine.'

She resolved never to think of it, of him, ever again. It would be as though he had never lived.

Or never died.

Acknowledgements

There are many people who deserve my gratitude. Jill, my literary mentor, I take my hat off to you for your unfailing and perceptive encouragement. My lovely writing group, *Writers of Our Age*, especially Joan, Bartle, Marcus, Hilary, Cherry and Clare, for sharing stories and laughter over so many years. Thanks to Claire W. for the smoke. Julia, the best agent ever, I'm grateful for your patience and support. Manpreet and your team, thanks for believing in me, and for your sensitive and clever editing.

I'm grateful to all of you who listened while I outlined plots and ideas over the years, especially Helen and my beloved family, Samuel and Hayley, Anna, Charlie, Molly, Joey, Bella, Matilda and Arthur Bear – and always remembering Tom and Georgia. Your support has meant everything. Thank you to my sisters, Carolyn, Amanda and Elizabeth, for listening to my stories for all these years. And thanks Dom, for being with me on the adventure.

ONE PLACE. MANY STORIES

Bold, innovative and
empowering publishing.

FOLLOW US ON:

@HQStories